A Love
and
Beyond

DAN SOFER

Winner of the
2016 Best Book Award
for Religious Fiction

In loving memory of

Brenda Lucille Miller

CHAPTER 1

On Tuesday, Dave Schwarz hit thirty and his best friend narrowly escaped a violent death.

The two events were probably unrelated, but both jolted Dave the way a sudden air pocket reminds nervous passengers that they're soaring above the clouds in a pressurized metal tube.

Realization number one: Welcome to the Middle East. Strangely, Dave never thought of his new home as the Middle East. Brutal attacks like the heavy blow to the back of the head that had nearly claimed his friend should not have surprised him.

Realization number two: I'm thirty years old and still single. In short, my life is over.

Dave shook the morbid thought from his head. This was no time for navel gazing. He perched on the edge of a bed in room 419C of the Shaare Zedek Medical Center. A plastic curtain divided the room into quarters and reeked of disinfectant and tragedy. Drops of indolent Jerusalem rain slid down the dark windowpane.

Ben's bulky form lay in the hospital bed, his eyes closed, a white bandage over his otherwise bald head, like an injured rugby fullback; the mind of an academic in the body of an East End bouncer.

According to the ward nurse, the ICU doctors had transferred Ben early Wednesday morning. He was in no mortal danger, but had his mind survived the trauma?

Dave cleared his throat. He whispered Ben's name for the tenth time in two minutes. Behind the curtain, a ventilator wheezed. A telephone rang down the hall and the nurse with the squeaky shoe continued her rounds.

Dave reached into the plastic bag from Steimatzky and placed a book on the nightstand. The Jewish War by Josephus. He had purchased the Penguin paperback at the hospital gift store on the ground floor. Ben's existing copy, a hefty side-by-side English translation of the original Greek, was thick with dog ears and split at the seams.

A bouquet of gerberas sat on the windowsill. Ben's wife had sent the flowers but it wasn't her flowing cursive that graced the message inside the card. The uneven block letters looked to Dave like a cryptic text copied by a blind scribe.

Yvette had called Dave at work half an hour ago. Would he stop by, make sure Ben was in one piece?

Dave plucked a yellow flower from the bouquet and dismembered it slowly.

If Dave lay in hospital, who would send him flowers? If he died, what would his lonely life have achieved?

"Looks bad. Doesn't it?" said Ben, his eyes still shut.

Dave almost swallowed his tongue. "No, not at all." He tossed the naked flower stem into the waste bin to join its petals. "I was thinking about myself."

"Oh," Ben said, as though that explained everything.

How long had Ben been conscious?

Dave searched the poky room for a cheerful thought.

"No shortage of Jewish doctors here." His laugh was lame even to his own ears.

"Muhammad," Ben said.

The hairs on the back of Dave's neck stiffened. He had heard anecdotes of near-death experiences but he had not expected the bright light at the end of the tunnel to be the founder of Islam.

"What?"

Ben worked his mouth, as if chewing gum. Dave scanned the headboard for an emergency button.

"Doctor Muhammad. Nice guy."

Dave exhaled, his worldview intact.

He scratched his head. Ben usually drove the conversation. A laconic Ben concerned Dave.

"I met a girl," Dave said in desperation and waited for the bomb to detonate. Ben devoured tidbits of Dave's bachelor misadventures with the voracity typical of safely married men.

The patient in the sick bed merely grunted.

Had Ben recognized Dave at all?

Dave bit his lip and drew his last card.

"You made the Jerusalem Post," he said.

Ben opened his eyes. "What did they say?"

Dave retrieved the folded printout from his shoulder bag.

"'Break-in at the City of David,'" Dave read aloud. "'An apparent break-in at the City of David Institute Tuesday night caused minor structural damage. All artifacts are accounted for, according to Dr. Erez Lazarus, curator of the museum in East Jerusalem. An employee who was present at the time sustained mild injuries. The police have opened an investigation and at this point suspect local vandals.'"

"Mild injuries," Ben mumbled and shook his head.

In a sequence of fluid movements, he sat up, propped his back against the wall with a pillow, and snatched the article from Dave's hands.

Not for the first time, Dave felt the sting of his so-called friend's so-called sense of humor.

"How long have you known I was here?"

Ben didn't look up from the article.

"And what were you doing at work so late?"

"Preparing an itinerary. Yvette's away so I wasn't rushing home. I heard a commotion outside and went to investigate. Next thing I know, I'm lying here with the mother of all hangovers. They didn't even mention my name, the bastards. Erez probably saw to that."

Dave had met Erez, Ben's boss, a number of times at the

City of David Institute, or the COD, as Erez referred to the popular tourist attraction. Erez was not known for his tact.

"You should carry a gun," Dave said, feeling suddenly vengeful.

"A gun?" Ben said, outraged. "I'm an archaeologist, Dave. Not a hit man."

Dave pictured Ben behind a heavy-duty revolver. The image made a certain amount of visual sense. His shaved head and beefy, don't-mess-with-me build called to mind the thugs of a Guy Ritchie film, rather than the rabbi's son enamored with academic nuance and scientific enquiry.

"Indiana Jones had a gun." A shameless smirk twisted Dave's lips as he said it.

"Indiana Jones." Ben lowered the printout and rolled his eyes. "God, I'm tired of that name. 'Found the Ark of the Covenant yet? Been to the Temple of Doom?' For Heaven's sake. Indiana Jones is a fictional character. Archaeology, on the other hand, is a very real, painstaking process of scientific research. Hypothesis. Excavation. Analysis. Well-founded conclusions. No stunt men. No special effects. We fight our battles in academic journals, not dark alleys... Ouch!"

Ben's hand shot to the back of his head and Dave felt a small stab of remorse. He also felt relief. This was the Ben he knew and... well, the Ben he knew.

Not that Dave was a man of adventure either. He failed to comprehend why some people tied ropes to their legs and dove off bridges, or out of perfectly good airplanes. Dave was a confirmed serotonin junkie. Any day of the year, he chose a good book, a hot cupper, and air-conditioning over jeopardy to life and limb. But the opportunity to ruffle his friend's feathers had been too good to pass up.

"What ever happened to the Ark, anyway?"

Ben raised a sarcastic eyebrow, then relented.

"Not a trace in the archaeological record. The Talmud mentions two theories. Rabbi Eliezer said the Babylonians carried it off after they destroyed the first Temple in 586 BC. Rabbi Shimon Bar Yochai claimed King Josiah hid the Ark in tunnels beneath the Temple Mount shortly before. In either event," Ben added meaningfully, "there's no mention of lost Egyptian cities or Nazi plots."

"Beneath the Temple Mount? Can't you just dig there and find out?"

"Not since Moshe Dayan gave the keys of the Temple Mount to the Waqf as a gesture of good will. Now they renovate with abandon and all we can do is sift national treasures, or fragments thereof, out of their rubble. But don't get me started on that."

Dave didn't. Instead, he asked, "When does Yvette get back from Madrid?"

"Paris," Ben said. "She'll be back tonight."

Ben's wife was, quite literally, a supermodel. She spent her days flitting between the catwalks of the world's fashion centers.

"Oh, good," Dave replied, a study of casual innocence. "So you'll both be home for Shabbat."

This was Ben's cue to invite Dave over for a Sabbath meal. Of the many banes of bachelorhood, the weekly scrabble for meal invitations pressed Dave the most. Few things were as miserable as a festive Shabbat dinner-for-one at home.

Ben didn't take the hint.

"All right," he said, "let's have it."

"Have what?"

"The girl you met."

Dave was no longer desperate enough to bare his dating soul. "Just some girl I met on Shabbat after shul."

The synagogue buffet after Saturday morning prayers was the closest Dave would get to a singles bar. The slender waterfall blond had stood beside a foldout table of herring and Jerusalem kugel—pizza slices of caramelized pasta—on plastic plates. Her free-flowing hair meant she was unmarried. The ringless fingers ruled out an engagement. But was she available?

Dave had meandered closer, a plastic shot glass of Black

Label in hand. He intercepted snatches of her conversation with a girlfriend. American accent. West Coast.

"And?" Ben said. "Tell me you made a move."

"Well..."

He had drained his glass. He placed her in his sights. The world focused around him. The moment swelled with destiny. It was now or never.

"Not as such," Dave admitted. "She's American, anyway. And probably too young."

Ben covered his face in his hands. "Dave, Dave, Dave."

"But I might know someone who knows her," Dave continued.

"Dave, oh, Dave."

"Stop it, Ben. I don't want to be the scary older guy who can't take a hint."

Ben removed his hands from his face and glared at Dave, the large, repulsive cockroach. "Why do you keep doing that?"

"Don't tell me I'm picky."

"You are picky but that's beside the point. Imagine you're a good-looking, single girl. Would you be interested in a *nebekh* who doesn't have the guts to ask you out in person?"

Dave had no sisters. He had attended Hasmonean Boys. His insights into the psyche of the fairer sex derived from acquaintances at the Hampstead Garden Suburb Hebrew Congregation, Bnei Akiva summer camps, and more blind dates than he cared to remember. Hollywood filled in the blanks. But Dave could see where this was going and he would not go down quietly.

"They want to get married, don't they?"

"True," Ben conceded. "Marriage. Kids. The whole package. But what else do they want?"

Dave shrugged. "Security?"

"Fireworks, Dave. Romance. A man to sweep them off their feet. They want to fall in love but not with Mr. Nobody. They want the leader of the pack. Mr. Numero Uno. Mr. Top Dog."

"Mr. Top Dog? You hit your head harder than I thought. What ever happened to 'just be yourself'?"

"Be yourself. But differently. You can't sit on the sidelines. You've got to put yourself out there."

"I am out there," Dave said, louder than he had intended. The plastic curtain rippled behind him and the ventilator quickened its pace.

Why do people always blame the victim? Dave looked at his watch. "Which reminds me. I've got Rabbi Levi tonight."

"Excellent," said Ben. "Here's your chance. One telephone number. That's all I ask."

"You're not dying, Ben. You don't get a last wish."

"Don't you dare leave that shul without one new telephone number."

"What if I don't fancy anyone?"

"Who cares? Think of it as practice. A game. I wish you'd just read the damned book."

Dave felt his shoulders tense. The Pickup Artist's Bible was the only paperback in Ben's library with more mileage than Josephus. In a moment of despair, Dave had agreed to read it. He had stopped on page two of the introduction.

"Ben. I'm not prowling bars for a one-night stand. I'm looking for a wife, for Heaven's sake. My soul mate. The woman who will share my life and sit at my Shabbos table."

"It's just a foot in the door," said Ben. "And girls are girls. Give her a reason to get to know you."

Dave drew a long, frustrated breath. Why did he confide in Ben in matters of the heart? Dave looked at the bouquet of flowers and remembered.

"Hypothetically speaking," he said, "if I get the number, I don't have to call it, right?"

"That's the spirit." Ben smiled, no doubt anticipating future field reports of humiliation.

Humiliation: the constant in Dave's life. How had it happened? All his childhood friends were married plus two or three kids. Somewhere along the tracks of life, Dave had derailed.

"Ben, is something wrong with me?"

Ben looked him squarely in the eyes. "You left a civilized Western country to live in the Middle East. You tell me."

Dave's Ford hatchback gunned down Herzog Boulevard. The light drizzle had faded into the night. In the opposite lane, a steady stream of cars flowed toward Teddy Kollek Stadium. Black and yellow scarves trailed from the windows and horns honked the Morse code of football heathens.

The football gene had skipped over Dave and he hid this aberration like a sixth finger. Only Ben shared the condition; a fact that had solidified their early friendship.

Ben would be back on his feet before long but the break-in cast an ominous shadow. Dave had visited Ben's office at the COD countless times and, over the years, he had explored every stone ruin, stairway, and tunnel. The archaeological site with its signposts and safety banisters had been, in Dave's mind, a beacon of normalcy in the sea of short fuses and itchy trigger fingers that was East Jerusalem.

Why would anyone break into the City of David? Dave could not recall any displays of gold or silver. The center's main attractions included the geological chasm known as Warren's Shaft, King Hezekiah's water tunnel, and a rooftop observatory. Although perfect for tour groups and dating activities, the COD offered little of interest to criminal elements.

Dave pressed his foot to the brake when traffic slowed at the intersection of Gaza Street and Ben Zvi.

Vandalism, the papers had written. But bodily assault was not typical of vandalism, however mean-spirited. Had Ben surprised them? Had they panicked? Botched robberies often turned violent.

Dave veered right at the light. Tchernichovsky climbed and meandered into the heart of Katamon.

Palmach. Fighter Pilots. Nili. The Jewish Brigade. Conquerors of Katamon. The street names echoed the struggles of a People returning to its Promised Land. Over the years, the four-story apartment blocks in chunky, white Jerusalem stone—a mix of Jewish slums and Christian-Arab mansions—had accumulated a patina of carbon pollution and a tenancy of students and yuppies, completing the transformation into a hive of Jewish singles.

"One phone number," Dave said, aloud.

The mantra made his task no less daunting. Dave was fairly sure that weekly Torah lectures with separate seating did not feature prominently in the Pickup Artist's Bible.

He made a left onto Emek Refaim with its trendy restaurants and boutique stores and then turned right onto Derekh Harakevet, a forgotten back road beside the grassy tracks of a defunct railway. He eased the Ford Focus into the unpaved parking lot outside his apartment building.

Dave's flat on the first floor comprised a small, square living room, tiny kitchenette, bathroom, and single bedroom.

He threw his shoulder bag onto the foldout couch that had come with the rental along with the ancient fridge, stove, and closet and went straight for the shower, maneuvering past the miniature TV, its low stand, and the rickety coffee table he'd purchased on Janglo, an email list for Jerusalem Anglos. He'd invest in real furniture after he married.

Freshly shaved, he chose an ironed shirt out of the closet when the house phone rang.

"David, darling!" The breathless voice oozed enthusiasm like crude oil. "It's your mother."

Dave cringed. His mother, the only person on the planet who called him David, packed her words with subliminal messages. The current subtext read: the prodigal son hasn't bothered to call his poor mother since the last Ice Age.

Dave lodged the portable receiver between ear and shoulder and buttoned his shirt.

"I know who you are, Mother."

"How *are* you?"

"Good. How are you?"

Dave's mental countdown started. His mother took an average of ten seconds to start poking around his love life.

The toaster oven pinged. Dave had five minutes to gobble his vegetable pâté if he was to get to Rabbi Levi's on time.

"Going out tonight?" Dave's mother asked.

Nine seconds.

"Yes," Dave said, injecting the monosyllable with enough venom to collapse a charging rhinoceros.

"A young lady?"

"No. Just a *shiur.*"

"Aw, David. When are you going to get married?"

"I'll be sure to notify the media when I do."

"I don't understand why you have to be so picky."

Subtext: crowds of irresistible, eligible girls surround Dave and vie for his attention.

"This isn't a pair of socks, Mum. It's marriage. 'Til death do us part. You want me to be happy, don't you?"

"Happy?" His mother tittered. Subtext: what a quaint idea. "I didn't say happy, David, darling. I said *married.*"

"Mother," Dave interrupted. Cracks appeared along the dam walls of his patience. "I really have to run."

"Your father wants to speak to you."

A short commotion on the other end produced a familiar gruff voice.

"Hello, boy. Everything all right?"

"All good. You?"

"Fine. Fine. Need anything?"

"Nope. All under control."

A muffled conversation. "Your mother says you should try to settle down soon."

"Will do."

The telephone changed hands again.

"David," his mom said, "what ever happened to that lovely girl from London you dated years ago? What was her name?"

Blood fled Dave's cheeks. Once, he had made the mistake of sharing his dating life with his mother. That's how certain he had been. He would not repeat the mistake. He could only hope and pray his mother would not remember her name. Dave himself tried never to think of it, never mind utter it out loud.

"Have to go, Mum. Sorry."

"You should take this seriously, David. You're not getting any younger."

"I'm hanging up now."

Dave replaced the receiver in the charger pad.

Little wonder he was still single, given the marital model of his parents. How had his parents ever gotten together? How had they endured thirty-five years?

The phone rang again. Deep inside Dave's brain stem, something snapped.

"What now?"

"That's a strange way to answer the phone," said a much younger female voice.

Dave slumped on the couch. "Sorry, Nat. I thought you were my mother."

"Ouch," said Nat, who had met Dave's mother. Dave had known Nat since Hasmonean Primary and she was his last remaining single friend from London.

"I'll keep it short, then," she said. "I'm hosting Friday night and you're invited."

"Great," Dave said. "Thanks."

One meal down; one to go.

"Wait a minute. Is it going to be one of those Katamon meals?"

"Well, we do live in Katamon."

"You know what I mean."

Dave heard Nat inhale. She knew exactly what he meant. Friday night was the time for family, Shabbos songs, and insights into the weekly Bible reading. It did not involve ten random singles drooling at each other and peacocking over infantile conversation.

"You know I only keep the most mature and intellectual of company. They can't help it if they're single. What do you have against single people anyway?"

"Nothing," Dave said: the single person.

"It's a small meal. Promise. One flatmate. Two select friends."

Dave hesitated. Two days before Friday night, alternatives to a miserable candlelit dinner for one were fading fast. And Nat knew her way around a kitchen.

"What can I bring to the meal?"

No stranger to bachelor culinary ineptitude, Natalie suggested he buy two large *challah* loaves.

"Oh, and we're meeting at Ohel Nechama."

Dave opened his mouth to protest. Ohel Nechama, also known as The Meat Market, topped Dave's synagogue avoidance list but he struggled to phrase his disapproval without sounding petty.

"Coming to Rav Levi's tonight?" Nat asked.

"Yes. Why?"

"No reason."

The Ramban Synagogue on King Amaziah Street reminded Dave of a small, rectangular theater. Rows of pine wood pews formed a large U around the central platform, offering congregants clear views of the Torah altar, the Holy Ark, the congregants in the facing pews, and the women's gallery upstairs. Dave often wondered what Rabbi Moses Nachmanides, the thirteenth-century commentator and cabbalist, would think of the house of prayer that bore his name.

He pushed through the large pine door at the foot of the synagogue and onto center stage.

During public lectures, the women sat on one arm of the U, and Dave, as he dashed toward the other arm, felt the press of their eyeballs until he found an aisle seat.

Rabbi Levi's podium stood empty on the platform. The women fell into three categories: retirees in prim hats like inverted baskets, teenagers in long skirts and sleeves, and, the largest group by far, bareheaded single women primped and primed for display.

Dave tried to imagine the view from across the gender divide. What betrayed the single men? The well-scrubbed desperation? The furtive glances?

He scanned the murmuring crowd for the waterfall blond.

The three dark girls in the front row showed promise. Not marriage material—if Dave brought home an Israeli, his parents would disown him—but fair game for Dave's phone number mission.

The lectures, at least, maintained a semblance of normalcy. For forty-five minutes a week, Dave could pretend his life didn't revolve entirely around dating. And, if he failed to discover a fresh face, he would still have gained insights into the weekly Torah reading. This was Dave's *hishtadlut*, the token human effort required for God's unfathomable Intervention to kick in.

Natalie entered and shuffled along a central pew. A year ago, she had cropped her hair short, opting for low maintenance and practicality over pandering to male sensibilities. She sat down. Her eyes met Dave's and she waved her hand discreetly. He returned an equivocal nod. He already had Nat's number and Ben knew that. But he now had a contact beyond enemy lines. If all else failed, Dave could ask her about the blond.

A cloud of cologne settled onto the seat beside him.

"Hey, Dave," Mike said.

Although tall, confident, and handsome, the amiable Midwesterner posed no threat. He was five years older than Dave and had a thing for thin Yemenite twenty-year-olds.

Mike placed a Pentateuch on the bookrack along the back of the next pew and scanned the talent.

He ran a hand through his blow-dried blond hair. "Who's the new girl?" he said. "She's quite cute."

Dave followed his line of sight. "Natalie?"

"The English girl? No. Behind her. Eleven o'clock."

The new girl had a mane of auburn curls, soft facial features, and, Dave had to admit, a certain charm. The leather jacket implied *ba'alat teshuva*, the starry-eyed newly religious types Dave avoided. Frum-From-Recent or Frum-From-Birth, either way she probably owned a phone.

"Not my type," Mike said, "but cute."

The girl touched Nat on the shoulder and they exchanged a few words.

Bingo.

"Made any plans for Shabbat?" Mike asked.

"Nothing special."

"Great. Jeff found a deal at the Queen of Sheba. He's driving."

"Eilat?"

"The one and only. Yitz is in too. We could do with a fourth."

Dave's idea of a weekend getaway involved exotic locations and his future wife. In no way did it involve a bungalow shared with three single men. But Eilat offered a refreshing break from Katamon unreality and Dave was still one meal short.

"I'd like to, but I already accepted a dinner invitation."

Mike jiggled an eyebrow. "What happens in Eilat stays in Eilat. Katamon will still be here when you get back."

Dave juggled guilt and cowardice. Katamon, on the one hand, with its contrived Shabbat meals and continual reminders of his bachelorhood failure; Eilat, on the other, promised sumptuous buffet meals, single malt whiskey, poker, Perudo, Settlers, water volleyball, girls at the pool, and the spectacle of Mike hitting on the pretty hotel staff.

Dave glanced at Nat in the women's section and bit his lip.

"OK," he said. "I'm in."

"Great, I'll call you tomorrow with details."

Dave didn't have to cancel Natalie straight after the *shiur*, he decided. He'd call her tomorrow morning.

Rabbi Levi strode into the synagogue and the chatter subsided. The young, clean-shaven rabbi placed his notes on the lectern and faced his audience.

"Vayeh'tzeh Yaakov mi Be'er Sheva," he read. *And Jacob left Beer Sheba.*

Every head in the women's section trained on the rabbi, including Nat, who now partially blocked Dave's view of New Girl.

The rabbi spoke a clear and precise Hebrew. Dave understood most of it; Jacob had fled the murderous wrath of his brother Esau to his uncle Laban in Haran, on the pretext of finding a wife.

If he was going to call Nat to cancel anyway, he could ask for New Girl's number at the same time and avoid the awkward face-to-face. He would need a pretext.

Jacob camped on a hilltop. In his dream, a ladder rose from the earth to the heavens. Angels shot up and down the spiritual highway. When Jacob awoke, he erected a pillar and called it Bet El, the House of God.

He remembered the story from the previous year. He had attended the *shiur* for over a year now. Each week he hoped to find The One. Each week he returned home empty-handed. Was this hard luck? Or had Dave misplayed his cards, folding out early, waiting for that miraculous perfect hand? Once upon a time, dating had meant excitement and anticipation. The thrill of the hunt. Where had that old Dave gone?

Jacob stopped at a well outside the city. Shepherds waited with their flocks. Then Rachel appeared on the horizon. In a single-handed show of gallantry, Jacob pushed the boulder from the mouth of the well. He ran to Rachel and introduced himself. Then he kissed her and broke down in tears. He worked seven years for her hand in marriage and they flitted by like days, so deep was his love.

Had Dave already met his soul mate? Had he failed to recognize her? In his gap year, he'd studied in an Israeli yeshiva. He'd met Ayelet at the till of her father's mini-market. The quirky American-Israeli loved all things British. She knew Monty Python's Dead Parrot Sketch by heart. She printed her number on Dave's receipt and they spoke every night for weeks. Without warning, he stopped calling her. What was the point? They were nineteen and Dave had registered at London City University.

Then there was Sarah, one of three *frum* souls in Psychology 101. Slender and graceful as a gazelle in her long dark skirts, Sarah would have made a gentle if not terribly intelligent wife. But Dave dreamed of *aliya*—of *rising up*, relocating to the Holy Land, the land of his forefathers, as the Bible commanded—while Sarah clung to her family in Golders Green.

Had karma punished Dave for dropping Ayelet? Should he have been more flexible with Sarah? He didn't think so. A third flame loomed in Dave's mind. Dave divided his life into the years before and the years after their meeting like a cataclysmic geological event. By her burning light, Dave's myriad blind dates, even the Ayelets and Sarahs, fell into shadow. His mother may have forgotten the girl's name but memories of her had been branded into Dave's heart and soul. Two years since their brief encounter, he still refused to utter her name.

Rabbi Levi turned a page in his notes. Jacob's dramatic courtship of Rachel formed a stark contrast to that of his parents, Isaac and Rebecca. Isaac didn't lift a finger. Father

Abraham dispatched his servant to Haran and arranged the marriage by proxy. Only after Isaac took Rebecca as his wife do we read of their love.

Nat shifted forward, clearing Dave's line of sight. For an instant, New Girl's eyes locked with his.

Dave's head snapped back toward the rabbi. He felt the color drain from his face.

Crap, crap, crap! Caught staring. Perfect. Dave, the leering weirdo. Before he even had the chance to make a fool of himself. Crap!

He focused on Rabbi Levi as though his life depended on the rabbi's every word.

"Two dating models exist," the rabbi said, no stranger to the demographics of his audience. "One is full of fireworks, adventure, and drama; the passion of Jacob and Rachel. The second model is quiet and calm; practical and rational. The pairing of Isaac and Rebecca. Both models are equally valid."

Dave hazarded a glance at the women's section. New Girl trained her eyes on the rabbi, with no indication that anything untoward had occurred.

"In recent times," Rabbi Levi continued, "books and films have idealized romance. Fireworks and adventure are no longer an option but a necessity. Young men and women discard relationships when there is no spark, no immediate passion."

Elderly heads nodded in agreement. Embarrassed smiles spread on many of the younger listeners. The façade of normalcy shattered on the tiles of the synagogue floor. More than ever, Dave wanted to be alone in his bachelor pad, away from probing eyes and good Samaritans.

Rabbi Levi hammered the point home. "Young men and women need to realize that another courtship model exists, slow and steady but just as likely to foster long-term marital content. Getting along, enjoying each other's company, can be the basis for a life-long, satisfying relationship, even without the thunder and lightning, heroic acts, or superhuman feats."

The rabbi wished them *Shabbat Shalom* and collected his notes. Before long, a chattering human sea filled the floor and blocked Dave's escape route. Mike had already engaged a young, dark Israeli in conversation, while Dave drifted, buffeted toward the great wooden door.

Nat and New Girl bobbed toward the exit. Their trajectory would converge with his at the door. Nat raised a hand and signaled at Dave.

Too late to duck out now.

New Girl whispered in Nat's ear. They smirked. Dave's beating heart rose up his throat. Crap, crap, crap!

"Hi, Dave," Nat said.

"Hi, Nat." Dave kept his eyes on Nat. The stream of bodies bumped against him. The expectant lull in conversation sucked on his mind. He searched for something witty to say. A pivotal moment welled up. *Ask her number. Ask her name. Make your move.*

He opened his mouth. "Got to run," he said and slipped out the door and into the night.

Deep within the Talpiot industrial zone, two men entered a dark alley and prepared to face their destiny. Their shadows stretched along the wet tarmac strip that squeezed between dormant warehouses. Passing traffic on Pierre Koenig threw Doppler echoes against the hoods of their anoraks. The deserted street smelled of trash and cat piss. Raised loading platforms watched them pass in the gloom.

Beyond a single, flickering fluorescent lurked a large white transit van. The van had seen better days.

"Stone the crows," Jay said. Clouds of mist formed at his mouth and evaporated. He had copied the directions onto a Falafel King napkin in an Internet café off Ben Yehuda Street. This was the right address, but he had expected something... well, different. Scratched and dented, the vehicle did not look like the ride of the prophet, whom Jay knew only as "the Teacher." Then again, God favored the humble and the meek. And the meek would inherit it all.

"What a bomb," said his companion, who was shorter and stockier than Jay, his coffee-toned skin foreign to this continent. "I don't like the looks of this, Jay."

Time for another pep talk.

"O ye of little faith," Jay began.

He had memorized a handful of quotes from the Scriptures, and this one had come in particularly useful.

"All right, all right," said his friend. "Let's have a gink and be done with it. This place gives me the willies."

The driver's compartment was empty. Jay reached for the Falafel King napkin in his pocket to recheck the directions when he heard the clunk of a heavy door unlocking at the back of the van.

The two men circled the vehicle. The doors swung easily.

"Get in," said a deep voice in the darkness. "And shut the door."

They climbed inside and sat opposite one another on metal benches built into the interior of the van.

As the doors closed, there was a click and white light flooded the interior.

Jay squinted. At the back of the van, beneath the ceiling light, a cloak of gray sackcloth faced them. A black void filled the cowl where a face should be.

That's more like it.

"You didn't mention your friend." The voice spoke with a slight British accent.

"This is John, my cuzzy bro," Jay said. "He's no trouble."

The dark cowl considered this for a few breaths, then said,

"Do you have it?"

Jay slid the knapsack off his shoulder.

"Here you go. Right where you said it would be."

Jay handed over the bag. The object he had pinched was too plain and simple to be of any real value. Jay's mission had been a rite of passage, nothing more, or so he had thought, but the long gloved fingers in the sleeves of the cloak trembled as they snatched the bag.

Time to collect.

"Now then," Jay said, "about this Hidden Treasure—"

"I believe," the cloak interrupted, "there was an incident."

Jay blinked.

"The security bloke? I wouldn't worry about him." Jay winked at John, who studied the corrugated floor of the van. "He won't remember a thing." Jay had floored the baldy in the official City of David polo shirt with a single blow.

The cloak was not impressed.

"Assault was not part of the plan. We don't want to… attract attention."

Jay gritted his teeth. He had expected praise. A coronation. Anointment with Sacred Oil. But this first meeting had to go well if Jay was to move to the next level.

"I understand," Jay said.

"Very well. But you must keep a low profile. People will not understand your… unique gifts. Not until the End."

"The End?"

"The End of Days. You will learn more in due time, my son."

My son.

Jay hadn't heard those words in what seemed a lifetime.

"And the treasure?"

"The treasure, yes. We are very close and this"—the Teacher raised the knapsack—"brings us one step closer. More steps remain. You must learn The Way and then you will change the world forever. We have waited centuries. We must wait a little longer. Patience, my son."

Jay nodded. He felt the tingle of destiny spread though his

bones. The Teacher understood. The Teacher would show him The Way.

"Enough for now," the Teacher said. "I will send further instructions in the usual manner."

John didn't need to be told a second time. He pulled the handle of the door and bailed out. Jay's head swam with questions but his time was up.

"One last thing," he said on the threshold. "What's your name?"

The cloak straightened. The deep voice uttered two unfamiliar words. Jay repeated them. Hebrew always tripped up his tongue.

"What does it mean?"

"Teacher. The Teacher of Righteousness."

DAN SOFER

CHAPTER 2

Dave awoke Thursday morning determined not to think about dating. Not under any circumstances. Not until his return from Eilat.

He needed a break. He *deserved* a break. Only two hurdles stood in his way: nine hours at work and one brief phone call to Nat.

Dave leaned over the side of the bed and washed his hands into the plastic tub stowed beneath. He brushed his teeth, dressed, tucked the embroidered phylactery bag he had received for his Bar Mitzvah under one arm, and braved the morning chill.

Cars choked Emek Refaim. Egged buses creaked and hissed. Storeowners rolled up security gates and set out chairs. Pedestrians bustled.

Dave's walk to the Great Synagogue averaged seven minutes. His route passed three other synagogues but only the Great Synagogue started after 8 AM.

He rounded the Paz gas station at Bell Park and climbed Keren Hayesod. He picked his way between bulldozers and torn sidewalks courtesy of the long overdue "light rail" project.

Dave passed the Kings Hotel opposite France Square. On Fridays, a gaggle of aging Israelis in black T-shirts overran the square and urged Dave to "end the occupation." He always smiled at them and accepted their pamphlets. At least they weren't trying to marry him off.

He veered into a courtyard and said good morning to the elderly guard. The towering Great Synagogue was modeled after Solomon's Temple. The main domed synagogue seated a thousand on Sabbath services, cantorial events, and weddings. Weekday prayers took place in the cozy oak-paneled study center two floors down.

Dave found an empty seat at one of the long pressboard tables and unzipped his *tefilin* bag. The congregation consisted mostly of retirees in varying degrees of gray hair and bent posture. They swayed and mumbled prayers beneath white prayer shawls. He wound the black leather phylactery strap around his left arm. He straightened the black box on the crown of his head. Then he wrapped the end of the strap over his fingers like rings.

"Ve'erastikh li le'olam…"

The words rolled off his tongue.

I betroth you to me forever; I betroth you to me in righteousness and justice, in loving kindness and compassion. I betroth you to me in faithfulness…

The symbols of marriage hounded him at every turn. Judaism was no religion for single men. Dave needed a wife and fast, and not just to get his mother off his back or even to fulfill the Divine command to "be fruitful and multiply." Family life was the only path to normalcy.

Rabbi Hendler nodded at Dave from his seat beside the Holy Ark. After thirty years of community service in New York state, the rabbi with the tidy white beard and John Lennon glasses retired to Jerusalem to write, teach, and introduce Dave to the congregation's granddaughters.

Rabbi Hendler smiled and beckoned. He wanted a word with Dave after the service. Dave remembered his morning resolution. He smiled, feigned stupidity, and kept his head down.

The men stood for the silent prayer of Eighteen Blessings.

Dave took three steps forward and closed his eyes.

The rabbi meant well. Dave, as a bachelor, was the only congregant without the protective cover of a prayer shawl, besides one gangly teenager and two Philippine caregivers. He must have stood out like a missing tooth.

He found his mind wandering like a flickering projector. Intelligent emerald eyes. The hint of slender legs beneath the dark, elegant fabric of her dress. Exquisite lips. Ivory neck. Silky black hair. A manicured eyebrow arched in surprise.

Dave pulled the projector cord; he sucked air into his lungs.

God had offered him Heaven on a silver platter and Dave had tripped up the waiter.

He took three steps backward and bowed to his left. *He who makes peace in His heights.* To the right. *May He bring peace upon us.* Forward. *And upon all Israel.* He straightened. *Amen.*

The offices of TikTech lay deep within the mushroom patch of hi-tech buildings known as the Har Hotzvim Industrial Park.

Dave's keyboard, mouse, and stationery had shifted to the foot of the monitor, a sign that the cleaning staff, a team of lanky, soft-spoken Ethiopians, had visited their sanitary wrath upon his workstation.

He nursed a paper cup of instant coffee and scanned the Jerusalem Post headlines for news of the City of David. Finding none, he reviewed the contents of his inbox.

He dropped the cup in the waste bin and dialed Nat's

number on his desk phone. The call cut to voice mail, as he'd expected. At this time of the morning, Nat was busy introducing thirty Israeli high schoolers to the joys of the English past participle.

He left his message: Dreadfully sorry... Something came up... You know how it is... He'd be happy to drop off the bread regardless, just say the word.

From beyond the cubicle divider, the voice of Kermit the Frog yelled, "What do you want?"

Five years on the job, Dave still jumped at the sound of his boss. From the volley of terse answers, curt demands, harsh recriminations, and abject denials, Dave could tell that Avi, the forty-year-old American-Israeli team leader, was talking to his wife on the phone.

Avi kept photos of his two teenagers, bucktoothed creatures with wild hair, on his desk with no images of his wife, and Dave pictured her as a disgruntled Miss Piggy.

There was trouble in Muppet Land.

Dave clamped headphones over his ears and played Genesis' Greatest Hits on his computer disk drive. He clicked open the document for his current work project. All work documents followed a standardized format known by the unfortunate name of Standard Test Document, or STD.

Phil Collins sang "Another Day in Paradise."

Nine hours and counting. Eilat, baby, here we come.

An email notification popped onto the screen: a new message from Frumster.com.

Ben had convinced Dave to open an account two years before and although Dave had met a handful of girls on the site, none had ended well.

The mouse cursor circled the email as he considered.

Don't bother. You're on a break.

The chances that his soul mate was reaching out to him this very moment were negligible. Still...

Dave clicked the link. A girl named Nili had written him the usual drivel.

Hi. Liked your profile. Be in touch.

Dave clicked her profile link. Thirty years old. Few extra pounds. No photo.

Delete.

Dave slumped back in his chair. His iron resolve had lasted all of two hours.

Be proactive, Dave.

He clicked his own profile and reviewed his selections: Modern Orthodox; Three Daily Prayers; Eats Kosher at Home and Out; Strict Sabbath Observance.

He downgraded Torah Learning from Daily to Weekly. Between work, groceries, laundry, jogging, ironing, and, of course, dating, spiritual growth had to take a number and stand in line.

He hardly recognized what he had written in the *About Me* box. He increased his *aliya* seniority from five years to seven.

He checked the boxes of a few hypothetical hobbies to round out his virtual self and clicked *Save*.

"What do you mean, 'no bugs'?"

The irate voice of Kermit the Frog triggered a reflex response in Dave's finger muscles. They pressed the Tab and Alt keys, replacing Frumster.com with his current STD.

"But it works," a young Russian said.

Dave's shoulders relaxed. Alex, the new recruit in the Quality Assurance Team, had made a classic mistake.

"What did I tell you?" Avi demanded, his voice quavering. "A test with no bugs is what?"

Alex said nothing. Poor sod.

"Dave?!" Avi hollered.

"A test with no bugs," Dave said, raising his voice, "is a failed test."

The quote originated from an old QA textbook, Avi's Bible, Koran, and Veda combined.

"Thank you! A *failed* test. Your test has failed, Alex. See this."

Dave heard a clatter of keystrokes. The coast clear, he toggled back to Frumster and clicked the Saved Search link.

Twenty profile tiles materialized on the screen. He'd viewed most of them before. The remaining girls he'd already met, judging by the photo or other telling details.

He broadened his search. His current criteria specified Single (Never Been Married), English Speakers who lived in the Jerusalem Area, described themselves as Slim or Athletic, wore Skirts Only and planned to cover their hair Fully after they married.

Now he added Average Figure, Skirts and Trousers, and Undecided vis-à-vis Hair Covering.

And people said he was picky. No need to search outside Jerusalem, though. He wasn't *that* desperate.

Dave clicked the button.

Thirty-three results. Nothing new. Apparently, he had run the search previously.

Eilat crawled half an hour closer.

Strangely, he couldn't find Nat among the profiles.

A throat cleared behind him.

Alt-Tab! Alt-Tab!

Dave craned his neck. He released the air in his lungs.

"Yoram, you've got to stop sneaking up on me."

"I have a girl for you," said Yoram, Israeli programmer and father of three.

Dave eased back in his chair. Battle stations.

"I'm on a break."

Yoram leaned his elbow on the cubicle wall.

"This one is special," he said.

He ran his hand over his close-cropped salt-and-pepper hair and smirked. Yoram always smirked. An unlit cigarette waved at the corner of his mouth.

Dave sighed. "How old?"

"Twenty-five."

"Religious?"

"Yes, but not crazy."

Dave had to give him credit. Yoram had done his homework and breached Dave's first line of defense.

"Looks?"

"You know. Two arms. Two legs. A nose."

Bingo.

"But she's attractive?"

Yoram frowned. "She's not a *supermodel*."

Dave considered arguing for the existence of a spectrum of women spanning between Bar Refaeli and the Elephant Woman but gave up before he started.

Time for the big guns. "Does she speak English?"

"A little." The smirk dropped. "Not much," Yoram admitted.

"Sorry, not my type."

Yoram shook his head. "You know where I sit, if you change your mind." He padded off toward the stairwell for a drag

A message arrived on Dave's phone. It was Nat.

Pity that. Another time. Don't worry about the bread. Laters.

Dave pondered Nat's missing profile. He searched her text message for clues.

In the cubicle opposite, Kermit uttered expletives in English, Hebrew, and then Arabic.

"Dave!" Avi shouted. Swivel chairs creaked and Avi appeared at Dave's side with Alex in tow.

"Break something for me, Dave."

He leaned over and commandeered Dave's keyboard.

"If Dave can't bring her down, nobody can."

He opened a browser window and navigated to a login screen.

"All yours," Avi said and shoved the keyboard at Dave.

Dave cracked his knuckles. He flexed his fingers. He entered random text in the User Name and Password fields.

Access denied.

He entered the test user credentials.

Welcome, Member.

Dave logged out. He clicked the Password Reminder and, dammit, that worked as well.

Tricky. Little. Bastard.

"It work," Alex muttered. "No problem." English was his

third language.

"You don't get it, Alex," said Avi. "Everything has bugs. If you can't find them, you're not looking hard enough."

Dave tested and retested. He entered Greek characters and Chinese. He served his best shots; they all bounced back. The system was flawless. Of course, the buttons were too small. But Dave refused to settle for cosmetic defects, the QA engineer's equivalent of a white flag.

"C'mon," Kermit growled in Dave's ear.

Dave wiped his brow on his shirtsleeve. Match point. Time for desperate measures.

He jammed his fingers onto the keyboard and jabbed keys at random like a crazed Captain Nemo at the organ, twenty thousand leagues beneath the sea.

The Members Only page blinked onto the screen.

"Yes!" He punched the air.

His input frenzy had kicked open a back door. An ace at the deciding moment. Inexplicable? Yes. Impossible to reproduce? Probably. But a bug is a bug.

Avi slapped Dave on the shoulder. "The Bugmeister strikes again." He loped back to his cubicle, trailed by a hangdog Alex. "I hope you took notes."

Dave's phone rang.

"Hi, Loverboy."

He stiffened. "Hi, Ben."

"And how is Jerusalem's most eligible bachelor?"

"I'll be sure to ask him if I meet him."

"They released me this morning."

"Good." He hoped his curt reply implied that he was very busy and therefore unable to answer questions about last night.

"Join us for lunch this Shabbat?"

"Can't. I'm in Eilat with Mike and the gang."

"Eilat? Are you out of your tree? Shabbat is your chance to meet new girls. You've got to get out there. Play the field."

"I'm on a break."

"Break-shmake. Breaks are for closers. There's a reason

Mike and his gang aren't married. Do you want to be single at forty?"

Dave's feelers tingled. "Are you trying to set me up? Who's coming over?"

"Just the three of us."

"But I've made plans, Ben. I even canceled dinner at Nat's."

"Un-cancel it, then. There. Now you've got both meals sorted. No excuses. Do me a favor, do your unborn children a favor, and stay in."

Dave groaned. "All right. I'll stay."

First his short-lived resolution. Now his bachelor weekend.

"God, I hate changing my mind all the time."

"Pity that," Ben said. "It's what you do best."

"And I can't believe I'm agreeing to another Katamon singles meal."

"Cheer up. How bad could it be?"

The Friday sun sank lazily over Jerusalem, bathing the stone apartment blocks in soft, gold light. Another springlike day had snuck into December and chased away the clouds.

Of all Diaspora comforts, Dave missed Sundays the most. Fridays and their manic errands offered a poor substitute.

At dusk, however, silence descended on the streets. Cafés stacked their chairs, shops rolled down their security doors, and the city exhaled the tensions of the workweek. The aromas of warm bread and simmering chicken soup wafted through the windows as housewives lit candles and ushered in the Sabbath.

Dave stepped onto Emek Refaim, a plaid sweater over his Sunday—or rather Saturday—best and the plastic bag from Ne'eman's Bakery in his hand.

Ahead of him, a father exchanged kind words with his two small children; the little girl wore a white-frilled dress, the boy a suit, a miniature version of his father. The ironed collars and personalized white yarmulkes spoke of a loving wife and mother.

Dave, the outsider, the leering vagrant at the gates, clamped his lips. He turned left on Rachel Imenu, climbed Kovshei Katamon and Palmach to the intersection of Jabotinsky and Chopin, a stone's throw from the Jerusalem Theater.

The Ohel Nechama synagogue rose in tiers about a central staircase like a ziggurat. A fitting design, in Dave's opinion, for this altar would be used to sacrifice what remained of his human dignity.

He selected a prayer book in the foyer and entered the inner sanctum. The walls, thirty feet high, tapered to a central square of ceiling like the inside of a snub-nosed pyramid.

Men packed the pews and the air swam with the surging waltz of their voices.

Le-e-kha Do-di. Li-i-i-krat Kal-lah. Ah-ah-ah. Pe-e-nay Shabbat ne-e-e-ka-belah. Let us go, my beloved, toward the bride. Let us greet the Sabbath day.

Dave hurried to a vacant aisle seat beside a little boy in a starched white-collared shirt. The boy held a prayer book open on his lap.

Dave placed his own *siddur* on the wood-paneled support affixed to the next pew and paged to the Friday night service.

The boy's father, about the same age as Dave, whispered instructions in French. Dave remembered sitting, as a young boy, next to his own father in the Hampstead Garden Suburb synagogue in London. The synagogue hall had seemed so large, the world so inviting and ripe for the picking. His plan:

complete the Talmud by eighteen, marry by twenty, kids at twenty-one, conquer the world by twenty-five. Tops.

The congregation stood for the Mourners' Prayer. Dave swiveled at the waist, as if to stretch his back; a practiced gesture that allowed him to steal a glance at the women's gallery above. No sign of the Waterfall Blond. Nor of the New Girl from Rabbi Levi's lecture. Nat stood in her usual front row spot, a prayer book resting in open hands, her gaze focused on a point in the center of the men's section. Was that lipstick? Dave tried to follow Nat's line of sight but then the congregation sat and fell silent.

A graying man dressed for the opera took the podium and read Hebrew from printed pages.

Dave thought of Nat's missing Frumster profile and the floor fell out of his stomach. Was Nat seeing someone? And if she was, what of it? Dave often shared details of his own dating escapades with her, although Nat never spoke of hers. For years, he had sensed that Nat was keen on him but he had never considered her seriously. Nat was the familiar tree in the backdrop of Dave's life. She would always be there. Or would she?

Three hundred kilometers away, Dave thought, in an Eilat hotel, three bachelors planned their assault on the buffet, blissfully unaware of the Ohel Nechama women's section.

The service concluded with the singing of *Yigdal* and Dave joined the outpouring of men and women onto the wide, outer stairway. The night air buzzed with greetings and chitchat under the canary yellow of street lamps.

"Good Shabbos, Dave," Chezi said.

The American economist had shared an apartment with Dave on Palmach four years earlier. His eyes worked the crowd.

"Good Shabbos," Dave replied. "How are you?"

"What?"

"Never mind."

"Dave," Chezi said, "have you seen Jessie?"

Jessica Marcus, Chezi's mythological ex, had featured in a

snatch of recent gossip.

Dave bunched his eyebrows, unsure whether or not to smile. "Didn't she get married?"

Chezi's eyes kept roving.

"She's just playing hard to get."

"In fact, I heard she's expecting."

"*Real* hard to get," Chezi mumbled. He patted Dave on the shoulder and sidled away, leaving Dave to run the gauntlet alone.

The mass of singles broke into pockets along the tiered stairway. Dave clutched his bag of *challah* loaves and marched down the central banister. Chemical clouds of perfume and hairspray burned his nostrils. Strangers pelted him with invasive glances. Snatches of mindless small talk snagged his ears. He kept moving until eventually he ran out of stairs.

Natalie stood at the street curb, guests in orbit, each with a plastic bag in hand. Dave said hello. He pretended not to notice Nat's flowing dress—a dramatic departure from her signature stiff skirts—or the neckline and the hint of cleavage or the fact that she was, he realized, beautiful.

"Dave," she said and clasped her hands. "This is Saul."

The lanky man at her side shot out his hand and shook Dave's. Vigorous. Overeager. Dave's limbs ossified. He forced a smile.

"I've heard a lot about you," said the gawky, bespectacled American.

Dave, who had heard nothing of Saul, lost his faculty of speech. He avoided Nat's eyes. Was he sparing her or himself?

He extricated his hand and turned to the other guests.

"Hi, Miriam," he said. The girl in the floral dress and oversized glasses nodded. Her haphazard hair dropped to her shoulders. Nat's longtime American friend collected academic degrees at the Hebrew University like butterflies, but little in the way of social graces.

A younger girl stood beside her and showed more promise. Her dark curls caught the streetlight and hinted at hairspray and hours at a mirror. Glitter sparkled on her eyelids.

"This is Ahuva," Nat said, the hostess, "Miriam's sister."

Dave introduced himself, his spirits rising, his earlier befuddlement forgotten. For the only unattached male at the meal, the night was young.

"Shall we?" Nat said, waving a hand to indicate the street.

"What about the others?" Miriam asked.

"What others?" Dave had counted five. Five was bearable.

"We'll meet them at the flat," Nat said.

They crossed the quiet intersection and set out, down Palmach, past the Islamic Art Museum.

Nat stepped within whispering distance. "Sorry, Dave, it started out as a small meal. Honest it did."

"It's fine," he lied. "How many others are we talking about?"

"Leah is home for Shabbat and didn't have plans. And she invited a friend. Then Saul's roommate got stuck for a meal. I hope that's OK."

Dave put five and three together and swallowed hard.

"Of course."

He knew Leah, Nat's rough-cut Australian roommate, well enough. Her mystery friend was unlikely to be the waterfall blond, but she might be the girl with the auburn curls from Rabbi Levi's *shiur*.

Nat and Saul picked up the pace along the fissured, car-lined pavement, leaving Dave to the sisters.

"How's Hebrew U?" he asked Miriam.

"Good," she replied, the mistress of conversation.

He cleared his throat and turned to the younger sister.

"Ahuva. What do you do?"

"I'm at Pardes for the year."

"Oh," he said.

Pardes offered coed study programs to Americans tourists. Although technically committed to Jewish Law and practice, the institute had an aura of pluralism.

Strike one.

A man in a hoodie and sweatpants punched the buttons of a DVD vending machine outside a darkly Mr. Zol minimarket on Palmach; a small reminder that not all denizens of Katamon observed the Sabbath.

"What do you do?" Ahuva asked.

"Hi-tech," Dave said.

"Ah."

He savored the awe in her voice. *Hi-tech* implied magical technology and million-dollar exits. The *hi-tech* elite created worlds and ruled them. At a minimum, they could pay the bills. Dave felt no urge to expose the reality of failed startups and mass layoffs. His own job provided zero advancement and, when explained in detail, sounded drop-dead boring.

He relaxed. He and Ahuva had hit it off, even if she didn't fit the checklist item-for-item. For starters, her age. Twenty-one, maximum, judging by the year abroad and the glitter. Was a nine-year age gap pushing the limit?

They turned right on Nili Street. Too late to pick up the thread of the earlier conversation. He needed a new starter for the hundred meters between them and Nat's apartment. Their footsteps echoed against the silent, modest apartment blocks. Dave could almost hear snatches of Nat's conversation with Saul.

Fifty meters.

The silence grew into a large, pink elephant with a mean streak, ready to charge at ice-breakers and brand them as desperation.

They entered Nat's building and climbed the stairs to the cozy first-floor apartment. Nat stowed their coats, scarves, and shawls in her bedroom.

She had set the oval dinner table with a white tablecloth, disposable plates, and paper napkins. No two pieces of silverware matched, neither did the chairs.

The girls disappeared into the kitchen to assist Nat with the salads. In the lamp light of the salon, Dave and Saul settled on the overstuffed couch. A Jerusalem Post lay folded on the coffee table.

"So, um," Saul began. "What do you do?"

"Hi-tech."

"Ah."

"You?"

"Accountant. Ernst & Young."

This sounded like a question. Dave nodded grimly. Stable. Dependable. Seemed nice enough. But Nat deserved better. Someone like... well, like Dave.

A chill of panic shot down his spine. Had he been blind? Was Nat the girl of his dreams all along? Had the one obvious choice slipped away right under his nose, lost to the man twiddling his thumbs on the couch beside him? Or was Saul a ploy, a wakeup call designed to spur him into action?

Calm down, Dave. Get a grip.

He took a deep breath and listened to the kitchen sounds. Four tea lights flickered on the mantelpiece and filled the room with their waxy scent. The Shabbat water urn hissed quietly.

Dave *had* considered Nat. Many times. And each time, an indefinable intuition had slammed on the brakes.

Dave slid the Jerusalem Post off the ring-marked coffee table and turned pages in the soft light: A new round of peace talks. A thwarted bomb attack. Another Gazan missile had landed near a kindergarten in Sederot. Politicians under investigation. Another day in the Middle East. Again, Dave looked in vain for news of the City of David.

The front door opened to the trailing edge of laughter and Leah exploded into the room, all tangles of carrot hair and energy. Her guest was slender and feminine, and had tied her hair up above a proud, aristocratic brow. Although neither the Waterfall Blond nor the New Girl, the guest was uncannily familiar.

"Good Shabbos, Saul," Leah said. "Dave," she added with mild disappointment. "Everyone, this is Sarit."

Sarit smiled at Saul, then at Dave and immediately she glanced away, flushed.

Dave sat up in his seat. *Hello!*

A man stepped through the open doorway. His baby face and freckles reminded Dave of Alfred E. Neuman. Alfred E. Neuman with a crew cut. His eyes darted to the two girls.

"Am I the last one?" he said. A New Yorker. Loud voice. Dave shifted in his seat.

Leah gave the newcomer the once-over and seemed to like what she saw. "Last but not least," she said. "You must be Saul's roommate."

He held out a bottle of wine in a plastic bag. "The one and only. I'm Josh."

Dave should have guessed. Half the Americans he knew were called Josh.

"Leah," she replied. "This is Sarit. And over there is Dave. Old friend of Nat's."

Dave winced at the "old." He rose, shook hands with Josh, and smiled briefly. Sarit kept her eyes on her feet.

Nat emerged from the kitchen. "Hi, Josh," she said. "Shall we start?"

The eight singles converged on the dinner table.

Nat herded Saul to the seat at the head of the table. Dave vied for the seat next to Sarit but was blocked by Saul on one side and Leah on the other. He landed up between Nat and Miriam on the other side. Josh stood at the foot of the table, placed strategically between Leah and Ahuva. At least Dave had a clear view of Sarit.

Nat filled a silver wine cup with King David Concord, the ubiquitous sugary *kiddush* wine, and the glancing game began.

Leah grinned knowingly at Josh, who eyed Ahuva, who stood out of Dave's line of sight. Miriam stared ahead vacantly. Dave focused on Sarit. She must have sensed Dave's attentions but didn't return the eye contact. Instead, she studied her plastic dinner plate. Bashful? Or a demure invitation?

Saul cleared his throat.

"Vaheyi erev, veyehi boker. Yom hashishi."

Saul concluded the prayer, poured wine from the cup into plastic shot glasses, and passed them down the table.

An awkward silence.

Nat directed her guests to the kitchen and bathroom where they washed their hands before breaking bread.

At the table, Nat removed a colorful, tie-dyed *challah* cover, lifted the plaited loaves in her hands, and recited the blessing. She cut the bread, dipped the slices in a pinch of salt, and distributed them in a little wicker breadbasket. Nat had commandeered the bread-breaking ritual, a task traditionally designated to men. Saul did not seem too scandalized. By now, he must be aware of Nat's Torah readings at the egalitarian *minyan* too.

The guests munched in silence. Dave spread hummus on a slice, still warm from the Shabbat hot tray, and bit into the sweet, soft bread. He felt the red wine enter his bloodstream.

Ben's voice rang in his ears.

Put yourself out there. Make a move.

Dave swallowed his mouthful.

Numero Uno. Mr. Top Dog.

"Sarit," he said. The vacuum of silence sucked at his words. "You look familiar."

Sarit raised her eyes. Her mouth contorted into a wan, piercing grin.

"That's because we've dated."

Dave felt his face drain. "Oh," he said, parrying with humor. "How embarrassing."

"Ha!" Josh slapped the table top. "Welcome to the swamp."

Saul gave a loud, whooping laugh, which elicited chuckles all round. Nat's cheeks reddened but then she laughed as well.

"The swamp?" Ahuva asked.

"Yeah," Josh said. "That's what the Israelis call Katamon. The *bee'tsah*."

"Too many frogs, not enough princes?" offered Leah.

"Or," Miriam said, the irrepressible academic, "a place you get stuck."

Dave's faux pas had burst the dam walls, granting free

speech to all. None of them could possibly shove their feet down their throats further than he already had.

Sarit sat opposite. Silent. Seething. Dave remembered her. One date. No, two. He had ended it and not well.

"I'm terrible with names and faces," he apologized, but no one was listening.

"Stuck," Josh said. "Exactly. People get stuck in Katamon."

Nat got up to serve the soup.

"Although," Miriam said, "technically we're in Kiryat Shmuel, not Katamon."

"Katamon isn't just a neighborhood." Josh had probably rehearsed this. "It's a state of mind. Kiryat Shmuel. Talbieh. The German Colony. Even San Simon. Wherever you have singles getting older and older and not settling down."

"Why aren't they getting married?" Ahuva asked, touched by the plight of older singles. No doubt, she already considered herself to be sitting on a dusty shelf.

"Fear of commitment," Sarit said. She focused her firebrand glance on Dave. It must have ended very badly. Had he even called?

"Fear of intimacy?" Miriam suggested.

Leah said, "It's not our fault. There's a shortage of single guys. Normal ones, anyway."

"You can say that again," said Sarit. Her eyes were still on Dave.

"Actually," Miriam said, "statistically speaking, each year slightly more males are born than females. But males have a lower life expectancy, so over time females overtake them."

Josh slapped the table again. "I've got the solution." His Alfred E. Neuman grin made prurient promises. "Thanks," he said to Nat, who had placed a bowl of mashed pumpkin soup before him.

"*Nu?*" Leah prodded, employing the Yiddish all-purpose prompt.

"The answer is simple." Josh drew out the suspense. "Concubines."

Leah squawked with outrage...or ecstasy, Dave couldn't tell. He just shook his head.

Ahuva said, "What's a concubine?"

"Like in the Bible," Josh said. "Wives, but without marriage."

"Let me get this straight," Nat said, delivering more bowls of soup. "You plan to rescue single women by throwing them in your harem?"

Saul, the hoopoe, let rip another fit of nervous laughter. "Why not?"

Giggles circulated the table. Half-digested pumpkin soup churned in Dave's stomach.

Nat took her seat. "The real cause of the problem," she said, "is that no one is willing to compromise."

Dave looked at Nat, surprised by her turn of conversation.

"Define *compromise*," Miriam said.

Nat swallowed a spoonful. "We've all got our lists even if we don't write them down. The guy or girl of our dreams. We search and search until one day we reach a certain age and we compromise. We pare the list down until finally someone fits."

Dave returned his spoon to his half-empty bowl. Nat had struck him with her candidness, her obvious confession and, he realized, her maturity. Neither Nat nor Saul seemed perturbed.

Nat: intelligent, talented, idealistic. And single. She had moved to the Upper West Side for a year and returned, still single. Crease lines marked the base of her neck. Dave could always date younger girls but the options for a thirty-year-old spinster diminished fast. Dave felt partially responsible. He had passed on asking Nat out on a hundred occasions. And, for the first time, he understood why. There was no spark. No flash. No primal quickening of excitement.

"I'm not going to compromise," Ahuva said. "My *beshert* is out there."

Leah laughed. "Let's talk when you're thirty."

Nat returned to the kitchen.

"Everybody compromises," Josh said. "Think of the Katamon couples you know. Jeff and Tamara? They got married a month ago."

Pumpkin soup threatened to erupt through Dave's nostrils. Thankfully, he didn't know Jeff and Tamara.

Leah said, "Jeff is a nice guy."

"But is Tamara the girl of his dreams? What about Julie and What's-His-Name? Iddo."

"Compromise," Leah said, warming to the game. "And then there's Shmuel and Rachel."

Dave glared at Leah. Shmuel was a good friend. They had shared a flat for a year before Shmuel disappeared into Married Land.

"I happen to know Shmuel and Rachel," he said. "They seem very happy to me."

"Seem," Josh said. "All couples seem happy. You never know what goes on behind closed doors."

"Bonnie and Lior?" Sarit had joined the melee. Dave was right to have dumped her.

"Definite compromise," Leah said.

Dave mumbled an excuse and fled to the kitchen.

Nat shoveled rice from a tinfoil tub into a serving bowl.

"How can I help?" he asked.

She gave him a sympathetic grin. "Sorry, Dave, not quite the meal I had planned."

He leaned against the fridge. "Thing's don't always work out the way we plan."

She pulled a tray of steaming vegetables off the hot tray and tilted the contents into a white platter.

Saul's hoopoe laugh echoed out again. Josh had enlisted Leah's stash of flavored vodka for a drinking game.

Dave decided to camp out in the kitchen for the rest of the meal. His dating prospects had burned to the ground anyway.

Nat finished fussing over the serving dishes and straightened. "I have a confession to make," she said. "I had an ulterior motive for inviting you."

"I'm a guinea pig for new recipes?" He had heard enough confessions for one night.

"More insidious, I'm afraid. I wanted to introduce you to someone. Mandy Rosenberg. A good friend. We shared a flat in New York. Great girl. You may have noticed her at Rabbi Levi's *shiur*."

"Really?" New Girl now had a name. Mandy Rosenberg. Dave had never dated a Mandy. Nat's consideration touched him. She was a true friend. And she had moved on.

Time to move on too, Dave.

"This whole meal was just a pretext," she continued. "But after you canceled she took up an earlier invitation and couldn't back out again."

"She didn't, by any chance, go to Eilat?"

"No. Why do you ask?"

"You still owe me a telephone number," Ben said, between mouthfuls of baked chicken.

After Saturday morning prayers at the Ramban synagogue, Dave had strolled down Emek Refaim to join the Greens for an early Shabbat lunch. Their home off Graetz Street consisted of large cylindrical rooms and thick, stone walls and had once served as a wine cellar and water cistern of the Templars who had settled the German Colony in the nineteenth century.

"Poor, Dave," said the blond goddess beside Ben at the dining room table.

Yvette, in her mild French accent, referred to Dave's

account of the previous night. In her presence, Dave felt as though he had wandered onto a movie set and found himself face-to-face with the dazzling female lead. Often, he forgot to close his mouth.

Ben's marriage to Yvette remained one of the unsolved mysteries of the modern era, on par with the Pyramids of Giza, Stonehenge, and Einstein's hair.

Ben belched softly. "Why don't you call this, what's her name?"

"Mandy." He spooned more *cholent* onto his plate. Yvette's version of the traditional beef stew hit the spot. *Cholent* solved two pressing problems: to feed many mouths with little meat, and to provide a hot meal without lighting a fire, a forbidden act on the Sabbath day. In this sense, the slow-cooked goulash joined the ranks of Gefilte fish, which obviated the need to pick out unwanted fish bones, yet another prohibition.

Yvette brushed strands of perfect hair from the face that had launched three perfumes and a dozen lines of designer clothing. "Call her. If it's meant to be, you'll come together."

Dave snorted beef stew out his nose and fumbled for a napkin.

"Sorry," he said. "I'm not sure I believe all that *beshert* business."

Yvette looked at him in shock.

Dave waved his fork conversationally. "It's a dangerous idea. How do you know if you've found The One? What if your marriage has problems? Did you make a mistake? Is your True Love still waiting?"

"That's so sad," Yvette said.

"It's not rational." Dave turned to his friend. "Tell her, Ben."

Ben frowned and stared at his plate. "Many religious concepts are not strictly rational," he said, in his lecture-hall tone.

Dave could not believe his ears. Ben's perfidy whet his appetite for battle.

"All right," he said. "If everyone has one soul mate, how can anyone remarry? Are soul mates exchangeable? And, back in the day when it was legal, how could one man marry two or more women? Were they all his soul mates?"

"Interestingly enough," Ben said, "the Dead Sea scrolls forbid bigamy outright and partly for this reason. After all, the animals entered Noah's ark two by two. They even interpret the verse against marrying two sisters as referring to any two…"

Ben noticed the blank stares and cut short his academic discourse. "Professor Barkley's class at Hebrew U," he added by way of apology.

"Don't give up, Dave," Yvette said. "You'll know when the right girl comes along. Be open-minded." She leaned on Ben and caressed his ear. "You never know when love will arrive."

Dave watched the happy couple like a hungry kid outside a candy store window. Married people belonged to an elite club that rejected him. They lived on a verdant planet, light years from his barren, solitary moon. They breathed different air. They were a different species. After the dinner fiasco at Nat's, the distance between worlds seemed unbridgeable.

"Remember how we met, Beni?"

Ben helped himself to more cabbage salad. "We don't want to bore Dave with all that, love."

"You never did tell me exactly how you met."

Dave remembered Ben's wedding. Yvette's family, a pride of tall, tanned Belgians, wore designer suits and shell-shocked expressions. Of all the eligible, successful men in the world, and after a fast-track courtship, how had their precious Yvette decided to spend her life with this short, brutish academic?

Yvette sipped her chardonnay and sighed. "I had flown in for a two-day shoot." Her eyes sparkled at the memory. "Middle Eastern theme. Beni guided the tour the agency had arranged."

Ben, a hunted expression fleeting across his face, pulled a

large volume of Gemara—the Talmud's gloss on Jewish law written in the style of a lively debate—from a shelf and hurriedly turned the pages.

"I didn't notice him at first, poor thing," Yvette continued, "but then he swept me off my feet. I just knew he was The One."

"Here it is," said Ben. "Here's your source."

He translated as he read.

"A man marries the woman he deserves... Skipping a few lines... And it's as difficult as splitting the sea... Some verses... Here we go. The Gemara quotes an apparent contradiction. Forty days before the fetus is formed, a Heavenly voice decrees: the daughter of So-and-So will marry So-and-So. There," Ben concluded triumphantly. "It's pre-determined. Beshert."

Yvette asked, "What was the contradiction?"

"Well, if a man marries the girl he deserves, then it depends on his deeds. It can't be pre-determined because of Free Choice."

"And the answer?"

Ben read on: "The one refers to the First Pairing, the other to the Second Pairing."

"Hold on," Dave said. "So your first marriage is made in Heaven but a second marriage isn't?"

"And as difficult as splitting the sea," Ben said. "Major headache for God. So do us a favor, don't get divorced."

Dave wouldn't let Ben off that lightly. "But if the first marriage was made in Heaven, why didn't it work out?"

"Death? There's another interpretation, though." He flipped to the back of the book and ran his finger along a column of fine print.

"*Ya'avetz,*" Ben said. "Rabbi Ya'akov Emden. Eighteenth-century Talmudist. No intellectual slouch. According to him, the two marriages are not necessarily chronological. Souls arrive in this world in pairs, male and female. The First Pairing mentioned by the Gemara refers to the reunion of twin souls. Made in Heaven, as you put it. But a man's actions might render him unworthy of his true soul mate. He may end up marrying another woman altogether, a Second Pairing, although chronologically his first marriage."

"That's terrible," Yvette said.

"So we *can* mess it up," Dave said. He had won the argument. Vindication left a bitter aftertaste.

Dave had met his soul mate. Two years ago, he had dated her. Hers was the name his mother had searched for, the sacred mantra he hesitated to utter even in his mind.

Shira Cohen. There. He had thought it. Shira Cohen. Shira Cohen. Shira Cohen. Only now she went by a different name. Because he had blown his only chance at true happiness out of the water. His First Pairing sunk, Dave would have to settle for second best, and even that after an arduous splitting of the Red Sea.

Unless. Unless he was mistaken.

"How do you know if you've found your twin soul?"

"According to Rabbi Emden"—Ben snapped the book shut—"you don't. Only God, the Maker of Souls, knows."

They sang *zemirot*, Dave's tenor harmonizing over Ben's baritone. They devoured Yvette's homemade Halva ice cream and chocolate brownies. After the Grace After Meals, Yvette excused herself to her ladies' afternoon *shiur* a few blocks away, and the two men retired to the living room for a postprandial whisky.

Dave sank onto a leather couch, his belly heavy with *cholent*. Glenmorangie washed over his tongue and slipped down his throat. The vapors numbed his brain pleasantly.

The salon walls, stone masses three feet thick, rounded toward a central ceiling shaft and recalled the old cistern the Greens had renovated and now called home. Sections of native rock peeked through smooth plaster on one side. On the other, the wall receded, forming a niche where a spotlight illuminated a slender earthenware jar of a familiar Middle Eastern style. The jar had a matching cap and its rounded bottom sat on a wire stand. Dave marveled at Yvette's good taste. Sitting there felt like lying in the lap of history.

Ben flopped beside him and peered into his whisky glass.

"Something was stolen from the City of David."

He processed Ben's words. "During the break-in? The papers didn't say anything about that."

"They didn't know because Erez didn't tell them. Bad publicity, he says. Piss off the donors."

"What was taken?"

"A clay jar. Two thousand years old."

"Valuable?"

Ben shot him an injured look. "It's history, Dave. It's priceless. Although," he admitted, "not in a strictly monetary sense. Few hundred dollars on the black market."

Robbery made more sense than vandalism. But why attack Ben for a few hundred dollars?

"Do you think Erez is involved?"

Ben weighed his words. "Unlikely. Erez could study it whenever he wanted. And he could make it disappear with little noise. Take it down for cleaning or restoration and keep it on his mantelpiece for a year or two."

Dave's quality assurance intuition kicked in, a honed sixth sense that sniffed out the most unimaginable and unlikely of computer glitches. "Unless Erez wanted to divert suspicion."

Dave would not put black market dabbling past Erez but not for a paltry sum.

"You sure there's nothing special about the jar?"

Ben smiled. "Ever hear of the Copper Scroll?"

Dave hazarded a guess. "One of the Dead Sea Scrolls?"

He had seen the long scrolls on display at the Israel Museum in Jerusalem. The ancient texts began surfacing in 1947 in the caves of Qumran thanks to the serendipity of a Bedouin shepherd.

"Yes and no. The Dead Sea Scrolls contain biblical texts and apocalyptic ramblings. They were written on parchment and papyrus scrolls, remarkably well preserved thanks to earthenware storage jars.

"One scroll stands apart. Firstly, it consists of two rolled-up copper plates found on a stone ledge and not in jars. The script is sloppy and riddled with errors. The Hebrew is markedly different to anything known, the spelling unorthodox. More importantly, instead of holy texts, the scroll lists deposits of gold and silver along with their locations. In today's currency, the hoard totals over a billion dollars."

"Buried treasure?" Dave smirked. "This sounds like Indiana Jones."

Ben's cheeks turned scarlet. "The treasure is a fiction, Dave. Most authorities identify the Judean Desert Cult that wrote the scrolls with the Essenes, ascetic monks more interested in ritual purity and apocalyptic visions than pots of gold. They fled to the desert to protest the so-called corruption of the Sadducee Temple management."

Dave had learned about the Sadducees in a high school Jewish History class. Sadducees were the bad guys, the ritualistic Temple-crazy literalists. After the Romans burned the Second Temple of Jerusalem in 70 C.E., the Sadducees all but evaporated and gave way to the Pharisees, the guardians of rabbinic tradition and the forerunners of modern Judaism.

"Even if the treasure exists," Ben continued, "it's practically impossible to find. The locations are too specific, tied to landmarks that are long gone. Some people, however, believe in the Copper Scroll. Enough to break into the COD."

Dave sipped his whisky but still failed to connect the dots. "You said the Copper Scroll was found on a ledge and not in a jar. Why would treasure hunters steal a scroll jar?"

Ben lifted his bulk from the couch. "This was no ordinary scroll jar."

He walked over to the recess in the wall and raised the clay urn from its wire throne. Cradling the vessel like a newborn, he rejoined Dave on the couch.

Dave realized why the urn had looked familiar. He had seen similar jars at the Israel Museum.

"Wait a minute. Do you mean to tell me that you stole the scroll jar?"

"Very funny, Dave. Although this is exactly like the one

stolen from the COD."

"Shouldn't it be in a museum?"

Ben hesitated. "That's not the question you want to ask."

"It's not?"

"What you really want to ask," Ben said, "is about this." He pointed to three angular characters etched into the urn's grainy surface. Three vertical lines: one bisected a circle; the second formed a triangle; the last met a wavy line at the top. A lollipop, a flag, and a streamer.

"Guess what language that is."

"Cuneiform?"

Ben shook his head at his ignorance. "It's Hebrew."

"Hebrew?" Dave had spent ten years in Hebrew Day School. Thrice daily, he read Hebrew prayers from his Hebrew prayer book. He lived in a country that listed Hebrew as one of its three official languages. He recognized Hebrew when he saw it and the twenty-two blocky characters shared nothing with the three glyphs on the side of the urn.

"Yes," Ben said. "Hebrew. And cuneiform is a script, a set of characters, not a language. What we have here is *Ktav Ivri*, the early Hebrew script. Today's Hebrew letters, *Ktav Ashuri* or Assyrian script, replaced *Ktav Ivri* two and a half thousand years ago. But the language of both is Hebrew."

Ben pointed out each letter from right to left. "*Tsadi. Dalet. Qof.*"

Dave had read the symbols in the wrong direction. He scrawled the Hebrew letters on the whiteboard of his mind and scrabbled for the little dots and lines, the vowel points necessary to vocalize the consonants. He tackled this feat whenever he read a Hebrew newspaper.

"*Zedek*," he said. "Justice."

"That's one reading," said Ben. "And one translation. *Zedek* also means Jupiter, the planet or the Roman god. Another reading is *Zeduki*, or Sadducee. The more interesting one, however, is *Zadok*."

"A name?"

"Exactly. A number of biblical characters went by the

name Zadok, the earliest being King David's High Priest. But Zadok also appears in the Dead Sea Scrolls as the leader of the Judean Desert Cult, usually referred to as *Moreh Zedek*, or the Teacher of Righteousness."

"I still don't see the connection to the Copper Scroll."

Ben placed the jar on his lap. "These jars have something in common besides the letters. None of them contained scrolls. And all of them originated in a single cave: Cave Three."

"Let me guess. The same cave as the Copper Scroll."

"Correct."

Not a strong link, in Dave's opinion. He considered the jar's cratered surface. The clay urn would not have drawn a second glance in a curio store and yet, according to Ben, it sat in the eye of a tornado.

"Assuming you're right," he said. "Assuming someone believes the urn is tied to the Copper Scroll. How would an empty jar help them find the treasure?"

Ben smiled like the Cheshire cat.

"I don't know." Like many hopeless academics, Ben preferred one good question to a dozen simple answers.

"But you have a theory?"

Ben stroked his imaginary beard. "Not yet."

Ben rose and restored the urn, empty of scrolls but overflowing with secrets, to its place of honor.

God knows what crimes men would *not* commit for a billion dollars.

"You sure you want that lying around the house?"

Ben shrugged. "It's safer here than at the COD."

Dave downed the rest of his whisky. "It's not the jar I'm worried about."

At mid-day in a Jerusalem apartment, a man drew the curtains and turned to the knapsack on the worktable.

At last.

He had dreamed of this moment.

Fingers of sunlight thrust between the curtains and groped at countless motes of dust. The man reached into the bag, unfurled a large gray cloak on the desk, and uncovered the treasure within. He lifted the earthenware jar into the air. His fingers caressed the rough surface and traced the three characters etched into the side.

You have waited long too, my little treasure.

Jay had done well. It had taken a few days for the hubbub to settle but suspicion had not turned his way.

Now nothing can stop me.

With this simple clay vessel, he would change the world forever.

He cleared the desktop and laid the urn on its side. He opened a drawer, placed a hammer on the table, and pulled garden gloves over his hands. He gripped the base of the urn and held it steady.

Then, the Teacher of Righteousness raised the hammer over his head.

Time to make history.

CHAPTER 3

Dave opened his eyes. Darkness filled his living room. Street-lights projected yellow Morse code through the window shades and onto the wall.

He had dozed through the Afternoon Service. The Evening Service too.

After lunch, he had stretched out on his couch to read, his mind abuzz with whisky, scroll jars, and the ghost of Shira Cohen.

A copy of Rabbi Soloveitchik's *Lonely Man of Faith* lay open on his chest.

Mandy Rosenberg.

Mike had pointed her out in Rabbi Levi's *shiur*. Nat wanted to set Dave up with her. She was American, around Dave's age, and probably Frum-From-Recent. How long would she be in Israel? Was she here to stay?

Dave needed more data.

A shuffling sound within the walls, like the patter of little rat feet, grew louder and then faded away. One of the upper neighbors had flushed the toilet.

Enough pottering around.

Dave got to his feet. He recited the *Havdalah* prayer that marked the conclusion of the Sabbath day over a glass of grape juice, a spice box filled with cloves, and a torch made of four interwoven candles. He clicked the shower boiler button, picked up his cordless phone, and settled on the couch.

Nat answered on the second ring.

"The girl you wanted to introduce me to," he said after exchanging post-Shabbat pleasantries. "Mandy Rosenberg. How long is she in the country?"

"You can ask her yourself," Nat said. "She's right here."

"Wait—" Dave said, too late.

The phone changed hands.

"Hi there," said a female voice with a Southern twang.

Dave shot to his feet.

Oh, God. Say something clever. Say something funny. For Heaven's sake, Dave, say something!

"Hi," he squeaked.

Breathe, Dave! Breathe!

He cleared his throat. "Mandy, right? How are you?"

He wanted to dash his head against the wall.

"All good. How about you?" There was a smile in her voice. Not derisive. Encouraging.

"Great. Just great. Thanks." Dave paced the length of the salon. "You shared a flat with Nat, right, but you don't sound like a New Yorker."

"Houston, Texas," she said with pride. "I moved east five years ago."

"Right," he said. "Good."

Don't ramble. Keep it short.

"I, um, was wondering. Do you drink coffee?"

"I've been known to," she said. "But you're British. Shouldn't we have tea?"

"Oh, no. We got rid of that years ago. Along with manners and the monarchy."

She laughed. The girl actually *laughed.*

He stormed ahead. "How about tomorrow night, eight o'clock? At Café Atara on Gaza Street."

"Sure," she said. "It's a date. Here's my number, just in case."

A full four minutes after the call ended, Dave removed the

wet handset from his ear and stopped pacing.

He had acquired not only a telephone number but a date with Mandy Rosenberg. And he liked her. She was down-to-earth and had a sense of humor. She was cute, even in Mike's objective opinion. And Mandy Rosenberg was the only girl on Dave's thirty-year-old desert island. He could not afford to screw this up.

He sank onto the couch. He slowed his breathing down to a mild panic attack. With pale, trembling fingers, he dialed a number.

"Ben," he said. "I need your help."

Mandy was not in the habit of arguing with rabbis, although, at times, their parables and interpretations pushed the limits of her credulity. This rabbi had gone too far.

"But Rabbi Jeremy," she said, "doesn't that contradict the Bible?"

A stunned silence filled the classroom of young women.

The thin British rabbi smiled behind his glasses and long, ginger beard, and leaned on the podium. His black hat and jacket rested on a chair and the collar of his white shirt rose toward his ears. He resembled a benevolent Yorkshire terrier.

"Our Sages say," he repeated in his soft voice, "*He who says David sinned is mistaken.*"

"What about Bathsheba? And Uriah?"

Mandy happened to know about King David. As a child, she had begged her father to tell and retell the stories: David and Goliath; David's flight from King Saul; his friendship with Jonathan; his conquest of Jerusalem; the betrayal at the hands of Absalom, his son. And, of course, the affair with Bathsheba and subsequent elimination of her pesky Hittite husband.

"Those are good questions," said Rabbi Jeremy. "Hold onto them for later in the course. For now, I'd like to finish the outline."

Mandy let it go. First day in seminary and already hassling the rabbis.

Her schedule at *She'arim* started at eight-thirty. The class consisted of twelve girls, mostly nineteen-year-olds on their year abroad who lived in the dorms. Mandy had opted out of the dorms. Been there, done that, bought the T-shirt.

Rabbi Jeremy taught the first class of the day, Introduction to the Prophets. He was recapping the background of the course for Mandy's benefit when she had felt compelled to interrupt.

What's with you today, Mands?

The girls broke into pairs. The rabbi introduced Mandy to her study partner, Esty, a painfully sweet New Yorker of about twenty with big eyes and straight black hair tied back. Mandy would have killed for hair like that. For years, she had struggled with dryers and flat irons before she had learned to embrace her natural curls.

"Rabbi Jeremy is amazing," Esty said after the teacher moved off to assist another pair of girls.

"Yeah?" Mandy raised an eyebrow but held back on the sarcasm. What had ticked her off this time? Was it the rabbi's gloss of King David or the stardust in the younger girl's eyes?

"Amazing," Esty repeated. "Just wait and see. He knows *so* much. You're going to *love* it here."

The rest of the day flowed without incident. Rabbis and Rebbetzins lectured on Women in *Tanakh*, the Laws of Cooking on Shabbat, Interpersonal Relationships, and Fundamentals of Faith, interrupted by short breaks and a canteen lunch of chicken schnitzel and mashed potatoes.

Mandy had smiled more than once at the not-so-subtle

subliminal messaging of the subject matter: how to be a good Jewish wife.

At five o'clock Mandy skipped the last lecture and the Ask the Rabbi session, and called a cab. She planned to keep her evenings free. This winter break was both a spiritual refresher and a much-needed hiatus from the office. But beyond that, four months in Jerusalem held other promises for a single Jewish girl.

Night had fallen over the concrete jungle of Har Nof. A white Mercedes idled at the curb, a yellow half-circle with the word "taxi" on the roof. Mandy opened the back door and got in.

"Mendele Street," she said to the driver, a graying, bareheaded man who nodded and started the meter.

She relaxed on the plush leather upholstery as the engine purred and white stone apartment buildings panned across the window.

Five days after her arrival, the sight of Hebrew street signs and storefronts still warmed her heart. Welcome to the Promised Land, the Land of Milk and Honey, the miraculous ingathering of Jews of all shapes, sizes, and colors after two thousand years of exile. Jewish police officers patrolled the streets. Jewish soldiers guarded the borders. Jewish judges resided over the courts. Even the garbage collectors and bus drivers spoke the language of Abraham, Isaac, and Jacob, celebrated Jewish festivals, and, each day, wrote a fresh page in the story of the Jewish People.

This was Mandy's first trip to Israel but, inexplicably, she felt at home.

And she loved her new flatmates, despite her initial concerns.

The Internet listing had sought a Sabbath-observant, kosher-eating, female non-smoker. Between the lines, Mandy read "straitlaced" and "uptight." A brief email exchange with Ruchama, who added a twelve o'clock curfew on visiting boyfriends and displayed great interest in how exactly Mandy planned to cover her share of the expenses, did nothing to dispel Mandy's first impression.

That first Tuesday morning, Mandy, exhausted from the flight, took an hour-long shuttle ride from Ben Gurion airport to Mendele Street. The apartment building stood four stories high in grubby Jerusalem stone and straddled a tiny parking yard on stone stilts. Mandy dragged her suitcases up the two flights of stairs and pressed the buzzer.

As the door swung open, her concerns evaporated.

A blond bombshell in a pink bikini leaned in the doorway. She threw a nonchalant arm behind her head like a lingerie model and sized up the newcomer with radiant blue eyes.

"Mandy, I presume." Her voice was rough, sensual, the accent a flawless Bostonian.

"You must be Shani."

"Very good." The sapphire eyes sparkled and Mandy knew they would be friends. "Ruchama is the short, fat, mousy one. She means badly but she's harmless enough. Come on in." She pulled Mandy inside by her scarf and reached for the suitcase handles. "I'll help you with these bad boys."

Mandy shed her coat.

Shani pointed at the ancient radiator fixed to a corner wall. "Central heating," she explained. "There's a diesel boiler in the belly of the beast. Keeps things toasty."

She gave Mandy the cook's tour. Mandy's tail wind of adrenaline survived the dank kitchen with its stained twin sinks, rickety cupboards, greasy gas oven, and gargantuan, ancient fridge.

She delighted in the Hebrew terms Shani used. The service balcony beyond the tiny bathroom was a *mirpeset sherut*; the oblong living room, a *sa'lon*.

Mandy collapsed onto the couch draped with a flower print dustcover. The owners of the apartment had decorated tastefully in the fifties and then let nature take its course. The fibrous, brown wallpaper peeled away in places and was blackened above the low telephone shelf where, Mandy guessed, the girls lit Shabbat candles. The dirt-stained floor tiles, warped cupboards, and sagging mattress of Mandy's narrow bedroom fell several leagues below the smooth parquet and steel four-poster of her 62nd Street apartment. To Mandy it was all part of the adventure.

Shani returned from the kitchen with two mugs of hot chocolate.

Mandy sipped her cocoa on the couch. Her eyelids drooped as the ten-hour flight caught up with her. Outside, the sun climbed in the sky but her body still thought it was time to go to bed. The radiators creaked as they cooled. Winter air seeped through the single-glaze French window at the balcony.

She watched Shani through a haze of chocolate steam. Shani had slipped on a silky kimono and curled up on the armchair. Her luxuriant golden curls cascaded over her shoulders.

"How long have you been in Israel?" Mandy asked.

"My parents moved here before I was born. I had no say in the matter."

"Any tips for the new girl in town?"

Shani read the answer off the small ersatz crystal chandelier. "When you take a cab," she said, "sit in the back. Cabbies can't keep their hands to themselves."

Mandy added Jewish Perverts to her mental list.

A key rattled in the front door and a rotund woman stormed in and pulled off layers of clothing.

"It's cold dogs outside," she said to the room at large.

Mandy directed her confused expression at Shani, who just rolled her eyes.

The woman still hadn't noticed them. "If I get another night shift this week…"

She turned around, smiled, and walked over to Mandy.

"Ruchama," she said, extending a large, cold but welcoming hand. She was the negative image of Shani: plain and pudgy but far friendlier than Mandy had expected.

As Mandy soon discovered, Ruchama was also the child of immigrants, and Mandy would learn more Hebrew from Ruchama's English than from any Ulpan class Mandy had taken in college.

Ruchama placed her hands on her hips and eyed her flatmates like a hen surveying her brood. "Shani hasn't broken you already, I hope."

"Give me time," Shani purred. "We've just met."

The cab ran over a pothole and Mandy bounced on the leather upholstery. They had mounted a bridge over a highway intersection.

Mandy recalled her spat with Rabbi Jeremy and squirmed.

Grumpy, argumentative, and cynical. What had gotten into her?

Had the novelty of the adventure worn off? Was reality slowly sinking in? She was a thousand miles away from her home, her life, and all she held dear.

Was there a deeper cause?

Her thoughts drifted to her father. He had loved Israel. He'd worked on a kibbutz for a year before returning home to start college, where he had met Mandy's mom. In her earliest memories, her dad promised to take her to the Holy Land and show her around. Was that why she had traveled so far? To fulfill her father's dream?

The cab dipped down Jabotinsky, made a sharp left onto Mendele Street, and pulled up outside Mandy's building. She paid the driver and climbed the stairs. She aimed the key at the front door when it opened and a thirty-something man stepped out. He wore a crocheted *kippa* on his head and an embarrassed expression on his face. Their eyes met for an instant, and then he rushed past Mandy and down the stairwell.

Mandy stepped inside, placed her bag on the living room table, and took off her coat. The radiators were working overtime again.

A boyfriend?

She was pretty sure Ruchama wasn't seeing anyone and Shani seemed to date a different lawyer or hotshot executive every night and this guy didn't fit the mold.

A brother?

Shani emerged from her room in her trademark pink bikini, a large red apple in her hand. As the bedroom door closed, Mandy spied a camera mounted on a tripod.

"Who was that?" Mandy asked.

"Who was who?"

Shani sashayed past Mandy into the living room and settled on the armchair. She took a large bite of the apple.

"The guy who just left in a hurry."

"Oh," Shani said, her mouth full. She waved the apple dismissively and swallowed. "A client." She took another bite.

Mandy had never considered that Shani had an actual job. The buxom beauty seemed to laze around the apartment all day.

"Oh," Mandy said. She considered the pink bikini and mounted camera. *What exactly do you do, Shani Weis?* Ask no questions, hear no lies. And Mandy needed to shower and dress, pronto.

Ruchama bustled through the living room en route to the kitchen.

"Hi, Mandy," she said. "Want pasta? I'm making mushrooms in cream."

"I'd love to," Mandy said, "but I have a date."

Ruchama stuck her head out of the kitchen, her eyes wide. "A date? Already?"

"Who's the lucky guy?" said Shani.

"David Schwarz."

Shani frowned. "Never heard of him."

"He's British. Old friend of Natalie."

"Blind date?"

"Not really. I saw him at the *shiur* last week."

"And?"

Mandy thought of the guy with the neatly parted hair and button-down in the men's section. A smug first impression raised its hand in the back of Mandy's mind. Mandy ignored it. Dave was Nat's good friend. With a haircut and a change of wardrobe, he could look good. After all the stolen glances, Mandy had been sure he would talk to her after the lecture but he had slipped away with barely a word. Did that count as mysterious?

"I don't know," Mandy said. "He has potential."

Dave never had trouble with first-date small talk. He had notched up countless flight hours and flew most first dates on autopilot. But he didn't usually find himself at a table for two with Mandy Rosenberg.

The soft light of Café Atara on Gaza Street glinted on her relaxed auburn curls. Elevator music played in the background. Mandy sipped her latte and smiled.

Dave smiled back and said nothing.

Mike was right. Mandy was cute. Not the classic elegance of Shira Cohen, mind you, but beautiful in a girl-next-door sort of way.

Dave said nothing again. He said more nothing. He had obsessed the entire day over this moment. He had endured a late-night session with Ben and the Pickup Artist's Bible. Despite all of that, his mind drew blanks.

"So," Mandy said. "What brings you to Israel?"

Oh, thank God!

But his relief shriveled in mid-bloom. Mandy had asked The Question.

Over the years, Dave's first date Q and A had evolved a small set of one-liners that served as litmus tests, and a girl's reactions predicted the outcome of the relationship with depressing accuracy. His answer to this particular question mixed irony and social commentary and often elicited blank stares or raised eyebrows, especially in Americans, who remained largely uninitiated in the joys of British humor.

He cleared his throat.

Here goes.

"The usual story," he said, deadpan. "I was brainwashed by Bnei Akiva."

Then a miracle occurred. The beautiful girl across the table *laughed*.

"It's true, I suppose," she said. "The summer camps. Seminars. You should file a class action suit." Her eyes narrowed, bemused. "What?"

Dave blinked away his stunned expression.

"Nothing," he said. "I'm just not used to people understanding my sense of humor. Not without diagrams. By this point they've usually called for the men in white coats."

Another delicate laugh.

"Thank you," she said. "I'll take that as a compliment."

She swept a strand of hair behind her ear. According to the Pickup Artist's Bible, a grooming gesture counted as an Indicator of Interest. Three IOIs and Dave could invite her back to his place. If Dave was that sort of guy, which he wasn't.

Mandy returned to her latte. Dave liked the Southern twang of her voice, at once familiar and exotic. He wished she would speak some more.

The uniformed security guard at the glass door of the coffee shop ushered in a young couple. The awkward body language said First Date.

The silence grew. It developed limbs and eyes and opened its hungry, toothy maw.

What had Ben said? Remember, dammit!

The Pickup Artist's Bible had said to feign disinterest in the target. Chat up her girlfriends instead. But Dave and Mandy were alone at the table.

What came next?

Dave ordered his fingers to stop fidgeting with the sugar sachets in the little white basin.

Don't focus on you. Ask about her.

He sucked in a lungful of air.

"How about you?" he asked. "What brings you to Israel?"

"I'm at *She'arim* for four months," she said. "But I haven't made *aliya* yet. Just trying it out."

Just trying it out. Code words for Husband Shopping.

He had heard good reports of the seminary in Har Nof, although it was not as *frum* as *Bnos Chava*, where Shira Cohen had studied that fateful summer two years before.

"Do you like it there?"

"So far. Although I had an argument with the rabbi on my first day. He said that King David never sinned, which is obviously not true."

"Bathsheba," Dave said. "And Uriah."

"Exactly! If he didn't sin, why the cover-up? Nathan the Prophet called him on it. He even confessed. Why do the rabbis feel the need to whitewash him?"

Dave had heard the midrashic explanations. The king's men routinely divorced their wives before setting out to battle in case they went missing in action. Bathsheba, technically, was a divorcee at the time the king got to her. But Dave decided not to play rabbi's advocate.

Mandy smiled at him. "David is my favorite biblical character."

Dave chalked up another IOI. He had earned points simply for his name, and finally his parents had justified their existence.

Mandy said, "How about you?"

"Me?"

"Your favorite character."

"Oh."

He ransacked the drawers of his Bible knowledge for a safe and worthy answer. Dave didn't play favorites in scripture. He liked the good guys, disliked the bad.

Just pick a hero. Abraham. Isaac. Jacob. Moses.

"Elijah," he said, surprising even himself. "Direct line to God. Miracles. Chariot of fire. And he never screwed up."

"It's OK to screw up. It's what I like about King David. His flaws make him real. He's a hero because he overcame his failings."

"Nah," Dave said. "Screwing up is overrated."

He had meant to be witty but he sounded jaded and cynical. His hard-earned points crumbled to dust.

His neck itched against his collar. Had they turned up the heat?

Mandy placed her empty cup on the table.

"What do you do?" she asked him.

She had steered the conversation back to safe, familiar waters, probably out of pity.

"Hi-tech," he said with pride and waited for the awed sigh.

Mandy looked confused. "Hi-tech is a big field. Can you narrow it down?"

Dave swallowed hard. "QA. Quality assurance at a software company."

"Ah. You're the guys who test the code. I worked in HR in New York. QA is always hard to find. They keep burning out."

Ouch. So much for impressing her. She probably knows how much I earn too. Perfect.

"How long have you been at it?"

"Seven years." Dave looked at his hands. "Ever since I moved here."

"And your current job?"

"Five."

Five years.

That sounded long. Too long. Dead-End-Job long.

Mandy, however, seemed upbeat. "That's great job security," she said.

"Yes."

Another lull in conversation.

Ask about her!

"Do you have family in Israel?"

"Nope. My mom's in Houston and I'm an only child."

Mandy hadn't mentioned her father. Were her parents

divorced? On bad terms?

"And your father?"

"My dad died fourteen years ago."

"Oh," he said. "I'm sorry." *Great job, Dave.*

"It's OK."

He needed a change of direction.

Compliment her but don't overdo it.

Her hair? Too personal. The jacket?

The glass door of the restaurant caught his eye again and fear rippled through him. A woman had just walked in. Unruly hair, so blond it was almost white. Toothy smile. Crazy eyes. Dave didn't know her name. He didn't want to. In his mind, she was simply *The Katamonster.*

The Katamonster scanned the coffee shop with hungry ferret eyes. Deep within Dave's brain stem, primal synapses triggered and he ducked his head to the tabletop.

"Is everything OK?" Mandy asked.

A waiter approached Katamonster and blocked her line of sight.

"Yes," he said, straightening slowly.

A year ago. Friday night. Outside Ohel Nechama. The aging spinster had accosted Dave on the street and, by way of introduction, asked for his home address. He had managed, with difficulty, to brush her off. He ran from her ever since.

The waiter directed the woman to a table about ten feet away.

Was the Katamonster on a date? A blind date, no doubt. The bloke was in for a surprise.

Mandy looked over her shoulder, toward the door, then turned a quizzical expression at Dave.

"An ex?" she asked.

"No! No."

How to explain this without sounding pathetic?

"More like a stalker."

Mandy's eyes widened. Then she raised a skeptical eyebrow.

His point balance hit zero and kept falling. He squeezed

his brain for another of Ben's dating nuggets.

Change location!

He waved to the waiter like a drowning man and scribbled in the air, the international gesture for "check, please."

Mandy looked surprised. Or disappointed. Did she think Dave was bailing on her?

He said, "Shall we go for a walk?"

Dave stepped out of Café Atara, onto the cracked sidewalk and into the crisp night air. He held the door for Mandy, who wrapped a gray scarf about her neck and swung the end over the shoulder of her leather jacket. They waited at the light as cars lurched up Gaza Street toward the city center. Mandy's perfume smelled fruity and fresh. Dave regained his composure. Best to pretend nothing had happened.

In the unreality of the Pickup Artist's Bible, a change of location involved questions like "your place or mine?" Seclusion with a girl was not an option for Dave, so Ben had found a substitute for him.

"Have you been to Yemin Mosheh?" Dave asked.

"No."

"It has a great view of the Old City. A bit far by foot. My car's around the corner."

"OK," she said.

They got into his Ford Focus, cruised up Gaza, then turned right at France Square onto Keren Hayesod.

Display value.

He had almost forgotten that point.

Reveal your added value, the qualities that raise you above the pack.

Dave had a car. Not many Anglo new arrivals did. Dave was established. And knowledgeable.

"Yemin Mosheh," Dave said, "was one of the first neighborhoods outside the Old City. Sir Moses Montefiore built it and named it after himself. Quaint stone houses."

Mandy didn't say anything. Since the Katamonster debacle, she had spoken in monosyllables. Had he freaked her out? Or was she just comfortable?

The possibility that he had blown the date calmed him. He

had nothing left to lose.

"I'd be nervous to drive in Israel," Mandy said. "People are so aggressive."

"The rules are simple. Never indicate. Never give way unless death is the only alternative. You get used to it. Frankly, I think the locals have to watch out for me now."

Mandy laughed. Dave heard the *cha-ching* of bonus points. Perhaps he hadn't blown it after all.

They crossed King David Street, drove down the tree-lined cul-de-sac of Yemin Mosheh, and parked opposite Montefiore's windmill. They walked onto the wide stone promenade under the expanse of starry sky.

Across a short valley, the buttressed walls of the Old City glowed in gold spotlight, immense and majestic. A young ultra-Orthodox couple sat on a metal bench under a street lamp and engaged in a whispered conversation. Dave and Mandy continued to the low wall at the edge of the promenade and absorbed the view.

A soft breeze animated the tendrils of Mandy's hair.

"It's beautiful." She turned to Dave and the streetlight caught her smile.

God bless you, Ben Green.

"So that," she continued, "is where it all began. The Jerusalem of King David."

"Actually," Dave said, "King David never lived in the Old City." For once Dave was glad for Ben's archaeological prowess. "And the so-called Tower of David"—he pointed to a lone minaret on the left—"has nothing to do with King David either. Suleiman the Great set up the Old City walls against the Crusaders. The original city of Jerusalem lies just south of the walls. It's known as the City of David."

Mandy didn't say anything for a while. Had he bored her?

"Wow," she said, eventually. "That *is* interesting."

"The inhabitants at the time of King David," Dave said, spurred on, "the Jebusites, or *Yevusim* in Hebrew, felt so secure behind the walls that they guarded them with the blind and the lame. Eventually, David conquered it by—"

"By sending a man through the water duct," Mandy said. She winked at him. "Favorite biblical character, remember?"

Ouch.

He had not been listening.

"But I didn't know about the City of David. You're a walking encyclopedia."

Ouch again.

Dave felt a need to apologize.

"A friend of mine is a program co-coordinator at the City of David."

Mandy seemed strangely contemplative. "Your Hebrew seems pretty good."

"Thanks."

"My Hebrew sucks. You probably understood Rabbi Levi's *shiur* last week."

She had remembered Dave at the *shiur*. Was that an Indicator of Interest or had he made her feel stupid?

"Not really," he said. "Not all of it. Well. Most of it. Except the poetic bits."

Mandy sighed.

"OK," she said. "Time for the big question." She inclined her head playfully at him.

"The big question?"

Mandy had a litmus test of her own.

"Yes," she said. "Man United or Liverpool?"

Oh, crap.

Of all the single women in the world, he had landed a soccer groupie.

"Um. Ah. Well. You see. As it happens. I'm not much of a football fan."

"You're kidding me."

"Nope. I kid you not."

"You don't like soccer?"

"Never have."

"What kind of a Brit are you?"

His reserve of witty comebacks ran dry.

"Not a very good one? I used to play in school but never

quite got the hang of spectating."

He was apologizing again, another Pickup Artist no-no. He wished they had built the promenade wall higher so he could bash his head against it.

He scrutinized Mandy's silhouette. She stared out at the Old City walls, her mood unfathomable. He no longer had a clue whether he was in the black or the red.

Mandy drew a deep breath.

"I should get back," she said. "Early start tomorrow."

She had passed her verdict, but had she found him innocent or guilty?

"Right. I'll drop you off."

"That's OK," she said. "My apartment isn't far. I'll walk."

Jay pulled the drawstrings on his hoodie and traipsed along the damp sidewalk. His stomach ached for food. Night had fallen over downtown Jerusalem and the moist air threatened more rain. Tall walls of weathered stone hedged the street in on both sides.

John kept pace with him in silence. Jay knew what he was thinking. Jay thought it too. They were low on cash and the Teacher had sent no word since their meeting in the back of a transit van that night in Talpiot. Jay's emails bounced back as though the Teacher had been a daydream.

Great things, a woman's voice whispered. *You will do great things.* Jay wasn't so sure anymore. The situation was bad. Very bad. Otherwise, Jay would never have agreed to this.

They paused at an intersection. The plaque across the road

read Street of the Prophets. A white taxicab cruised by.

"This it?"

"Yeah," said John. "First left and then a right."

A busker on Ben Yehuda Street had given them directions. Keep this up and Jay would have to work the streets as well. He had played the guitar once but his fingers remembered nothing. He wasn't much for dance or song. He could preach.

Keep a low profile, the Teacher had said.

John stopped at a large hole in the wall. Rusted metal doors stood open on each side and sagged against the hinges. Rubber flaps dangled like the strip curtains of the walk-in freezers they kept on sheep farms.

John gawked at him, waiting for the go-ahead. Jay inhaled. "OK." He tightened the hood over his head. "Let's make this an in-and-out job."

They pushed through the strips. The interior felt warm and musky and glowed with dim, amber light. The oblong hovel contained four wooden tables, two a side. Behind the counter at the back, people got busy at tinfoil trays and large pots. A microwave hummed.

The two men walked between the tables to the counter. White rice filled one of the pots and a tantalizing whiff of sweet-and-sour chicken made Jay salivate.

An immense woman frowned at them, her gray, frizzled hair tied in a bun.

"New ones," she said to herself and huffed. "Go on and sit down there with Sid. Sid!" she yelled.

"Yes'm," said a dark bundle of rags and blankets at the table by the door.

"Sid. Take care of these young fellas. I'm Maggie," she added and smiled for a split second. "Go on now and have a seat."

Jay obeyed, stepping away from the counter. He had stumbled into the saloon of a hick town in the Wild West.

Jay and John swung their legs over the wooden bench opposite the ragman. Sid had a face like a black raisin and good white teeth. "Over here they serve it out," he said, all whispers and smiles.

"Who does?" said Jay.

"Them young 'uns. Volunteers. They got Chinese tonight. From that place on Ben Seera. Mmm-mmm-mmm!" He rocked from side to side and licked his lips. The old man liked to talk. This would be a long night.

Sid nodded at the counter and lowered his voice. "Maggie got a heart o' gold. Jus' don' piss her off. Where you from?"

"Far away," said Jay.

The old man wrinkled his nose. The mongrel had caught a scent. "Australia?"

"Thereabouts," said Jay through clenched teeth. New Zealand was the correct answer. People always got it wrong.

Sid laughed. "I seen Australians here. Russians. South Africans too." He eyed John with suspicion. "Your friend here ain't no aborigine." He turned to John. "What are you then? Mexican? Ain't no Mexicans round here. Say, what cat dragged you to the Holy Land? You Jewish?"

A girl of twenty in an ankle-length skirt and hair down to her shoulders appeared at their table. She filled out her sweater well enough but Jay's eyes fixed on the tray in her hands, the steaming rice and chicken pieces, and that dizzying sweet-and-sour sauce. The girl slid a heaped disposable plate and a plastic cup of cordial before each of them. Jay grabbed a plastic fork.

"Thanks, Malki," Sid said. "You got ketchup?"

Jay looked up at the girl. An aura of gold light enveloped her head. The fork paused halfway to his mouth. He knew her. But where? When?

"Mary?" he said. "Is that you?"

The girl's eyes opened wide and she hurried back toward the counter. The spell broke.

"Hey!" Sid hissed at him. "You crazy? You *ha*rass the girls and Maggie'll send you packing. What's with you?"

Jay resisted the urge to slap the old man.

Instead, he said, "I forgive you."

"You for*give* me," Sid repeated and hooted. "Who d'you

think you are? Jesus Christ?"

Jay dropped his fork on his plate. He sat erect and peeled back the hood. In the bathroom mirror, Jay had monitored the progress of his hair. Down his neck. Over his shoulders. The brown oily locks, wispy beard, and gaunt cheeks matched the likeness known around the globe. Understanding hatched in Sid's black rheumy eyes.

"Holy crap," the old man said. "Hey, Maggie! Got us here another crazyass thinks he's Jesus Christ. Ha!"

Jay pulled the hood over his head and stood. He collected his plate and cup. "C'mon, John."

The two men walked the damp street and ate in silence. The Teacher was right. The world wasn't ready yet. Jay would have to be discreet. Until the End of Days. He liked the sound of it. He'd like to see Sid's face then.

"Jay," John said on Rabbi Kook Street. "It's not too late. We can get on a plane. Start over."

Jay slammed the remains of his meal into a garbage bin. He had lost his appetite. "We've been through this, John. We can't go back."

Only chaos waited behind that door. But John wasn't giving in.

"There's a flight to Greece," he said. "We can just about afford it. Find an island. Jobs—"

"John," Jay said. "Our job is here. Our destiny. This was our home. *Is* our home."

John stared at the cracked sidewalk and said nothing. He had gone through fire and ice for Jay but now he needed a sign and a miracle to stoke his faith. Jay was running low on both.

Teacher, where are you?

"A week," Jay said. "Let's give it another week and then we'll talk about planes. OK?"

They stopped at the Internet café off Ben Yehuda. Behind the desk, the balding Israeli owner didn't look up from his newspaper. A Chinese man in sunglasses sat in Jay's regular spot playing roulette, so Jay moved two seats down. An empty seat on either side was all the privacy he would get.

He signed in to his Gmail account. At the top of his inbox waited an unread message. Jay's heart galloped. The Teacher had sensed his distress.

Jay read the message.

"Oh, bugger," he said, and won a glare from the Chinese.

The End of Days had not arrived. Instead, Jay had received another mission. This one would not be so easy.

CHAPTER 4

Never call the next day.

Dave stared at the Standard Test Document on his flat-screen monitor. Page thirty-two stared back. The clatter of busy keyboards in the other cubicles circled his head like a swarm of plastic bees.

Two hours into the day and still on page thirty-two.

In his mind's eye, Mandy Rosenberg brushed a stray lock of hair behind her ear. Her silhouette gazed at the Old City walls. He searched her every word and gesture for hidden meanings.

Never call the next day.

Ben's advice, copied word-for-word from the Pickup Artist's Bible, made sense. Let her stew a while. Don't appear desperate. But Dave wanted to know—he needed to know—where he stood.

Dave logged into his Frumster account and suspended his profile.

Yes, they had just met. And, yes, she was an American. But a girl had walked into his life and she was normal, religious, and cute. Mandy Rosenberg was a statistical impossibility.

He eyed the phone on his desk. He picked it up. He put it down. He picked it up.

He had not felt this way since…

Since Shira Cohen.

He put the phone down again.

Rule Number One: It's a game. Do not become attached.

But this game toyed with his future happiness.

A quick call to say "hi, I had a good time" seemed harmless enough. Expected. Good manners.

He'd call her after work. Right now, he needed to get through the day.

He browsed the Jerusalem Post online. Still no follow-up on the City of David.

A Google search for the Copper Scroll returned photos of flattened metal sheets with rough, weathered surfaces and vertical incision lines. He recognized Hebrew block letters among the rows of carved symbols, and an occasional Greek symbol, but not the older *Ktav Ivri* of Ben's scroll jar.

Wikipedia corroborated Ben's account of the treasure scroll.

Then Dave found the mother lode: a full English translation. The first paragraph made his inner pirate drool:

At the ruin in the Valley of Akhor,

Under the steps, forty paces eastward:

A chest of silver and vessels. Seventeen talents.

Dave ran another search. In ancient Israel, a talent measured thirty kilograms. His heart rate doubled. He was ready to grab a sword and a barrel of rum and set sail.

He read on.

In the tomb of Ben Rabba the Third:

One hundred gold ingots.

The list rolled on. Dave lost count of the deposits of silver and gold, each with precise locations. None of the landmarks in the scroll rang a bell. According to Wikipedia, all attempts to date at discovering the hoard had failed.

The last item on the list caught Dave's eye, although it mentioned neither silver nor gold.

A copy of the scroll,

The meanings and omissions,

And each...

The text ended abruptly.

Dave heard a desk chair swivel.

Alt-Tab.

The screen switched back to page thirty-two.

Silence in the cubicle.

According to Ben, the scroll jars might hold the key to the treasure. Had the jars once contained scrolls? The copy of the scroll mentioned at the end of the list?

A finger tapped Dave on the shoulder and he jumped.

"See what I'm talking about?" Avi said in his Kermit voice. "That's focus. That's what it means to be caught in the hunt."

Alex stood beside the team leader and rolled his eyes.

"You coming?" Avi asked Dave. "Sushi day."

"Nah," Dave said. "I want to finish this Use Case. I'll catch you up later."

Avi nodded his head with admiration. "Look and learn, Alex," he said. "Look and learn." The two traipsed off.

Dave had no appetite for food.

Did Mandy feel the same? Had she checked and rechecked her phone all morning? Did she think he was just not into her?

A cold shiver shook his torso. He slapped his forehead. Why had he ever listened to Ben? Dave's First Pairing had slipped away. Now he stood to lose his second and final chance.

Dave peeked over the cubicle divider. The coast was clear. He seized his phone.

To hell with Ben and his games.

Dave had to trust his instincts. He had to show Mandy how he felt.

He dialed Mandy's number.

"Hi. This is Mandy's phone..."

He exhaled, relieved. Of course. She was at She'arim, probably in the middle of a lecture. Don't leave a message. Hang up before—

Beep!

Dave cut the call a half-second too late.

Oh, crap!

Crap, crap, crap!

Dave had called and not left a message. No message meant breakup. To call and leave a second message would scream desperation. Crowding. Creepiness.

Dave was not a creep. Dave was sincere. Sensitive. Romantic.

The ballpoint pen in Dave's hands snapped in two. He didn't remember picking it up. He had to lay his cards on the table. Face his destiny like a man.

He opened a fresh browser window and reached for his wallet.

Three minutes and a few mouse clicks later, he'd ruined his life.

"Roooochaaaaaammmmmaaaaaaaa..."

The moan came from the living room. The *sa'lon*, Mandy corrected herself. Mandy sat on her bed with her MacBook and finished an account of her first week in Israel for a few of her girlfriends. Her second day at sem had gone smoother. She had warmed to the lecturers and to Ester, her *chevrusa*. It was great to be a student again.

"Roooochaaaaaammmmmaaaaaaaa..."

"I'm not hearing!"

Ruchama's irate voice echoed down the hallway.

Shani and Ruchama reminded Mandy of an elderly couple

after fifty years of dysfunctional marriage.

Silence reigned for five pregnant seconds.

"Maaaannnnnndeeeee…"

Mandy hit send and closed the laptop.

"Don't listen to her," Ruchama's voice warned but Mandy had already stepped into the living room.

Shani sprawled over the couch, clad only in her lingerie. Her Marylyn Monroe hair pooled over the cushions and spilled to the floor. Her arms stretched past her head in a display of exhaustion or ecstasy. Mandy paused to admire Shani Weis, the living advert for Victoria's Secret.

A pencil lay on the floor a few centimeters beyond Shani's fingers. Mandy scooped it up and placed it in her flatmate's hand.

"Mands, you're an *angel*," Shani said, in her sultry, breathless, Angelina Jolie voice. "A *life* saver."

"You're welcome," Mandy said and dropped onto the armchair.

Shani, still flat on her back, gripped the pencil and scribbled in a large black ledger, and Mandy's curiosity as to her flatmate's line of work pricked up its ears.

Shani closed the notebook, held it to her ample bosom, and peered out the French window of the balcony.

"Ruchama," she yelled. "Your boyfriend's home."

Mandy turned to look. In the third-floor apartment across the street, a man sat on a couch. He wore leather sandals, blue jeans, a white undershirt, and a domed knitted yarmulke in primary colors. A sparse beard dusted his jaw and curled sideburns fell past his nose. He leaned over a guitar and adjusted the tuning pegs.

Mandy heard the thump of Ruchama's feet down the hallway. She shoved Shani's legs aside and took her place on the sofa.

"How long has he been there?"

"Is he a Chassid?" Mandy asked.

"Breslover," Shani said. "Chassidim on speed. They smile like crazy and spray-paint mantras on turnpikes. At red lights, don't be surprised if they get out and dance around the car. I swear to God."

The man across the street strummed his guitar, oblivious to his three spectators. He seemed harmless enough.

Mandy said, "Go for it, Ruchama."

Shani snorted.

"Go on," Mandy continued. "Invite him to a meal."

"That," Shani said, "would require guts."

Ruchama frowned. "I don't know how they call him. On the mailbox it's written Yitzi, Dani, and Ben. I think he is Yitzi. And maybe he has a girlfriend?"

Mandy said, "There's one way to find out."

Ruchama rested her jowls on her knuckles and sighed.

"I should have moved into Mandy's room."

"What? Why?"

Mandy's room was the smallest of the three bedrooms and had only one window.

Shani coughed. "Your room is the *segula* room."

"*Segula* room?"

"You know. A lucky charm. Like praying at the tomb in Amuka. Reading Psalms at the Kotel for forty days. Holding the *havdala* candle at the desired height of your future husband. They are all supposed to get you married within the month."

Ruchama's cheeks became two large tomatoes. "Our last three flatmates all got married and they stayed in your room."

Mandy didn't believe in lucky charms, for good or bad.

"Ruchama," she said, not without compassion, "the only *segula* that will get you married is dating."

"That reminds me," Shani said. "How did it go last night?"

The question caught Mandy off guard. The date with David Schwarz had slipped her mind. She had even left him out of her email.

Dave was well mannered, intelligent, and funny, on the phone and in person. And, unlike many of the New Yorkers she had dated, Dave wasn't trying to worm his way into her jeans skirt.

But…

But that first impression stuck.

"*Nu?*" Shani prodded.

"Um."

Mandy hated first impressions. They sat in the back row of her mind and snickered as their predictions came true. And they always did.

She had hoped for a spark on their first date, but that first impression, formed at Rabbi Levi's *shiur*, still smelled of stagnation and desperation.

"I don't know," Mandy said. She wrinkled her nose. "He hasn't called. Maybe it's just as well."

Unless that mysterious blank message this morning was Dave. Mandy had not jotted down the number. Unlikely. Guys never called that soon.

A phone rang in Mandy's bedroom.

"Talk of the devil," Shani said.

She walked to her room. Dave didn't have her home number. Or did he? She picked up the phone.

"Mandy!"

Mandy sat on her bed. "Hi, Mom."

She glanced at her watch and made a quick calculation. Eight in the morning, Houston time. Her mom had called yesterday as well. Mandy summed up the last twenty-four hours in a few brief sentences.

"I miss you, Mands."

"I left home years ago, Mom. We're still just a phone call away."

"I know. You haven't taken any buses, have you?"

"No, Mom. Just cabs." The last suicide bomber had struck over three years ago, thanks, according to Shani, to the new security fence, but a deal was a deal. "I promise, Mom, I'll be careful."

The doorbell rang. Ruchama's footfalls plodded across the living room.

"Remember what your dad used to say."

"I remember, Mom, heroes are dead." It was his standard

warning whenever Mandy climbed a tree or slid down a banister.

"*Heroes are dead*," her mom repeated, her voice tearing up.

Ruchama knocked on the door. "Mandy," she hissed, her eyes wide. "It's for you."

"Gotta go, Mom," Mandy said. "I love you."

Mandy put down the phone and hurried to the front door. Nothing had prepared her for what waited there.

Dave parked his car in the makeshift lot opposite the City of David Institute and turned off the headlights. The City of David was a stony wedge of land shaped by two valleys and the southern wall of the Old City. Over the millennia, the proud walls had crumbled, the Western valley filled in with rubble and dirt. Across the Kidron Valley to the east, ancient tombs dotted the hillside and, more recently, the hostile Arab neighborhood of Silwan.

By nightfall, the tourist bustle had subsided and a dark silence descended on the stone ruins.

The Old City walls towered above him, bathed in regal floodlight.

Immense. Imposing. Impenetrable.

The adrenaline high of that morning had worn off toward the afternoon. By the time Dave realized what he had done, it was too late.

He got out of the car and crossed the street. Neat stone arches topped with jasmine marked the entrance of the Institute. A large inverted omega in bronze adorned the gate;

a David's harp, the symbol of the City of David.

The security guard had left for the day. Dave pushed through the unlocked gate. A staircase led to the rooftop observatory. The ticket booths and snack shop stood eerily empty in the glow of nightlights. A hole in the floor, hedged in by a railing, provided glimpses of the ancient citadel foundations. At night, the hole became a gaping black abyss.

Dave followed the footpath that led to Hezekiah's aqueduct and Warren's Shaft, then veered right toward an administrative building. Dave opened a door labeled Staff Only. The lights were on. He made for the third office down the hallway.

Ben looked up from his desk and shoved piles of schedules and itineraries aside. He reached for the two volumes of Gemara on a shelf.

Dave and Ben had studied Talmud together every Monday night for the past six years. They had covered tractates dealing with Jewish festivals, the return of lost items, and compensation for injured livestock.

The bookmark pointed to a discussion of the *Shma Yisra'el* prayer, the twice-daily reaffirmation of faith.

Ben read the text in the familiar singsong of Yeshiva learning halls and translated as necessary.

"From what time can the Shma be recited in the evening?"

Dave's head sank to his book on the desk.

First Shira. Now Mandy.

If Shira had been his First Soul Mate, then Mandy was his Second. He had squandered both. Dave had reached the end of the road.

Ben's book clapped shut.

"I thought you said last night went well."

"That was yesterday."

"Want to tell me what happened?"

"I screwed it up."

It took a moment for the penny to drop.

"You didn't," Ben said, incredulous. "Tell me you didn't call her, Dave. Not the next day. It's a Golden Rule."

"Call her?" Dave laughed. "I wish I'd just called her."

"No," Ben said, still in denial.

Dave raised his head from the table and prepared to face his shame like a man.

Ben raised his eyebrows. "Chocolates?"

Dave shook his head.

"Flowers?"

"Roses. Five pink roses. White box. Ribbon. Bow. The full monty."

"Pink?" said Ben, brightening. "Pink isn't too bad."

"And a poem."

Ben hid his face in his hands. "Dear God."

Dave felt his mind detach from his body, to watch his train wreck from a safe distance.

"'The Rose Family' by Robert Frost. 'You, of course, are a rose; But were always a rose.' I always liked that one."

"Why?" Ben asked. "Do you do it on purpose? Every time a great girl comes along you lose it. You self-destruct. This is exactly what happened with the other one, what's-her-name. The Cohen girl."

"Shira." Dave's voice belonged to a ghost.

"Right. Shira Cohen. She was a real catch."

"Yes."

"You could have married Shira Cohen."

"I know."

Ben threw up his hands. "Arggh!"

"You're right," Dave whispered. He needed to blow his nose. He searched his pocket for a tissue.

The office door swung open.

Erez Lazarus hovered in the doorway, a wiry, forty-year-old buzzard.

"Benjamin," he said. Erez enjoyed ruffling Ben's feathers. "I need those brochures first thing tomorrow. Can't keep the Crusaders waiting. What's with him?" He indicated Dave with a toss of his beak.

"Woman trouble."

"Ah." His empathy lasted a split second. "Don't stay too

late," he warned Ben and grinned. "Remember what happened the last time you worked late." He mimed a baseball swing at Ben's head and then disappeared out the door.

"Idiot," Ben muttered.

Dave grunted in agreement. His suspicions regarding Erez and the break-in dissolved. No one that annoying could do any harm.

"Crusaders?" Dave asked.

"Evangelist nutters. They schedule private tours at odd hours. Erez indulges them. Big donors, probably." Ben sighed. "Anyway. How did Mandy take it?"

Dave handed over his mobile phone.

Ben read the text message aloud. "*Thanks for the lovely gesture. Mandy.* Hmmm. Formal. Measured. I like her already. Pity you blew it, Dave. Time to move on. Plenty of fish and all that."

Dave's future stretched out ahead, an endless corridor of locked doors.

Then the heavens opened. Sunbeams of revelation warmed his mind. A choir of cherubs gave forth. Years of angst slipped from his shoulders.

How had he not thought of it before?

He said, "No."

"What do you mean, no?"

"I mean no. No more. Game over. The end. I give up."

"You can't just give up."

"Why not? Some people marry; some don't. I can still lead a happy life, can't I?"

Dave chuckled. Every so often, Dave dreamt that he was sitting an O-Level exam but had forgotten to study. When he awoke, he realized that it didn't matter; he had graduated long ago. He felt that same sense of joyous relief now.

The dark side of the coin spun into view. Poor old Dave, people would say. Loveless. Childless. A virgin to the bitter end.

That hurt, but after a few seconds, the sting faded. This

was Dave's de facto reality. Now he had tenure.

"Seven years," Dave said. He shook his head in awe. "I wasted seven of the best years of my life on dating. I could have traveled. Studied half day. Read more. Written a novel. Lived! I won't make that mistake again."

"Dave," Ben said. "You're depressed. You'll get over it. I was there too, remember? Don't lose hope."

"This is hope. Can't you see?"

The shackles fell to the ground. He rubbed his chafed wrists and savored the weightless freedom.

First, a safari in Kenya. Then, the month in New Zealand. He had saved money for his honeymoon and future kids. No need for nest eggs now. Mike may be interested. Worst case, Dave would go it alone.

Ben slammed his fist on the table.

"How badly do you want her?" he asked.

Veins swelled over Ben's forehead. He had taken this harder than Dave.

Dave said, "It's OK, Ben. It's over. And thanks for your help over the years. Really. You did your best."

"Listen to me," Ben almost shouted. Something dark and violent within him strained at the leash, like a werewolf at full moon. His breath came in fitful bouts. "Is Mandy the one you want?"

"What?"

Dave felt confused. Frightened.

Ben jumped to his feet, knocking his chair against the wall. He hurried to the office door, opened it, and scanned the corridor. Satisfied that they were alone, he returned to his seat. A trail of sweat glistened down his cheek.

"Is she The One?" he asked again.

"I suppose. But it doesn't matter."

"Listen," said Ben. "There's one last thing you can do. And this time, it's guaranteed to work."

Dave didn't like the sound of this.

"I'm not going to slip things into her drink, Ben, if that's what you have in mind."

Ben swatted Dave's words with his hand. "No. Nothing like that. But if you do this, she's yours. Forever."

Dave peered around for the hidden camera. He hazarded a smile. The punch line moment came and went and Ben still locked Dave in a ferocious gaze.

Ben had Dave's full, sober attention. The promise of redemption sparked within.

"Guaranteed to work?"

"Yes. But swear to me one thing."

"All right. What?" He braced for the fit of scornful laughter. None followed.

Instead, Ben said, "Nobody can know about this. Ever."

"Done." He swallowed hard. "I swear."

"Good." Ben leaned in and Dave felt the full force of his friend's mobster exterior.

"Because," Ben continued, his voice dangerously low, "if anyone learns of this, and I do mean anyone, Dave, as much as I love you, I'll kill you."

Jay stepped off an Egged bus and onto an unfamiliar sidewalk. Across the road, hugged by forested hills, the Israel Museum complex basked in the soft glow of the setting sun. The short, white funnel of the Shrine of the Book pointed skyward. Designed to resemble the lid of a scroll jar, the building housed the first seven Dead Sea Scrolls.

Jay's business, however, lay behind him in the broad building like a long wall of Jerusalem stone.

He and John climbed the steps of the wide courtyard

before the large glass box, the entrance to the Bible Lands Museum.

A graying guard with a thick mustache waved and said something in Hebrew.

"What?" Jay said.

The guard switched to English. "Close. Ten minutes."

Jay removed the hood from his head. "No worries."

The guard shook his head at the wasteful youth of today. He waved a wand up and down Jay's anorak and repeated the procedure on John. They walked through a doorframe metal detector. Nothing beeped.

At the ticket desk, an old woman with blond hair peered at them over half-moon glasses.

"We close in—"

"Yeah, yeah. We know."

"The tour is closed."

"That's OK. This'll be a quickie."

The woman shook her head and pressed a touch screen.

"Student?" she asked.

Jay shrugged.

"Eighty shekel."

"Blimey!"

"Adult forty shekel. Student twenty shekel."

"We're students."

That was true enough.

The woman raised her eyebrows but didn't ask for ID. Jay placed two crumpled twenty-shekel notes on the counter and pocketed the tickets.

They walked down a wide, ramped corridor that opened onto the main hall. The design was modern and minimalist: high ceilings, white walls and plaster panels, steel railings, and sunken spotlights. The floor was a maze of white cubicles and glass display cabinets, reliefs and three-dimensional models.

A knot of Spanish-speaking tourists passed the two men on their way out. Jay and John were the only ones left.

Two oldies and an empty room. Piece of piss.

This was no City of David. All the pieces lay indoors. Tiny

cameras peeked from the corners where walls met ceiling. The hint of a lockdown gate protruded above the lintel of the entrance passage like the portcullis of a medieval castle.

Jay pulled his hoodie over his head. John did the same. He put his index fingers together side-by-side, and then moved them forward and apart. He had learned the gesture from a SWAT team in an action movie. John understood and they split up.

Jay scanned a display case of stone hunting tools, figurines of fertility goddesses and primitive, cylindrical seals. The next enclosure contained household vessels and animal statuettes. The dates on the explanatory notes ranged from five to two thousand years BCE. That was like BC.

Before Christ.

Jay smiled.

He passed the model of a pyramid surrounded by steel railing, a sarcophagus, and a wall mural. A bird-headed god placed a man's heart on the cup of a scale. The other cup held a feather.

"Psst!"

Jay turned around. John waved for him to follow and marched off. He stopped in an enclosure labeled Rome and Judea. The cubicle contained a stone box, a wall of corroded coins, and mosaics of animals. In the center stood a white pillar, waist-high, that supported a rimless glass display case.

Jay whistled softly.

The case contained three rounded jars. The lids looked like acorn stems. The rightmost jar, shorter than the others, wore three etched characters proudly on its belly. The note read, "Scroll jars, Qumran. Circa 100 BCE. Caves 4 and 3."

Jay's hand touched the hidden pocket in the lining of his anorak. He looked around. He nodded at John, who extracted a smooth rock from his pocket, wrapped it in a sock, and drew his arm back.

A speck of black caught Jay's eye.

"Wait," he said.

"What?" John whispered. Sweat shone over the triangle of

forehead visible under his hood.

Jay weighed the options.

The Teacher's words echoed in his mind.

Patience, my son.

"Abort," he said.

"Come again?"

Jay pointed at the upper corner of the case. Barely visible along the black lining of the glass pane ran a thin, black wire.

"Closing time," he said. "C'mon. Rattle your dags." He made for the exit.

"But..."

"Not today, mate," Jay said, "or your five-fingered checkbook will land us both in the boob."

Mandy tossed her mobile phone into the sleek DKNY handbag on her bed. She added a pocket pack of Kleenex and a can of mace the size of a lipstick.

Heroes are dead.

She intended to be neither a hero nor dead.

She usually agreed to a second date, especially when the matchmaker was a close friend like Nat; a change of place and time let her intuition settle.

This second date would probably be her last with Dave. The box of roses had set off alarm bells. God alone knew what he was capable of next.

She swung the handbag over her shoulder and left her bedroom. The living room couch lay empty; an unusual silence filled the apartment. She stepped out the front door, locking it behind her, and her heels echoed down the stairwell.

Mandy hated breaking up. Guys had a sixth sense for approaching breakups that drove them to buy stuffed animals and heart-shaped cushions. She felt bad for them.

She pushed through the door of the apartment building. Dave's silver hatchback idled on the curb. Too late to leave a note on the dining room table.

She climbed in.

Dave gave her a closed-lip smile. His aftershave filled the car with the scent of coconuts.

No stuffed animals. So far so good.

"Where are we heading?"

Dave stepped on the accelerator.

"Where are we all?" he said.

Mandy squirmed in her seat. She remembered what she had disliked about Brits. They worked double meanings into every sentence. She enjoyed kidding around as much as the next girl but right now she wanted a straight answer to a simple question.

"Dinner," Dave added in an apologetic tone. "A very nice place. You'll like it." He avoided eye contact. He seemed distant. Detached. The false bravado of the male sixth sense?

Her conscience twinged.

"Dave," she said. "We don't have to go anywhere expensive."

"It's all right," Dave interrupted. "Please."

She sighed and resigned herself to the evening. Fancy dinners beat stuffed animals.

The motor of the car murmured as he negotiated corners between stone buildings and a rocky outcrop. An old, abandoned train station whizzed by the window. They made a left at a light. A sign indicated the Mount Zion hotel. The road dropped sharply and meandered onto a short bridge over a shallow valley.

"Ben Hinnom," Mandy read the street sign aloud. "That sounds familiar."

They stopped at a red light at the end of the bridge.

"The Valley of Ben Hinnom," Dave said. "Or *Gey Ben Hinnom* in Hebrew. Idol worshippers used to build fires here for human sacrifice. Over time, the name became Gehinnom. Or Hell."

Mandy sank deeper into her seat.

"Nowadays," Dave continued, "they use it for rock concerts."

A nervous laugh escaped her lips. Dave laughed too and drew a deep breath. The tension in the air evaporated.

The light turned green. They followed the road left along the edge of the valley. To their right, the tall, crenellated walls of the Old City rose in spotlight. Dave drove up a steep road and passed under the enormous, arched lintel of Jaffa Gate. They negotiated a herd of tourist caps, kaffiyehs, and a robed priest.

The Old City. Mandy had visited the Jewish Quarter and the Western Wall for the first time on Thursday morning. She wandered the narrow alleys and courtyards. Night added a layer of romance.

The car tires pattered over cobblestones. They rounded the Tower of David and then barreled down a narrow one-way between tall walls of stone.

Dave slowed at a tunnel-like archway, letting a tall, bearded priest in black robes, a white belt, and a square, black hat cross their path.

The road meandered on, sheer walls on each side, then emptied into a broad parking lot, speckled with trees and crammed with cars, which Mandy recognized as the edge of the Jewish Quarter.

A romantic dinner in the Old City?

On her first visit, Mandy had noticed pizza and falafel joints but no fancy kosher restaurants.

Dave didn't park. Instead, he followed the sharp descent to the Western Wall plaza. Only permit-holding cars entered the plaza. Had he made special arrangements to impress her?

He plowed on and exited through Dung Gate.

They had passed right through the Old City!

Was this his idea of a romantic car tour?

He made a sharp left and drove alongside the Old City wall. Ahead, haphazard electric lights lit a hillside like stars, and Mandy glimpsed the edges of rough, chaotic buildings. Two men on the sidewalk, dark-skinned and mustachioed, looked them over. Mandy squeezed her handbag. They had left the safe familiarity of the Jewish Quarter for Arab East Jerusalem.

Dave made a right down a narrow side street lined with crumbling walls and cement barricades marred by graffiti.

Her hand slipped into her bag and touched the cold canister of mace.

"Dave," she began to say but Dave stopped the car on the side of the road.

"We're here," he said.

"Where are we?"

"Look." He pointed out his window at a façade of clean Jerusalem stone. In the glow of the Old City light, she made out three white arches topped by bushes. The middle arch contained a large bronze David's harp. Golden letters on the wall read, in English and in Hebrew, The City of David.

"Oh," Mandy said. Dave had remembered her interest in the City of David Institute. Sweet. But beyond the arches the site sank into darkness.

"Is it open this late?"

"No," he said and opened the car door.

She got out but kept her hand in her bag. The thump of the car doors echoed in the alley. She looked around. They had parked beside an empty, gated lot with a dirt floor and a perimeter of abused corrugated sheeting. Below the City of David Institute, the road descended into blackness.

The car beeped as Dave locked it and he proceeded on foot down the dark street.

Mandy stood her ground.

Twenty feet down the street, Dave paused and turned to her. He smiled and spread his arms. "Welcome to *Ir Da'vid.*"

She didn't budge.

"Just a few more steps," Dave added. "Over there." He pointed to the glowing outline of a doorframe that she had not noticed in the darkness.

She let the canister slip from her fingers in her bag. Dave had made an extra effort tonight. She could at least hear him out.

"So this is where David lived," Mandy said. She descended the slope carefully in her heels. Her dad would have loved to stand here. Perhaps he had.

They walked the rest of the way together in silence.

A lantern illuminated a heavy wooden door in a stone wall, like the entrance to a castle. Or dungeon. The stone of the wall was rougher and grimier than that of the City of David Institute. A sign on the door in thick silver Roman letters read Ornan's.

Dave pulled the brass knob and the door creaked open. They stood at the top of a stone stairway. Flaming torches lined the walls. Dave started the descent and she followed. Her fingers trailed the walls for support. Her heartbeat accelerated. They had entered another dimension, crossed the portal into a mysterious parallel world.

She neared the first torch. What had appeared to be fire was an electric flicker flame bulb. The fake torches reassured her. They reminded her of Disneyland's Haunted Mansion or the Revenge of the Mummy Roller Coaster at Universal Studios.

Sit back, honey, and enjoy the ride.

Above their footfalls, she heard the clatter of cutlery. Aromas of fresh bread and spices wafted up and her stomach stirred.

The staircase ended in a circular, cave-like landing. Patterned rugs covered the stone floor. A floor-to-ceiling honeycomb of wine bottles rose behind a teak concierge desk. Behind the desk, a muscular, tanned man in opulent gray robes and a red fez on his head turned his bright eyes to them.

"Good evening," he said in a Middle Eastern accent. "Your name?"

"Schwarz," Dave said. "Dave Schwarz."

Their host searched a leather-bound ledger on the desk.

The slow plucking of a harp and the thump of a drum drifted on the air, the music of massage parlors at high-end hotels but with an oriental touch.

"One moment," said the concierge. "I will call the manager."

He disappeared down an arched passageway.

Mandy looked at Dave, who shrugged.

Had they lost his reservation?

A framed document hung on the wall behind them. A kosher certificate.

Oh, good.

Not that Mandy had suspected Dave of taking her to a *treif* restaurant. In Café Atara, Dave had recited the blessing on his coffee aloud.

Consistency. Attention to detail. Good traits in a QA engineer. Not necessarily Mandy's scoop of ice cream.

Dave remained silent. He stared at the tapestry on the wall to their right. Two figures stood upon a wall. They wielded spears. One leaned on a fork-like crutch; the other turned his head heavenward, his eyes closed.

Mandy shivered. Before she could process the scene, the concierge reappeared with the manager, a short, dark, mustachioed man with a scarlet diagonal sash over his impeccable black suit. He looked like one of the Mario brothers from the arcade game.

He spoke a few sharp words at the concierge in a guttural language Mandy assumed to be Arabic.

"Good evening," he said and he bowed at the hips, displaying an oily comb-over. He flashed rows of white chisel teeth. "We have reserved the VIP room. Please. Follow me."

Mario marched off.

Dave and Mandy followed.

The VIP room? Oh, brother.

She should have come clean and wrapped this up before Dave had gone to any trouble.

"Dave," she whispered, as they tried to keep up with the manager. "You don't have to do this."

He waved her objection aside with a hand and smiled briefly.

"It's fine. Really." Then he focused on the little man ahead of them. An emotion had clouded his face. Nerves. Or fear.

Mario hurried along the corridor. Arched doorways opened onto dining areas. Mandy caught glimpses of elaborate tapestries and flowing curtains; tables for two set in rich, white cotton; heavy silverware; women in evening dresses, men in collared shirts; intimate words over aromatic cuisine and large wineglasses; and in the backdrop the lull of harps and the heartbeat of a bass drum.

The arches ended. Mario drove on, following the lines of ersatz flaming torches. A barrier of thick rope between two golden poles blocked the corridor. Beyond the barrier, the torches ended and the corridor faded to black. Mario moved one of the poles aside and led them through an arched doorway of overlapping crimson curtains.

"Ladies first," Dave said with a flourish of his arms. Mandy clutched her handbag and pushed through the curtains.

The room resembled a jewelry box, ten feet wide and padded with Bordeaux tapestries and rugs. A bronze floor lamp cast a cozy glow over a two-seater couch of carved wood and velvet cushions. Mandy stepped around the small table draped in white cotton that reached the floor, and sat on the couch. Dave sat down beside her, his hands on his knees, a safe empty strip of couch between them.

The soothing harp music permeated the air from hidden speakers.

The tapestries depicted biblical scenes. A young man slept on a hilltop at the foot of an impossibly tall ladder flanked by rows of winged men. A ram snagged his horns in a thicket beside a rocky altar. A pair of lovers embraced, their naked limbs entwined, like the interlacing branches of the enormous tree behind them.

The couch was surprisingly comfortable. All tension drained from Mandy. Anticipation and a sense of heightened awareness tingled along her body. She breathed in the air and the scent of history about to unfold.

Wow.

This was unlike any restaurant Mandy knew.

She broke the silence. "How did you find this place?"

"A friend," Dave said.

She turned to him. His shoulders had relaxed. His fingers had moved to the silky cushions. She'd wanted to tell him something but she couldn't remember what.

Never mind.

From this angle, he looked different. His solid jawline and manly cleft chin brought to mind a young Michael Douglas in the swashbuckling romance movies of the eighties.

Mandy breathed in his aftershave, which hinted at sun-drenched beaches and luxury yachts in tropical, azure waters.

A dark-skinned young woman in flowing red robes entered the chamber. She placed two leather-bound menus and tall wineglasses on the table. She filled the glasses with red wine and hurried away in a ripple of red fabric without once making eye contact.

Dave handed Mandy a glass of wine and raised his.

"Here's to us," he said, his voice deep and compelling. His confident eyes caressed her face and said that he liked what he saw.

She felt a flutter in her stomach. Wine teetered at the rim of her glass.

"So," Mandy said, recovering. A playful lilt had jumped into her voice. "Is this your plan? Lead a girl to an exotic restaurant in an Arab neighborhood and ply her with wine?"

You're flirting, Mands, and you haven't even tasted the wine!

Dave's eyebrows hitched with amusement and mild concern.

"I wouldn't put you in any danger," he said. "No need to

play the hero." He contemplated his wineglass. Then, as an afterthought, he added, "Heroes are dead."

Goose bumps broke out over Mandy's body. Her lungs refused to inflate. She was sure he could hear her pulsating heart.

"What did you just say?" Mandy asked when she remembered how to breathe.

"Hmm?"

Mandy put down the glass.

"That saying. *Heroes are dead.* How do you know that?"

Had Nat primed Dave for the date? No. Not even Nat knew that one. It was a family motto. An heirloom. A secret handshake.

"I don't know," Dave said, still contemplative. "I thought I made it up. But I may have heard it somewhere."

A haze of confusion like the white noise of an untuned television jumbled Mandy's mind.

Then it cleared.

Everything was clear.

Oh, God. So this is how it feels!

She surrendered herself to Dave's irresistible magnetic field. Her cheeks burned at her sudden urge to rip open his shirt, send the buttons flying, to run her fingers over the hard muscles of his abdomen and nestle in the warmth of his chest.

He recited the blessing over wine, *borey peri hagafen.*

She answered *amen*, reclaimed her wineglass, and gulped down half its contents.

The girl in scarlet robes returned to the room, her eyes lowered.

"Is everything all right?" she asked.

"Oh, yes," Mandy replied.

She settled her glass on the table and reached for a menu.

Mandy was ready to order.

CHAPTER 5

A leather ball bounced over a white chalk line on a grassy field and into a net.

Five thousand people jumped to their feet and roared.

In the stands high above the field, Dave jumped with them. He had expected the Neanderthal in the yellow tank top beside him to mug him at some point during the ninety minutes, but now the giant grabbed Dave by the ears and kissed him on the forehead.

Dave grinned at Mandy and shrugged.

The Yellow Shirts had tied the score with five minutes left on the clock. Tension rippled through the hot summer's night air. It was good to be alive.

The crowd chanted slurs regarding the parentage of the White Shirts.

"Seven years," Dave shouted to Mandy. "I've lived here seven years and this is my first game."

Mandy shouted back, "I'm glad your first time was with me." She winked at him.

Dave jabbed a finger at her ribs but didn't dare make physical contact.

Instead, he helped himself to another handful of salted sunflower seeds from the jumbo bag in Mandy's hand. Dave had mastered the technique. He held a shell between thumb and forefinger, splintered the casing with his incisors, and extracted the little gray seed with his tongue. A lot of work for a bellyful of birdfeed and salt-caked lips but a ritual was a ritual.

Football and *garinim*, two of the many firsts Dave had notched up over the four months he and Mandy had dated.

The night after their dinner in the City of David, he had taken her to the bowling alley in the Talpiot industrial zone and broken that elusive third date barrier.

And never looked back.

Museums and movies followed. Then a rock concert: Ben Draiman at the Yellow Submarine. After date number eleven, Dave stopped counting. They spent every spare moment together, usually at Mandy's apartment, where her ever-present flatmates kept them out of trouble.

Time flew by. On Purim, they had crashed a fancy dress party wearing matching cow suits. How had she persuaded him to do that?

They parted company for the week of Passover to visit their families overseas. The distance had hurt. Dave, fearful of jinxing the relationship, breathed not a word to his parents and, strangely, his mother never inquired into his love life; although, during the long Pesach meals, whenever she looked at him a smug grin spread across her face and Dave suspected she had spies in Jerusalem.

The football game ended in a tie. He and Mandy followed the crowd down the concrete steps and through the tunnels that led to the parking lot. She smiled blissfully at him as they walked, and bumped against him at every opportunity.

Indeed, life had changed. Dave even looked different. He wore his hair swept back. No more nerdy parting. That had been Mandy's idea. She had helped him select a new wardrobe of polo shirts and O-neck sweaters and donated his old button-downs.

Dave had quit his job and signed with a smaller company more likely to offer advancement opportunities, again on Mandy's advice. Tonight was Wednesday, which meant he had exactly three workdays left under a devastated Kermit the Frog.

He unlocked his Ford hatchback and they joined the jam of cars between Teddy Stadium and Malcha Mall.

He enjoyed their comfortable silences, although recently a large pink elephant had tiptoed in.

Four months.

Long enough to get to know a girl. Many of Dave's friends had proposed in less. And Mandy had only two weeks left in Israel. Dave had the girl. The motive. The opportunity.

What am I waiting for?

Mandy said, "That wasn't so bad, was it?"

"Football? I actually enjoyed it. Ben will be shocked."

"Ben. Your friend at the City of David?"

"The one and only."

Dave hadn't seen Ben in months. He had suspended their weekly *chevruta* after date number three. Dating trumped Gemara.

That was half the truth.

The other half lay deep within the City of David.

That fateful winter night at Ornan's, four months earlier, something had shifted the balance of affection in Dave's favor sharply and absolutely. Try as he might, he could not explain it away. Neither the atmosphere nor the food accounted for it. Not even the Pickup Artist's Bible.

Although he didn't understand the mechanics, he did feel responsible. He had tricked Mandy. Taken advantage. Tampered with her destiny.

One fine day, the spell would break. The piper would come knocking. Mysterious forces had given; mysterious forces would take away.

And, considering his recent behavior, maybe Mandy wasn't the only victim.

One man stood at the center of the enigma and Dave had avoided him ever since. Ben seemed in no hurry to see Dave either.

A car pulled up beside them at the traffic light. Four

passengers dressed in yellow-and-black shirts and scarves hung out the windows, all catcalls and cheers. The driver drummed the horn.

Dave answered with three short bursts.

His internal critic scolded him.

Very mature, Dave.

Other girls he knew would have agreed. His mother, for one.

But Mandy giggled. In her eyes, he could do no wrong.

The light changed and he pulled away.

"You and Ben go way back, don't you?" Mandy asked

"He was a year ahead of me in high school. We became friends in Yeshiva. I returned home to start my degree and Ben stayed on to study archaeology at Hebrew U. We bumped into each other when I made *aliya*. I've been trying to shake him off ever since."

Another giggle. "We should meet up with him."

Dave's foot slipped onto the accelerator, spinning the wheels for a second.

"What?"

"I'd love to see the City of David. Maybe Ben can show us around?" she said.

"Sure." He fixed his eyes on the road.

Don't fuss. She'll probably forget. It'll blow over.

"How about Friday? We're both free. Ruchama invited us for both meals this Shabbat, so we don't have to cook."

Dave's stomach squirmed. Ten ways to dodge the question came to mind, none of them honest.

Bollocks!

"Sounds good," he said. His voice had climbed an octave.

"Great. An archaeologist *and* an old friend. I've got a lot of questions for him."

Dave's fist clenched on the wheel.

"Yeah," he said. "Me too."

Mandy doodled in her notebook. Rabbi Jeremy's voice carried her thoughts.

Over the last four months, the biblical David had risen to prominence, fled attempts on his life by a deranged King Saul, and unified the tribes of Israel under his leadership.

It was during this long-awaited period of calm that the new king faced his most difficult trial.

"And so," Rabbi Jeremy concluded, "Uriah had divorced Bathsheba before he set out for battle. David may have abused his power, but he had not committed adultery. As our Sages write: *He who says David sinned is mistaken.*"

The rabbi beamed at the class. "Any questions?" His eyes drifted to Mandy.

Mandy returned the smile and lowered her eyes. She did not raise her hand.

The written text told only part of the story. The oral traditions of the rabbis lay between the lines.

Mandy had traveled far since her first day at She'arim. Her impulsive rebellion had masked deep cuts in her soul. Frustration. Anger. Hurt.

Healing had followed. The insights and introspection of her Torah study routine had helped. But mostly she thanked Dave.

He had filled the void in her heart. He powered her newfound serenity.

The girls split into study pairs.

Esty's eyes shone brighter than usual. Her smile threatened to burst her cheeks. Lately, she had skipped classes and Mandy had guessed something was up.

"Mandy," she gushed. Unable to find words, Esty placed her left hand on the desk. The gold band on her ring finger held a large, clear and colorless stone. "I wanted to tell you first."

Mandy hugged her. "Esty, mazal tov! That's awesome!"

"I know," Esty said, her eyes tearing up. "His name is Shmuel. He's at the Mir."

"Wow." The Mir was an ultra-Orthodox yeshiva in Jerusalem's Me'ah She'arim neighborhood.

"It's glass," Esty whispered, referring to the stone. "Until we get on our feet."

The other girls quickly surrounded Esty and bombarded her with questions.

No more studying for today.

Mandy watched her twenty-year-old study partner glow. She felt no envy.

Good for you, Esty.

She looked at her notebook. Two words repeated down the page: Mandy Schwarz.

The sun still hung high in the sky during the cab ride home that evening. Mandy plugged her earphones into her iPhone. Diana Ross sang "Upside Down."

Her playlist of eighties hits transported her to the happy years of her childhood. A thousand sunny days lay ahead, filled with trust in the goodness of life. Tragedy was a distant rumor. She'd thought she'd lost that feeling forever.

The song ended and a dance rhythm of drum and piano thundered in her ears. Her favorite: Bonnie Tyler's "Holding Out for a Hero."

Dave didn't drive a fancy sports car. He didn't fly his own helicopter. His family seemed well off but he was no billionaire. And he had his quirks. But he lived his ideals. He had moved to Israel alone, left behind a comfortable life. He resisted her attempts at holding hands with a quiet cowboy resolve and each day his inner hero shone brighter.

Besides, according to the romance novels on Ruchama's shelf, billionaires were a dime a dozen.

The cab reached Mendele Street and Mandy paid the driver. Shani pushed through the door of the apartment building in tights and a loose tank top.

"Hi, Mands," she said. "You're just in time to go shopping. Ruchama ran out of Rich's Cream. Come along?"

"Sure," Mandy said and climbed out of the car.

Ruchama cooked and calculated the expenses. Shani did the groceries. The girls split the Friday cleaning three ways.

Mandy had never shopped with Shani before and it promised to be an interesting experience.

"Hey," Shani snapped at the cabby. "Move it along, pal." The driver stopped staring and drove off.

Shani beamed at Mandy. "Is my strap showing?" she asked.

"Yeah." The pink bra strap was hard to miss.

"Good," she said. "This way."

Shani turned left up Keren Hayesod.

"Is Dave joining us for meals?" she asked.

"Uh-huh."

"I don't know what you see in him, Mands. You are so out of his league."

Mandy smiled. Shani had disliked Dave the moment she laid eyes on him, and, whether Shani loved or hated, her opinions were absolute. Mandy didn't take it personally. Shani was looking out for her like a protective big sister.

"Look at it this way," Mandy said. "If it weren't for Dave, I'd be leaving in two weeks."

Shani halted and grabbed Mandy by the hands. "You extended your ticket?"

Mandy nodded. Shani hugged her. Mandy could hardly breathe. "It's a year ticket anyway. I just haven't booked the return leg."

Shani held Mandy at arm's length. Her smile faded. "Don't get your hopes up. It's been four months. If he hasn't proposed by now, chances are he won't. Trust me. Have you met his friends yet?"

"As a matter of fact," Mandy said, "we're meeting his best friend tomorrow morning."

Shani pursed her lips. "Maybe he's smarter than I thought.

But if he doesn't propose soon, I'll shoot him. Now, Mandy, dear. Watch and learn."

Shani headed for the hole-in-a-wall convenience store on the corner of Sokolow Street. A Coca-Cola refrigerator stood beneath a jutting tin roof. The store was a long walk-in closet of cool storage and shelves packed to the ceiling. A hairy, overweight man slouched behind the counter in a dirty undershirt.

"Mah inyanim, motek?" he said. What's up, sweetie?

Shani ignored him. She sashayed through the store, swinging her hips.

Mandy waited at the entrance.

Four months.

That counted as a long-term relationship in these parts.

Was Dave holding back?

Shani reached for the sliding door of a low-lying cooler, bending at the waist, her shapely behind aimed at the counter. The storeowner patted his forehead with a greasy handkerchief.

Mandy stifled her smile.

Shani pulled a bag of breadcrumbs from a shelf and dropped it on the counter next to the carton of non-dairy cream.

Something felt out of place. Shani wasn't carrying a bag, and her tights hid nothing, not even a roll of bills.

Mandy reached into her bag. "Let me get that."

"No, no," said the man. He waved a beefy hand at her when he saw her purse.

How did they always know she spoke English?

The man placed the items in a white plastic bag but didn't touch the till. "On da house," he said. His smile was wide and yellow.

Shani swung the bag over her shoulder and pranced out the store.

"Bye, Yossi," she said with a playful lilt in her voice.

Mandy fell into step beside her. "Shani, you are one of a kind."

Shani winked. "God helps those who strut their stuff."
Mandy laughed.
Shani had no fear. She always got what she wanted.
Mandy bit her lip. With a bit of imagination, so could she.

Jay pulled a black ski mask over his face and scaled the perimeter fence. He dropped to other side, a black shadow in the night, and hunkered down on untrimmed grass. He located the Capewell grapple hook and ran his fingers over the braided length of the BlueWater Assaultline. Tactical teams used the black kernmantle rope for its high tensility and low visibility. The gear had always been far out of Jay's budget.

How times change, he thought.

He lobbed the hook onto the roof of the three-story building. It held. He fed the rope through the harness of his black bodysuit and walked up the wall.

The roof was wide and flat in the dim moonlight and dotted with the bulging rectangles of skylights and air-conditioning units. Jay felt a tug on the line: a sign for him to haul up the black duffel bag. John followed a minute later.

The men worked wordlessly with the quick confidence bred by months of planning and surveillance. John carried the bag to the second skylight. Jay held the padlock straight while John applied the bolt cutter. After five seconds of strain, the shackle snapped.

John secured the grapple hook around an angle clip that bolted an air conditioner to the roof, while Jay fed the

Assaultline through the figure-eight descender on his harness.

He studied his wristwatch.

9:04 PM.

Two minutes from now the guard would conclude his rounds, granting them sixty seconds of grace before the motion sensors activated.

The Teacher had approved Jay's shopping list without question. Despite appearances, the Sons of Light had come into money.

The Sons of Light.

He had known that destiny would draw him to distant lands and ancient secrets. His new brotherhood lived up to his every expectation. His initiation into The Way had not passed without difficulty. Handing over his worldly possessions was the easy bit, Jay and John having little left between them, but the regimen of ritual and study tried his patience. The vows of silence. Immersions in cold, purifying waters. The endless chanting of Psalms and Isaiah. Communal meals with their motley crew of new brothers. Jay suffered it all. The End of Days neared. When the Teacher finally revealed Jay to the world, the Sons of Light would be his personal guard. Thankfully, Jay and John spent most of their time away from the community called the *Yachad*, searching for scroll jars, then scouting their target. Planning. Training.

John swung the skylight open on its hinges and dropped the end of the Assaultline into the darkness below.

Jay stepped into the void. He slid down the rope, through the shaft of moonlight. In the inky blackness around him, exit signs glowed and, as his eyes adjusted, the edges of partition walls and cabinets materialized in the gloom.

The rubber soles of his shoes touched the floor.

Fifty seconds.

He broke a glow stick strapped to his chest, quickly covered the six paces to a tall display case, and unfurled his equipment pouch on the floor.

Forty seconds.

He pressed a suction pad against the center of the glass pane and flipped the vacuum lever. He attached the metal arm, unsheathed the diamond-edged cutter, and traced a perfect circle around the suction pad.

Thirty seconds.

Slower than their best rehearsal time, but still good.

The glass around the sucker gave way. Jay laid the contraption and the glass circle on the floor and reached an arm through the hole. First the clay cap, then the jar.

Twenty seconds.

Enough time to place the jar in the padded specimen bag, secure the bag to his harness, and climb the rope.

Bzzzzzzzzzzzzzz.

An electronic hum rang from every direction.

Jay's heart sank to his stomach. His mouth dried up. Metal cogs whirred and heavy security gates thumped to the floor.

Impossible.

Had he miscalculated the times?

Then it hit.

Obvious, you ning-nong!

There must have been sensors beneath the jar.

John's silhouette peered down from the skylight hole. Jay urged him away with a wave of his free arm. John hauled up the rope.

A switch clicked. Bright light flooded the museum.

Jay hit the floor and rolled to the nearest cubicle wall.

Footsteps echoed on marble, far behind him, from the direction of the entrance.

An electric motor whirred and then halted.

The footsteps grew louder.

Jay's future stretched out before him. Jail. Extradition. Persecution.

Oh, Father. Please. Not again.

Was the world still not ready? Would he again sacrifice his destiny for an unworthy planet?

The footsteps stopped behind the partition. Jay heard the guard's uneven breath.

Then, another sound.

Meow.

"*Kishta, Chatula!*" the guard said. Scat, cat!

Little paws scampered and skidded over polished marble.

The guard grumbled in Hebrew and shuffled off. His footfalls faded. Jay's pulse still galloped.

The security doors rose. The lights dimmed.

He exhaled long and slow. The countdown had reset.

Patience, my son.

Finally, the stars had aligned behind Jay. Destiny smiled.

Morning light washed over the white stone façade of the City of David Institute. Dave wore sunglasses against the glare and followed Mandy through the arched threshold and the sweet scent of jasmine.

He felt like a criminal returning to the scene of the crime.

A crowd of elderly Japanese tourists in shorts, colorful shirts, and cameras filled the courtyard and listened to their guide jabber away.

An arm waved above the crowd and Ben waded toward them. He wore a cap embroidered with the David's harp emblem. For the first time, Dave glimpsed the Ben that tour groups knew: a bald, rounded Brit, all smiles and boyish passion for archaeology. Endearing. Harmless.

If they only knew.

"We meet at last," Ben said to Mandy. "You're Dave's best-kept secret, you know?"

"Watch out," Dave said. "Ben has a sense of humor and

he's not afraid to use it."

She giggled. "That's OK. I like English jokes."

"Then you'll love Dave. Come on. If we hurry we'll make the next screening."

They watched the 3D documentary in the movie theater, climbed to the rooftop observatory, and then hiked through the knee-deep icy waters of King Hezekiah's tunnel.

Dave waited for a knowing wink from Ben.

None came.

Was Ben toying with him? Pretending he knew nothing?

"This place is amazing," Mandy said. "I have so many questions."

They sat on couches in the refreshment lounge Erez used to entertain his VIP groups.

Ben gulped down a plastic cup of Coca-Cola. "Shoot."

"What can you tell me about the Jebusites?" she asked.

"Not much. Some identify them as Hittites. They ruled a large area around today's Turkey. Their kingdom declined shortly before David's time."

"Uriah was a Hittite. What was a Hittite doing in David's army?"

Ben poked Dave on the shoulder. "The girl's a real catch."

"Thanks," Dave said, through clenched teeth. Mandy blushed.

Ben explained. "King David accepted many nations into his ranks and he had close ties with the northern kingdoms. But Hittites is just one theory.

"More recently, scholars have identified Jebusites with Amorites, a far older Semitic nation and native to the region. In fact, the ceramic evidence in the City of David goes back to the Copper Age, over six thousand years ago, and Jerusalem may have served as an ancient holy city, predating even the Jebusites."

"Wow, that's really interesting." She looked at her wristwatch and frowned. "I should get going before the stores close. Continue another time?"

"How about lunch tomorrow?"

Dave cleared his throat. "I don't know about that."

"We don't want to impose," Mandy said.

"It's no trouble," Ben assured her. "Yvette is dying to meet you. I think you'll get along great."

"The thing is..." Dave searched desperately for some reason to decline the invitation. "We already have plans for lunch."

Mandy looked at him and shrugged. "Nothing we can't get out of."

Dave fumbled for an excuse; Ruchama was a good backup plan, but no contract etched in stone. He sighed, defeated.

Mandy smiled at Ben. "We'd love to."

She collected her handbag and waved goodbye at the door. Dave would drop off her gym bag of soaked clothes later.

He helped Ben dispose of the plastic cups and refreshments and followed him to his office, closing the door behind him.

"We need to talk."

Ben shuffled the paperwork on his desk. "Are we breaking up?"

"I'm serious, Ben."

Ben's lips curled into a smile. Dave had his full attention.

How to say this?

"I went to a football game this week."

Ben stared at him. "And?"

"And I enjoyed it."

"I'm very happy for you."

"Since when do I like football, Ben?"

"Is there a point to all this? Friday is a short day."

"Ben, what's happened to me? And Mandy? One minute she's about to dump me. The next, she can't get enough."

Ben leaned back in his chair. He shook his head. "You are one screwed-up puppy, Dave. I'll tell you what's *happened* to you. You've been single for too long. Your life is changing and it terrifies you."

Dave put his hands on his hips.

"So this is just fear of the unknown?"

"Yes. That and the Groucho effect."

Dave rolled his eyes. "The Groucho effect?"

"Groucho Marx said he would never join a club that would have him as a member. Mandy likes you, so something must be wrong with her. Snap out of it! Mandy's a great girl. She loves you. Deal with it. 'You've been born into royalty, baby. Now you just gotta wear the ring.'"

Ben recited the last bit in an American accent. He had stolen the line from a movie. Everything about Ben was a lie and Dave was sick of it.

"This isn't another dating crisis, Ben. This is real."

Ben laughed. "You know what? You haven't changed a bit, Dave. Paranoid as ever."

"Bullshit."

"Whoa." Ben spread out his hands and glanced at the shut door. "Dave, calm down."

"Don't tell me to calm down. What happened that night at Ornan's?"

"I said, *calm down.*" Ben looked at the door again.

Dave leaned forward, his fists on the desk. "Tell me what's going on."

Ben worked his jaw like an ox chewing the cud. "OK," he said. "You want a secret. I'll tell you a secret. Here it is: *Nothing* is going on. Ornan's is just a restaurant."

Dave folded his arms. "So this is pure coincidence?"

"No, Dave. Not coincidence. More of a lucky coin. Magic feather. You were falling apart at the seams. I gave you something to believe in. Add a pinch of ambience and a glass of wine and voila."

A part of Dave clung to Ben's words like a drowning man to a lifesaver.

"I don't believe you."

"All right," Ben said, losing his patience. "Tell me how you did it. Did you slip her a love potion or wave a magic wand?"

Dave had obsessed over every detail of that night. He had

considered everything from drugs in the air vents to hypnotic suggestion, but nothing added up.

Even Ornan raised no red flags. The little manager had reminded Dave of Manuel from Fawlty Towers. Obsequious. Comic. Pitiful.

Dave said, "Something's not right with that place."

"'Something's not right with that place,'" Ben repeated. "You're not being rational."

Dave ignored the insult.

"You're the archaeologist. Someone must have dug beneath Ornan's. What did they find?"

The mention of archaeology defused Ben and shifted him into lecture gear.

"Hard to tell," he said. "The excavation site was destroyed."

"Destroyed? How?"

"When you dig, you damage. That's why you document everything. Layers. Artifacts. Everything. And you never excavate an entire site. You leave something for future archaeologists and their more advanced techniques.

"Anyway, Kathleen Kenyon excavated large sections of Ir Da'vid in the sixties and she destroyed them."

"She never wrote things down?"

"She never published her findings. For all practical purposes, the site is lost. But if she had found anything momentous, we would know by now. Shortly afterwards some local Arabs moved in and built over the site."

Dave sensed a maneuver. The sensation occurred whenever he played chess with Ben, and it always preceded a checkmate. Dave had moves of his own.

"All right," he said. "If that was all a mind game, why the secrecy? Why the threats?"

Ben looked disappointed. "Would you have believed me otherwise?"

Dave ground his teeth. If you miss the head, aim for the heart.

"So you tricked me? You betrayed my trust?"

"That's what friends are for," Ben said. "Don't mention it."

"Then you won't mind if I tell Yvette?"

Ben shrugged. "Be my guest. You're the one who swore an oath."

"OK. Then I'll have a word with Ornan. He should be able to set the record straight."

"No way. Do you have any idea how fragile our relations with the local Arabs are? All we need is you poking your nose around, making accusations, and we'll have riots on the streets. Decades of delicate symbiosis down the drain of your twisted imagination."

Dave opened his mouth. He closed it.

Checkmate.

Ben leaned forward.

"Can't you see? You've done nothing wrong. You got the girl. Just ride off into the sunset. Happily ever after."

Dave's vision blurred.

Was Ben right?

Was the conspiracy theory all in Dave's mind?

Ben had opened the escape passage and Dave longed to crawl through.

"I wish I could believe you, Ben," he said.

Ben sagged in his chair. "Ouch. I do have feelings, you know?"

"I'm sorry. But I know what I know."

Ben ran his fingers over the cracks in the wooden desktop. He pushed back in the chair and studied the ceiling, his head resting against the wall.

This had been a bad idea. Now he had to sit through a Shabbat lunch with Ben and Mandy and Yvette and pretend he had said nothing.

Ben sat up. He clicked the joints of his neck. "What if I have proof?"

"What?"

"What if I prove to you that no magic in the world can make someone fall in love?"

"How?"

"I know a guy in Me'ah She'arim. A Cabbalist. Not some haggard old baba selling red strings. The real deal. If there's a way, he'll know. He's a real genius."

An unbiased third party. Dave liked the sound of that. It was the closest he would get to scientific certainty.

"OK. When do we meet him?"

"He doesn't have a phone so we'll have to try him tonight and hope we get lucky. He only talks Cabbala on Shabbat anyway."

Ben drummed his fingers on the desk and chewed his lip.

"What's the matter?"

Ben glanced at him. "Like I said, the guy's a real genius."

"So?"

"Have you ever met a real genius?"

Mandy climbed the road along the Old City walls and psyched herself up for the task ahead.

First stop: the Western Wall.

I need all the help I can get.

She passed beneath the tall arch of Dung Gate and along a walkway that overlooked the remains of stone foundations and broken pillars arranged among tidy patches of green grass, tall cypresses, and pergolas. Together they formed an unlikely landscaped garden at the foot of the Southern Wall of the enormous stone block that was the Temple Mount.

At the women's entrance, she opened her handbag for the security guard and stepped through a metal-detector.

She had made a good impression on Ben, she was certain. For immigrants, friends were family. Today Dave had done the equivalent of taking her home to meet the folks.

And Mandy had a plan to bump their relationship up one more level.

Unless it backfired, that is.

She entered the expansive Western Wall plaza. Pigeons fluttered over the long tiles of white stone and the small pockets of tourists. In the markets, stores, and kitchens of the city, Jews bustled about their Sabbath preparations but the ruined enclosure wall of the Second Temple basked in sunlight and quiet.

A tiny, wrinkled woman approached her. Whispers of gray hair strayed from the kerchief on her head. She extended an olive-colored hand while Mandy fished in her bag. The woman pocketed the five-shekel coin, muttered a blessing, and shuffled off.

Mandy entered the women's section of the outdoor synagogue. As she drew near the Wall, the golden roof and pine trees of the Dome of the Rock dropped out of view. She selected a book of Psalms from a trolley and found a vacant plastic chair.

She reached out her hand to touch the ancient wall. The stone felt smooth and cool on her fingertips. Thousands of folded paper notes filled the cracks between the enormous stone slabs.

Mandy turned to a page at random and whispered the Hebrew prayers. Her mind filled with gratitude for the present, acceptance of the past, and trust in the future.

The sun warmed her back and caressed her hair. Overhead, swifts dived and darted, and found refuge in bushes between the upper boulders.

Each of God's creations had a time and place. Mandy had found hers.

She kissed the book and returned it to the trolley. She crossed the square toward the turnstile where taxis idled.

As she walked, she heard a sound, the soft strum of a

harp. Then another. Two more followed, louder now, as she veered toward the source of the music.

The melody mingled hope and regret in a romantic, unrushed trickle that whispered of flowing brooks, thick forests, and medieval castles.

At the foot of the staircase to the Jewish Quarter, she found the source. The man wore a white toga lined with gold. Biblical sandals strapped his feet. A glittering plastic crown sat on the ginger curls of his head. Long, thin fingers plucked the strings of a wooden David's harp.

Mandy drew closer. Sparse, rust-colored beard; milky skin; eyes closed in rapture. A few coppers lay in the upturned hat at his feet. The tune rose, quickened, and then ended.

Mandy clapped. "'Greensleeves,'" she said. "Great song."

The man blinked at her and smiled. His eyes were pale blue and now they intensified. His mouth moved as if to ask a question.

A memory jolted her. She had passed him on the campus corridors of the University of Texas ten years ago. Loner. Pothead. Mandy searched for his name.

"Damian, right?" she said. "It's Mandy. Mandy Rosenberg. We were in Art History together. At UT."

The man shook his head.

"David," he said. "Son of Jesse."

Mandy laughed. Still in character. The guy was good.

"What brings you to Jerusalem?" she asked

Damian's face contorted with emotion. He pointed a finger at Mandy.

"I know you," he said, far too emphatically.

Don't weird out on me, Damian.

"Bathsheba!" he said.

A shudder rippled down her back. Damian was either an excellent actor or seriously disturbed.

OK. Time to go.

She glanced at her wristwatch.

"Gotta go. Nice to see you again."

Mandy turned around and made for the turnstile.

"Wait!" Coins tinkled. Sandaled feet slapped the tiles. Slow, at first. Then faster.

She pushed through the iron bars of the turnstile. She dove into the nearest cab and locked the door. After the car pulled off, she looked back. Damian stared at her from the curb, his face a mix of confusion and anguish, the David's harp at his heart.

Mandy took a deep breath and told the driver the address.

That was creepy.

Damian had made a journey of his own, it seemed. She preferred to stay out of it.

By the time the cab stopped, she'd calmed down. She'd passed this busy street and office block many times on the way to She'arim.

She paid the driver and climbed out of the cab.

Kanfey Nesharim, the street sign read. The Wings of Eagles.

How appropriate.

Mandy took the stairs two at a time to the second-floor office and pressed the buzzer. The lettering on the window read *Nefesh B'nefesh*.

The girl at the desk held a folder in her hand and smiled at Mandy.

"Can I help you?" she said in a Canadian accent.

She wore a denim skirt and a cotton T-shirt with three-quarter sleeves. Straight out of high school, Mandy guessed.

She returned the smile. "I hope so. I'm here to make *aliya*."

DAN SOFER

CHAPTER 6

Streetlamps hummed as they flickered on and off, casting jaundiced light over the sidewalks of downtown Jerusalem. Bus shelters stood empty on islands between the vacant lanes.

Dave kept pace with Ben on Keren Hayesod. Both men wore Shabbat trousers and collared shirts.

Let's get this over with, he thought.

He had excused himself after a cozy Friday night dinner at Mandy's and strolled to the Greens. Ruchama's sweet chili chicken and steaming almond rice still warmed his stomach. The buzz of sugary Kiddush wine circled his head. Mandy had brushed her foot against his leg under the table. Even Shani seemed to have softened. All was well in the world.

Ben marched in silence, retaining full sulking rights.

Perhaps he was right and Dave had overreacted, imagining trolls under every bridge. He considered apologizing to Ben and turning back, but the least he could do was to see it through. Wrap up the visit. Tuck his conscience in. Call it a night.

Keren Hayesod became King George. They passed the Great Synagogue and the green edge of Independence Park.

Shutters sealed the fronts of tourist stores and fast food joints on the Ben Yehuda pedestrian walkway.

A black hat whisked by. Trimmed beard. Eyes to the

ground. Brow tense with concentration.

Years had passed since Dave had forayed into the ultra-Orthodox underworld and he was not looking forward to the prospect.

"Remind me," he said, to break the silence. "How do you know him?"

"I used to guide tours in Me'ah She'arim. 'A cross-cultural Shabbat experience.' We'd stroll the streets and crash a few *tishen*. The finale was a Q and A in the home of a genuine Charedi couple. Mishi was one of the few willing to host tourists."

"Mishi?" Dave said. "Our Cabbalist's name is Mishi?"

"What did you expect?"

"I don't know. An Isaac. Aharon. Maybe a Nachman. Something more conventional."

"He's conventional enough," Ben said.

Dave tried to lighten the mood. "He lives in a two-room apartment with a wife and ten kids?"

"Six kids. All under the age of eight."

Dave and his older brother had spent their childhoods at each other's throats and *they* had slept in separate rooms. The thought of a two-room warren made him cringe.

"They must be miserable."

"Actually, they're extremely happy."

"Well, the thought makes *me* feel miserable."

A yellow Volkswagen Golf sped by and Dave had a glimpse of peroxide hair and an earful of trance music. The tires screeched as the car veered right at the blinking red light on Jaffa Road and the pulsating beat faded.

Ben and Dave crossed on the painted lines. Far down the street, a crowd of long-legged teenage girls in painted-on jeans chattered outside a nightclub.

In a way, Dave had as much in common with secular Israelis as with *Charedim*: pop culture; university; modern clothing; concern for the world beyond the four cubits of Jewish Law.

After the ghetto walls had crumbled, some Jews, wary of

the temptations of the big wide world, had raised unseen walls of their own. Dave had Charedi cousins in Gateshead and he had whiled away many an evening in the men's sections of their frequent weddings, like an anthropologist among a tribe of bearded, smiling wizards.

His British cousins, however, were regular cosmopolitans compared to their Israeli counterparts, who were known for draft dodging, the siphoning of government budgets, and spitting at immodestly clad women on buses. On Independence Day, some of them burned Israeli flags.

Dave's annoyance with the ultra-orthodox *Charedim* went beyond the bad name they gave religion, beyond their chronic poverty and single-minded conclusions.

Dave loathed the almost palpable sense of superiority and entitlement. They turned their noses at hard-working, tax-paying, fully observant Jews such as Dave, who straddled both worlds. In their eyes, these Modern Orthodox were capitulators, Secularists in disguise, a device of the evil Other Side, whose filthy lips suckled at the teat of Sanctity.

And tonight, he needed them. He needed the kind of specialist who could germinate only in their sterile Torah incubator.

Ben and Dave climbed Strauss Street. More black hats bustled by. Darkened storefronts displayed religious books and Judaica.

Ben and Dave stepped over the peak of the hill and two hundred years back in time.

Me'ah She'arim Street teamed with humanity. Bearded men in satin robes and furry *shtreimels*—the hat worn by married Charedi men. Women in formless gowns and shower cap head coverings. Strollers rolled along the middle of the street. Young boys in white stockings and waistcoats played tag, weaving between pedestrians, their ear locks flying, black skullcaps held to their heads with their hands. Young girls with braided hair and ankle-length Victorian dresses chatted excitedly.

Dave's wristwatch read 11:30 PM but it could have been

the middle of the afternoon on those cobbled streets.

A banner in severe black letters warned visitors against immodest dress unbecoming the Daughters of Israel.

Ben and Dave joined the throng and the scents of pressed clothing and recent showers. The color and length of the robes and stockings distinguished the Chassidic bloodlines, but ultimately their dress code aped that of the Polish gentile nobilities of a forgotten age.

Makeshift balconies jutted overhead like sewn-on appendages, suspended by rusted steel rods and a miracle.

Despite his ideological misgivings, Dave found comfort in this pocket of simple, childlike faith.

Ben stopped at a public notice board thick with layers of paper and glue. Dave studied the harsh Hebrew font but knew little Yiddish.

"What is it?" Dave asked.

"A *Pashkevil*," said Ben. "Readers beware. Some book about evolution. They've excommunicated the author for heresy."

"Anyone I know?"

Ben frowned. "Never heard of him. Until now. C'mon."

Ben ducked into a dark alley and paused at a weathered wooden door a full foot above street level. He tried the handle and the door gave way.

Low voices echoed down the long, dark passageway.

Ben stepped into the void. Dave's lungs rebelled.

"Coming?" Ben said.

Dave wiped his palms on his thighs. "I'll wait out here."

"Come on. Don't be a muggle. We're almost there."

The corridor reeked of damp, mothballs, and old plywood. Doorways spilled rectangles of light across their path. Dave felt like the detective in a crime thriller, braving the derelict hallways of a rundown tenement, but instead of trigger-itchy drug dealers, bearded men pored over heavy tomes on narrow tables and rickety podiums in the small study rooms and makeshift synagogues.

After a few turns, Dave lost his sense of direction. He

would have trouble finding his way out without Ben. Could this Mishi be trusted even if he told him what he wanted to hear? *Especially* if he did. Ben could easily have staged the meeting, or at least primed the witness. Again, he walked onto a chessboard filled with Ben's pawns.

The voices grew louder, rising and falling to a seemingly random tune, as the two men ventured deeper into the alternate universe.

The corridor emptied into a large marble foyer. The voices resonated from behind two large wooden doors.

Ben pushed through the doors and released waves of sound and blinding light. The hall was the size of a basketball arena. A mammoth chandelier hung from the ceiling. Wooden grandstands lined three of the walls, packing row upon row of men in cloaks and hats and beards. Many of them swayed at the waist like frenzied metronomes, fingers curling their ear locks to the wordless song that carried on five hundred throats.

A tight jam of Charedi teenagers blocked the standing room. They tiptoed and craned their necks to win a better view of the central court, entering and exiting the fray according to their own Brownian motion. Dave felt like a scuba diver in a cloud of sardines.

Ben pushed through the mass of bodies and disappeared. A moment later he reappeared, grabbed Dave's wrist, and pulled him in. The smell of fabric, sweat, and awe assaulted his nostrils. The coats and hats jostled him and each other without apology.

None of the boys seemed bothered by the culture tourists and their white *kippas* which, from above, must have looked like seagulls on a sea of black. Every eye and ear strained toward the center of the hall.

Ben halted at the edge of a clearing. Plastic platters of fruit, pretzels, wafers, and assorted pastries covered a long table set with a white cloth. A row of seated, aging rabbis in *shtreimels* lined the table but none touched the food. A rabbi in robes of cream and gold and an adventitious white beard sat at the center. He looked very frail and sat perfectly still, his eyes and mouth closed in deep meditation. Or sleep.

"That him?" Dave whispered in Ben's ear.

Ben shook his head. "That's the Rebbeh. Our man is next to him. The redhead."

The man to the Rebbeh's left had a ginger beard and side locks, and looked three decades younger than the other seated rabbis. He *shochelled* back and forth on his chair, his eyes clenched with concentration.

Mishi.

The Golden Rabbi raised his hand and the hall fell into a silence so complete Dave could hear his own heartbeat.

The Golden Rabbi spoke in Yiddish, his voice hardly above a whisper. The hall soaked up each word, eyes straining through spectacles, ears cupped to collect each drop of holy wisdom.

One figure remained in motion, rocking to a soundless melody of his own.

Mishi.

The Rebbeh's speech dragged on. Dave understood only snatches: *Riboyno shel Oylom*. Master of the World. *Oraysoh*. The Torah.

Dave's knees hurt. He shifted his weight from leg to leg. Then the Golden Rabbi mumbled a blessing over a chocolate wafer and bit into it.

Pandemonium ripped through the hall. Men pushed toward the table and almost knocked him to the ground. Arms snatched at the snacks on the dishes and lifted the plastic trays into the air. The sardines had turned into sharks at feeding time. The rabbi with the red beard rose to his feet.

"Quick," Ben said. "He's on the move."

They fought the surge and ebb of bodies, and chased the *shtreimel* out a back door.

They pursued Mishi along a dark passageway, down a dingy stairwell, and squeezed past a band of hats barreling in the opposite direction.

As they turned a corner, another set of double doors

swung shut.

"Stay close," Ben said, and he slipped through.

Dave followed and found himself adrift in deep space. The room had no light source and, judging by the utter blackness, no windows either. He sensed an expanse ahead and above, like a cave.

He heard Ben's footfalls and the rustle of clothing. He didn't dare step forward. Then he heard the hum. A single human baritone. Then another. Five male voices. Twenty. A hundred. The voices rose and fell and meandered, then repeated. The tune sounded like "Three Blind Mice" on a stretched audio cassette.

Silhouettes emerged in the dark: men in coats, seated on chairs, distributed at random in the void. Their voices reverberated against the walls and through Dave's body. Ben's figure advanced delicately between the seated Chassidim toward a thin rectangle of light. Dave followed. For an instant, the outline became a block of blinding light and the man in the *shtreimel* exited.

Dave stumbled and felt his way across the hall.

"They're the Slonim Chassidim," Ben explained when they stepped out the door. They stood in yet another dimly lit corridor. The scrape of a chair leg sounded from a nearby room.

Ben nodded at the doorway. "Let me do the talking. Let's not sidetrack him, OK?"

Dave nodded.

Mishi sat behind a narrow table of chipped plywood, a large black *yarmulke* on his head. The *shtreimel* sat on the table like a curled up, sleeping fox.

Mishi looked up from a thick volume, smiled broadly, and rose to his feet.

"Binyomin," he said. He gave Ben's hand a vigorous double-handed shake. "*Gutten Shabbos.*" Ben introduced Dave, and Mishi pressed Dave's hand between thin, bony fingers. Mishi indicated the wooden bench opposite and closed his book.

Mishi, bright-eyed, pale-faced, and hatless, looked very young indeed. Dave had expected a wizened, benevolent Gandalf.

He beamed at them. "English, yes?"

"Please," Ben said.

Dave rejoiced. He would receive the truth unfiltered by Ben.

Ben inquired regarding the rabbi's family. Then he said, "My friend here, and I, we want to know if it's possible to make someone fall in love?"

Put in so many words, the question embarrassed Dave.

The smile dropped from the young rabbi's face.

"No magic," he said. "No amulet. I do not do this thing. Yes?"

"Oh, no," said Ben. "We don't want you to *do* anything. We just want to know if it's possible."

Mishi peered from Ben to Dave.

"Ahhh…"

He ran his long fingers through the sparse red beard of his chin. "Love? Yes? In beginning, God make man and woman. Not like today. No. No. One body. One soul. Then—"

Mishi performed a martial arts chop worthy of Bruce Lee. "Break in two. Lonely. Walk-da-walk-da-walk-da world." He clapped his hands together, startling Dave. "One again! This is love. Yes?"

Mishi giggled. He slapped his leg. He giggled some more. His torso rocked forward and sideways and threatened to floor both the young rabbi and the bench on which he sat.

Ben and Dave exchanged glances.

"Yes," said Ben. "But can you make a girl fall in love with you even if she's not your… soul mate?"

Mishi sobered up and wiped his eyes. "Make girl fall in love?" He scratched his beard. He stared at the ceiling. He frowned. His eyes fell on Dave. "No," he said.

"No?"

Mishi smiled like an escaped lunatic. He found the question incredibly amusing. "God make soul. And man. And woman. No magic. No amulet. Yes?"

No magic.

Dave savored the words. He felt his shoulders relax. It was official. It was all in his head.

"Thanks, Mishi," Ben said. "That's all we needed to hear. Regards to Rochelleh." Ben patted Dave on the knee. "Let's go."

"Maybe," Mishi said.

The two men froze. Mishi stared at the ceiling, as if listening.

"Maybe?" Ben said.

Mishi sighed, searching for adequate words. He raised his hand above his head, the palm level with the ground.

"World Above," he said. "Soul."

He placed his other hand below the first.

"World Below. Body."

He moved his bottom hand and the top hand kept up. "Move Below, move Above."

Dave understood. Actions in the physical world affect the spiritual. It was the principal behind every *mitzvah*—good deed.

Mishi positioned his hands in the air, side by side. "Two body. Two soul." He moved his hands together and entwined the fingers. "Body and soul togeda."

"But how?" Dave asked and won a first-class scowl from Ben.

Mishi smiled. "One place," he said. "First place. Togeda Below. Togeda Above."

Mishi slapped his leg again and surrendered to another fit of laughter.

"Where?" Ben asked, as Mishi showed signs of recovery. "Where is this place?"

Mishi coughed and drew a deep breath.

"Where?" he repeated, as if the answer was obvious.

"One place. Holy Holy. One place. *Even shesiya.*"

Dave jogged down Strauss Street. He tried to keep up with Ben and his own scattered thoughts.

His intestines writhed and threatened to push Ruchama's home-cooked meal up his throat. The short foray into the unreality of Me'ah She'arim had turned his world on its head once again.

Even shesiya.

The Shesiya Stone, the holy place where Heaven and Earth collide. Finally, Dave had a name for the mechanism behind the worst mistake of his life.

"I hope that settles it," Ben said, as they rounded the hill and approached the Jaffa Road intersection.

He had hotfooted his way through the hive of corridors and side streets, leaving little time, or breath, for questions.

"What do you mean *'that settles it'*? Mishi explained everything. Maybe this place, this *Even Shesiya*, is in Ir David."

"*Even shtiya*," Ben corrected, using the Israeli pronunciation.

Dave translated as best he could. "The Drinking Stone?"

"Foundation Stone," Ben said. "Or Weaving Stone. The point where Creation began. The site of the binding of Isaac and Jacob's dream of the ladder to Heaven. The stone upon which the Ark of the Covenant rested in Solomon's Temple. The stone that commands deep waters and one day will cause a river to flow through the Holy of Holies and reveal the lost Temple treasures."

Ben spoke in an exaggerated, cynical tone, but Dave's mind locked on target.

A magical stone. Unassuming. Easily overlooked.

"That's it," Dave said. "The stone must be in Ir David."

"Forget about it. The stone is a dead-end. A wild goose

chase."

"Why?"

"Because we know exactly where it is. It fills most of the shrine built in its honor on the Temple Mount. Maybe you've heard of it? They call it *The Dome of the Rock*."

Dave paused at the mouth of Ben Yehuda and fell behind.

The large golden dome lay beyond the Western Wall, a few hundred meters North of Ir David.

Of course!

Dave had not set foot on the Temple Mount and, he was sure, neither had Mandy. The Arabs in charge restricted the entry of non-Muslims, and Halacha prohibited Jews from treading on the holy site.

"Wait." Dave ran and caught Ben at the edge of Independence Park.

"How do we know that's the Foundation Stone?"

"It's the only Foundation Stone we know of. Huge, rough lump of bedrock. Little cave underneath. No known magical properties."

Dave read the Torah portion each week. He knew enough about the Ark of the Covenant to realize that something did not fit.

"You said the Ark rested on the stone. But the Ark wasn't nearly that big, was it? Two-and-a-half by one-and-a-half cubits. Neither was the Holy of Holies. And if this stone is so uneven—"

Ben turned on his heels and gripped Dave by his shirt collar.

"What's the matter with you? Can't you just let it go? You've got the girl. You've even got your precious conscience back. Isn't that enough?"

A pair of passing black hats ogled them. Ben released him.

"I'm sorry," he said.

Dave felt the need to explain. "Mandy goes back to the States in two weeks."

"Do you love her?"

"Yes. I think so. I don't know. I want to know for sure."

"You never will. You know why? Because the problem is in your head."

"If we could just speak to Ornan—"

Ben raised his hand for Dave to stop.

"Tell you what. I'll take you to a real expert this time. Professor Barkley."

"The Dead Sea Scroll guy?"

Ben had studied under the professor at Hebrew U and he mentioned him at every opportunity.

"Yes. I'm meeting him Sunday night to discuss another matter. You can tag along. Maybe *he* can talk some sense into you."

It is the happiest day of Dave's life.

As he steps forward, the chorus line of friends and relatives in suits and smiles retreats. A trumpeter keeps pace and blares his song. The scene moves in slow motion, the sounds muffled, as though he's underwater, but he can make out the tune. *Keizad Merakdin Lifnei Ha'Kala*—How We Dance Before the Bride.

Dave nods and smiles at his guests. A tear of sweat slips down his brow. He wears a long white *kittel* over a blue suit and white tie. His mother, in a salmon evening dress and wide-brimmed hat, locks his left arm in hers, and his father grips his right. Dave has never seen them both so happy at the same time.

A doubt pulls at his mind like a terrier at his sleeve. He's forgotten an important detail. He shakes it off.

The wedding parade rounds a corner of the closed hall and there it is. White silken sheets form the canopy and colorful bouquets adorn the corner posts.

The dancers fall back. Dave and his parents walk the red carpet, passing between rows of chairs. Under the *chuppah*, the traditional wedding canopy, a red-haired rabbi in a furry *shtreimel* bares his teeth.

Mishi!

The silver goblet in the rabbi's hand brims with thick, red liquid.

Ben stands by. He wears a white robe and turban like the Genie of the Lamp. He winks at Dave, then cracks open a velvet jewelry box. A gold wedding band glints in the spotlight. Three letters in an ancient script dance along the surface—Tsadi-Dalet-Qof—then fade away.

The doubt returns. It gnaws at the edge of his awareness.

Not now. This is my day. Leave me alone!

Friends and relatives peer expectantly from the rows of chairs. The red carpet stretches away for miles and at the end stands a tall slender figure all in white. She holds a round bouquet to her bosom; a wispy veil hides her face. She glides along the carpet. Dave squints and strains his eyes but cannot penetrate the screen of lace.

Rivulets of cold sweat trickle down his forehead and drench his cheeks. The doubt has grown into panic.

The bride mounts the steps of the *chuppah*. She circles Dave. The white satin train of her dress scratches his polished shoes, wraps his ankles, and winds around his legs.

He needs help. Ben winks and smiles. His parents smile. The rabbi smiles. Faces in the crowd smile. None of them hear his silent cry.

The bride halts beside him. She stares ahead. The rabbi raises his goblet and utters the sacred words.

He shivers. Too late he grasps the slippery question. This is his wedding day, but he still has no idea. He wants to ask, but terror clamps his throat. *Please*, his thoughts beg. *Please, someone, tell me who she is!*

DAN SOFER

∽

Mandy gaped at the supermodel across the dinner table.

"How do you do it?" she asked and passed the salad to Dave.

First an archaeologist; now a Jewish Claudia Schiffer. How had Dave kept them secret so long?

She had a secret too and it itched to burst the gift wrapping.

Later.

"I only accept modest assignments," Yvette explained in her sophisticated Belgian accent. "No lingerie. No swimsuits. And no Saturdays. Some cholent?"

"Sure."

The girl knew her way around a kitchen. Mandy had devoured the sautéed chicken strips. "That must be pretty limiting," she said.

"I've had to turn down a few jobs. But if they really want you, they get over it."

"You're amazing." She turned to Dave. "Isn't she amazing? You sure know how to pick your friends."

"Uh-huh," he mumbled. He had hardly spoken a word all morning.

"Don't bother with them," Yvette said. "They wandered around Me'ah She'arim all night."

Me'ah She'arim?

Dave hadn't mentioned that when he had left her apartment after dinner. He had displayed no special interest in Chassidism. The surprises kept coming. Each day she discovered another facet of Dave Schwarz.

"Thanks for the invite," she said.

Dave produced a sheepish smile. "The Tish was strictly men only."

"I'm thinking of doing night tours of Me'ah She'arim again. Dave was my test group." Ben gave Dave a tired look. "Thanks for your help, Dave."

Dave didn't look up from his plate of cholent. "Don't mention it."

Mandy wrote off the resentful undertone to British Humor. "Yvette, I wish I had a glamorous job full of travel and interesting people."

Yvette cradled her chin in her palm. "Too much travel, if you ask me. I fly again on Sunday for a week. And the people? Pffff. So-so. Some are kind. Most are shallow. Once this old Italian man tried to chat me up and I told him to get lost. One of the girls came up to me after. 'What did he say to you?' she says, so I told her. Then she says, 'Don't you know who that is? That's Giorgio Armani!' I was so embarrassed."

After lunch, Dave walked Mandy home along Emek Refaim. Birds dipped overhead and sang of spring. Violet and white *Rakefet* flowers peeked over walls and brightened up the sidewalk flowerbeds. Joggers and Sabbath strollers passed them. The promise of new beginnings and fresh horizons hung in the air.

Dave's string tassels peeked out the belt of his trousers and Mandy's thoughts drifted to the world underneath his clothes. She felt her cheeks heat up.

Oh, my.

She let her hand brush against his but he didn't seem to notice.

They walked past Bell Park. Only a short stretch of sidewalk remained to Mandy's street, where Shani and Ruchama awaited.

"Guess what?" she said.

"What?"

"You're looking at an Israeli citizen."

Dave stopped in his tracks. "You made aliya?"

"Uh-huh."

Dave seemed confused. The circles under his eyes deepened. "I thought you were just trying it out."

139

No smile. No mazal tov.

"I did. And I like it."

His eyes glazed over as he sank into dark thoughts.

"We have more time now," she said. "That's all. No pressure."

He ran a hand over his face. He looked exhausted.

"Are you OK?"

He blinked as though waking up. "I'm just… surprised. That's… great news. I'm happy for you."

They crossed King David Street and climbed Keren Hayesod.

Not the reaction she had hoped for but her timing could have been better. Dave had slept little and he was about to start a new job. A dose of not-so-subtle relationship pressure was all he needed.

Way to go, Mands.

"Tuesday night is Independence Day," she said, artfully changing the topic. "Let's do something fun. A hike. Or a picnic. What do you prefer?"

"Yes," Dave said, his voice distant. "That's a great idea. Let's talk after Shabbos."

Of course! Shouldn't make plans on Shabbat. Silly girl.

They walked in silence and soon reached the stilts of Mandy's apartment building on Mendele.

"Want to come upstairs?"

He shook his head. "I should get some rest."

She'd seen that coming.

"I love you," she said.

The words bypassed her brain and slipped out her mouth before she knew what she was saying. She and Dave had never used the L-word. Mandy needed to hear it more than ever.

He smiled and his eyes filled with a secret sadness. Or hurt.

She had hoped for four words; she settled for two.

"Me too," he said.

Dave plodded down Keren Hayesod in a daze. The afternoon sun reflected harsh light off the apartment blocks. A cloudless blue sky studied him without mercy.

Oh, God. What have I done?

He had endured lunch with a growing sense of disgust. Countless times, he had sat at Ben's Shabbat table in awe of Ben and his beautiful wife, unaware of the deception beneath the veneer of marital bliss.

He had discovered, if not the whole truth, enough loose ends to make out the thread.

Dave's love for Mandy, for he *had* loved her, was an illusion. Ben clung to his rationalizations but Dave could not escape his conscience. He woke at night in a cold pool of doubt that destroyed the peace of mind necessary for sleep.

He had toyed with Mandy's heart. Her soul. Changed the course of her life. Turned her into a Stepford Wife. But unlike in Dave's nightmare, it was not too late.

He paused for breath on Emek Refaim.

His stomach cramped. The dry taste of death filled his mouth.

Someone was calling his name.

"Geez, Dave," said a stocky Australian. "I called you three times."

"Shmuel." Dave shook his friend's hand. He felt his face redden. He had last thought of Shmuel and Rochel at Nat's Shabbat dinner catastrophe when Alfred E. Neuman had added their names to a rogues' gallery of compromise. "Long time no see. You look good."

Shmuel had cropped his hair short. His cheeks had shed their soft edges. "Thanks. What's news?"

"All good." He waited for Shmuel to address the obvious

141

absence of his wife. Was Rochel pregnant? In labor at a Jerusalem hospital?

"What brings you back to Jerusalem?" Dave asked.

Shmuel and Rochel, like many young couples, had left exorbitant Jerusalem for the yuppie suburbia of Modiin.

"I moved back," Shmuel said. "Around the corner from here. We should get together."

I moved back. The words grated on Dave's nerves. He could take no more. "How is Rochel?" he asked.

"You haven't heard?" Shmuel's smile faded. "We got divorced a few months ago."

The universe tilted off balance. Dave fumbled for words. "I... I'm sorry. I didn't know."

"No worries. It's not the kind of news you spread around." He placed a consoling hand on Dave's shoulder. "It's all right," he said.

"Sorry," Dave said again. "You seemed so happy."

"Yeah, well." Shmuel studied the trees across the street. He did not seem too broken up about it. "We had issues from the start. I feel relieved, actually. You'd be surprised how often it happens. There's a bunch of divorcees in Katamon. I'm just glad it's over. You know? Get on with my life."

"That's good," Dave said, still reeling.

"A word of advice," Shmuel said. "Listen to your heart. Don't compromise."

Shmuel walked off and left Dave gagging on his words.

I can't believe it.

Dave had envied Shmuel. His wife Rochel—his ex-wife— was a dark American-Israeli beauty with a needlepoint wit. He had enjoyed a Shabbat lunch at their table six months ago before they'd relocated. He replayed the table talk, the body language, in his mind and searched for signs of impending doom.

Nothing.

Dave stopped walking. He stood beside a shaded square of grass at the far end of Emek Refaim. He had passed the walkway to his building. Two goats of flat, hammered metal, nailed together in the name of art, hung atop a pole like cadavers on a stake; a gruesome warning to passersby.

Dave sat down on a steel bench. He held his head in his hands. Small birds pecked at breadcrumbs in the speckled shade of trees. The Sabbath shoes of passersby drummed the sidewalk.

Dave knew of divorce among young, religious couples the way he knew of car accidents. Tragic. Regretful. Happened to other people. Never people he knew.

What shook him most was Shmuel's nonchalance. His relief. Was Dave heading off the same cliff?

Just breathe, Dave. You're tired. You're in shock. You are in no state to make rash decisions.

He became aware of changes in the ambient sounds. A pair of high heels had paused on the sidewalk. A scratch on the asphalt and then the footfalls continued.

Cla-clack, cla-clack, cla-clack.

Instead of fading into the street noise, the steps grew louder, more decisive. The birds scattered. A pair of elegant black sandals and pedicured feet entered his visual field. His eyes followed the sandals, up the ankles of flawless ivory, the Barbie legs, the elegant dress and shapely form. Sunlight danced on her flowing, black-satin hair. Dave stared: a hobbit spellbound in the presence of an Elven princess.

Could it be?

The remnants of his sanity had snapped and now tortured his poor mind with the most sweet and cruel of delusions.

The apparition parted her perfect red lips.

"Dave?"

Now he heard a voice, too. Precise. Feminine. British. The voice that had haunted his regrets.

He fought for air. He fought for words. Questions queued up and bottlenecked his brain. How? What? Why?

Finally, he managed one word, the last desperate gasp of a man whose lungs had filled with freezing, salty water.

He said: "Shira?"

CHAPTER 7

Blessed is He who divides between Sacred and Mundane.

Shani sipped from the silver goblet and spilled grape juice into the tin saucer. Ruchama extinguished the *Havdalah* candle in the puddle and with it the Sabbath sanctity.

Shavua tov! A good week.

Mandy yawned. She had slept through the afternoon. She powered up her mobile. No messages yet. Dave would return from synagogue in a few minutes.

The post-Sabbath cleanup began. Mandy helped Ruchama scour the dishes and shove the dinner table to the corner of the living room.

The languor of Saturday afternoon gave way to the anticipation of Saturday night.

"Princess Bride?" Ruchama suggested.

"Nah," said Mandy. "I'll probably go out with Dave."

After all that sleep, Mandy was in the mood for a night on the town. She selected two skirts from her closet, stepped under a hot shower, and settled on the living room couch while her hair dried. The microwave hummed in the kitchen.

Mandy glanced at her phone in the soft lamplight. No missed calls.

Dave must have overslept.

Poor thing.

She typed a text message.

Shavua tov! Need coffee. Say when. Xxx. M.

Send.

The bathroom shower hissed. Shani always spent at least half an hour in the shower, turning the bathroom into a steaming rainforest, with wet towels draped over doors and faucets like the branches of tropical plants.

Ruchama bustled into the living room with a large bowl of buttered popcorn, collapsed beside Mandy, and turned on the TV with the remote. Mandy reached for a handful of popcorn and leaned back.

According to the laws of physics, Ruchama's Princess Bride DVD should have worn away long ago. Mandy had walked in on enough snatches of the movie to piece the plot together: Buttercup and Westley fall in love. Westley leaves to find his fortune. Pirates attack his ship and these particular pirates never leave survivors. Buttercup must marry the mean Prince Humperdinck. Outlaws kidnap Buttercup.

All her life Mandy had consumed movies and books about love but never truly understood.

Until now.

"Not that dreck again." Shani stood in the corridor wearing a short red dress. She leaned against the wall and slipped on a pair of black stilettos with heels long and sharp enough to kill a man.

"*Too 'ove!*" Ruchama protested, her mouth packed with popcorn.

"Who's the lucky guy?" Mandy asked.

"Some CEO looking for a trophy wife." Shani spoke of her dates as though they were dentist appointments. Her meticulous makeup told a different tale.

Five dates a week, at Mandy's count. No wonder the girl had never learned to cook.

A horn honked outside, the high-pitched trumpeting of a Porsche or Ferrari.

"That's my ride," Shani said and she click-clacked out the front door.

Shani and Ruchama returned to their movie.

A pirate rescues Buttercup from the outlaws. The pirate is her beloved Westley! They flee the outlaws and cross the Fire Swamp.

Mandy needed a plan for Independence Day. Her options included a walk along the stream of Wadi Kelt and a concert at Safra Square. Which would Dave like best?

Mandy glanced at her watch.

9:30 PM.

Strange.

She got up, walked to her room, and dialed Dave's number.

It rang.

So you're up after all.

Café Hillel would do nicely. Or Aroma.

Then, on the second ring, before Mandy had decided on a venue, the call cut to voice mail.

Dave stood at the glass doors of Café Hillel like a man in urgent need of the loo.

Shira Cohen had returned to Jerusalem.

Shira Cohen wanted to talk.

Dave filled with joy. And dread.

A waitress in a black T-shirt and jeans unlocked and opened the doors. Dave secured a table at the back.

Ten minutes early. Time enough for his adrenaline to settle.

Why had Shira Cohen spared a few minutes for her old

flame? A few reasons bubbled in Dave's brain. Morbid curiosity. A chance to show off her perfect husband. Guilt. But Shira was above all that. She was not cruel. And she had no cause for shame. The worst possible scenario remained: pity.

A middle-aged security guard took up his station outside the doors. A few years earlier, the American doctor David Applebaum, legendary for his care for all races, had sat by those doors to drink coffee with his daughter, Nava, the night before her wedding. Then a suicide bomber had walked in.

The waitress placed three menus on the table but Dave declined to order.

Couples entered the coffee shop, ordered cappuccinos, salads, and toasted sandwiches. Dave fidgeted with the white sachets in the porcelain holder. He studied the menu without appetite.

Still no Shira.

Had he imagined the whole encounter?

His phone buzzed.

Had Shira changed her mind?

His heart lurched with disappointment and relief.

The text was not from Shira. Mandy wanted to go out for coffee.

At least he had Mandy. Dave would tell Shira about Mandy. Let her know that he had moved on. Retain a shred of self-respect.

In the park that afternoon, he had gaped like a stunned fish. *We should catch up*, she had said and Dave had gulped down the invitation without chewing.

A thought occurred. Would they need room for a stroller? Dave's stomach juices bubbled and boiled.

This was a very bad idea.

He looked up. Shira Cohen stood in the doorway. Her eyes searched the room and fell on Dave. She smiled. Dimpled. Demure.

How he loved her smile.

She walked over to his table.

How he loved the way she walked.

Shira Cohen. Smiling. Walking toward him.

Alone.

Dave's lungs cramped in his chest.

Either her wig was flawless or she was not wearing a head covering. He searched her fingers for the glint of a wedding ring.

Could it be?

Shira Cohen sat opposite Dave, her posture erect. Silky black hair pooled over the shoulders of her blouse. Her emerald eyes focused on him with a warm intensity that unnerved him.

"Bit unreal, isn't it?" she said.

How he loved her voice. Precise. Intelligent. Familiar.

"Indeed," he replied. That's it. Stay cool.

Shira looked at the menus on the table and for a split-second she seemed crestfallen.

"Is anyone joining us?" she asked with polite interest.

"Oh, no. I just thought... I had heard..."

Shira dipped her head.

"We called it off a few months before the wedding," she said. "If you don't mind, I'd prefer not to talk about it."

"No problem."

Dave's heart seemed to have stopped.

Oh. My. God. OhmyGodOhmyGodOhmyGod!

The waitress came to his rescue.

Shira ordered a latte—weak, with soy milk and in a glass cup—and Dave a hot cider.

They took each other in.

God, she is so beautiful.

Shira Cohen. Single and out for drinks with Dave.

Don't do it, Dave. Don't hope. Don't even dream. Your heart won't survive another shattering.

"How long are you here?" he said.

"I'm at *Neveh* for a month. But I could stay through the summer."

Hints danced at the corners of her lips. Her eyes smiled.

Dave nodded, none the wiser.

"You've changed," she said.

"Have I?"

"*Hot cider.* You always took tea."

"Now and again, I do daring things."

Her lips curled upward again. Dave basked in the intense interest of her gaze.

"It's more than that. You're… relaxed. Confident."

He said nothing, fearful to disturb that impression.

"I've changed too," she said. "I've done a lot of thinking over the last year. About the choices I've made. Relationships. I have very fond memories of our time together."

He still remained silent.

"I had to find you," she said. "To ask for another chance."

Ask for another chance.

Dave considered pinching his thigh or stabbing the back of his hand with a fork.

Shira Cohen was pleading with him to get back together. This was no dream. This was the splitting of the Red Sea, the sun standing still over Gibeon. This was an open miracle.

The waitress placed their drinks on the mahogany tabletop.

"Well?" Shira said.

"Well what?"

She shrugged her shoulders. "Can we have another go?"

"Yes," he said. "Yes, of course."

Shira leaned back in the chair. Her chest heaved with pent-up air. Her smile was glorious.

Dave's own cheeks threatened to crack.

Don't let this moment end. Please.

A dark cloud loomed at the edge of his awareness but he ignored it and sailed into the eyes of emerald green.

She parted her divine lips again. "It's as though we traveled back in time."

Da-dee-da-da da-dee-da-dee-ee-dah.

Dave's phone sang "Jerusalem of Gold."

Mandy! Mandy had added the ringtone to Dave's phone

and he silenced it with a single jab.

"Who was that?" she asked.

"No one," Dave said, pocketing the phone. "No one at all."

∽

"Maybe they stole his phone?"

Ruchama placed her dish of spaghetti next to the empty mugs and popcorn bowl on the ring-marked coffee table.

Over the last hour, Westley had defeated Humperdinck and saved Buttercup. They kissed and rode off into the sunset.

Mandy's hero, however, was a no-show. Her second attempt to call Dave redirected to voice mail without even ringing.

She shook her head. Something was wrong. She could feel it.

"Maybe he broke the leg?" Ruchama suggested brightly. "Dave is a nice guy. Don't worry, Mandy."

Ruchama picked up her own phone, a Nokia brick a few generations older than Mandy's iPhone.

"Look," she said. "And promise you won't tell Shani."

Mandy shifted closer.

Ruchama started a text message. "Dave," she said. "D. A. V...."

"What are you doing?"

"There is a message in every name," Ruchama whispered. "Look."

Ruchama thumbed a button that iterated between letter

151

combinations.

"The first words are *eat* and *fat*. Hmm. Dave isn't that fat."

Mandy smiled. Names reflect essence, Rabbi Jeremy had told her She'arim class, but Mandy was sure the Sages had not had this in mind. She felt a tug of compassion for her flatmate, so orderly and sensible in all things except love.

"Ruchama," she said as kindly as possible. "Predictive text doesn't actually mean—"

"Wait. Here's the last letter. E. That gives: *date*."

Mandy forgot her objections. "OK. I'm impressed. What else?"

Ruchama pressed a key. "*Fate*. I told you, Mandy!"

An irrational sense of relief snuggled in Mandy's breast.

"That's all there is," Ruchama said. "Wait. What's his full name?"

"David Schwarz."

Ruchama's fingers got to work. "I. D. S. That gives: *father*. Freud would love that one... Oh. I'm sorry." She had noticed Mandy's expression.

Mention of her father had drained Mandy's optimism into a deep, dark place.

The front door clicked open and Ruchama stiffened. Shani sailed in, her high heels dangling over her shoulder by her fingertips.

"I'm home," she sang. "And don't ask. Some men have no... OK." The shoes dropped to the floor. She placed her hands on her hips. "Who died? And what, Ruchama, for God's sake, are you hiding behind your back?"

Ruchama produced the cell phone.

"Oh brother." She collapsed onto the armchair. "It's Dave, isn't it?"

Mandy filled her in. "Something's happened to him. I can feel it."

Shani smiled at her sadly. "I wouldn't lose any sleep, Mands. I'm sure he's not in any mortal danger." She grinned. "But I can get him to pick up if you like."

"How?"

Shani slid her arm down the length of her thigh, then held up her hand. "With this."

"A phone?" Mandy's hopes wavered. Shani's Samsung Galaxy had a touch screen but it was no magic wand.

"This is no ordinary phone. It's *my* phone."

"Very funny. So now Dave's screening me?"

"Twenty shekels says he picks up."

Shani tossed the phone into the air and Mandy caught it.

"You're on." Soon Mandy would be twenty shekels richer, although a large slice of her just wanted to hear Dave's voice.

Mandy dialed Dave's number by heart. It rang. Twice.

"Hello?"

"Dave?"

Shani punched the air and launched from the armchair into a victory dance.

"Dumb luck," Mandy whispered at Shani, her hand over the receiver.

"Who is this?"

Dave didn't recognize her voice.

"It's Mandy. I'm on Shani's phone. Been trying to reach you all night. Are you OK?"

"Oh, yeah. Hi, Mandy. I'm fine. Sorry I didn't get back to you. Something came up."

Mandy felt a steel anvil lift from her shoulders. Dave was alive and well. That's what mattered. She waited for Dave to say *what* had come up.

Silence multiplied on the line.

"*Yom Ha'Atzma'ut* is still around the corner. I was think-ing—"

"Yes," Dave interrupted. "Actually, I've been meaning to speak with you."

He sounded formal. Distant.

"OK," she said. "Speak away."

"We should take a break."

Mandy's brain struggled with the sentence, then shoved it into an available mental compartment. "OK. A long weekend should do the trick."

"No," Dave said. "I mean a timeout. You know. To think things over."

"To think what over?"

"I feel confused."

"Confused? About what?"

"I'm sorry. Let me start again."

He spoke for a while and Mandy listened. She muttered *OK* and *sure* a few times but her brain had turned to jello. She understood each of Dave's words but their combined meaning fluttered beyond her grasp. By the time the message settled, Dave had hung up.

Mandy looked into the worried faces of her flatmates.

"That was Dave," she said. "I think he just broke up with me."

Sunday morning Dave leaned back in his office chair and gazed out the window at the office buildings. His heart floated on a cloud of bliss. Images of Shira Cohen looped in his mind.

He was Mr. Numero Uno. Mr. Top Dog. He exuded manliness and charm. He had displayed decisiveness and resolve. He had made a clean break with Mandy, surgical almost, although at first he had tried to duck and dive.

Mandy was a great girl. Attractive. Smart. Fun. Down-to-earth. She'd make an excellent life partner. But she was not his First Pairing. His true Other Half had appeared in designer sandals, moments before disaster.

Thank you, God!

Dave had changed; Shira had noticed. Last night was, in a way, their first date. More than anyone, he knew the chasm that lay between a first date and a wedding ring.

Dave waited for the cubicles to empty at lunchtime.

He dialed Shira's number. She answered on the first ring. "Hello, Dave."

She had saved his number. Result! She sounded friendly, inviting.

Dave lowered his voice involuntarily. "Hi, Shira. How are you today?"

Pleasantries aside, Dave suggested they get together.

"How about tonight?" she said.

Wow, is she eager!

Dave notched up another Indicator of Interest.

"I can't tonight," he said. "How about tomorrow?"

Dave wasn't playing hard to get. He had arranged with Ben to meet Professor Barkley that night and his absence would raise questions.

"Tomorrow is fine. Speak then."

He hung up the phone and basked in another victory. The Pickup Artist's Bible nodded at him with approval.

Date number two, here we come.

He straightened in his chair and located another contact on his phone.

The name consisted of a single character: O.

O for Ornan.

Dave stared at the forbidden number. His stomach churned.

Ben had warned him not to contact Ornan. But Shira Cohen had slipped through Dave's fingers before and he could not let that happen again. If anything, Dave would be righting a wrong, restoring the spiritual-physical balance he had unsettled. Besides, as Ben protested, the magic was probably all in his mind. There was no harm in one more dinner date with romantic ambience.

He dialed the number.

Immediately, a hand gripped his shoulder. He canceled the

call.

"God, Yoram. Please don't sneak up on me like that."

Yoram, cigarette in hand, leaned on the cubicle wall and smirked. "I wanted to say good-bye. I'm on vacation tomorrow. Was that your girlfriend on the phone?"

"Yes, it was."

Dave smiled, safe at last from Yoram's setups.

"The American?"

"No. She's English."

"When did you break up with the American?"

"Last night."

Yoram's eyes bulged. "*Why, why, why!* Way to go, Dave! Don't forget the cake tomorrow."

"Cake?"

"For your farewell party."

"Why do I have to bring the cake?"

Yoram shrugged. "It's the same with birthdays here. This way at least you have a cake." He shook Dave's hand. "Good luck and send me your email." He looked over his shoulder. "I'll send you my résumé."

Yoram traipsed off. Dave got back to business.

The call connected.

"This is Ornan."

Dave recognized the voice of the mustachioed restaurateur. He even *sounded* like Manuel of Fawlty Towers.

"I'd like to make a reservation for tomorrow night. Seven-thirty. Table for two."

"Very good. Your name?"

"Schwarz. I'd like the VIP room."

Dave thought the line had died.

"Hello?"

"This is a mistake. There is no VIP room."

"It's Dave Schwarz. Ben Green gave me your number. Do you remember? I was at your restaurant a few months ago."

"Ahh. Yeess," the voice said slowly. "I remember. That one time only. Mr. Green tell you, no?"

"I know," Dave said. "But this time it's a different girl."

Another long pause.

"Mr. Schwarz," the voice said. "This is not a game."

"I know. I'm sorry. I made a mistake. Please. One last time. I'll be eternally grateful. Hello?"

This time the line did cut off.

Dave swore under his breath.

He had discarded Mandy and Shira was not yet Mrs. Schwarz. Dave had stepped onto the tightrope without a safety net.

Dave hit redial. A recorded message played in Hebrew and English: *The number you are trying to reach is not connected.*

"What the hell?"

The recorded message repeated in Russian and Arabic.

Dave ran his hand through his hair. This was not a good sign.

Crap, crap, crap!

An unseen hand clenched his insides. Would Ornan call Ben? Was he dangerous? Dave knew next to nothing about Ornan. What other secrets did he harbor? He had set a process in motion and he had no idea where it would end.

The telephone cord dangled in Ornan's hand like a dead snake. He let it drop to the stone floor. He leaned on the wall of his office. The rough slabs of cool rock seemed so solid yet they were crumbling. All things crumbled. With enough time.

Down the corridor came familiar sounds: shifting tables, the tinkle of stacked dishes, running water in the scullery.

Mr. Schwarz and Mr. Green.

Black and green. Not his lucky colors. Inquisitive weasels had pushed their noses into his affairs before. Ornan knew how to deal with weasels. But the timing had never been worse. There was no room for error.

Ornan dialed a number on his mobile phone.

"It's happening," he said in an ancient guttural tongue long forgotten by the world. "We must act now."

The doorbell rang. Dave put his eye to the telescopic peephole. A bald Quasimodo stooped in the hall.

He had rehearsed his confession all afternoon but when he opened the door his attention turned to the large orange box in Ben's arms.

"I thought we were going to the professor."

"We are," Ben said, offloading the box—a cooler with a white lid—onto the couch. "But first you're going to do me a favor."

"A picnic in Gan Sacher?"

Ben shut the front door and fastened the security latch. He walked over to the living room window and rolled down the shutters. Then he removed the white lid of the cooler and withdrew a mass of bubble wrap.

"Oh, goody. I love bubbles."

Ben unwound the wrapping and extracted a cylindrical earthenware jar.

"It's safer here," he said.

Dave lost his sense of humor.

"Ben, I don't think that's a good idea."

"C'mon Dave. It's just a jar. About time you did something for *me* for a change."

"Let me see," Dave said. "In gratitude for messing with my soul and my chances of a happy marriage, I should harbor your dodgy artifacts and put my life in jeopardy?"

Ben smiled. "Glad you agree."

He repacked the scroll jar and lugged the cooler into the kitchen. Dave followed. Ben stood in the service balcony at the end of the kitchen. He frowned at a set of rickety storage shelves, then placed the box on the lowest ledge.

"Just for a few days," he said, dusting off his hands. "Until I figure out what they want with it."

"But it's been perfectly safe at your place for years."

Ben camouflaged the box with a checkered dishcloth. "There was another break-in Thursday night. Bible Lands Museum. Of all the priceless displays, they only took one item. Guess what it was."

Two minutes later Dave watched the flow of life on Emek Refaim through the passenger window of Ben's Toyota Yaris. Pedestrians at crossings. Friends chatting in restaurants. He waited for the right moment to mention his call to Ornan.

"A word about Professor Barkley," Ben said.

"Let me guess, he's a real genius."

Ben turned left off Emek Refaim and toward the apartment block suburbia of Talbieh.

"He's an expert on the Dead Sea Scrolls, a student of John Allegro, a member of the original group of scholars who pieced together the scrolls and deciphered their texts.

"A few years ago Professor Barkley published a controversial paper on the scrolls and lost his post at Hebrew U."

They passed the Jerusalem Theater on the rise of Marcus Street.

"His career never really recovered. So let's try to avoid subjects like the university."

They made a right at a flowery traffic circle and descended Jabotinsky. Soon they would pass Mendele Street. Mandy's street. Dave felt a twinge of guilt. Mandy had called a few times during the day. He'd let the phone ring. She'd get over him. Mandy was a trouper.

Trouper. A word Dave had learned from Mandy.

Ben turned into Sokolow Street.

He remembered his apology. He opened his mouth to speak when Ben parked the car beside a large island of trees, grass and swings in the middle of the road.

He closed his mouth.

No rush. Best to mention Ornan on the way home. Less time to cook in Ben's wrath.

They got out the car. A footpath joined Sokolow and Mendele. Dave had spent many Shabbat afternoons with Mandy on the benches and swings of the small park. She could walk by any moment. A thrill passed through him, not of anxiety, but anticipation. One whole day had passed since their last meeting. It felt longer. It would be good to see that she was OK. In time, maybe they could be friends.

Ben approached a four-story apartment building on the corner of Keren Hayesod. Air pollution stained the Jerusalem stone like nicotine on a smoker's fingers. Ben pressed the buzzer of apartment number three. An intercom coughed.

"Yes?" said the voice of an elderly British male.

"Ben Green, Professor."

An electric lock clicked and Ben pushed through.

Up one flight of stairs, an apartment door stood ajar.

"Come in," the professor called from within.

The two men stood in the middle of a shoebox apartment. Ahead of them, a doorway opened onto a kitchen with rickety closets and an old gas stove. To their right, the hallway flowed into a living room. Rows of well-thumbed volumes and journals strained the floor-to-ceiling shelves. A large, carved writing desk sat by the far wall. Behind the desk sat an old man in a paisley bathrobe.

"Please excuse the mess," the professor said. He fussed over papers and writing implements on the desktop, raising small clouds of dust in the meager glow of a naked incandescent bulb. "Early retirement has scattered my sense of order along with my thoughts."

The professor looked up. His eyes sparkled. A rakish mop of hair topped a face still handsome beneath the creases and sagging skin. His gaze shifted to Dave and a momentary cloud of disappointment passed over him.

"You've brought a friend," he said.

"I hope you don't mind, Professor. Dave here needs an expert opinion on another matter."

"No. Not at all. But we'll need another chair." The professor grinned expectantly at Dave. "Whisky?"

Soon they sat before the desk on kitchen chairs and nursed glass tumblers of Laphroaig. A bit smoky for Dave's palate but a fine single malt nonetheless. The spirits numbed Dave's brain pleasantly. He liked the aging professor already.

Frames of dust marked the former resting places of papers on the desktop. The Oriental rug beneath Dave's feet had faded, and tattered strands stuck out at the edges.

A clock ticked, unseen.

A young Barkley smiled from a photo on a bookshelf. He and his friends wore Victorian dress and neck collars. The label read: Macbeth, Oxford University Dramatic Society, 1973.

The scent of regret and former greatness filled the room.

Above the professor and beside the shuttered windows hung a frame containing a square scrap of parchment between glass panes, but Dave could not read the blurred black characters.

"I see you've noticed the famous fragment from Cave Four," the professor said. "Deuteronomy 32:8. 'He set the boundaries of nations according to the number of the Children of Israel.' In this particular copy, however, the text reads not the 'Children of Israel' but the 'Children of God.' In one stroke, it affirms the text of the Septuagint and exposes the pagan roots of our treasured first monotheism."

The professor smiled at Dave. A challenge glinted in his eyes.

Dave squirmed involuntarily. Bible criticism did that. He was all for enlightenment and reason, but academic scholarship often undermined the traditional Jewish narrative. His personal solution was to ignore the academics. Scientific theories changed every other day, unlike the timeless teachings of the Torah.

"One word variation," the professor continued, "and our understanding of the Bible changes forever. Behold the power of the written word." The professor raised his glass and drained it.

"Now," he said, "what is this delicate matter you wanted to discuss?"

Ben withdrew newspaper clippings from his pocket and spread them on the desk.

"Scroll jars," he said. "Recently two were stolen, first from Ir Da'vid, then the Bible Lands Museum. Both jars were from—"

"Cave Three," the professor said. His smile disappeared. "Has your boss put you up to this?"

The professor's vehemence startled Dave.

"Who?" Ben said. "Erez?"

"Yes. Dr. Erez Lazarus. He's been pestering me about scroll jars for months. 'How many are there? Where are they?'"

Ben caught Dave's eye for a fleeting moment.

"Erez didn't send me, Professor. I didn't know he was interested in the jars."

"Obsessed is the word. At the bidding of his Evangelical sponsors, obviously. They stop at nothing. I should know. They ousted me from my post at the university when I dared cast aspersions on their precious faith. I wouldn't be surprised if they've resorted to thievery to get what they want."

"Why would Christian fundamentalists want the scroll jars?" Ben asked.

The professor licked his lips and glanced at Dave.

"Two thousand years ago, Jewish society was unrecognizable. With no single Bible canon to unite them, Jewish subcultures abounded. Those were chaotic days. The biblical texts were still in flux. The shadow of Rome fell over Judea. Apocalyptic groups sprouted like mushrooms. Each kept strict regimens of ritual purity and asceticism. Many of them united around a charismatic leader. The Judean Desert Cult that authored the scrolls was no different. Known as *Moreh Zedek*, the Teacher of Righteousness, he preached penitence, poverty, humility, and neighborly love. He condemned the priestly classes of Jerusalem for their perceived iniquity. His followers called him *Mashiach*, or Messiah, which in Greek translates to..."

The professor paused for dramatic effect.

"*Christos*," Ben said.

"Wait a minute," Dave said, unable to restrain his curiosity. "Are you saying that this Teacher of Righteousness was Jesus?"

"No," said the professor. "The scrolls *predate* Jesus by a hundred years. Early Christians must have based their theology on this earlier sect. Which explains the many parallels between Christian teachings and the Dead Sea Scrolls. Both propound legends of the dead rising and read them into identical verses from Psalms and Isaiah. The same sermons and beatitudes, almost word for word. Put differently, there was no historical Jesus, only a poor imitation of this earlier Teacher of Righteousness."

Dave whistled. He could see how that theory could ruffle a few feathers.

"Now you may be wondering," the professor continued, "what does this have to do with the scroll jars? Each of the jars from Cave Three bears an inscription comprised of three letters."

"*Zedek*," Dave blurted and Professor Barkley eyed him with renewed interest.

"Yes," he said. "As in *Moreh Zedek*. This may connect the jars with the Teacher of Righteousness. Either they belonged to the gifted leader or contained his special message."

"So the thieves need the jars to find the message?" Ben said.

The professor frowned.

"Or they collect them as relics, assuming they have warmed to the idea that he really was the original Jesus. In all likelihood they have not and their goal may be simpler: to destroy all references in the archaeological record to the man who undermines their beliefs."

The professor refilled his tumbler.

"This would not be the first time. 1948. Six Arab nations invaded the nascent Jewish State. Jordan captured the West Bank, including Jerusalem and the Dead Sea valley. When Bedouin shepherds discovered the scrolls, the Jordanian government confined their study to a group of foreign scholars that consisted almost entirely of Catholic priests. With the Six Day War in 1967, the West Bank fell into Israeli possession and with it the scrolls. The Israeli authorities, however, respected the Christian scholars' prerogative to independent study and publication.

"Which, I may add, took some time. The group delayed publication of their materials for over thirty years. The world first heard of the Teacher of Righteousness only thanks to the bravery of one member of the team, John Allegro, under whom I studied."

"So these scholars," Dave said, "were trying to hide the references to Jesus in the scrolls?"

"Not really," Ben said. "The final texts were published in their entirety in the early nineties and contained nothing that controversial."

"That," the professor said, "is not fully accurate. Many scroll fragments made their way onto the black market. Who acquired them? What did they contain? And then there is the matter of Father Roland de Vaux."

The professor indulged Dave's blank look.

"De Vaux was a Frenchman. A Dominican monk. President of the Palestine Archaeological Museum. Head of the team that studied the scrolls. He searched the scroll caves of wadi Qumran that the Bedouin had looted and discovered additional scroll caves. In the fifties he fully excavated the ruins of Qumran itself."

"I thought archaeologists never excavate an entire site," Dave said.

"Precisely. De Vaux prevented future researchers from corroborating his finds and theories. And it gets better."

Dave hazarded a guess. "He never published his findings?"

"Very good! He died in 1971 without sharing a scrap, except for rumors of elaborate earthenware and coins. The scant materials that were eventually released, mere photographs and plans, revealed that de Vaux had committed another archaeological crime: he had failed to apply the principals of stratigraphy."

"Stratigraphy," Ben explained, 'is excavation by layers. Each layer is dated and interpreted separately."

Professor Barkley cut in. "A method developed, incidentally, by Thomas Jefferson over a half century earlier, and already applied in Palestine by the likes of Kathleen Kenyon, who excavated Jericho at the same time de Vaux dug Qumran. According to their correspondence, de Vaux and Kenyon were close colleagues."

"Kathleen Kenyon," Dave said. "Didn't she excavate the City of David?"

"My, my," the professor said. "Your friend is an excellent student."

"Professor," Ben said, "are you suggesting that de Vaux sabotaged the excavation of Qumran in order to erase the tracks of whatever he found there?"

Professor Barkley sank back in his chair.

"I have no proof for any of this, of course, but a pattern emerges. Nameless forces within the Christian world have taken great pains to silence the truths connected to the scrolls."

Professor Barkley let his words sink in.

"If you happen to come into possession of any such jars,"

he added, "I would tread carefully. Very carefully."

Dave felt his palms moisten.

A telephone rang down the hall and the professor excused himself.

The new information flooded Dave's mind. Fanatical Christians prowled the streets of Jerusalem, searching for the contents of the cooler bag that sat in his service balcony.

"Ben," he hissed. "I want it out of my flat. Now."

Ben chewed his fingernails. "Don't worry. It's safer there than anywhere."

"I don't care about the damn jar—" He was unable to complete the sentence.

Professor Barkley returned to his chair behind the desk.

"My apologies," the professor said. He turned to Dave. "What was the other matter you wanted to discuss?"

Dave had almost forgotten.

"The Foundation Stone," he began.

"Ah. *Even Shtiya*. The Weaving Stone. The point from which God wove the world. Or the Drinking Stone. The legendary source of watery depths beneath the Temple Mount."

"I told Dave that the stone itself lies within the Dome of the Rock," Ben said.

The professor hesitated.

"That is the common consensus, yes."

"But?" Dave prompted. His insides twisted.

"But," the professor continued, "the full picture is more complex.

"The Talmud claims that the stone served as a stand for the Ark of the Covenant. In order to support the Ark, the stone would have had to be flat and smaller than the Holy of Holies. The rock beneath the dome is neither. It is a large irregular mound of bedrock. The Talmud sets the stone's height at only twenty-five centimeters."

"Where is it then?"

The professor chuckled at Dave. "A student and a treasure hunter. Many have spent their lives in pursuit of lesser treasures. Ask Ben about the Copper Scroll. That should keep you occupied.

"But to answer your question: no one knows. The Foundation Stone was last sighted during the Middle Ages. A number of eyewitness accounts exist."

Professor Barkley pulled a worn paperback from a shelf and turned the pages.

"The Arab Judge Mujir ed-Din in the fifteenth century; Rabbi Moses Hagiz in the sixteenth. The Karaite voyager, Samuel son of David a century later. They all reported seeing a peculiar stone at the Temple Mount, a Foundation Stone that floated miraculously in the air and instilled awe in the hearts of all who beheld it."

The professor returned the book to the shelf. "Where the Foundation Stone traveled from there, I'm afraid, is anyone's guess."

"I see," Dave said.

He could guess better than most where the Foundation Stone had landed and he had burned the one bridge that led there.

Darkness had descended on the streets of Jerusalem as Ben drove Dave home. Beneath the mundane surface activity a world of biblical secrets and covert struggles simmered and slowly sucked him in.

"Hidden scrolls," he said. "Secret Christian societies. I feel like we've walked into The Da Vinci Code."

"If this were The Da Vinci Code, you'd be a beautiful

female forensic specialist. And you might actually be of use."

"You're the specialist, Ben. I'm the lead character. It's my soul that's on the line, remember?"

Ben shook his head, then fell quiet. "Seems I owe you an apology. Maybe you *are* onto something."

Ben's about-face gave Dave whiplash.

"You think so?"

"Yeah. We need to speak with Ornan and settle this once and for all."

Oh, brother. No way out now.

"That might not be a good idea."

"Why not?"

Dave told Ben of Shira's reappearance. By the time he reached the bit about Ornan disconnecting his phone, the Toyota Yaris idled in the lot opposite his apartment.

Ben drummed his head against the steering wheel.

"What do we do now?" Dave asked.

"Throw you off the nearest bridge, that's what."

Dave sat in silence. On the whole, all was well with the world. He had Shira. Miraculously, the train of his life had jumped back on track. He had no desire to derail his destiny again.

"Ben," he said. "I'm sorry. Really, I am. I've driven you up the wall with all this hocus-pocus. But maybe you were right all along. Ornan was all in my head. I just needed a little push, a little confidence. That's all. Let's just let it go."

Dave pulled on the door handle. It didn't open.

"We're going to finish what you started. Ornan won't pick up? Fine. We'll meet him in person."

"What about the delicate balance in the City of David?"

"Screw that. If Ornan has the Foundation Stone, I want to see it. Lord knows what other artifacts he has stashed there. And I want to find out what he knows about the break-ins."

"Why would Ornan have anything to do with the break-ins?"

Ben sucked in air. "There's something I haven't told you. I got the jar from Ornan. Said he bought it from a dealer. I didn't make much of it until now."

"This isn't really about the Foundation Stone, is it?"

Ben ignored Dave's question.

"Let's go Tuesday morning. Memorial Day. You'll be in between jobs anyway."

"You go ahead, Ben. You don't need me."

"I need you to watch my back. We've been friends for years, Dave. I've always been there for you. When have I ever asked a favor?"

"About an hour ago. The jar in my home?"

Ben waved that way. "Before that?" He didn't wait for an answer. "Good. Tuesday. At the COD. Nine o'clock. Don't be late."

Night cloaked the driver's seat of the white Hyundai H1 minivan that lurked in the small parking lot off Emek Refaim. Jay and John had munched through a jumbo bag of *Tapu-Chips* and emptied a six-pack of Corona, luxuries Jay savored when away from the *Yachad*. After an hour of waiting, his hunch paid off.

The metallic blue Yaris pulled up and idled beside the apartment building. The driver and passenger wore knitted skullcaps of the West Bank settler kind.

Jay recognized the bald driver. Their paths had crossed months ago in the City of David and Jay had knocked him out. His name was Ben Green. Jay did not know the name of the passenger.

He had first sighted the Yaris outside the address off

Graetz Street. He followed the hatchback onto Emek Refaim, then Derekh Harakevet. When the Yaris veered into the lot, Jay continued down the narrow, bumpy road to avoid detection. By the time he doubled back, the car had disappeared and his stakeout began.

The passenger got out of the car. He had his polo shirt tucked into his jeans. He entered the building without looking back and the Yaris backed out of the lot.

"Aren't we gonna follow?" John asked, his only words that evening besides "give us another."

Jay didn't answer. Lights turned on in the ground floor apartment. Jay caught shards of the man through the shutters of the service balcony as he moved around the privacy of his home. Eventually the lights darkened.

Jay slipped out of the van.

He walked up to the entrance of the building but did not try the door. Instead, he studied the rows of mailboxes. The tag for apartment number one bore a name in both English and Hebrew. It read, *David Schwarz.*

CHAPTER 8

Afternoon light pierced the shutters of Mandy's bedroom window but she didn't have the energy to get out of bed.

Dave was gone.

Her life had no meaning.

It's all my fault.

Mandy checked her phone.

One message from Esty: *Are you OK?*

She had no energy to reply.

Two days in pajamas. Mandy drifted in and out of fitful sleep. She was a little girl again—she soared into the air, then fell. Each time she rocketed skyward, she felt the joy of weightlessness and the fear that she would slip through her father's arms.

Knuckles rapped on the door. Shani stood in the opening.

"Hey, Mands."

"Mmmm."

"You should eat something."

Mandy's stomach felt hollow but she had no desire to eat. The shadow of a migraine pulsed behind her right eye.

"What time is it?"

"Five o'clock. Sit up."

Shani held the door open. Ruchama entered carrying a tray. The aroma of hot, buttered toast and fresh coffee filled the room.

Mandy sat up, not wanting to be impolite.

Ruchama placed the tray on Mandy's lap.

"Thanks, guys." She stared at the meal without appetite. "I don't know why I'm like this."

Mandy had weathered breakups before, although usually she was on the other side of the equation. Why was she falling apart?

"It doesn't seem real," she said.

"I also can't believe," Ruchama said. "It doesn't look like the end of the story."

"Well, it is," Shani said. "And good riddance."

Mandy shook her head at her own idiocy. "I should never have told him I made *aliya*."

"Hey," Shani said. "You did nothing wrong. This isn't commitment phobia. You didn't scare him away. He's with another girl."

Shani's tough love came in one style: extra strong.

"Dave? No way."

"Seen it a hundred times. My clients never believe it when it happens either, but I'm never wrong."

"Your clients?"

Shani looked surprised. "I never told you?" She placed her hands on her hips and tossed back her head. "I'm a life coach. I help people get their shit together. Personal development. Dating. Self-confidence. Dating, mostly."

Ruchama placed her hand over her mouth to hide a smile.

Mandy had wondered about the flow of young, bashful men through their apartment.

"You're a psychologist?"

"Sort of."

"A psychologist without a degree," Ruchama said.

"More of a big sister," Shani said, ignoring Ruchama. Her eyes narrowed with bemused curiosity. "What did you think I did for money, Mands?"

Mandy felt her cheeks warm. "I had no idea," she said.

Ruchama snickered. "She never thought you sorted out

other people's lives. You, with difficulty, sort out your own."

Shani stood erect. "Just because I teach geometry doesn't make me a square. And I'm good at what I do. Trust me, Dave has found himself another girlfriend."

Without warning, tears welled in Mandy's eyes.

"He said he loved me."

"You're better off without the creep. Mands. You'll get over him."

"I don't want to get over him."

"You must, and you will. I guarantee it." Shani's eyebrows arched with mischief. She grinned. "I have just the thing for breakup blues."

Dave had shaved, showered, and was ironing a collared shirt when the doorbell rang.

"Just a minute."

He placed the iron on its stand. Dressed in a white undershirt and bath towel, Dave approached the door. In ten minutes his second date with Shira started on Emek Refaim.

He put his eye to the peephole and swore under his breath. He opened the door.

A middle-aged woman smiled up at him. She wore a designer suit. Her blond hair spiked like porcupine quills. She glanced at the towel around his waist.

"David, darling. Is that the way you answer the door?"

His mother walked right in.

His father followed. "Hello, boy."

Dave locked the door. "Mom. Dad. What are you doing

here?"

"We thought we'd surprise you," his mother said.

She studied the small living room and the ironing board. His father sat on the fold-out couch.

"Well," Dave said. "I'm surprised."

"You should do something with the place. Fresh paint, a pot plant. It needs a woman's touch." She smirked. "I don't know why you refuse to let us buy you a decent apartment. Anything is better than this hovel."

A gossamer thread held Dave's patience together. He clapped his hands together. "It's really good to see you. I'd offer you a drink but I have to rush out soon."

"I'd put some clothes on first." She smirked again. "You can't show up to a date like that."

Dave's father got to his feet. "We only dropped by to say hello, let you know we're in town."

"And," his mother continued, "we're treating you to a few days at the Dead Sea. We leave tomorrow. You're in between jobs, aren't you? And Wednesday is Independence Day. We'll have a nice long family weekend."

The gossamer thread snapped.

"Mother, I'm a grown man. Don't you think I might have plans of my own?"

"Plans? Don't be ridiculous. What plans?"

"Well..." Dave said. He had not suggested anything to Shira yet. One date at a time. But he had planned to have plans. And there was the matter of the City of David. "I have a meeting tomorrow morning."

"Then come straight after. You have a car. The rooms are ready at two o'clock."

"*And*," he added, "I have tentative plans for later on."

A plan for a plan qualified as tentative plans, didn't it?

"It means a lot to your mother, son," his father said.

Dave looked into his father's tired eyes. If he didn't give way, his father would bear the brunt.

"OK," he said. "But I may have to cancel last minute."

"There's a dear." She pecked him on the cheek on her way

out the door and grinned knowingly. Again. "Have a good time."

A high-pitched horn honked twice outside.

"That's our ride," Shani said.

"I thought you ordered a cab."

Mandy knew the sound of a white Jerusalem taxi when she heard it. This sounded more like a red Ferrari.

"I did," Shani said. "Sort of."

The three girls had showered and dressed for a night out. Their heels clacked down the stairwell.

Mandy had been wrong. On the curb, a yellow Porsche waited.

Shani swung the door open, shoved the passenger seat forward, and pulled Mandy after her into the back. The car smelled of new leather and Dolce & Gabbana. Ruchama settled in the front bucket seat and smiled at the driver, a handsome twenty-something with gelled hair, a black leather jacket, and a shocked expression.

"Mands and Ruchama," Shani said, "meet Jake. Jake, Mands and Ruchama."

Jake turned to Shani. "Aren't we—?"

"Malcha Mall," Shani said. "Pronto. This is an emergency."

The engine growled pleasantly and g-forces pressed the girls back in their seats. Two minutes later the car growled to a stop at the main entrance of Kanyon Malcha, the shopping mall across the road from Teddy Stadium.

"No need to park," Shani told the driver when they climbed out of the car. "Girls' night out."

Ruchama waved at Jake. "Thanks."

The girls joined the line for the security inspection.

"He's nice," Ruchama said.

"Stay focused," Shani said. "Tonight is about Mandy."

They opened their handbags for the security guard and stepped inside.

Shani appraised the storefronts, a hungry lioness eying a herd of impala. "Ready, girls?"

"Shopping won't change anything," Mandy said. The thrill of the ride had worn off.

Shani didn't falter. "This kind of shopping will. Ladies, take no prisoners."

Shani strode into Bonita and pulled an evening dress off a rack. "Try this on," she instructed Mandy.

"I could never wear that," Mandy protested.

"Why not?"

"Too many sequins. It's sleeveless. And above the knee. Way too skimpy for a *frum* girl."

"Perfect," Shani said. "You're trying it on."

Mandy knew better than to argue with a force of nature. She found a changing stall and pulled back the curtain. Shani meant well but this was ridiculous. She stripped down and stepped into the minimalist dress, which, she discovered, was not only sleeveless but strapless too. The snug fit lifted her bust like a Wonder Woman costume.

Do people actually wear these?

At least the store was empty. Less embarrassment all round.

Mandy stepped through the curtain.

Her flatmates sat on stools and applauded. The store attendant clapped her hands as well.

Shani wolf-whistled. "That is one hot lady," she said.

"Wow, Mandy," Ruchama said, her eyes wide. "You look like a bomb."

"That's a compliment," Shani added.

Mandy's cheeks burned. "Cut it out. I'm never going to wear this."

"You just have."

She consulted the full-length mirror.

The dark glitzy material brought out her neck and forearms and the curve of her behind. The hem tickled her thighs.

"Some lace gloves," Shani said, "and leather boots and you're good to go. Now. My turn."

Shani emerged from the booth in a snaking trail of pink frills that covered most of the critical bits but without hampering the imagination. She struck a Marilyn Monroe pose.

"Go Shani," Mandy said. She laughed. Shani blew kisses at the clump of spectators that had accumulated at the store-front window.

Mandy examined the price tag of her dress.

"This will end," she said, "with us in debt or in jail. Or both."

She didn't really care. Shani's retail therapy was a fun distraction but every few minutes her thoughts drifted back to Dave.

But Shani wasn't done with her yet.

She placed their selections on the counter

"Ring that up," Shani told the attendant. "We're on a tight schedule."

The show went on. After the designer boutiques—Dafna Levinson, Lord Kitsch, and Renoir—they graduated to lingerie: Intima, Pituyim, La Senza.

The motley crowd of admirers grew and shadowed the girls from store to store. Among them Mandy noted a few excitable young men with black yarmulkes on their heads.

Two hours later, the three women marched toward Pizza Hut, their arms and hands heavy with their loot of oversized shopping bags.

"Feeling better?" Shani asked, melted cheese dripping from her mouth.

"Yeah," Mandy said. "I am. But I think I'm going to have

a serious credit card hangover."

A couple of women walked by the restaurant. At least Mandy assumed they were women. Black burkas covered their bodies from head to toe. In the comfort of the mall, she had forgotten she was in the Middle East and she was glad for the security guards and metal detectors at the mall's entrance.

This is home now, Mandy.

With Dave out of the picture, Mandy's decision to go native seemed hasty.

"Strange world," she said. "I wonder if they're as frightened of us as we are of them."

"I wouldn't feel too sorry for them," Shani said. "They get government handouts. Health insurance. The vote. Religious tolerance. More than they'd get in any Arab country."

"Right," said Ruchama. "The hospitals are filled with Arab doctors and nurses. They get special scholarships. Their life is honey."

"But," Shani continued, "if we so much as wander into Ramallah by mistake, their brothers will lynch us without blinking."

Shani dusted her palms free of pizza crumbs and thoughts of Arabs. "Phase One complete."

"There's a Phase Two?"

"You betcha." Shani pulled her phone from her handbag. "I'll call Jake. Phase two: Emek Refaim."

Dave walked down Emek Refaim trailing a cloud of coconut-scented Hugo Boss.

He was used to his mother prying into his love life but this time she sounded more playful than petulant. She was up to no good.

He passed a restored Templar building that housed Aldo Ice Cream and climbed the staircase to the Latin steakhouse above called La Boca.

The hostess showed him to the table for two he had reserved on the balcony. He settled on an armless leather chair and peered at the street below. The restaurant was empty. Bossa nova music played softly in the background. Ambience: check. Good food: check. Magical love stones: not even on the list.

He had come a long way since that night at Ornan's. That afternoon he'd left his cubicle at TikTech for the last time and with no regrets. The ambient stress of his work projects evaporated from his mind. He breathed in the fresh, heady scent of a new chapter in his life.

Dave glanced up.

Shira appeared in the doorway, bright-eyed and made up. She strode toward him. The silky green fabric of her dress matched the emerald of her eyes and hinted at toned legs and a full bosom.

She sat opposite him. Her perfume whispered of money and sophistication, a league above Mandy's fruity scent.

They smiled at each other in silence.

"Nice place," she said.

The building across Emek Refaim caught her eye. On the second floor a dozen women in leotards performed jumping jacks with varying degrees of success.

"So that's the women's gym," she said.

He had never associated her with exercise, or any other mundane physical activity for that matter. Shira Cohen breathed the same air as he did, after all. She ate the same food. She probably used the ladies' room as did other mortals.

"Are you going to join?"

"Heavens no." She laughed. "I feel tired just watching them. Never been one for sports. Some men are obsessed with all that. Football. Basketball. At least I don't have to worry about that with you." She glanced at him with sudden apprehension. "Do I?"

"No, of course not. I jog a few times a week," he admitted. "Around Katamon. Nothing obsessive."

For years Ben had lectured Dave on the correlation between a toned body and dating success. For years Dave had resisted. Until Mandy. He and Mandy had taken walks together. She had introduced him to the joys of spectator football. He decided it best not to mention his experiences at Teddy Stadium.

A waitress handed them their leather-bound menus and explained in English about the day's specials. Dave ordered the entrecote. Shira selected the salmon fillet on a bed of saffron rice but without the pine nuts and dried fruit and with the dressing on the side.

Mandy would have gone for the steak. At least Shira wasn't vegetarian.

She sat back in her seat. She looked completely relaxed and content to be with him.

He looked about the restaurant with what he hoped was suave distraction. Their waitress stood at attention against a far wall. "The Girl from Ipanema" drifted through the air.

"Bit empty isn't it," she said.

"What?"

"I think we're the only ones here."

The penny dropped. Israeli holidays started, as did Jewish festivals, at sundown.

"Memorial Day," he said. "Most Israelis are at memorial services or watching them on television."

"Oh." They sat in somber silence. Wars and terror attacks. Not ideal dating conversation.

"Which reminds me," he said. "Tomorrow night is Independence Day. We can do something together if you like."

He had a few hours left to dodge the weekend with his parents.

Shira looked askance at him. "But we have plans already."

"What plans?"

"Didn't your parents tell you?"

"My parents?"

"We're going to the Dead Sea tomorrow, Dave. All of us. Your parents. My parents."

"Our parents have met?"

She nodded. "In London. A few months ago. They're quite close."

"Oh. And our parents know that we...?"

Shira nodded again.

Dave remembered his mother's innuendo. Shira had told her parents. That was a good sign.

"Is everything all right?" she asked.

"Yes. Of course. I just don't usually share my dating life with my parents. You know how parents can be. Well, *some* parents."

Shira's family was probably functional and well-adjusted.

"Our parents need to meet eventually," she said. "At least we know that they get along."

She had a point.

His dreams of Shira Cohen had involved many things but never his parents. Elopement had always been a valid option. A romantic weekend for six with his mother's constant smirk did not make him feel all warm and fuzzy inside. Dave's mother had a talent for ruining his mood.

Shira must have read his thoughts.

"Don't worry," she said. "I'm sure we'll have a lovely time."

Mandy stepped out of the Porsche and onto a cracked pavement. Twilight descended on the German Colony.

Emek Refaim. Dave territory.

The three girls left their shopping bags in the back seat and Shani dismissed Jake with a noncommittal "Call you later."

Mandy's knees quivered.

What if Dave went to the minimarket right now?

How awkward.

Would he think she was stalking him?

She longed to see him again, even from a distance.

Shani herded her into Aldo's chocolate and ice cream emporium. "Welcome to heaven, ladies."

Shani selected a thick candy-sprinkled cone filled with balls of Belgian chocolate and toffee. Mandy settled on cookies and cream and mocha. Ruchama ordered three balls of fruit sorbet in a cup but her willpower collapsed when the steaming waffle arrived, covered in syrup and rich vanilla ice cream.

They sat at the counter against the window and faced the street.

"There's more to life than men," Shani said, licking syrup from a long dessert spoon.

"Mush more," Ruchama mumbled through her full mouth.

Mandy lifted another square of waffle onto her spoon.

Shani was right. Heaven was served with ice cream and tasted of maple. She would need to double her jogging schedule. She had no excuses now that her evenings had freed up. Shani never seemed to exercise but then again, until tonight, Shani had never seemed to eat.

Streetlights bathed Emek Refaim in yellow. Across the street, at a table outside Café Aroma, a man held a newspaper. A waitress approached but he waved her away. The straw hair and sparse beard registered in Mandy's memory.

"Oh my God," she said. "I know that guy."

"The *gingi* at eleven o'clock?" Shani asked. "He's been watching us the whole time."

Ruchama almost choked on her waffle. "A stalker?"

"How do you know him?"

Mandy remembered the long robe and crazy blue eyes.

"We studied at the same college campus. Now he plays the harp at the *kotel*."

"The King David guy," Shani said. "Great."

"How do you know he's stalking us?" Ruchama asked.

"First of all," Shani said, "he hasn't ordered anything. And he's holding the newspaper upside down."

As they watched, King David dropped the newspaper on the table and got up. He pulled the hood of his shirt over his head, shoved his hands in his jeans pockets, and crossed the street. He headed right for them.

"He's coming!" Ruchama said.

The hair on Mandy's neck prickled.

"Easy, girls," Shani said. "We stay put until he's gone."

"What if he follows us?"

"Shhh. Don't make eye contact."

King David reached the sidewalk, meters from their window seats. Then he turned his back to them and ducked his head, as though studying his running shoes.

What is he doing?

A young couple crossed their view, smiling and engaged in close, animated conversation.

It took a few seconds for Mandy to process the image.

The girl dressed well, had straight, dark hair and a great figure. The man wore a casual collared shirt, like the one she had picked out for...

Dave?

Shani lay her hand on Mandy's forearm.

Outside the store window, King David lifted his head. He glanced to the side and strode off. After the couple.

"Phew," Ruchama said. "Maybe he wasn't following us after all."

Mandy stood. "I've got to go."

"What? You're going after him?"

Shani's grip tightened. "Don't, Mands."

Mandy shook her arm free and dropped a fifty-shekel note on the bar.

"I've got to warn him," she said.

"Mandy!"

"Warn who?"

She had no time to explain. She grabbed her bag and sped out the store.

A group of high school kids with New York accents blocked her way. She squeezed through.

Dave and the girl were already far down the road. King David followed a few paces behind. She wanted to cry out, to call Dave's name.

Dave stopped at a pedestrian crossing. He looked for oncoming cars in Mandy's direction but didn't see her.

Should she wave? Try to get his attention?

King David kept walking and passed by Dave. Doubt froze Mandy's arm.

Dave and the girl crossed the street and made for the path beside the little park with metal goats. Mandy knew it well; it led to Dave's apartment.

Her brain overloaded with conflicting emotions. How bizarre to watch Dave as an outsider. Like a stalker. The real stalker paused on the sidewalk. The hooded head watched the couple disappear between apartment buildings. He seemed to consider crossing the street. Then he turned around.

She spun on her heels.

Oh, brother.

She quickened her pace.

Don't run. Act calm.

The noise of passing cars made it difficult to hear his

footfalls.

She heard a thud behind her. She turned in time to see a white taxi swallow the stalker and cruise away.

Jay hung his towel over the metal banister and stepped down the steps, naked. His skin prickled at the touch of the chilly waters. Calves. Thighs. Stomach. Chest. At the bottom of the steps, the water reached his neck. His breath came in quivering snatches. The square indoor pool was large enough for one man.

The light of a single fluorescent danced on the water. Jay closed his eyes, held his breath and sank. He lifted his legs off the tiled floor and spread his limbs. The purifying waters kissed every inch of his body.

He came up for air.

One.

He dipped beneath the surface again.

Two.

Three.

He repeated the motion, faster now, the waters surging and spraying with each dive.

Forty.

Jay held his breath. He savored the last immersion, floating like a fetus in the shifting fluid of the womb.

He climbed the steps, a new man, and toweled off.

John cracked the door open.

"Head sherang wants a word," he said.

Jay lifted the gray sackcloth cloak from a hook on the wall

and slipped his feet into his jandals.

He walked down a corridor of stone tiles and dangling incandescent bulbs.

Home.

Jay had not had a place to call home in a very long time. Here he ate, slept, studied, and meditated. He prepared his current incarnation for the revelation of his great soul. Any day now.

He paused outside a large reinforced door.

Perhaps today?

He knocked once and turned the brass knob.

A single lamp cast amber light over the spartan furnishings of the square chamber: a wooden desk, bare storage shelves, naked walls of rough stone. Stars twinkled through the iron bars of a single raised window.

A white hooded cloak sat behind the desk. The dark cowl tilted to the side, lost in thought.

Jay stood at attention and waited. The Teacher had outlawed mundane speech in the *Yachad*.

The notes of Jay's report lay on the desk.

He had never seen the leader eat or sleep. He seemed to subsist on meditation alone. He saw what others failed to see.

"Tomorrow," the Teacher said. "Mr. Green."

Jay knew what he must do. He nodded.

"We are close," the Teacher continued. "Stay invisible."

Jay's fingers twitched.

"What about Schwarz?"

He had distrusted Green's straight-laced accomplice the moment he had set eyes on him. In his report, he had recommended moving on Schwarz first.

The cowl straightened and gray whiskers glinted in the light. The Teacher lit a match. He held the pages in the air and watched as the fire consumed the edges. He dropped the burning words into the tin waste bin.

"His day will come, my son," the Teacher said. "Soon enough."

Tuesday morning, Dave opened the door of Ben's office at the COD.

Ben slouched at his desk.

"Your girlfriend called last night," he said without looking up.

Dave hesitated. "Shira?"

Ben shut his laptop. "Your *other* girlfriend, Casanova."

Great. Mandy had given up calling Dave and moved on to his friends.

"What did she say?"

"She's worried about you. She thinks you might be in danger." Ben shook his head. "Poor thing. You've really messed with her head."

Dave closed his eyes and counted to ten. He had not wanted to hurt Mandy. Ben knew that. And he didn't want to hurt her any more than he had, but the whole truth would really sting.

"What did you tell her?"

"That you're an idiot and not worthy of her. Besides that, nothing."

He gave Ben a pleading look.

"Relax," Ben said. "I didn't mention your new flame. She was really upset. She's coming over to the house later to talk. You're welcome to join us."

He wasn't falling for that. He looked at his wristwatch. "We need to finish in an hour. I'm off to the Dead Sea."

His overnight bag waited in his car outside.

"Romantic weekend with Shira?"

"And our parents."

Ben frowned. "Crime and punishment." He stood. "Now. Time for our chat with Ornan."

Ben swung a deflated City of David backpack on his shoulder and led the way out of the office and through a group of camera-toting Chinese.

"What's with the bag?"

"Just in case. Who knows what treasures Ornan has stashed away. We might be able to salvage something."

"The way you salvaged the scroll jar."

Ben stopped beside the huge David's Harp at the Institute gates.

"Listen, we're in this together. Soon we'll be sitting with Ornan, pressing him for answers. We have to present a unified front. Remember *The Godfather*?"

"The movie?"

"Don Corleone meets with a rival mafia boss. In the middle of the negotiation, Corleone's son argues with the Don. The rival Mafioso sees the split as weakness. So he orders a hit on the Don, thinking that if he gets the Don out of the way, he can cut a deal with the son. See what I'm saying?"

Dave raised his eyebrows. "I should keep quiet so Ornan doesn't try to whack you?"

"Good," Ben said and strode down the slope.

Dave almost slammed into him when he suddenly stopped.

"Dammit," Ben said. "We're too late."

Two black vans hugged the wall of Ornan's. They reminded Dave of the *A-Team* van from the eighties action series.

They hurried down the hill.

Through the tinted windows of the van, Dave made out the forms of wooden packing crates.

"You must have spooked him," Ben said. "We've got to get to him and fast, or whatever he has will be lost forever."

Ben reached for the handle of the cast-iron dungeon door, but abruptly leaped to the side of the door and pulled Dave after him.

"What—?"

"Shhh."

The door swung open. Ben grasped the handle as it neared his belly and kept the door from shutting. A van beeped twice and a car door opened. Boxes shifted. Words were exchanged in a gruff guttural language.

Ben stepped around the door and tugged Dave after him by the arm. Two muscular men in jeans and T-shirts leaned into the back of a van.

Ben put his finger to his lips and snuck through the open door and down the stone steps. The electric torches flickered on the walls. This time they hissed warnings of imminent danger, not romantic possibilities.

This was a bad idea.

"They call this breaking and entering," Dave whispered.

"Didn't break anything," Ben whispered in reply. "Work with me. It's the only way we'll get answers."

The landing had not changed: the concierge desk, the hive of wine bottles, and the mounted tapestry of blind soldiers on a castle wall. Wine and furniture were not at the top of Ornan's moving list. Gone were the aromas of spicy food and soft background music.

Ben did not tap the bell on the counter.

The thud of a distant hammer sounded further inside. Ben flexed his fingers at Dave in a *follow me* gesture.

Dave opened his mouth to protest. They should ring the bell, make their presence known; but then he might never see the VIP room again.

He followed Ben down the arched corridor.

Still no sign of life.

Ben stalked down the passageway. Beyond arched door-ways, tables and chairs stood in disarray. Something had interrupted the waiters' work unexpectedly.

Down a long corridor, a satin boundary rope blocked their advance. The curtained doorway of the VIP room beckoned.

Ben parted the curtains an inch with his fingers, then disappeared into the chamber.

Dave hesitated. The first time he had entered that room his life had changed course. Who knew what a second visit would do?

Voices echoed down the corridor. He drew a deep breath and pushed through the curtains.

The freestanding bronze lamp burned in the corner. The chamber had not changed: the Bordeaux curtains, the wooden two-seater, the round coffee table.

Ben dropped to all fours and peered under the table.

"Nothing there," he said, dusting his trousers off. "I can't see under the couch."

Ben gave the two-seater a heave. Nothing gave. He frisked the cushions and shrugged.

Dave peeked between the tapestries but found only a narrow gap and a wall of solid stone. "Nothing behind the curtains."

The room was smaller than he remembered.

On one tapestry, a young shepherd slept and used a rock like a cushion. The ladder behind him stretched to the heavens. Winged men peered down at him.

Mishi's words rang in Dave's head.

Move Below, move Above.

"Was the light on when you came in?" Dave asked.

"Yes."

"Then they'll be back soon. We should go. "

"It's got to be here somewhere. Hidden in plain sight."

"Unless there is no stone."

Ben raised his hand, tilted his head.

Dave heard the voices too. They were drawing closer.

Ben looked about the room for a place to hide.

"Here," Dave said. He slipped behind the silky curtains and pressed his back to the wall. The curtain hung an inch from his nose and smelled of old fabric and dust. Ben quickly took position beside him. Through the blade of light between the hanging curtains Dave could see most of the couch and table.

Two burly men crossed Dave's line of sight. Dave recognized one of them as the concierge who had handled his reservation. He wore jeans and a T-shirt and a brown sash across his back—which was in fact the carry strap of a machine gun.

Oh, crap.

Dave stopped breathing. His heart beat like a drum in his ears. He watched the scene like a disembodied soul.

The men got to work. They picked up the table and carried it out of sight.

A third, unseen man spoke. His gruff voice commanded the others with harsh, guttural words. The men returned and put their shoulders against the side of the couch and heaved. It shifted a few feet on hidden tracks.

Unseen Man spoke again. The concierge stepped out of view and returned with a crow bar.

Dave shifted his head for a better vantage point and bumped his head against Ben's.

The concierge inserted the iron rod between the stone tiles where the couch had sat. A heavy slab lifted. The other man caught the edge and soon laid the square stone beside the hole in the ground.

Dave exchanged a glance with Ben.

Is this really happening?

Unseen Man issued another command and the two helpers filed out of sight and earshot.

Unseen Man stepped into view. He was short, balding, and had a greasy mustache.

Ornan.

A handgun peeked out of his belt. This was no Manuel of *Fawlty Towers* now. This was one secretive and dangerous little man.

Ornan gave the room a sweeping glance. At one point he seemed to stare directly at Dave. Then he stood over the hole in the ground and gazed downward.

He dropped to his knees. Slowly, he reached his arms forward and into the hole. He straightened and turned slowly at the waist. At arm's length he held a cylindrical metallic container like a very small hat box.

Dave's breathing quickened.

Ornan placed the box on the floor. He reached back into the hole, fetched a metal lid, and sealed the box. He got to his feet. He pulled a handkerchief from a trouser pocket and mopped his forehead. Then he left the room.

Dave sucked in a lungful of air.

"Now," Ben said. He stepped from behind the curtain and made for the box.

Dave stuck his head out. The coast was clear so he joined Ben. They looked at the metal box.

Ben lowered the bag from his shoulder. "Hold it open."

"Are you crazy?" Dave hissed. "They've got guns."

"This is our history, Dave. Our heritage. The stone should be studied, and placed in a museum, not flogged on the black market. If they move it, we'll lose the stone forever. This is a once in a lifetime opportunity."

"*Lifetime* is the operative word."

Ben sighed. "They'll be back any second. Do you want to get out of here or not?"

Dave took the bag.

Ben lifted the box and eased it into the bag. He tightened the drawstring and strapped the backpack onto his shoulders.

"Not too heavy," he said.

Dave felt the blood drain from his face. "Guns. They've got guns."

"Kalashnikovs." Ben grinned. "Ready?"

He poked his head through the curtains at the exit. Then the rest of him. Hearing no sounds of catastrophe, Dave followed.

They padded carefully down the corridor.

How did Ben plan on explaining their presence in the restaurant? *Sorry, we lost our way. Can you show us to the nearest bathroom?*

Unlikely.

Ben paused at the first arch and leaned into the opening. He signaled the all-clear. Another fifty meters and they would reach the landing. Up the stairs and they were home free.

Voices echoed down the corridor. Louder now.

Oh, crap.

Ben made a backward gesture with his hand and they retreated down the torch-lit passageway.

Boots clomped on stone. More than one pair.

Ben shifted from a careful walk to a brisk march. The backpack danced over his shoulders. The VIP room came into view.

Voices behind them. Louder now. The boots quickened their pace.

Ben broke into a sprint. Dave kept pace. Ben vaulted the safety rope. Dave did the same.

The passage curved to the right. The flaming torches ended. Ben ran on. Dave kept up. Their bodies threw long, wild shadows on the walls.

Ornan's henchmen must be out of sight. Are they giving chase?

Dave looked back.

Then the floor disappeared beneath his feet.

Dave felt himself falling down, down into inky blackness.

CHAPTER 9

Jay parked the van on Graetz Street. John carried the black duffel bag; the handle of a cricket bat stuck out the zipper. Jay planned not to use it this time.

Stay invisible.

They walked down a quiet cul-de-sac called Moshe Gaster. Wild grasses sprouted along the roadside and between the low boundary walls of apartment blocks.

The alley ended in a clump of duplexes and a wall. An unlocked pedestrian gate stood beside a large number six.

No sign of the blue Yaris.

Jay unlatched the gate and padded down an L-shaped stairway into a private courtyard.

Perfect.

They could get to work without worrying about nosy neighbors.

The house mixed modern and ancient elements: large, uneven rocks; thick layers of smooth plaster; a domed roof alongside a belt of translucent square stones.

He crouched at the front door and rolled out his kit of long metal picks on the floor.

The lock gave little resistance.

Jay poked his head inside and listened.

Bird calls without. Silence within.

He held the door open for John and the equipment.

The narrow passage opened onto a modern kitchen in chrome and chocolate-colored wood paneling. Squares of light projected on the walls and floor.

The men split up.

Heavens knew why the Teacher wanted the clay jars. They were pieces of a puzzle and the third jar completed the picture. If Green yielded nothing, Jay would move on to Schwarz, orders or not. He was done with waiting.

Down three steps, he entered an oblong dining room. The walls were at least a meter thick. They curved upward and inward and met at a central square shaft. Hints of a former life.

The furnishings were stylish and expensive. Jay opened the cupboard beneath a buffet counter. Stacks of fancy dishes and crystal glasses. He uncorked a bottle of eighteen-year-old Glenmorangie and inhaled the pungent scent. Green knew his whisky.

Jay held onto the bottle for later.

In the lounge, a bulge of bedrock jutted from one of the walls. He eased back onto a brown leather couch.

The opposite wall contained a decorative niche. A spotlight illuminated an empty wire stand.

Jay stood and inspected the niche up close.

"Bingo," he said aloud.

John joined him.

"What? A bottle of whisky?"

"No, you nonger. This. Look. Green was expecting us."

"Crikey!"

"Took the word out of my mouth, John. Say, if you were an old jar, where would you hide?"

The doorbell rang.

He put a finger to his lips.

"Ben?" a woman's voice outside called. The visitor knocked on the door and it creaked open.

Jay smiled. Soon he would have the answers to his questions. *Batter up.*

One day he would die. Dave knew this. He had dropped the fact into a deep drawer of his mind and rarely reviewed it. When he did, he imagined a peaceful passing—in his sleep, at a ripe old age. Mourned by a tribe of children and grandchildren, maybe even a few great-grandchildren. At the present moment, a more likely and imminent scenario arose.

He was sprawled facedown in a foot of putrid mud at the bottom of a deep pit beneath the City of David in complete and utter darkness.

He lifted his head and gasped for air.

Thankfully, the mud had broken his fall. Death would come not by asphyxiation but, judging by the excited voices of the gunmen that echoed above, by bullet.

Soon Dave's life would flash before his eyes. It would not take long. He would never see daylight again. He would die here. Single. Childless.

He pushed his arms out and raised his torso from the mire. He lost balance and rolled onto his side. He wiped grime from his face and spat mud. His chest stung. His legs hurt. His body was wet and cold.

"Ben?"

"Here," Ben whispered. "Quick."

Dave crawled in the dark. Hands gripped his forearm and pulled him onto a hard ledge. A small square of white light snapped on. Ben's phone. His face was plastered with mud.

"You OK?"

"I think so. Where are we?"

"Some kind of tunnel. Come. We need to keep moving."

Ben crawled away and his body blocked most of the light.

Dave followed. He bumped his forehead on a rocky outcrop and swore. The floor of the tunnel was smooth and pebbly except for the muddy trail Ben left. A few meters on, Dave fished his phone out of the back pocket of his jeans. It lived! The tunnel was only a few feet high. Ben had stopped some distance ahead. Dave's phone displayed zero bars of cellular reception. So much for calling the police.

Were Ornan's men following?

He caught up with Ben on his knees and elbows.

"Why have we stopped?"

"Ran out of tunnel."

Oh, God. They were trapped.

"Wait," Ben said. "There's some loose dirt and rocks here. I'll try to chip through."

Stone scraped on stone.

Oh, thank God!

The sounds outside the tunnel were more distant and indistinct. Small patches of cobwebs hung between jutting edges in the tunnel roof.

"Turn off your phone," Ben said.

"Why?"

"Save the battery. We might be here for a while."

Mandy walked down Moshe Gaster and her heart thumped.

The Greens were Dave's friends. Without him, Mandy had no business knocking on their door.

Ben had sounded sympathetic on the phone. Mandy had shared few details. Enough to get her foot in the door. Not enough for Ben to file a restraining order.

She thought of Dave and the girl on Emek Refaim. Dave

had no sisters. No female cousins that she knew of. But body language doesn't lie.

He'd found another girl.

Mandy still found that hard to believe. They were meant for each other. Dave was her hero. He would never do that. There had to be more to it. And the wild-eyed King David was her only lead.

Mandy didn't care if she sounded crazy. She feared only that the truth would be as simple and bitter as Shani had said.

Either way, at the end of the grassy backstreet—her last foothold in Dave's life—closure waited.

Mandy unlatched the gate and descended the stone steps into the courtyard.

She rang the doorbell.

No movement inside.

She dialed Ben's mobile.

Voice mail.

She hung up.

"Ben," she called.

She knocked on the door. It moved.

A vision flashed in her mind: Dave waited for her inside with open arms. It was all a big misunderstanding.

Mandy walked inside.

The kitchen was empty. Yvette was overseas at work, Ben had said. Still no sound.

Why would Ben leave the door unlocked?

She slid her hand into her bag.

A few steps into the dining room, she stopped.

A short, stocky brown man stared at her. His chubby face was expressionless.

Her hand fished through tissues and lipsticks.

Why am I not more organized?

The man looked at her hand.

"Hi," she said. "Is Ben here?"

He took a step toward her.

"Stay where you are."

"No worries." He spread his hands slowly like a hunter

approaching a wary bird. "I won't hurt ya."

The accent was strong. Australian? A drop of sweat slipped down his brow.

Mandy's fingers closed around the small, cool canister of the pepper spray, when an arm wrapped around her torso from behind. A hand gripped her elbow, trapping her arm in the bag.

"Hey!" A gauze cloth clamped over her mouth and nose. She gasped, inhaling a pungent, sweet fragrance. For what seemed a long time, she struggled inside the iron embrace. Then the world tilted sideways and faded to white.

The scraping continued. Debris trickled in the dark.

The time on Dave's phone had read 10:13 AM. An hour had passed since then, although time was hard to measure in the darkness of the cramped tunnel.

The chill of wet mud and cold stone spread through his clothes, seeped through his skin, and invaded his bones. His stomach groaned. At least he didn't need the bathroom. Yet.

Why had he ever listened to Ben?

They had narrowly survived Ornan's henchmen and a free-fall into a slime pit, only to face a slow death in a damp, old worm hole.

"Any luck?" he said.

The scraping stopped. The pale glow ahead shifted.

"It's almost large enough to crawl through. The tunnel we're in seems to be a natural feature, like Warren's Shaft in the COD. The other tunnel is definitely man-made. Very early workmanship, like the Canaanite aqueduct we discovered nearby a few years ago."

"Ben," Dave said through gritted, chattering teeth. "I don't need a bloody guided tour. Just tell me when we're getting out of here."

"That's what I'm trying to explain to you. If the second tunnel is man-made, it might be an escape passage."

Dave brightened. "Escape passage?"

"King Zedekiah fled Jerusalem through secret tunnels and surfaced near Ein Gedi. Not that it helped. The Babylonians captured him, put out his eyes and dragged him to Babylon in chains. So cheer up, Your Highness. You might make it to the Dead Sea on time."

Dave had been chased by armed thugs. He had sky-dived into a mud pool and spent hours trapped in a dark tunnel. He was in no mood to let that comment pass.

"What's that supposed to mean?"

"That means I don't know exactly where we are and when or whether we'll get out of here. We'll have to wing it, OK? So grow up."

"Grow up? Excuse me if I'm not overjoyed about being stuck here."

The scraping continued.

"Here we go again," Ben said. "Everything revolves around you."

"Me? You got us into this, Ben. Just remember that."

Ben laughed to himself. "You've had it easy all your life. Silver spoons. Trust funds. You whine whenever you don't get your way."

If the tunnel was any wider, Dave would have reached out and wrung Ben's neck.

"I earn my own keep, thank you very much. Not like some people I know."

"What exactly do you mean by that?"

Four months of paranoia boiled over. "I mean that you took Yvette to Ornan's and now you're set for life. Why else would she fell in love with a bald, crazy pseudo-academic?"

The scraping halted.

Brilliant, Dave. Ben is your only ticket out of here and now you've pissed him off.

When Ben spoke, his voice was eerily calm.

"We're through, Dave," he said. "Once we get out of here, you're on your own."

"Good."

The scraping resumed.

No words passed between them for half an hour. Dave had been harsh. Ben was doing his best.

Ben's phone beeped, almost out of power. Good thing Dave had turned his phone off.

By now Shira and his parents would be at the Dead Sea. How long would it take them to realize something was wrong? Nobody but Ben knew where he was. Would Shira think Dave had got cold feet?

"Ben."

"What?"

"Can we go back the way we came? They must have left by now."

"That depends. How are you with rock-climbing? In the dark. And mud. A smooth cliff-face about, uh, two floors high."

"Right," Dave said.

More scraping. Rubble crumbled in the semi-darkness.

"There we go," Ben said.

He crawled ahead.

Dave sighed.

Thank God. They might get out alive after all.

"It's a larger tunnel." Ben's voice echoed. "I can stand. Here. Give me your hand."

He helped Dave through the hole.

Ben shone his phone about. The square, smooth hole stretched on beyond the light.

"This way," he said. "I think."

Then the light cut out.

Dave powered up his phone and handed it to Ben.

"Thanks."

A blue haze of phone light wrapped Ben like an aura. The tunnel rose and fell, turned this way and that. Dave had lost his sense of direction long ago. Were they going deeper underground? Ein Gedi was by the Dead Sea, an hour by car. How long would it take by foot?

Dave's stomach moaned again. His muddy shoes and socks squelched.

Ben halted.

"What's the matter?" Dave asked.

"Look." Ben pointed the light at the floor.

A large black hole blocked their path. Only a narrow ledge of rock remained on one side.

Ben picked up a stone and lobbed it into the hole. Dave counted seven seconds before he heard it clatter below.

"I think we can make it," Ben said. "Here."

Ben handed Dave the phone. He edged along the narrow strip of floor, his back to the tunnel wall, and reached the other side.

Dave handed the phone over and inched onto the ledge. He was not a man for heights but the darkness let him pretend the danger away. The ledge had held Ben's weight.

Squelch. Squelch.

Ben gripped Dave's arm and steadied him onto solid ground.

"Thanks."

They plodded onward.

At least the walking warmed him up. The air had cleared of damp. His ears picked out the occasional drip of water along with the echo of their footfalls.

If they got out, he decided, he would live differently. For starters, he'd never listen to Ben again. He'd settle down. Get on with his life. Raise a family with Mandy. With *Shira*! Raise a family with Shira.

What was the matter with him?

Dave collided with Ben. "Sorry."

The path had split into three. The tunnel was now a

network of interconnected tunnels. A subterranean labyrinth.

"Which one do we take?"

Ben shrugged. "Got a coin?"

Jay rummaged through the girl's handbag. Her auburn curls pooled on the floor as she slept. She had reached into the bag as if feeling for a weapon, so Jay had pinned her hand to her side before covering her mouth and nose with the pad of chloroform.

Instead of a gun and badge, he found a pocket pack of Kleenex, lipsticks, and a leather wallet.

He pulled the Texas driver's license from the window pocket.

Mandy Rosenberg.

The name did not register in his memory but the chestnut curls drew him back in time.

A yellow print dress with small, blue flowers close to his face. The smell of soap and the pine scent of cheap gin. The rust-colored locks towered over him. *You will do great things, my boy.* Her large hand smoothed his hair. *Great things.*

John tinkered with the girl's phone. "She called Green last," he said. "And lots of calls to Schwarz." He dropped the phone in her bag. "You OK?"

"Box a birds." Jay cleared his throat. "Check the bedrooms. Beds. Cupboards."

John trudged off.

Everything happened for a reason. He would not return to the Teacher empty-handed.

The wallet held a hundred shekels and a few cards: VISA, Mashbir. Jay found a square, wrinkled photograph. A man's face. Early forties. Thick curly hair. Wholesome smile. Mountains in the background.

Daddy's girl.

Jay considered the slender body on the floor, the bare legs protruding from the jeans skirt. The girl was there for a reason too. Another piece of the puzzle.

John reappeared. "Nothing."

Jay tossed him a bunch of keys. "Bring the van out front. She's coming with."

CHAPTER 10

Dave's phone bleated. Electronic death approached. Soon the darkness would swallow all hope. The tunnel walls closed in on him. Ben stood at the crossroads in the dim white light and scratched his chin. They had to find a way out and soon. But even Ben the Great was stumped.

"Where did it start?" Dave asked.

"Where did what start?"

"The escape tunnel."

Ben wrinkled his nose and the crust of mud cracked.

"Somewhere in the Old City. Sections may have collapsed or filled up over the years. Like the hole we crawled through."

"Great."

Dave searched his shadowy surroundings for clues. Nothing in his training or life experience had equipped him for this. Cavemen had a better chance of survival. All three tunnels might lead to dead ends. They had only a few minutes of light left, enough to explore one path at most.

Come on, Dave. Think!

"There must be a way of testing this," he said.

"Testing? This isn't a computer program."

"It's the same principle."

At work Dave tested hidden code logic. He had developed

a sixth sense for the right combinations of mouse clicks and input to ferret out the bugs that hid among the bits and bytes.

"One of these leads out of here."

"Or none," Ben said.

Dave's phone beeped again.

Dave said, "Let's head back and try the other end of the tunnel."

"That will take a long time without light."

Dave didn't fancy crossing that narrow ledge blind. "Wait a minute."

Dave remembered a movie scene. A pirate on a raft and a flat ocean.

Dave pushed past Ben to the crossroads. He wiped his forefinger on a dry patch of jeans and put it in his mouth. Mud particles swirled over his tongue. He extracted his saliva-coated digit and held it in the air. He entered the tunnel on the left.

Nothing.

He tried the middle.

More nothing.

Dammit!

He tried the third and last option.

A faint breeze tickled the wet skin on the edge of his finger.

"This one," he said. "There's air down there."

Ben looked at Dave with surprise. Without another word, he led the way with Dave's phone.

After a short march, the right wall fell away, turning the tunnel into a cave. They pressed on. The ground rose slowly and became a chiseled staircase. They pushed ahead, faster.

Distant footfalls echoed. Then hushed voices. Dim ambient light strengthened with every step.

In the gloom an object emerged that brought tears to Dave's eyes. A metal handrail.

Ben and Dave skipped up the stairs.

A circle of blinding, amber light opened ahead.

A crowd of people stood on a platform. They wore

peaked caps.

"Legend has it," the tour guide said, a scruffy string bean of an American with glasses, "that King Zedekiah—"

He stopped mid-sentence.

"Excuse me," Ben said. "*Slicha*. Coming through."

A woman gasped. The crowd parted for the two mud-plastered swamp monsters.

"Hey!" the tour guide said. "You're not allowed down there."

Ben steamed ahead.

"Are you with our group? You're not with our group."

The steps wound up the cavern. Garden lamps lit a path through the wide, tent-like cave. They passed through a turnstile and stepped into daylight.

The two friends collapsed on a bench at a street corner. They breathed. They laughed. The Old City walls towered above. Passersby eyed them with interest. Dave's feet ached. Relief warmed his body like the beautiful, hot sun above.

Ben placed the grimy backpack on his lap. "You look like crap."

"Thanks. You should have seen the other guy."

"Zedekiah's Cave," Ben said. "What did I tell you?"

"You were right." Dave's wristwatch read two o'clock.

"We should head back or you'll miss your Swedish massage."

They followed the walls to Jaffa Gate and limped through the Armenian quarter.

"I'm sorry," Dave said. "What I said earlier. I didn't mean…"

"Forget it. Nothing happened."

Dave waited for a counter apology. Perhaps Ben had folded one into his reply. Maybe Ben still thought Dave was a spoiled brat. Maybe he was right.

"What do we do now?"

Ben mulled over his answer. "Call the police, I suppose. Have Ornan's searched thoroughly. Salvage what we can, although I doubt they've left anything of value. But that tunnel will keep us busy for years. This too." Ben tapped the bag on his shoulder.

They walked in wordless understanding and descended the ramp from the Jewish quarter to Dung Gate and turned the corner of Ma'alot Ir David.

Ben froze at the top of the street.

"I don't believe it." Dave followed Ben's gaze past the COD. A large black A-Team van pulled off in a hurry.

"Here." Ben thrust the backpack into Dave's arms. "Hang onto this for a while. I've got to find out where they're going."

Ben sprinted down the street.

"Wait!" Dave held the bag at arm's length. "What am I supposed to do with it?"

Ben climbed into his Toyota Yaris. He revved the engine. The black van had disappeared down the road.

Ben rolled down his window. "Just keep it out of sight. I'll pick it up later."

He launched down the street and careened out of sight.

Ben spotted the black van deep within Abu Tor. The jumble of apartment blocks, streets strewn with uncollected garbage, and haphazard electric cables resembled an urban warfare training set, although many hailed the old neighborhood as a model of Jewish-Arab symbiosis.

The van showed no sign of slowing. Without indicating, it turned north onto the three-lane boulevard of Derekh Chevron and flanked the Old City to the west.

He shadowed the black van at a discreet distance.

Where are you going?

He'd already hit the jackpot once that day. The new tunnels beneath the City of David alone warranted a press release, research grants, his name in lights. All this before penning his first academic paper.

There were legal issues to iron out, granted. But Ben had been the right man in the right place at the right time.

Now he set his sights on a second, perhaps larger, jackpot.

The van hurtled past the Old City, through the *Tzanchanim* tunnel, and up Chaim Barlev toward the Mount Scopus campus of the Hebrew University.

Ornan, you sneaky snake.

Ben had first visited the restaurant in the City of David shortly after the sign went up.

Romantic ambience. An opportunity to display his value as an expert in archaeology.

His date, a plump New Yorker doused in makeup, had railed against Israeli hairdressers and Ben's attention drifted to the earthenware jar on a stand in the corner. He walked over to investigate. The date was not a total loss, after all. He called the restaurateur aside and explained the historical significance and the legal ramifications of his chosen decoration.

Ornan had played the part of the obsequious and servile Arab. The man deserved an Academy Award. The jar was a gift from a wealthy friend, he had said. He had no idea of its significance. As a gesture of remorse, Ornan gifted the artifact to Ben.

"And," Ornan added, "next time, VIP room."

"VIP?"

Ornan had Ben's full attention. Backstage passes. Executive lounges. Access to restricted benefits was the Demonstration of Value *par excellence*.

"Yes." Ornan's eyes twinkled. "*Special* room. Make girl fall in love. Guarantee!" He raised a cautionary finger. "One time only."

DANSOFER

Ben took the jar home that night for further study. He would report it to the Antiquities Authority once he figured out its provenance.

He forgot about the VIP room.

Until Yvette.

Ben's dream came true. A group of international models rounded out a weeklong fashion shoot for Vogue with a tour of the COD. Ben scheduled himself as their guide for the day and quickly honed in on the tall blond in the modest skirt.

"You're more knowledgeable than the others," Ben remarked offhand, as they negotiated Hezekiah's water duct by flashlight.

She had asked a question earlier while the others had studied their nails and posed with City of David caps and hiking shorts.

"That," she said in the Belgian accent that looped rosebud tendrils around his heart, "is because I'm Jewish."

"No kidding."

"Religious too."

"You don't say."

Ben didn't need any more hints from God.

But how to get her alone?

"There's a special place in the City of David. You'll love it. It's off limits to tourists but I can make an exception. How is this evening? It includes dinner."

Yvette didn't say anything for a while. In the beam-lit twilight of the water tunnel, Ben felt like the diggers must have felt twenty-five centuries before, chiseling away in the dark, unsure whether they would meet their colleagues, who burrowed toward them from the Shiloah spring.

"OK," she said. "Tonight is our free night. But you should know: we leave Israel tomorrow."

A declaration of non-interest? Or a hint at future possibilities?

Either way, Ben's heart soared.

He called Ornan. The little restaurateur led them to the VIP room. There was wine. There was laughter. And, two

212

months later, a wedding.

A red light flared on the dashboard. The gas dial touched empty. The emergency tank gave Ben another twenty kilometers.

No matter.

Any minute, the van would turn right and disappear into the chaos of Arab East Jerusalem but Ben would know where to send the cops.

He hadn't taken seriously Ornan's claims to love magic. He had chalked up the conquest to ambience, personal charm, and the Pickup Artist's Bible.

But the evidence was piling up. Ben and Yvette. Dave and Mandy. Mishi had provided the theoretical foundation, Professor Barkley the historical clues. And now Ben had acquired the Foundation Stone itself.

I earn my own keep, Ben. Not like some people I know.

Despite Dave's apology, his words in the tunnel added water, sunlight, and a bag of fertilizer to a dormant seed of guilt and now the sapling broke through Ben's subconscious.

The plant budded.

Dave was wrong. Ben had married Yvette for love, not money. But had he taken advantage? Had he tricked the person he loved most in the world?

He focused on the black van two cars ahead.

Ornan was going down. He had graduated from a single, incidental artifact to large-scale illegal excavation. Ben had fallen into the proof. Add a few Kalashnikovs and you had a network for antiquities smuggling, and perhaps even the bankrolling of fundamentalist violence.

The black van ramped onto road number one east.

"What the…?"

Ben followed the van as it crossed the Jerusalem city limits.

The highway began a long descent.

Ben eyed the gas dial with concern.

A large road sign sped by. It read: The Dead Sea.

Dave removed his mud-caked Skechers and socks before entering his apartment. He dropped them in the kitchen trash can. He did the same with his jeans and shirt.

He surveyed his living room. He felt as though he had returned from a long trip overseas. He never thought he would see his apartment again. Yet the small square room with the fold-out couch and rolling shutters at half-mast had not changed at all.

He stepped into the bathtub and drew the curtain. A long hot shower never felt so good.

He had survived. Cracks had appeared in his equanimity but he'd played a key role in the escape. *Enough adventure for one lifetime.* He had paid his dues, suffered for his sins. Time to put all that behind him.

Mandy.

At the peak of crisis, his mind had fled to Mandy. Understandable enough. A few days ago, Dave had planned to propose to her. Under immense pressure, the mind was liable to skip a track.

Dave put on fresh clothes and clean running shoes.

He scraped dirt from his wristwatch.

3:07 PM.

He wrote a text message to Shira and his mother.

Running late. Will be there in a few hours.

His overnight bag still sat in the trunk of his Ford Hatchback.

Time to head out.

Ben's backpack slouched beside the front door.

He slid his hands into the bag, taking care to avoid the muddy crust. The metal container shined, spotless. Ben was right, it weighed very little. Was it empty? After all they had

214

gone through, that would be funny.

He moved to the couch and placed the container on the coffee table. It reminded him of the round tin box his grandmother had kept stocked with chocolate bars.

Just a peek.

He wrested the lid loose and tilted it upward.

A large stone like an oversized hockey puck filled the container. The surface was smooth and dark like the igneous rocks formed by cooling lava. It begged to be touched. Held. Caressed. He could take it with him. Keep it near during a quiet moment with Shira. The universe seemed to rotate slowly around the mysterious stone.

Dave snapped the lid shut.

No more.

He fetched the orange cooler from the service balcony. The metal tin lodged comfortably beside the bubble-wrapped scroll jar.

You belong together.

Dave replaced the white cover, returned the cooler to its shelf, and covered the box with the dishcloth.

Stay here.

Dave locked his apartment and got in the car.

Ben shifted the Yaris into neutral and barreled down the winding highway. The Ma'aleh Adumim turnoff flew by.

The gas dial dropped below the empty line.

He was in no shape for a long haul. The old gym bag on the back seat contained shorts, a T-shirt, an official City of

David peaked cap, and rubber sandals—his emergency kit when a younger guide didn't show for the aqueduct tour. But fresh clothing was the least of his worries.

An army checkpoint rose in the distance like a four-lane toll gate. Cars entering the West Bank faced less scrutiny than those traveling in the opposite direction and the black van hardly slowed. Ben coasted through.

His phone rang in the docking station.

The caller ID read *Erez Lazarus*.

His boss didn't bother with hello. "Where are you?"

The faux British accent packed a double dose of peeve.

"I had to step out. Will be back soon."

"I've been looking for you all morning. Why was your phone off?"

"Battery ran out. I'll get back to you later, OK? I'm in transit."

"Where are you?"

What was Erez on about?

"Can't cope without me for a second, can you?"

"This isn't a joke, Benjamin. Either you come back right now or don't bother. Understand?"

"What's going on?"

"The police are here and they want to speak with you."

"The police?"

Erez hesitated. "About the missing jar."

"I thought you kept that quiet."

"I kept it out of the papers, but the detective thinks you might be able to help."

Police? The scroll jar? Months after the break-in? Ben remembered Professor Barkley's warning.

Obsessed is the word.

"My battery is running low again," he said. That much was true. "I have to hang up now. I'll be there as soon as I can."

He tapped the foot brake to slow the car around a sharp bend.

Ornan and Erez.

He'd never put the two together. How *had* the COD come

to possess a Cave Three scroll jar?

Ben had been asking the wrong questions.

Policemen, my ass.

Erez had his dodgy Christian connections. Was Ornan another dot in the picture? Had Ornan connected Ben with the missing Foundation Stone? Had he alerted Erez?

The northern edge of the Dead Sea rose into view, a flat inland bay at the foot of the Jordanian valley ridge.

The road leveled out. In a few kilometers, they would reach Qumran, the origin of the scrolls and their jars.

Returning to the source.

Poetic resonance aside, Ben found that unlikely. Today's Qumran was a tourist attraction complete with sound-and-light shows, souvenir stores, and dusty ruins, not an ideal base for militant antiquities looters.

And the caves were slippery death traps.

The black van slowed and, again without indicating, turned north onto the 90 toward Bet She'an and away from the Dead Sea. The sign post read King Hussein Bridge Border Crossing.

Of course!

If Ornan crossed the border, the chase would end. Ben's gym bag did not contain a passport. The Jordanians had controlled the scrolls until 1967 when Israel captured East Jerusalem and the scroll fragments in the Rockefeller Museum.

Was Ornan a Jordanian agent? That explained the unfamiliar guttural dialect. Had he sacrificed one measly jar in order to keep a larger hoard under wraps? Or was the neighboring Arab country merely a convenient safe haven?

Even without Dave, Ornan would have moved his treasure eventually. At least now Ben had a trail to follow.

He dialed 101 on his phone, then changed his mind. Border police might intercept smugglers but there was no such thing as an anonymous tip from a cell phone. Ben would have to explain how he had come upon his intel and he did not care to add fuel to the police's growing interest in his affairs.

"It's just you and me, Ornan."

Ben would tail them in the waiting line for border control. Cause a commotion. Slip away while the police cuffed Ornan and his thugs.

Ben stepped on the accelerator to keep moving. The gas dial slipped below the empty line and over the large E. The bridge was near Bet She'an. Would gas vapors take him that far?

It didn't matter. Ben would follow if he had to hitchhike the rest of the way.

Then the van veered left, off the 90 and toward a distant patch of palm trees against the mountain rise of the valley.

Jericho.

"Oh crap."

The City of Palms. The oldest known continuously inhabited city. Modern Jericho fell within Area C and the exclusive control of the Palestinian Authority.

Jericho was considered a calm city by Palestinian standards and even attracted a trickle of Christian tourists, but Jews wandering into Area C could expect a welcoming lynch mob and machetes. No Israeli citizen in his right mind entered Area C without an armored personnel carrier and helicopter extraction team.

Ben followed the van.

Signs in Arabic sped by as he approached the sprawling mass of Arab Jericho.

A loose roadblock of Palestinians in speckled army fatigues and Kalashnikovs flagged down the black van and its yellow Israeli license plates, and then waved it through.

Ben slowed. The van turned right and disappeared behind a clump of palms. He made a sharp right onto a dirt road that flanked the city along a dilapidated perimeter fence. He caught snatches of the van between trees and low, plastered buildings. It moved deeper into the city and he lost visual contact.

He idled on the dirt road for a few minutes. The engine

quavered and cut out. He turned the key. The car coughed twice but did not turn over.

Wonderful.

Ben got out. He opened the back door, changed clothes on the back seat, and did his best to remove the mud from his face and arms. He emerged wearing shorts, a T-shirt, and a COD cap.

If anyone asked, he would be a clueless British tourist.

He kept the muddy trainers on. He might need to run.

His phone rang.

He glanced at the caller ID.

Mandy Rosenberg.

He'd forgotten about their appointment. No time for apologies or explanations now. And the phone had charged only a little in the docking station. He put the phone on silent and slipped it into his pocket.

Fifty meters along the perimeter fence, Ben found a hole. He stepped through and his shirt sleeve snagged on a strand of rusted chicken wire.

He made for the nearest clump of houses.

Wild grass and low brush littered the uneven, broken earth. A woman in a brown burka pegged bed sheets to a clothesline. Arab children chased a football barefoot in the dirt. Three chickens waddled by. The asphalt street had neither shoulder nor sidewalk. The houses, bare cement walls and flat roofs, grew denser.

Ben walked up a side street, deeper into the city. Beyond a cement wall, he spotted the edge of a black van.

A metal sign on the wall contained the street name in Arabic. Ben snapped a photo for later analysis. He moved closer to the edge of the wall. His shoes crunched on loose gravel. He heard no voices. The men must be indoors, storing their loot, sure that they had made a clean break.

He peered around the corner. The second black van stood at the other edge of a long, single-story housing complex. He photographed the license plates. There were no windows on this side of the building.

Time to turn back, flag down a tour bus, and return to the safety of Israeli territory. He could call the towing service for the car. Did his insurance extend to Area C?

A hard nozzle pressed into the small of his back. A large, muscular hand closed over his shoulder.

Ben froze. He didn't dare raise his arms.

"*Wakif*," said a deep, Middle Eastern voice. The man breathed hot air on the back of Ben's neck.

"*Wakif willa batokh.*"

Over the years Ben had picked up snatches of Arabic. He had learned this particular phrase during his shortened service in the Israeli army.

Stop, the man had said. Stop or I'll shoot.

CHAPTER 11

Mandy woke and struggled to open her eyelids; they felt lined in lead. She lay on a hard bed and through blurred vision realized she was in a small room with gray walls and a large brown door.

Not her room on Mendele. Not her studio on 63rd Street. Definitely not her frilled childhood bedroom.

Her mouth tasted like glue.

An image rose in her mind: the brown man in Ben's house stepped toward her; an arm closed around her like strong rope; the sweet-smelling gauze over her mouth.

She had come to during the ride. She'd found herself under a heavy blanket in a dark, closed space that stank of motor oil, then drifted off again.

She lifted her head from the rough mattress. The springs creaked.

A man cleared his throat. A second bed stood perpendicular to hers and on it sat a gray hooded cloak; she couldn't see the face inside it.

"Hi," it said.

Mandy felt about for her bag.

"Don't bother," the cloak said. "You'll get your stuff back later. Great playlist, by the way. 'Upside-down you turn me.' 'Babooshka.' Takes me way back. Gotta love eighties music."

An awkward silence developed between her and her captor, who had broken into her iPhone. He seemed to be trying to chat her up.

"Where am I? Who are you?"

"I'm sorry." Remembering his manners, he pulled back the hood and Mandy stared into the blue eyes and sparse red beard of the Western Wall street performer.

Damian.

Or was it *King David?*

How was he connected to the men at Ben's home? And why had he followed Dave?

Damian smiled. "It's me. Don't you remember?"

Mandy hesitated. Was he still in character?

"Sure," she said. "We took Art History together."

Damian waved his hand in the air. "No, no, no." He chuckled. Wholesome. Good-natured. He reminded her of Owen Wilson. "Before that."

Here we go.

"Before that?"

She decided to play dumb. Best not to argue with the madman in the cloak who held the key to her prison cell.

"Yeah," he said. "Before all this. Before I was Damian. Before you were Mandy Rosenberg."

So you've been through my purse too.

He stared at her. Or through her.

He made another generous sweeping movement with his hand. "It'll come back to you. I brought you a little something. "

Mandy braced herself for a fluffy teddy bear, but he produced a glass of water and a plate of apple slices. "Eat up. We'll have plenty of time to catch up later."

She didn't like the sound of that but she *was* starving.

He placed the plate and glass at her feet and returned to the other bed.

"Go on," he said. "It's not poison."

Mandy gulped down the glass of cloudy water and devoured the fruit. Damian, or rather King David, watched her closely.

"Can I go now?"

He frowned.

"What do you want from me?"

"You know," he said and stood. "We're going to be best friends, you and I. And believe me, you're gonna need friends here."

"Why?"

"'Cause the other guys, the guys who brought you here? They're *crazy*."

Mandy sighed inwardly. "Crazy?"

"Uh-huh," said the man who thought he was King David. "They'll do anything to get what they want."

"What do they want?"

Damian licked his lips. "A scroll jar. We got two already but we need the third. They think you know where it is. But you don't. I know you don't. You were sent here for a higher purpose."

Mandy forced a poker face. She didn't want to know about this *higher purpose*, and the game of Crazy Cop/Crazier Cop did nothing to comfort her.

King David seemed satisfied for the moment. He got to his feet and collected the plate and cup.

"I'll see you later." He winked at her. "Think on what I said."

He entered a code on the keypad beside the door; it clicked open and he closed it behind him.

Scroll jars? What did they want with scroll jars?

Ben was the archaeologist. Mandy had fallen into a trap Damian's pals had set for Ben.

Had Damian followed Dave to get to Ben? Had Dave tried to protect Mandy by breaking up with her?

That was it!

Mandy shared Dave's secret now. They were bound together. Dave no longer had to keep his distance. Any moment, he would sail in to rescue her.

Meanwhile, Mandy had a part to play. She'd find out what

she could. Unlock the mystery from within.

And this *King David* was her key.

The keypad beeped and the large door clicked open. Two gray cloaks walked in, the brown man from Ben's home and a taller, skinnier Caucasian with long slick hair and a wispy brown beard. He held a stick in his hand like a baseball bat but wide and flat.

"G'day, pretty." He had the same Australian accent as Shortie. His smile made Mandy cringe.

He slapped the bat on the palm of his hand.

"It's show time."

Dave stepped out of the elevator, into the lobby of the Dead Sea Crowne Plaza, and prepared to meet his future parents-in-law.

He had never met the parents of his other girlfriends, certainly not after a second date.

Clammy palms: check. Trembling fingers: check. These were no ordinary parents. These were the parents of Shira Cohen, the closest to royalty Dave would get.

At the window that overlooked the pool, a hand waved. Shira's hand. Dave recognized his mother and father at the table. The second couple faced the window: a balding man and a woman with satin black hair wound and held above her ivory neck by long pins. They grew larger and more intimidating with every step.

Just smile. And keep your mouth shut.

"There you are," his mother said. "We nearly called the

police. Steve and Beverly, this is our David."

The balding man shook Dave's hand. "A pleasure to meet you, David." He smiled warmly beneath a bushy mustache.

Shira's mother, Bev, gave Dave an amused smile and he understood where her daughter got her looks. Shira would age well.

"We've heard so much about you," she said, in an unexpectedly high-pitched voice.

"Nothing terrible, I hope."

He took the last vacant seat between the two fathers. Shira beamed at him from across the table and radiated elegance. Dave nodded at her politely.

Shira's father fixed him with an intense, questioning gaze.

Here it comes.

"So tell me, David," Steve said. "Who do you support, Manchester or Liverpool?"

His mouth dried up. His tongue squirmed uselessly like a beached whale. "Um."

Manchester or Liverpool?

A wrong answer would estrange his future father-in-law forever. He tried to divine the answer from the dark, expectant eyes. Neither were London teams. It was a fifty-fifty chance.

Pick one, any one.

Steve erupted with laughter and clapped Dave on the shoulder.

"Did you see his face?" Dave's mother said.

"What?" Dave said.

Shira smiled and lowered her eyes to the table.

"Relax, David," his mother said. "Steve and Bev know all about you and football. In fact, they know everything there is to know about you."

"Oh." He felt his cheeks burn.

What else had his mom shared with Steve and Bev? Every faux pas and embarrassing moment since birth, probably.

She squinted at him. "David. What happened to your forehead?"

His fingers flew to the scratch below his hairline. His mother didn't wait for an answer.

"Really, David. Try to be more careful." She turned to Steve and Bev. "Did I tell you about the time he walked into a street lamp on Golders Green?"

"Mother! I was four years old."

"He had a large red welt smack in the middle of his forehead for days. Anyway. What were we saying earlier?"

Bev replied, "You were telling us about the new painting."

"Oh, yes. I walked into the lobby and this poor sheep was staring at me. I had to have it. It's a Kadishman."

Dave's mom flaunted her interest in Israeli art at every opportunity.

"The sheep portraits with the colors?" Shira said. "I adore them."

Dave focused on the menu. He could do with a solid meal. That morning he'd faced armed gunmen and certain death beneath the City of David; now he perused a dinner menu. A funny thing, life.

His eye settled on the fish and fries. He looked around for a waiter.

"Our house is filled with them," his mother said.

"It feels as though a herd of sheep is crossing the living room," his father chimed in.

Laughter all round.

"*And* the dining room," his mother added.

"How do you ever serve lamb?" Bev said.

More laughter.

"Shira, my dear, when you're back in London come by and I'll give you the guided tour," his mother offered.

Shira, apparently, had hit it off with her, a fact that aroused mixed emotions in Dave.

A waiter arrived with a large tray of dishes. He placed one before Dave: a fillet of grilled fish and French fries.

"I haven't ordered yet."

"That's for you, David," his mother said.

Dave's blood boiled. "Mother! I think I'm old enough to

order for myself."

"It was getting late. No sense in you watching while the rest of us eat."

"But how do you know what I want?"

She laughed. "I've known you all your life, dear. I know what you need. Would you prefer something else?"

Dave opened his mouth but words didn't follow.

"I rest my case," she said.

The conversation returned to oil paintings of livestock. Dave stabbed the fillet with his fork and sliced off a piece. He chewed in silence.

The white fish was delicious. And Dave had been spared the traditional paternal grilling. Strangely, he felt cheated.

Through the French windows, swimsuits lay on sun chairs in the softening light. Children frolicked in the pool. The calm, salty waters of the Dead Sea lapped the sandy shore beyond and drew the eye to the blue haze of the Jordanian mountains. Six o'clock and daylight still reigned.

"What a lovely day," Dave's mother said. "And a lovely start to new relationships. Make a toast, darling."

Dave's father raised a glass of chardonnay. "To Shira and Dave."

Dave almost choked on his French fries.

"To Shira and Dave," the couples declared.

Dave looked around the table. Shira smiled and sipped her wine. He tried to spot the hidden camera.

"Shira, dear," his mother said. "I'm so glad you agreed to come to Israel."

Dave's fork clanged loudly on the plate. "Mother, can I have a word?"

She rolled her eyes and wiped her lips on the napkin.

"What's going on?" Dave said as soon as they were out of earshot.

"What do you mean?"

"I mean, Shira coming to Jerusalem, conveniently bump-ing into me, getting back together. Did you set this up?"

"David," she said, offended. "You've been heartbroken

over the girl for years. All I did was ask the right people a few questions. Make connections. I did what any concerned mother would do. Isn't this what you wanted?"

"I didn't want you to twist her arm."

"She's here of her own free will, David." Her voice softened. "You were made for each other. Now go sit down and stop making a fuss."

She pinched his cheek and marched back to the table.

He followed. He sat down. He smiled at Shira. He ate his fish.

Shira Cohen had fallen into his lap without any effort on his part. All the dates he had endured, the singles events, the stratagems, the stress, had amounted to nothing. He'd had only to fold his arms and wait.

Dave watched the people around the table. Their mouths talked and chewed, their cutlery processed the food. He heard not a word they said.

This is your life, Dave. Your future.

Yet, in a narrow tunnel below the City of David, when death had seemed imminent, he had not seen the face of Shira Cohen.

Dave's phone sang "Jerusalem of Gold."

"Excuse me." He wiped his mouth, got up, and stepped through the glass door to the pool deck.

He didn't know what he would say. He didn't even know what he felt. But he had to hear Mandy's voice and perhaps he would find out. He answered.

"Mandy," he said. "I've been meaning to call you."

On the other end of the line, a man laughed. "Mandy can't talk right now. But you can speak with me."

The voice was cruel and mocking, and clearly Australian.

"Who is this?"

The man laughed again. He took his time, enjoying the game.

"You have something of mine, David Schwarz. You and your friend at the City of David."

Ornan? No.

One of his men?

"What?" he asked.

The man on the phone lost his patience. "You know exactly what I'm talking about."

Dave did. The round black stone lay in an orange cooler on a shelf in his ground-floor Jerusalem apartment, a hundred kilometers away.

"You better cough it up if you ever want to see your girlfriend again."

Dave was about to protest that she wasn't, technically, his girl, when another voice spoke.

Mandy's voice. "Be careful, Dave. They're—"

The voice cut out.

Dave lowered his body onto the slate steps that descended to the pool area.

The cruel voice returned. "Call me when you're on the road."

"Wait," Dave said. "I don't have it with me. I'm out of town. It'll take a few hours at least."

The voice was silent a moment. "You've got till tomorrow morning. I'll call again. Come alone. Call the cops and your girl gets it. Understand?"

"Yes. But listen. I'm not the one who—"

The line disconnected.

Oh, God. Oh, my God.

For the second time that day, Dave wished he had never met Ben, had never heard of Ornan's and the Foundation Stone.

A woman in a yellow bikini and wrap-around sunglasses walked her toddler up the stairs.

Don't panic.

He looked through the tall lobby windows. Shira and their parents sat at the table. He couldn't just leave.

Ben had made this mess; let Ben clean it up.

He dialed Ben's number.

"You've reached Ben Green. Please leave a message."

Beep!

"Ben. Call me right away," Dave said.

Nothing too specific; you never knew who was listening.

"It's an emergency," he added, trusting his desperate tone would convey the urgency of the situation.

He ended the call.

He waited.

Mandy. I am so sorry.

Dumping her was bad enough. Putting her in harm's way was unforgivable.

While Ben was out swashbuckling, an innocent girl was picking up the bill.

It occurred to Dave that Ben had chased after Ornan's van. He might have seen her or discovered where she was being held. The police would be able to take over from there.

Call the cops and your girl gets it, the man had said.

But what choice did he have?

He called Ben's home line. It rang for a full two minutes.

He called Ben's mobile and left another message.

"Ben, you bastard, wherever you are. Call me right away."

Ben sat in a windowless room. The chair was not designed for comfort. Neither were the ropes that strapped his arms and legs to the steel frame. A single naked lightbulb hung from the ceiling.

So this is how it ends.

Ben had seen it before in film and on the evening news. Interrogation. Torture. Forced confession. Then, a large curved sword and game over.

His last moments might appear on YouTube for a few minutes before the moderators removed the clip.

Would his captors bother with demands?

Gilad Shalit had waited five years for a prisoner exchange. Nachshon Waxman died during the rescue mission. Which was worse?

Would he be able to send a farewell message to Yvette?

Yvette.

Yvette was all he'd ever wanted in life. But he couldn't leave well enough alone.

Ben, you idiot. When will you learn to stand down?

Behind him, a door opened.

He'd failed to get a good look at his captors. There were at least two guards with Kalashnikovs and they spoke among themselves in whispers.

Pay attention, Ben.

The details might mean the difference between escape and beheading.

Footsteps. A man stepped into view. He was short, dark-skinned, and sported an oily handlebar mustache.

Ornan!

Ben released a lungful of air.

He could strike a deal with Ornan. Ornan understood dollars and cents and the need for discretion. A pragmatic man, Ornan. And Ben had the stone. Ideal leverage for a negotiation.

Ornan studied him intensely. His brow crumpled with concern and determination. He looked almost scared. Then he spoke.

"I wouldn't make any hasty assumptions," he said.

Ben's jaw dropped. Ornan had spoken in a flawless British accent.

"Where is it, Mr. Green?"

"What...?" Ben said, still reeling from the man's perfect Oxford diction. "How...?"

"You took something from my property this morning. It's not in your car. I must have it back immediately. You have no

231

idea what you are dealing with."

"The Stone?" He felt his bargaining position strengthen. The Foundation Stone must be Ornan's star artifact.

"Yes," Ornan said, pointedly. "The Stone."

"I don't have it. But I can help you get it. I can even arrange a sale."

It was Ornan's turn to react with surprise.

"What?"

"Museums will pay millions for the stone. Much more than you'd get on the black market."

Ornan's expression darkened. His face flushed. Surprise turned to disgust. Ben had hit a nerve. Time to crank up the charm.

"That means more money for your cause."

"My cause?"

"You know. Freedom fighting. The Palestinian people."

Ornan turned crab red. His body trembled. His fists clenched. Disgust graduated into full-blown rage.

"We are not *Palestinians*!" A globule of saliva shot from his mouth like a stray bullet. "We are not *Arabs*."

Ben fumbled for a new theory.

MI5? Mossad?

That didn't make sense.

Iranian Revolutionary Guards?

What about Erez and his fundamentalist Christians?

Then it dawned on him. Whatever Ornan's affiliation, he had let down his guard. He was not even trying to hide his identity. This was no gesture of good faith designed to promote cooperation. Kidnappers always hide their identity unless they have nothing to lose, unless they have already decided to kill you.

If Ben was to die, at least he would die knowing the truth.

"Who are you?" he asked.

Mandy stood on the iron-framed bed with the squeaky mattress, but she could not reach the window. It wasn't large enough for an adult to pass through but at least it would give her a peek at the outside world. Maybe tell her where she was.

She might even be able to help Dave.

He was on his way to rescue her.

That much she had learned from the telephone call.

She felt like jumping on the mattress. Not a good idea. She'd probably fall right through. The man called Jay wanted something that Dave had, and Dave was giving it up for her.

The scroll jar.

Mandy pieced the scraps of information together.

The jar must be very valuable. Maybe not just dollar value. Her cloak-wearing captors didn't come across as a rational bunch.

She counted three men: Damian and the two Australians. Jay called the shots. Shortie seemed to fear him. But not Damian.

The keypad beeped six times and the door to her cell opened.

She jumped off the bed and sat down.

A gray cloak entered the room and closed the door. He lifted the hood. *Damian.*

"How are you, Bathsheba?"

Mandy let it slide. Damian was right, she needed friends.

"How does it work?" she said.

"What?"

"Damian and King David. Mandy and Bathsheba. Have we been wandering around the planet for centuries?"

He smiled. "It's more of a soul thing."

"Reincarnation?"

"Yeah. That. We just need to rediscover our true selves."

"Great." Mandy smiled expectantly.

Damian took the bait.

"We're at a critical point in history. The Sons of Light are the world's only hope."

The Sons of Light. What is this dude smoking?

Aloud, she said, "What critical point in history?"

It sounded like a phrase he had heard and repeated.

"You see the news. Tsunamis. Earthquakes. Tornados. Bombings. Mass murders. The world is falling apart. An energy is ripping through the Earth, driving nature wild. A critical point."

"And you're here to save the world?"

"*Heal* the world. To usher in the End of Days. To spread the Light. Teach The Way."

"And then you'll be king again?"

"Yeah. Well, not at first. The Teacher is our leader now. The Teacher of Righteousness. He has shown us The Way. When the world is ready, the Teacher will reveal my true identity."

Mandy held her smile. The End of Days. The gray robes. *These Sons of Light are walking clichés.* "Sounds great. Good luck with that."

He beamed at her. "Good luck to us both."

He placed a wad of folded gray cloth beside her on the bed. It was a cloak.

"Put it on," he said. "Time to meet the others."

Dave shifted down to second gear and accelerated up the steep hill. The sun had dipped below the Judean Mountains ahead and the light was fading fast over the open road.

He'd be home and back in an hour and a quarter, in time for the display of Nigerian acrobats in the hotel lobby and the sing-along of Israeli folk songs in honor of Independence Day.

Shira and their parents had split up to shower and primp for the performance. Dave's absence might not even be noticed.

He redialed Ben's number. Straight to voice mail. Was Ben's phone out of service? He was beginning to worry.

A signpost that marked sea level sped by.

Soon Independence Day celebrations would begin all over the country. Mandy had wanted to celebrate with Dave. Instead she'd spend the night in captivity.

Where was she?

How were they treating her?

There was only one way Dave could help her and by God he would do it.

Sorry, Ben. History and heritage or not, the Stone has to go.

Dave slowed as he approached the floodlit army checkpoint. Then he came to a complete stop.

A large concrete barrier blocked the road.

A bottomless pit opened in Dave's stomach.

What the hell...?

A soldier in a helmet and flak jacket approached Dave's car. A machine gun hung across his torso.

Dave rolled down his window.

"Hi there," he said in English. The Confused Tourist routine had gotten him out of a speeding fine once. It was worth a shot.

The soldier grinned. "Dave?"

Dave tried to place the smudged eyeglasses, dimpled cheeks, and two-day stubble. He drew a blank.

"Moshe," the soldier said. "Moshe Menkes. From the

Gush."

Click.

The gangly American-Israeli with blond hair and Woody Allen glasses had sat two rows ahead of Dave in the yeshiva study hall during Dave's gap-year in Israel.

"Moshe," Dave said. "Sorry. I didn't recognize you. How you doing?"

"Bored. But OK."

"You're still in the army?"

"No. I work at a law firm in Tel Aviv. Got stuck with reserve duty over the long weekend. Major bummer."

"Sorry to hear it. Any chance I can get through?"

"Not unless you have a bulldozer in the trunk. The road is closed over *Yom Ha'azma'ut.*"

Dave indicated the stream of cars traveling in the opposite direction. "What about them?"

"Cars can leave Israel for the Territories. But they can't go back. Not until tomorrow night."

Cement barriers blocked the road shoulder as well. He could make a U-turn through a break in the lane dividers, drive a few meters into oncoming traffic, and then return to his lane.

"Moshe," Dave said. "Maybe you can help me out. It's an emergency."

"I'd like to." Moshe pointed a thumb at the other soldiers. "But orders are orders. Unless you've got a beating heart in a bucket of ice, there's nothing much I can do."

"Got it. I'll head back. Thanks."

He maneuvered the car between the dividers. A bullet in his tires would not help Mandy. Neither would a bullet in his head.

He entered the opposite lane and drove away from Jerusalem. He pulled over and idled in the emergency lane.

He punched the wheel. "Dammit!"

The air-conditioning blew cool despair in his face.

He didn't have a day to spare. He could climb the hill on foot. There were no cars in that direction, let alone cabs, and

Dave had not thought to bring a bottle of water. A long night march was not wise in the rough West Bank outskirts of Jerusalem. Local Bedouin were bound to take an unhealthy interest in a lone, unarmed Jewish hiker.

He tried Ben's number again.

No luck.

"The road is blocked," he said, after the beep. "I'm turning back." His voice messages were a diary of complaints and demands. Soon Ben's voice mail would reach capacity.

He searched for Mandy's number on his phone. Would the man with the cruel voice agree to another delay?

Best not to upset him. He had a short fuse.

Dave needed help.

He scrolled through his list of contacts.

Nat!

Nat cared for Mandy. She could keep a secret. Dave hit Call. He braced for the angry berating he thoroughly deserved.

"This is Nat. I'm abroad for the week, so text me or I'll hear your message when I get back."

"No!"

Dave drummed the wheel like a raging King Kong. He folded his arms over the steering wheel and hid his face. Tears wet his forearms.

Why Mandy?

Damn you, Ben.

Darkness descended on the road.

How could he return to the hotel and pretend all was well. How could he sit through the hotel entertainment and talk of his future with Shira when Mandy sat, for all he knew, in chains?

He had failed her. He had failed himself.

He scrolled down his call history.

An unfamiliar number came into view. The number, technically, should never have been on his phone. He had never dreamed of using it. But now a world of hope squeezed into ten precious digits.

Call it Fate. Call it Cosmic Irony.

Dave selected the number.

He pressed the button.

The number rang.

It answered.

As fast as he could, he said, "Please don't hang up."

Mandy followed Damian down a stone corridor.

No windows.

No sign of the outside world.

His biblical sandals kicked up the hem of the gray cloak.

She had tossed the cloak's hood over her head and she was heating up. Did the others also wear clothes underneath? She hoped never to find out.

The corridor opened into a broad, bare-walled chamber. Three gray cloaks sat around a large wooden table: Jay, the brown man, and a blond balloon of a man with three chins.

The table was set with simple glass tumblers, a glass water pitcher, a tin pot on a trivet, and earthenware bowls. The men slurped soup with plastic spoons.

Jay looked up and swore.

"Brothers," Damian announced with a flourish. "I present to you, Bathsheba. You've met Jay and John. This is Sol."

Sol looked concerned.

"It's OK, Sol," Damian said. "You can speak to her. It's for the holy purpose of welcoming a new member to our clan."

Mandy swallowed. Her appeasement tactic had worked

better than she had intended.

Sol smiled broadly. "Pleased to meet you." He had a Texan drawl. Mandy shook his meaty hand.

"I have gold," he said and winked at her. "Lots of gold."

"And many wives," Damian said. He waved a finger at Sol. He pulled out the chair next to Sol for Mandy, opposite the other two men.

She sat. "King Solomon, right?" she said to Sol.

Sol inclined his head. "At your service, ma'am."

Two kings, two jacks, and a queen. No sign of this Teacher of Righteousness.

Jay glared at Damian.

"Are you insane? You can't just hand out invitations to the *Yachad*."

Damian seated himself at the end of the table between Mandy and Jay.

"Why not?"

Jay gaped like an incredulous fish.

"First off, we're the *Sons* of Light."

"*Children* of Light," Damian corrected. "*Bnei* can mean either *sons* or *children*. We are boys *and* girls."

Damian dished up two bowls of hot soup. He placed one in front of Mandy.

"Strictly vegetarian," he said. "John here is a wizard in the kitchen."

John bowed his head.

"Second of all," Jay said, "rule number four is celibacy. How do you expect us to be celibate with a girl in our ranks?"

Damian blew on a spoonful of soup.

"Use your imagination, Jay. We're doing you a favor. The Teacher won't be overjoyed that you kidnapped her. Lucky for you, God put your stupidity to good use."

"She was supposed to be out of here tomorrow morning," Jay said. "The Teacher didn't have to know."

Supposed to be out of here.

Mandy didn't like the sound of that.

She tasted the soup. A bit heavy on the salt but not bad.

The way the conversation was going, she would need her strength.

"Whatever," Damian said. "Let's just make her comfy and be on our best behavior."

Slurping sounds filled the air.

"Maybe you're right," Jay said. "Destiny brought her to us. But you're wrong about one thing."

"Oh yeah? What?"

"She's not Bathsheba. She's Mary."

Mandy almost sprayed soup out her mouth and over the table.

Jay did not look like he was joking.

"Dream on, Jay," Damian said.

"M is for Mary."

Mandy put two and two together. "You're *Jesus?*"

"See," Jay said. "She gets me already."

Damian winked at Mandy. "Ask him to walk on water. I'd like to see that."

"You will," Jay said. "Right after you learn to play that bloody harp."

King David shot Jesus a venomous glance. "The End of Days is close," he said, meaningfully.

Jesus smoldered, violence simmering beneath the surface. "Judgment Day. The Sons of Darkness will perish."

Silence stretched over the table like a bowstring ready to snap. The Sons of Light teetered on civil war and Mandy sat in the middle.

Then King Solomon spoke. "What's for dessert?"

Jay leaned toward John. "Bring the fruit."

John collected the empty soup bowls.

Here's your chance, Mands.

She lifted the pot off the trivet. None of the men objected. She followed John through a door. The kitchen smelled of kerosene and fried onion. Long stained counters, tired wooden closets, shutters closed. And a back door.

Slip outside. Disappear down the street. This is no place for a sane girl.

She placed the pot on the old gas stove. John lifted a platter of sliced fruit from a counter and Mandy lined up behind him as if to return to the dining room. Then she ran.

The back door opened easily. Hot air hit her face. The frenetic rattle of a generator rang in her ears. Spotlights lighted the skirts of the house. A white van. A dirt road. And beyond the circle of artificial light, darkness.

No houses. No buildings. Only the inky black of a moonless night.

Yellow lights blinked on a distant horizon like the dusty stars above.

Then shapes emerged in the gloom. The rise and fall of sloping dunes. Patches of low scrub. A lunar wilderness.

They were in the middle of the freaking desert!

She stepped off the threshold. Loose stones crunched beneath her sandals. The dirt road climbed into darkness.

Mandy ran blind. After a hundred yards, the voices started. The sounds reached her ears, clear and sharp in the still night air. Heavy feet on gravel. A car door opening and closing. An engine turning and spluttering to life.

Did they have weapons? Mandy hadn't seen any guns. She would make a difficult target in the dark.

Just keep going.

Her eyes adjusted to the night.

Leave the path. Take your chances in the open.

A bright light flickered ahead. It moved.

A flashlight?

Two lights now, two roving lights. And beyond, a dull yellow glow.

A road?

The lights grew larger. Closer.

"Hey," she called. "Over here!"

Had Dave found her?

She waved her arms. The headlights fell on her, blinding her. Wheels locked and skidded over the loose stones. The vehicle halted a few feet from her and kicked up a cloud of dust, the particles gleaming in the harsh beams of light.

Mandy shielded her eyes with her hands.

Then something hard and heavy hit her waist and knocked her to the ground. Wiry arms clamped around her and pinned her down.

She tasted dust. Her body pressed against the rough terrain.

A car door opened. A man stepped in front of the car and blocked the harsh light.

Mandy raised her head and squinted.

The man was not Dave. He wore a long white robe, translucent against the headlights. He raised his arms in a gesture of welcome or forgiveness.

The Teacher spoke. "What the Devil is going on here?"

CHAPTER 12

Early Wednesday morning, Dave said his prayers in the cozy hotel synagogue and hurried to the breakfast buffet.

He had taken his first bite of an omelet with mushroom, cheese, and onion when two girls sat down beside him at the large round table.

He almost choked. "I told you to call me."

Shani swept her blond locks over her shoulder. She wore an orange tank top. Dave felt the glances from the other tables.

"You got us up at the crack of dawn," she said. "You didn't expect us to wait at the bus stop, did you?"

"It's an oven outside," Ruchama added. She eyed Dave's plate.

Dave glanced at the concierge podium that guarded the entrance to the dining hall. Neither Shira nor her parents had surfaced yet.

"Do you have it?" Dave said.

"What kind of an idiot keeps his spare key in the electricity box?" Shani said.

"Where is it?"

"In the lobby."

"In the *lobby*?"

"Calm down, Dave. Nobody's going to swipe your

precious cooler bag."

Dave drew a deep breath.

He had the Stone. Now he must wait for the call. And get rid of some dead weight.

"How did you get in here?"

"I told them we're with you. Don't look at me like that, Dave Schwarz. You owe us. Big time. Breakfast is the least you can do. Now, where is Mandy? And what *grave danger* is she in exactly?"

Shani's sarcastic tone could not conceal the concern in her eyes.

Dave looked at the entrance again. Any minute Shira would walk in. Or worse: Dave's mother.

"Thanks for your help," he said. "I can take it from here."

"Oh no you don't. We're not leaving without her."

"Or without breakfast," Ruchama added.

Shani waved over a waiter and he poured two cups of coffee.

"It's complicated. I'll get Mandy to call you when it's over."

Shani and Ruchama sipped their coffees.

"That's OK." Shani leaned back on the chair. "We have all day."

Dave groaned.

What the hell.

The truth was unbelievable. Maybe they'd write him off as delusional and leave.

"Mandy's been kidnapped."

"Kidnapped?"

"Keep your voice down."

Shani lowered her coffee cup. "What do you mean *kidnapped?*"

"You know my friend Ben Green?"

Blank looks from the girls.

"He's an archeologist at the City of David. He discovered an ancient artifact called the Foundation Stone. It's supposed to have mystical powers."

Shani raised an eyebrow. "The rock in the cooler bag?"

"I told you not to open it. Whatever. Now the bad guys want the Stone and they're holding Mandy until they get it."

Shani looked him square in the eye. "The Bad Guys? Are you high?"

"What? No. I don't know who they are or where. All I know is that they have Mandy and they want the Stone. The guy called from her phone. I heard her voice. He's going to call any minute with instructions. He told me to come alone."

Shani sipped her coffee. "Remind me," she said. "What does this have to do with Mandy?"

"Nothing. She was just in the wrong place at the wrong time."

Shani chewed her lip and eyed Dave with mistrust. "Ruchama. Go get some food. We're not going anywhere."

Ruchama didn't need to be asked twice.

Out of the corner of his eye, Dave saw Steve and Beverly walk into the breakfast hall. Bev scanned the tables and waved at Dave.

"Oh, no," he said.

Shani followed his gaze. "What's the matter, Dave? Afraid to introduce us to your parents?"

"They're not my parents."

Shani's eyes narrowed. Then she smiled. "You. Little. Weasel. You're here with your new girlfriend, aren't you? And these are the in-laws. How sweet."

Dave's stomach did a nauseating double flip.

He should have seen that coming. The streets of Katamon have eyes and ears.

"Shani," he hissed. "Please! I'll get Mandy to call you as soon as it's over."

She leaned back and sipped her coffee.

Bev placed her handbag on the chair opposite Dave. "Good morning, David."

Her eyes moved from Dave to Shani and her sleeveless shirt. Steve waited in line at the latte counter.

"Hi, Mrs. Cohen. This is Shani. An old friend."

"Yeah, we go *way* back," Shani said.

"Oh, really?"

"Remind me, Dave. How did we meet? Oh, I remember. In rehab."

"She's joking," Dave said.

Bev's cheery expression froze. "I'll dish up." She strolled toward the buffet line.

Dave turned to Shani.

"You win," he said. "But you'll have to stay out of sight. Starting now."

Shani grinned.

His phone rang. He showed the display to Shani. It read *Mandy Rosenberg*.

He cleared his throat and answered. "This is Dave."

The cruel voice spoke. "Do you have it?"

Dave glanced at Shani. "Yes."

"Good. Now do exactly as I say."

Ornan paced over the oriental carpet of his office.

The building was old. Very old. Not as ancient as the City of David but old enough to have served twenty generations of his ancestors.

Their portraits lined the walls of his office. Men with noble features and impenetrable gazes. They wore turbans and headdresses. Ornan's grandfather sported a top hat, his father a bowler.

Ornan felt the weight of their legacy. This was no mere tradition. He had inherited a critical mission and secret charge.

His forebears had maneuvered far greater threats in the past and yet the bald archaeologist had penetrated Ornan's defenses deeper than any interloper had in decades.

Small wonder.

Resources had dwindled over the centuries. Weaponry. Bribes. Top-class education. Managing the present and preparing for the future carried a hefty price tag. Ornan had to do more with less. Invest in technology. Invent new revenue streams.

The restaurant had been a mistake. A colossal mistake.

Only once before had the Stone fallen into foreign hands. The recovery had cost much in blood and treasure.

That morning, Ornan had panicked. The anonymous tip to the police had aimed to flush Green out. Put him on the defensive. Separate him from his loot.

Ornan had not expected Ben to track his men to the second stronghold.

Ben Green was tenacious. Determined. Foolhardy.

For his trouble, he had spent the night strapped to a chair in the basement, the key to the Stone still sealed in his head.

Could he be trusted?

Ornan stopped pacing.

He lifted a ceremonial dagger from the wall, the black leather sheath inlaid with rubies and emeralds.

He withdrew the long silver blade. Letters of a covenant etched the surface in an old, forgotten tongue.

Ornan knew what he must do. In a way, he had made his decision yesterday the moment he had confronted his prisoner.

The blade gleamed in the morning light.

Ornan had no other option.

In an IDF tank base along the Jordanian valley, the surveillance operator rested her feet on the desk and waited for her toenails to dry. She closed the bottle of luminous pink polish. The desk chair eased back at a comfortable angle and allowed easy access to the keyboard and joystick.

She had transferred to Intelligence expecting a desk job and flexible hours. She was not disappointed. Usually.

That morning she was supposed to be recovering from an Independence Day hangover with her boyfriend. But high alert for Nakba Day had moved her observation balloon and control caravan to the small tank base near Jericho.

Nakba Day, the Day of the Catastrophe, was the Palestinian answer to Israel's Independence Day. The dubious festival followed the Gregorian calendar, not the Hebrew, and so the disturbances rarely managed to mar the Israeli celebrations.

The operator scanned the monitor for suspicious gatherings or signs of violence.

So far she had tracked three herds of sheep and a broken-down car on the 90.

8 AM. Her boyfriend had promised to visit that morning. He had called at 2 AM, the clink of beer bottles audible over the background beat of trance music. So far, no boyfriend.

Two hours until the end of her shift.

At least she had air-conditioning. The flow of cool air filled the caravan with the scent of nail polish.

She nudged the joystick.

Zoom out.

Road 90 cut along the valley in shades of gray.

Three vehicles moved along the line like ants. No sign of her boyfriend's little white car.

Pan right.

Palm groves. Square houses. A dark patch caught her eye next to the perimeter fence of Jericho.

Zoom in.

A hatchback.

Zoom in.

Israeli license plates.

In Area C.

She moved her feet off the desk and onto her socks and black sneakers and sat up.

She typed the numbers into the computer. After a few seconds the details displayed.

She picked up the green phone.

"This is Osprey," she said. "We have a situation."

Dave's Ford Focus sped along the 90. The road snaked along the valley between the Judean Mountains and the Dead Sea.

Head north, the man had said. I'll call in twenty minutes.

Dave rounded a bend in the snakelike road notorious for high-speed collisions.

Where are you taking us?

"You need gas," Shani said from the passenger seat. Ruchama sat in the back with the orange cooler.

Dave had half a tank but Shani was right. Who knew where the man would lead them.

"We can fill up along the way if we need to," he said.

The car engine groaned as it negotiated a hill.

Shani fished his old map book from the passenger door pocket and turned the pages. Ruchama munched the pastries she had snatched from the buffet.

"This is a bad idea," he said. "He told me to come alone. We're putting Mandy at risk."

Shani emitted a scoffing laugh. "As if you care."

"I do care."

He did care about Mandy. He'd sort out the dissonance later, but at that moment it was true.

"Right," Shani said. "But now she's made you leave your cushy hotel and future in-laws."

"Or saved me from them."

Ruchama chuckled. Dave had an ally on the back seat.

"Please," Shani said with a double dose of scorn. "You're just saving your own ass."

"I didn't mean for this to happen. I didn't want to hurt Mandy."

"Too late for that."

Right again.

Dave *had* hurt Mandy. He had rejected her out of the blue. How was she supposed to make sense of that? And yet, that morning, speeding along the one-lane motorway through semi-wilderness, Dave had no desire to be back at the hotel with his parents. With Shira.

Only one thing really mattered.

Oh, God. What have I done?

A factory for Dead Sea beauty products came into view.

Dave's phone rang on its cradle.

"It's him," Dave said to his passengers. "Keep quiet." He answered. "I just passed the Ahava factory."

"Take the next left. There's a parking lot at the end."

The man hung up.

Dave turned at the next left.

The sign read *Qumran*.

A shiver ran down Dave's spine. A circle was closing. Again, Dave felt like a pawn in a game, the full scope of which was beyond his grasp.

"Qumran," Ruchama said. "That's where they found the Dead Sea Scrolls."

The paved road climbed up a sandy slope, then leveled out and emptied into a circular parking lot filled with tour buses and cars.

"At least it's a public place," Shani said. "We'll be able to blend in."

"Blend in?" he said. "You stay in the car. I trade the Stone for Mandy. We leave. Got it?"

"You expect us to just sit here?"

"He told me to come alone. Don't screw this up."

Dave reversed the car into a spot between an Egged Tours bus and an old station wagon.

Time to set things right.

He left the keys in the ignition and the air-conditioning on. He got out, opened the back door, and got in beside Ruchama. He removed the white lid of the cooler bag and slid out the metallic box.

He drew a deep breath. "I'll be right back."

He tucked the tin under his arm and walked toward the clump of low buildings. A sign in three languages pointed arrows in the direction of a sound-and-light show, an excursion, a tourist shop, and restrooms.

He paused at a corridor filled with men and women, mostly gray of hair and wearing walking clothes, cameras, and sunhats. Many had necklaces with crucifix pendants. Tour guides bellowed explanations in heavy Israeli accents. None of them gave Dave a second look.

No sign of Mandy.

He called her number.

Voice mail.

OK. Let's play hide and seek.

Dave entered the souvenir store. Posters and carvings covered the walls. Jesus on a cross. Jesus with arms extended. Jesus with a halo. Baby Jesus in his mother's arms.

Stacks of glossy books covered the low display tables. Secrets of the Dead Sea Scrolls. The Dead Sea Scroll Conspiracy. Jesus in the Dead Sea Scrolls.

"Jesus," Dave said, under his breath.

The magnetic pull of the scrolls reached further than he'd imagined.

He stepped deeper into the store. Merchandise filled the shelves. Scroll jars, large and small, of pottery and even plastic.

He picked one up with his free hand. Tapered body. Pointed cap. Pockmarked surface. An exact replica of the jar in his car. Except for the three letters.

From the corner of his eye, Dave saw a head of auburn curls. A woman in the crowd. She walked past the shop, beyond the checkout tills, and disappeared behind the wall.

Dave's heart galloped.

He flanked the line of shoppers.

"Hey," a middle-aged American woman said. "Can't you see there's a line?" She eyed the box under Dave's arm.

"I'm not buying anything," he said.

Dave squeezed past and rushed out the door.

Tourists choked the cobbled street. Some waited below a WC sign. Dave rose to the tips of his toes and peered over their heads. Far ahead, the auburn girl turned a corner. A man walked at her side, an arm wrapped around her waist.

"Excuse me," Dave said. "Sorry. Coming through." He parted the crowd, jostled a few elderly tourists, and rounded the corner.

A quiet alley between the buildings, off the designated path. Beyond it lay desert dunes and wadis carved by long forgotten rain and the whispering wilderness breeze below clear azure skies.

A door slammed.

He continued along the walkway, staying close to the brick wall. His shoes scraped over the sandy floor. The dry air smelled of dust.

Another short alley to his right ended in a rough paved opening.

Along the side of the building, wooden packing crates warped in the sun on raised platforms beside service entrances. The rectangular air-conditioning units on the walls rattled loudly.

The delivery yard contained a single vehicle: an old white van. Dave stepped past the crates toward the van. The windows were tinted black.

He tried the handle.

The door opened. The interior had two low benches, a spare tire, and a pile of auburn hair.

A swish of movement behind Dave.

He turned. Something hard connected with the side of his face and floored him. The metal tin clanged to the ground and he watched it roll away, spinning on its rim.

A voice swore. A cruel voice.

The shadow of a man stood over Dave. The sun sparkled around the long hair of his head like a halo. Another, shorter man stepped up beside him.

"Dave, Dave, Dave," the kidnapper said. "'Am I disappointed in you."

Shani shifted on the passenger seat.

The digital clock on the dashboard read 10:02 AM. Dave had left the car twenty minutes ago.

Where is he?

If Dave had let anything happen to Mandy...

She balled her hands into fists.

"Five more minutes," she said aloud. "Five more and we follow."

She climbed over the gear stick and into the driver's seat. Just in case they needed a fast getaway.

"He loves her," Ruchama said, apropos nothing. She had devoured her takeaways and fallen into a thoughtful silence.

"Who?"

"Dave. He still loves Mandy."

"Please."

"He's here, no? He could have stayed in the hotel."

Shani sighed. "If Dave had loved Mandy, he wouldn't have dumped her. He's just covering his tracks. He doesn't want a scene with an old flame to upset his new girlfriend."

The car purred. Shani turned the vent and cool air blew on her face. Ruchama rapped her fingers on the lid of the cooler.

"Maybe he wants a second chance?"

"There are no second chances, Roo."

Shani stopped herself in time. She knew about second chances.

That was a long time ago. She had been young and naïve. It had kicked off a chain of events that had made her who she was today. But she was not going into that, not even with Ruchama.

Her phone rang. She snatched it up.

"Dave? Where are you?"

Silence.

"Hi," Dave said. "I need help."

"Is Mandy OK?"

Another pause.

"Can you come?"

"We're on our way."

"One more thing," Dave said. "Bring the cooler bag."

The keypad beeped six times and the door to Mandy's cell clicked open.

Mandy sat up on the stiff bed.

Since the previous night, she had had little interaction with the Sons of Light. She had heard a commotion of footsteps and angry voices beyond the door.

Heads would roll for her near escape. Or for taking her hostage in the first place. The Sons of Light made for one seriously dysfunctional family.

But, if what she had learned was true, she had cause for hope.

Dave was on his way. Had he negotiated her release already?

Damian stood in the doorway with a tray.

Not yet.

John had delivered her breakfast that morning. He had let her out for a short bathroom break and watched her eat without a word. Mandy had a better chance of squeezing information out of Damian.

That would prove easier than she had expected.

Damian walked up to her.

"Everything will be OK," he whispered.

He placed the tray beside her on the bed.

A few slices of whole-wheat bread, an apple, and a tumbler of milky water.

He hovered over her.

"I'll have a word with the Teacher," he said. "When things calm down."

"What about Dave?"

"Shh."

He placed a finger over his lips. He winked at her, pulled the hood over his head, and left the room.

The Teacher.

Mandy had hoped for a responsible adult and a fast track to freedom. Her hopes faded by the hour. With his white robes and graying goatee, the so-called Teacher of Righteousness seemed as delusional and unpredictable as the rest.

She ate her lunch.

One full day in prison. Would her flatmates worry about her yet? It *was* Independence Day. They wouldn't make anything of it until Sunday.

It didn't matter.

Dave was sure to rescue her by then.

They'd have one great story for their grandkids.

Six beeps and the heavy door clicked open again.

That was quick.

The man at the door pulled back his hood. It was Jay.

"G'day, Mary," he said. "Fancy some company?"

Mandy shuddered. She had feared this might happen. Jay would not be as subtle or hesitant as Damian.

But he didn't have romance on his mind. He pushed two figures wrapped in gray cloaks into the room and they sprawled on the floor.

He leered at Mandy before closing the door.

The figures wallowed and groaned, trying and failing to get up.

Mandy rushed to the nearest. Duct tape bound the wrists. She sat the figure up and pulled back the hood.

Mandy recoiled in shock.

She pulled back the hood of the other figure.

"Shani," she said. "Ruchama. What are you doing here?"

The Teacher of Righteousness arranged the documents in a row on the wooden desk.

Five paper rectangles. Five texts of varying size. Five windows on the future.

One scroll.

One Truth.

He had printed two off the Internet. Three he had acquired and scanned.

Number six still eluded him.

Jay had sworn to produce the final piece today, yet the sun had started to fall and the Teacher waited still.

Jay had shown promise. He had produced two jars. He had joined the Sons of Light, converted to The Way. But his zeal was a pile of gunpowder, and yesterday Jay had lit the fuse. He had ignored the Teacher's warnings. He had kidnapped a girl and brought her into the heart of the *Yachad*. He had fired a flare into the night sky and shattered the dome of invisibility the Teacher had worked so hard to construct.

Within twenty-four hours, his star disciple had become a liability.

If Jay kept his promise, none of this would matter. The Sons of Light would outlive their utility. The Teacher would seize the prize and shed his followers and their failings along with his white cloak.

There came a knock at the door.

He collected the papers together and shoved them into a drawer of the desk.

"Enter," he said.

Jay stood in the doorway. He smiled obsequiously. He held a large, orange box.

Was this some kind of joke?

"I have it," Jay said. "*We* have it." He placed the box on the desk with pride. He was panting.

"Good," the Teacher said. "Leave us."

Jay's smile dropped. He made no move to leave. He had more news and the Teacher would not like it.

"And?"

"Schwarz," Jay said. "I told him to come alone but he brought two girls."

"What of it?"

"Well…" Jay chuckled reflexively. "We got them too."

"What?"

"They saw us. And the jar. I couldn't let them go blabbing. I put them with Mandy for now."

The Teacher cleared his throat. "Now we have three prisoners?"

"Well. Four. We have Schwarz as well."

The Teacher inhaled long and deep. Four prisoners. One for each disciple.

"We'll deal with the Sons of Darkness later," he said. "Now let me be."

Jay hurried out the room and closed the door.

The Sons of Darkness. The Teacher smiled at the neatness of it all.

He pulled the lid off the box and peered inside. The jar lay on a bed of bubble wrap. The Teacher did not stand on ceremony. He extracted the jar, cleared the desktop of the box, and spread the bubble wrap on the table. From a drawer of the desk, he withdrew a hammer and rubber gloves.

He took a few moments to admire the jar and its inscription. Then he steadied the jar on the desk and brought the hammer down.

"These guys are crazy," Mandy told her flatmates, now her cell mates. "Certifiable. They all think they're biblical characters. King David. King Solomon. The one who brought you in thinks he's Jesus Christ."

Shani shook her head. She sat next to Ruchama on the

hard bed. "Jerusalem Syndrome. Happens to tourists all the time. The Kfar Shaul psychiatric hospital is full of them."

"*Our* King David?" Ruchama asked.

"Yeah," Mandy said. "But I wouldn't call him that, if I were you. He might fall in love. They've got their own weird religion. They call themselves the Sons of Light. And they're supposed to be celibate. I think they're vegan too. They're looking for a jar connected to the Dead Sea Scrolls. Don't ask me why."

The company of her friends gave Mandy a boost of energy and she almost forgot that she was a prisoner. Told this way, her story sounded like an adventure. It would have a happy ending.

"A scroll jar?" Shani said. "Dave said they were after a magic stone."

"Dave? You spoke to Dave?"

"Who do you think got us into this mess?"

Shani told her about Dave's phone call and their trip to Qumran.

"I told you there was more going on," she said. "Dave got into trouble with the Sons of Light. That's why he had to break up with me."

Shani and Ruchama exchanged glances. Ruchama looked at the floor.

"What?"

"Mands," Shani said. "Dave wasn't trying to protect you. He really has a new girlfriend."

"Come on, Shani."

"I'm serious. She was with Dave at the Crowne Plaza. Her parents too. We met them. And Dave was not happy to have us around."

Mandy felt the energy drain out her legs. This was Dave breaking up with her all over again.

"But he's coming to rescue us."

Shani shook her head.

"Don't count on it. He led us into their trap. The *meshugenas* got what they wanted. We haven't seen him since. He probably traded us for a few camels. For all we know he's on his way back to the hotel and his new girl."

Ruchama nodded.

It was true.

Dave had another girl. He was not riding to her rescue. Dave was... not who she thought he was.

Mandy broke into sobs. Her chest trembled. Tears burned tracks down her cheeks. Her friends embraced her on either side.

"I've been such a fool."

"It's not your fault."

"I can't believe it."

"Shh. It'll be OK."

She wiped at her tears. Things were not OK. She had followed Dave into hell and dragged her friends after.

"How are we going to get out of here?"

"We'll think of something. If they're as crazy as you say, they'll mess up."

The keypad beeped again. The door unlocked.

Jay had returned. Another cloak-wrapped figure tumbled into the holding cell and the door closed.

Shani stepped over to the writhing heap and pulled back the hood.

Dave Schwarz had joined the party.

The Teacher looked up from the desk. Before him lay the scroll in its entirety, the five pieces united for the first time in two thousand years. He had deciphered the final passage.

Laid bare its secrets.

I should have guessed. The solution was brilliant. Where else to hide such a trove?

Act now. While you can.

The Teacher sent a text message from his phone. He collected the sheets of paper and stowed them in the drawer along with the chunks of shattered pottery. He tucked the copper square into his canvas shoulder bag.

There was a knock at the door. Jay stood at attention.

"Gather the troops," the Teacher said. "We leave in five minutes. Bring all your equipment. Be ready for the unexpected."

Jay's eyes widened with lust but he hesitated. "Teacher," he said. "What about the Sons of Darkness? They could... get in our way."

They had discussed this before. The Teacher had accommodated Jay's requests for exotic supplies but he drew the line at weaponry. Jay was the sort of man to use it.

"Not by might," the Teacher quoted. "Nor by power, but by My Spirit, said the Lord of Hosts."

Jay's chest rose and fell. The Teacher had stretched his patience again. The anticipation made it hard for him to restrain his passions. *Careful now. You still need him.*

"But to be safe," the Teacher added, "tell John to stay behind and guard the prisoners."

Jay made to protest but the Teacher raised his hand.

"Hurry now. Your birthright awaits."

Jay nodded and fled the chamber. *So easily prodded.* Pity the fool.

The Teacher fished a small key from his pocket and unlocked the bottom drawer. A silver pistol lay among a clump of loose bullets. He lifted the pistol, unhinged the barrel, and inserted the silver slugs. He slipped the weapon into his shoulder bag. *Just in case.*

He was right to separate the two friends. A mutiny at this point would be fatal, although, by the night's end, the Sons of Light would cease to exist.

The End of Days. Irony curled the edges of his lips.

He looked about the chamber for the last time. The orange box caught his eye. He lifted the lid. A silvery glint. The other object in the cooler still sat in bubble wrap. The Teacher picked up the cylinder and pried the lid open.

A black stone, polished to perfection. The Teacher's face stared back. The stone seemed to hum pleasantly. It begged to be held.

"Hello," said the Teacher. "What do we have here?"

Dave squirmed on the hard floor. His arms ached.

He had lain in darkness, his wrists bound behind his back, his mouth sealed with tape, his head covered by a rough hood, for what seemed an eternity. Then the men had hauled him out of the van, up steps, and through a corridor.

Shani looked down at him.

"Hm-hrr-mm," he said. I'm sorry.

Shani made no effort to untie him. She looked at him as if he was a bug stuck to the underside of her shoe.

He wasn't getting his message across.

He struggled against the thick duct tape.

No luck.

He rolled onto his side, kicked his legs, stuck his elbow into the ground, and achieved a sitting position. A second figure approached him, Ruchama, and pulled the tape from his mouth.

"Ouch," he said. Then, "Thanks."

She got to work on his hands. A spiral fluorescent on the

wall cast a yellow glow over the stark room, which contained two steel-framed cots and...

Mandy!

Dave staggered to his feet.

"Thank God you're all right."

She glanced sideways at him. She had been crying.

"Keep your distance," Shani said. "If you know what's good for you."

Fear gripped Dave from head to toe.

If those bastards had hurt her in any way...

"Is she... Did they hurt her?"

"*They* haven't hurt her," Shani said. "But I told her the truth."

"What truth?"

Shani rolled her eyes. "About your girlfriend."

He breathed a sigh of relief.

Mandy was unharmed. That's what mattered. She might hate him. He deserved that. He could live with that. And he had a lifetime to make it up to her. He would need it. But the cruel man and his accomplices had not laid a hand on her.

Thank the Good Lord.

The road ahead was clear. The insight that had quickened in the tunnel below the City of David had stirred again on the road to Qumran. On the dark, hot floor of the van, the conviction had burst into the world.

There's nothing so powerful as a man who knows what he wants.

Dave knew what he wanted.

"Mandy," he said. "I can explain."

Mandy turned to face the wall.

Shani folded her arms. "This'll be good."

"Shani, stay out of this."

"I'd love to." Shani spread her arms indicating the prison cell. "But here I am. Thanks to you."

"I had no choice. They had seen you and they wanted the scroll jar. It was the only way to get Mandy back."

Mandy blew her nose and ignored him.

Shani had turned her against him. He didn't blame Shani, either. He'd have to work hard to earn back their trust.

He could start by setting them free.

There came the sound of beeping and the shifting of bolts. He turned toward the door.

The cruel man stood in the doorway. He slapped the cricket bat on the palm of his hand and smiled.

Dave could run at him, knock him down. But the memory of the bat still stung the side of his head. And behind the man stood others.

"You," the man said. He pointed the bat at Mandy. "Come with me."

Mandy glanced at Dave and made for the door.

"Mandy, no!"

But it was too late. Mandy had walked through the doorway.

"What do you want with her?"

The man winked at Dave. "Just a little insurance. Be good and she'll be home and hosed before you know it."

CHAPTER 13

The shift manager at the Crowne Plaza had looked forward to a quiet evening.

Hotel occupancy had dipped, the Israelis preferring the wild parties of Tel Aviv to mud massages and sulfur springs on Independence Day.

That suited him well.

The all-nighter also provided a convenient escape from the annual *Nakba* get-together at his in-laws', who seized every opportunity to mourn the existence of the Jewish State, the source of their gainful employment, health insurance, child stipends, and all other worldly evils.

He closed the door of his office, poured himself a generous serving of Johnnie Walker from the bottle he stashed in the desk drawer, and eased back on the padded leather armchair.

He breathed in the heady scent of Scottish *aqua vitae*. The second sip was always more palatable than the first, the third even more so.

He aimed the remote at the flat-screen television and flipped channels.

The Jerry Springer Show had just started.

His favorite.

He joined in the war cry: *Jer-ry. Jer-ry. Jer-ry.*

There was a knock at the door.

He slipped the whisky glass out of sight and muted the screen.

A head with close-cropped hair poked through the crack of the door.

"Excuse me, sir," the boy said in Arabic. "A woman at the desk demands to see you."

The desk hand, an eager lad from Jericho, was two days on the job and his English lacked polish. Probably a minor misunderstanding.

The manager sighed. "I'll be there right away. And next time use the phone. Understand?"

"Yes, sir."

He gargled Listerine and spat into the basin. He donned a new dress shirt, his uniform suit jacket, and tie in front of the full-length mirror. He paused at the door and sent a longing glance at the television.

A well-preserved, petite woman waited at the hotel desk, her hand on the counter, as alert as a terrier. The hangdog man at her side was the husband. Both wore serious expressions.

"Yes, madam?" said the manager in English. He applied his welcoming smile. "How may I assist you?"

"My son is missing," the woman said, with the irritation of one who has had to repeat the words countless times. "He was staying with us at your hotel."

Your hotel.

She meant trouble.

Guests never ceased to amaze the manager. They ordered freely from the pool restaurant but always reacted with surprise to the checkout bill. They let their kids roam wild and, when their precious progeny stubbed a toe, they blamed the hotel management.

Sometimes he felt like a schoolmaster.

The woman's blond hair stuck out like long, thin daggers.

He adjusted his expression to concern laced with polite skepticism.

"And how old is your son, madam?"

"Thirty."

"Oh." This would be simpler than he thought. He may still make the end of Jerry Springer.

"He was supposed to meet us for tennis at eleven. That was nine hours ago."

"And when did you see him last?"

"He was last seen at breakfast."

"You were not with him?"

"Friends of ours saw him at breakfast this morning," she said. "He was with two *young women*."

Her tone indicated her disapproval for the girls and implied that the manager was somehow responsible.

The manager hid his smile beneath the well-practiced veneer of cheerful hospitality.

"Could that explain his disappearance? He is no doubt an independent young man. Perhaps he made plans with his new friends and forgot to tell you?"

The woman's face reddened and her mouth gave a twist.

Her husband cleared his throat. "We don't think so." He lowered his voice. "You see"—he glanced at the nametag—"Muhammad, the friends who saw David are the parents of his girlfriend, practically his fiancée. They're also staying here."

"Ah, I see." Muhammad forced his lips together.

Step aside, Jerry Springer.

"Well?" the woman demanded. Her manicured fingernails rapped the marble countertop. "What are you going to do?"

"What am I going to do?"

"Yes. Before I call the police."

He thought of the whisky bottle in his drawer and coughed.

"There is no need for the police, madam. Not until twenty-four hours have passed. Only then will your son be considered a Missing Person."

"But what if he's been abducted?"

"I beg your pardon?"

"Kidnapped," she said. "By terrorists."

She gave him a meaningful look. By *terrorists* she had meant *Arabs*.

He took no offense. His brother-in-law, Id, was a card-carrying member of Hamas. After transporting a trunkload of explosive belts across the Green Line, he had won full board and lodging at an Israeli prison. Muhammad didn't hold it against the authorities. At least in prison Id had earned a B.A. in International Relations via the Open University.

He steered the conversation toward more practical measures.

"Have you checked his room?"

"The door is locked and his phone is off."

"I see."

Muhammad had a theory about the boy's disappearance.

"Your last name, madam?"

"Schwarz."

He tapped the computer keyboard. He found the room number for David Schwarz and configured an electronic key card.

"This way, madam," he said. "I think we can… put this mystery to bed."

Sometimes, Muhammad thought, *I really love this job.*

Jay shadowed the white Subaru down the dark valley road. The Teacher had completed the puzzle. Only time separated the Sons of Light from their treasure. Jay's treasure. Jay's destiny.

Pity that John was going to miss the historic moment. *Teacher knows best.* Jay wished he could ride with the Teacher instead of his fellow Sons of Light.

"We should have left her at the *Yachad*," King David, or *the Harper* as Jay preferred to think of him, said. He had moped in the passenger seat the whole way.

In the rearview mirror, King Solomon wore his ridiculous cowboy hat and stared out the window. Beside him sat the girl, her wrists taped, her eyes lowered, resigned to their company.

"She has no business coming along," the Harper whined.

"Shut ya gate," Jay said.

The road was quiet. A few cars passed in the opposite direction, their headlights like fiery eyes in the night. One car followed far behind.

"It could be dangerous."

"I'm the only danger you should worry about right now, so shut it. Remember your vow of silence."

That shut him up. For three whole seconds.

"Ooh-ooh," he said. "I'm so scared."

"Goodo."

"One day you'll regret talking to me like that."

Jay let it slide. *Don't let him ruin the moment.* He had tried forgiveness, turning the other cheek. A second slap didn't sting any less. When the Teacher revealed Jay's true colors, Jay would change the rules.

Not long now.

"Cheer up," Jay said. "She can help us dig."

"Very funny. Your future queen isn't going to dig holes."

Future queen?

Where did the Harper get his loony ideas? He made a mediocre foot soldier. Now he was starting to annoy. Good thing Jay had brought the girl. That would keep the Harper on his best behavior.

The Harper turned in his seat. "Don't worry," he told the girl. "You won't do any digging. When I'm king again, and you're my queen, you'll have servants and castles. You won't have to lift a finger, unless it's to flip Jay off."

"Whoa," Jay said. "What did you say?"

The Harper straightened. "Nothing. Forget it."

"When you're king? When *you're* king?"

Jay strangled the rubber steering wheel.

"I told you you shouldn't talk like that to me. I'll remember."

Jay was not letting *that* slide. "Why do you think you'll be king?"

"I wasn't supposed to tell you. I have to be invisible. Until the time is right."

Invisible.

The Teacher's word.

Jay swore quietly.

He felt like stopping the van and braining the ning-nong on the sidewalk, but the Subaru hurtled on and he had no idea where it led.

"Just keep quiet and do your job," he said. He ran his tongue over his incisors and pumped the accelerator. *And when the time comes,* he thought, *when you least expect it, I'll do mine.*

Dave pressed his ear to the iron door of the holding cell.

Silence.

"They've gone," he said.

He had heard two engines start up and drive off.

He lowered his body to a bed and held his head in his hands.

"Where are they taking her?" Ruchama said. The question

was on all their minds.

Dave had seen the hurt in Mandy's eyes as she had left the room. It no longer mattered whether she was his First Coupling or Second, or whether the Foundation Stone had magical powers. Even if Dave could save her from her kidnappers, the result remained the same.

Dave had lost her.

Forever.

He would marry Shira. Within a decade, he would turn into his father. He didn't want that. Not after he had tasted a life with Mandy.

All his days, he'd chased the dream of perfection only to attain nothing.

"This is all your fault," Shani said.

"I know."

"You really screwed things up."

He nodded, his face still buried in his hands.

"You made every possible mistake."

Ruchama exhaled the contents of her lungs. "And she still loves you."

The words took a moment to sink in.

Dave raised his head.

"What did you say?"

"You're to blame," Shani said.

"I got that bit." He turned to Ruchama. "What did you say?"

Ruchama looked from Dave to Shani and back.

"She still loves you," she said. "Don't you see?"

The four words kept Dave above water.

"She does?"

He turned to Shani. Of all people, Shan would not bullshit him.

Her jaw tensed. "She'll get over it."

That was all he needed.

Warmth spread through his body.

"Well, don't just sit there hugging your arms," Ruchama said. "Do something."

Dave sprang to his feet.

Mandy loved him. She needed him, now more than ever. He had to get out of the cell.

He sized up the room. The window was too high and small to squeeze through.

Think, Dave, think!

Prisoners escaped all the time. Dave needed a sharp implement, a large poster of Audrey Hepburn, and six months.

He had none of those.

But if the house was deserted, he didn't need them.

He walked to the end of the cell and flattened his back against the wall. He had never kicked down a door before.

There's a first time for everything, Dave.

He bolted across the room and threw his full weight at the iron door. Pain needled through his shoulder and he crumpled to the floor. He got up and caressed his injured arm.

The iron door hadn't budged.

He studied the keypad beside the door.

"I don't suppose you know the code or part of it."

"It has six digits," Shani said.

Six digits. Ten keys. Dave did a quick calculation.

"That's a million possible combinations."

What the hell.

Dave entered one through six. An angry red light flared. He tried the reverse. Six ones. Six sixes. Odd numbers. Even numbers. Prime numbers. Fibonacci.

The red light blinked.

He needed more data.

"What do we know about these guys?" he said.

"Nut cases," Shani said. "One thinks he's King David. The meanie thinks he's Jesus Christ. They run a cult called the Sons of Light."

Dave tried all sixes, sevens, and eights. He tried six-thirteen and twelve, and combinations of the two.

"What else?"

"That's it," Shani said. "What do they want with the scroll

jars?"

"The Copper Scroll. The jars were discovered in the same cave as the Copper Scroll, a list of buried treasures worth a billion dollars."

Shani whistled.

"Each jar has an inscription with three letters: Tsadi. Dalet. Qof."

"Zedek," Shani said.

"Is that the code?" Ruchama asked.

"What do you mean?" Dave said.

"You know," Shani said. "*Gematria.*"

Gematria. Why hadn't he thought of that?

Each letter of the Hebrew alphabet had a symbolic numeric value. Bible commentaries wove reams of esoteric conclusions based on these number games.

It was worth a shot.

He thought aloud.

"Tsadi is ninety. Plus four for Dalet and Qof is a hundred. One hundred ninety-four."

He entered one-nine-four twice.

The red light blinked again.

"Dammit."

"Break it open. Hold the wires together," Ruchama suggested.

"That could put the damn thing out of order," Shani said. "And we'll be stuck here for a lot longer."

The voice of Kermit the Frog echoed in Dave's brain.

Break this for me, Dave.

The keypad expanded until it seemed to fill his mind. He felt the pull of destiny. His years of hi-tech experience were part of a cosmic plan that converged on this moment.

"I've got an idea," he said. "I test software for a living. Bugs always slip into products. Maybe we can open it even without the combination."

Shani mulled this over. "Like a back door?"

"Exactly."

He flexed his fingers. He rubbed them together.

"Come on," he whispered. "Don't let me down."

Then he shoved his fingers into the keypad. He wriggled them and moved them around, pressing keys together.

Dave prayed. He made a wish. He held his breath.

The little red light flared once more and went dark.

"There goes that," Shani said.

Ruchama dropped to her knees. "We're never going to get out. We're going to die here."

"No one's going to die here, Roo. They can't keep us in here forever."

"Oh, yeah? What about those kids they kept in a basement for thirty years?" Ruchama inhaled sharply. "It's just as well. No one will marry me anyway."

"Roo—"

"I'm fat and ugly."

Shani joined her friend on the floor. "Don't say that. Every pot has a lid."

"Maybe I'm a frying pan!" Ruchama wailed.

Shani shot Dave an urgent look that was both a plea and a threat.

He knelt on one knee. "You'll be OK, Ruchama. Look at me. I thought I had dated every single Jewish girl in the world. I had just turned thirty. I was hopeless. Then, out of nowhere, I met Mandy and everything changed. She didn't match my grocery list. In some ways she was the opposite of what I thought I wanted. But she made me feel alive and loved. And it scared the crap out of me. So I messed it up. And here I am."

Dave doubted that his words had consoled her, but she stopped crying. Shani stared at him, her mouth slightly open.

Behind him, the door beeped six times and the bolts shifted.

John frowned at them from the doorway. So, Dave thought, the house wasn't empty, after all. John had probably come over to tell them to keep it down.

Instead, he said, "Come on, you lot." He indicated for them to follow with a flick of his head.

"Where are we going?"

The brown man shrugged. "Wherever you like," he said. "I won't stop you."

❧

The van sped through the night.

Mandy sat in the back, her hands and mouth covered in tape. Occasionally, the headlights of a passing car lit the interior and faded.

The Sons of Light had traded their cloaks for jeans and T-shirts. King Solomon filled the two seats beside her, his breaths deep and slow. Damian and Jay sat in the front. Vaguely she heard them argue.

She didn't care.

Dave had a girlfriend. He went away with her for the weekend. He'd met her parents.

How long had he led this double life? How had she been so blind?

Mandy was glad to be out of the prison house, and to put some space between her and Dave.

Better to have loved and lost, they said. She was not convinced. Even if you wanted to die? Even if you could never love again?

The Teacher's car made a sharp right and they followed. The road climbed and leveled out. Then the vehicles stopped. A gate blocked the way. The sign read *Qumran*.

Jay got out. He opened the back of the van, rummaged among the tools, and walked to the gate carrying a double-handed chain cutter.

A metal chain clinked and the gates swung open.

He returned to the driver's seat and the convoy plowed on. The circular parking lot was empty except for a single white hatchback.

Dave's car.

The car had featured prominently in their relationship. Dates started and ended in that car. It had witnessed their endless talk of dreams and plans. The back seat had played a key part in Mandy's fantasies. The scent of the upholstery and purr of the engine were forever bound to Dave.

Tonight, in the abandoned parking lot, the car looked alone and lost.

Jay parked beside the Teacher's car at the edge of the clump of low, dark buildings.

The men got out.

King David opened the door at the back of the van.

"Don't worry," he whispered. "I'll keep an eye on you."

He helped her out of the van.

Flashlights sprung to life and danced over the terrain.

The Teacher strode ahead. He wore a deerstalker on his head, loose trousers, and a button-down shirt. He held a shoulder bag close to his side. He bypassed the buildings and sidewalk, and struck out into the wilderness.

Sol followed wearing an oversized cowboy hat and shouldering a heavy-looking black duffel bag.

Jay strapped a second bag to his back, then shined a light in Mandy's eyes. He gestured with a steel shovel.

"After you, chook," he said. "I'm right behind you."

Mandy kept up with Damian.

A thin sickle moon hung in the sky. The air was dry and still. She could run but she wouldn't get far. Rocks and crevices waited to trip her up or send her off hidden cliffs. Jay followed close behind, metal shovel at the ready. And Mandy had no energy for an escape.

The Teacher stepped over a low wall of old square rocks. Damian helped her over, no easy task in a denim skirt and with her hands tied.

The crumbling foundations of houses and rooms emerged in the gloom. People had lived here once. Now only ruins marked the spot.

The Teacher turned from the structures and stepped down a gentle slope. The field before them filled with row upon neat row of low stone mounds, the work of a hundred giant gophers.

The Teacher paused to consult a folded piece of paper with his flashlight.

Was he lost?

What in God's name did he expect to find in this wilderness desolation?

The Teacher directed a beam of light over the mound at the end of a row and marched on. The Sons of Light followed.

"Here." He panted quietly. "This is it."

The men dropped their duffel bags on the ground, opened the zippers, and handed out shovels.

A shiver ran down Mandy's spine. This was no field. They stood in a graveyard.

The men removed the stones and dug into the earth.

Mandy stepped backward, beyond the graves, and kneeled, then sat, on the flinty ground.

The rows of silent mounds waited patiently beneath the stars and hid their secrets. There were easily over a thousand graves.

She preferred her prison cell.

Let them find whatever they're looking for fast so we can leave this place.

It was hard to believe that the Sons of Light would find anything of value.

The diggers stood waist deep in the dirt. Jay removed his shirt. His body gleamed in the moonlight, all sinew and muscle.

"We got somethin'." Sol grabbed a flashlight and dropped out of sight. "There's a shelf on the side and—*ah!*" the big man shrieked.

"What is it?" the Teacher demanded.

"Any gold?" Damian asked.

Sol surfaced, pale in the torchlight. "There's a skeleton down here."

"What did you expect, genius?" Jay said.

"Keep going." The Teacher returned to his resting spot on the next mound.

He looked Mandy over, his hand inside the shoulder bag. Mandy avoided his gaze and studied the stones on the ground.

The crunch and scrape of digging filled the night air.

Then a shovel hit solid rock.

The Teacher sprang to his feet.

Jay scraped the dirt aside. "It's a floor."

The Teacher aimed his flashlight into the hole. "Or a door. Find the edges."

Mandy struggled to her feet. Her left leg had gone to sleep so she limped to the edge of the hole.

A long smooth slab of stone emerged from the grime, three large angular letters etched in the surface.

"Yes," the Teacher said, urging them on. "Yes!"

The men worked faster, widening the hole around the white rectangle.

"My sons," he said. "We've waited two thousand years for this moment."

He rummaged in the equipment bags and lowered two crowbars into the pit.

Jay, Damian, and Sol leaned on the crowbars. The stone slab shifted and rose. With a great deal of effort, the men stood the slab on its side.

The Sons of Light looked at each other with ecstatic smiles. Sol and Damian exchanged a high-five.

A staircase, chiseled in stone, descended into darkness.

"Down the rabbit hole we go," the Teacher said. He dangled his legs over the edge, slid into the hole, and led the way. Sol and Damian followed.

Jay dragged his duffel bag to the edge of the open grave.

He turned to Mandy and held out his hand.
He grinned. "Ladies first."

"I'm sorry," John told Dave, Shani, and Ruchama. "I never meant for any of this to happen."

They sat at a long dinner table of unpolished wood, decked with plastic plates of chocolate wafers and glasses of water.

Dave didn't touch the food.

Was this a trap?

"Where have they taken Mandy?" he asked.

John shrugged.

"I dunno. They're going after the treasure."

"What treasure?" said Shani.

John raised a sarcastic eyebrow. "According to the Teacher, the first Sons of Light hid a huge stash of gold and silver. He said the scroll jars would lead us to it. Then we'd bring the End of Days, yada yada yada."

"The Copper Scroll," Dave said.

Shani picked up a wafer. "And you're letting us go because..."

John's chest heaved. "I've known Jay since kindy. We've done some crazy shit but I draw the line at kidnapping. We're in enough trouble back home."

Dave wasn't sure he wanted to know about the trouble back home.

"And where is home?" Shani asked.

"Christchurch." John gave a wry smile.

Dave looked at Shani and Ruchama.

New Zealand. That explained the accent.

John, the Maori, looked miserable.

"I thought it was a phase, you know? His way of dealing. But now he's a sandwich short of a picnic." He sighed again. "Anyway, better chow down and move on. Can't say when they'll be back. They took the rust-buckets. The main road is ten minutes by foot." He stood. "Here's your phone, Dave. You'll be wanting the rest of your stuff."

John led them to a square room that contained a wooden desk and little else. "Teacher's office," he said. "We weren't allowed in much."

On a set of shelves, they found the two girls' phones.

Shani picked up a handbag. "This is Mandy's."

John's pals still had her. To find her, Dave would have to find them. A layer of fine dust covered the desk and the floor around it.

He stepped behind the desk and opened the drawers.

A pile of printer paper. Sharpened pencils. Ballpoint pens. Harmless enough. A hammer and heavy rubber gloves. He opened the third drawer.

Hello.

"I don't believe it." Dave picked up a large shard of broken pottery. Three characters were etched into the surface.

"Your scroll jar?" Shani said.

"What's left of it."

He remembered the reverence Ben had lavished on the urn in his living room.

Why would the Teacher destroy the jar?

Professor Barkley had talked of extremists who wanted to wipe out evidence of a precursor to Jesus Christ.

"John," Dave said. "Did the Teacher talk of Christianity, or of Jesus in the Dead Sea Scrolls?"

John shrugged. "No. He went on about The Way. Modesty. Silence. Cleanliness. The war against the Sons of Darkness at the End of Days. And he had a rat about the jars. The jars are the key to the treasure."

Dave arranged the pottery fragments on the desktop. A jigsaw puzzle of a thousand pieces and countless particles of dust. Even if he put the jar together again, what then?

Start at the edges.

Two pieces stood out. Large and round, they had formed the base of the jar. Dave slid one over the other.

A perfect fit. Almost perfect. A gap remained between the pieces. Dave turned them over. Red pigment stained the inner surfaces. Tiny lines and ridges rose and met. The answer sparked in his head.

"Look! Something was baked into the clay. There's writing. Not very legible and probably inverted. No wonder no one ever found the treasure. The Copper Scroll was incomplete."

Shani double-checked the drawers and peeked under the desk. "Nothing here. They must have taken it."

"Dammit."

Ruchama took the pottery circles from Dave and squinted at them. "It looks like Hebrew. But I can't read it. Too much noise."

Dave groaned. They were so close. There had to be a way.

He opened the top drawer and grabbed a piece of paper and a pencil. He laid the clay circle on the desk, flat side down. Then he covered it with the sheet of paper.

"What are you doing?" Shani asked.

Dave picked up the pencil.

"We did this in art class at primary school."

He held the side of the pencil nib close to the page and shaded over the inner plane of the pottery.

"We used coins," he said. "But any raised surface will do. The lead catches the raised bits and brings out the impressions."

Lines emerged beneath the pencil and combined. Soon two rows of Hebrew letters appeared on the page.

Shani and Ruchama looked over Dave's shoulder.

"Yeru," Dave read. "Yerushalem."

"Jerusalem," Shani said.

"De," Dave continued. "De-ta-ta."

Ruchama wrinkled her nose. "Yerushalayim de-ta-ta?"

Dave knew that one from the Talmud. "That's Aramaic. It means *below*. The Jerusalem Below."

Mishi's words rang in Dave's ears, words he had heard late one Friday night deep in the halls of Me'ah She'arim.

World Above. World Below. Move Below, move Above.

Was there a Jerusalem Above and a Jerusalem Below?

Dave read on. He had to skip a few illegible words. "Kav...Kav-ra-ya."

"*Kevarot?*" Ruchama suggested. "*Bet Kevarot?*"

"Cemetery," Shani translated.

Dave read the last word. "De-mad-ba-ra."

Shani pieced it together. "*Midbar* is desert. The desert cemetery."

"That's it," Dave said. "I know where they've gone. Let's go."

"Crikey," John said, incredulous. "You're going after them?"

"They've got Mandy," Dave said. "It's the only way."

"You could just wait here," John suggested. "I doubt they'll actually find anything. You can dong 'em when they get back."

John had a point.

"I think it's time we called the cops," Shani said.

"Shh," Ruchama said. "Do you hear that?"

Dave did.

A soft thud. From inside the building.

Dave had not heard cars outside.

Had someone else stayed behind?

The door swung open.

First, Dave saw the guns, the long nozzles of machine guns. Two heavy-set men in army fatigues burst into the room. A smaller man entered after them. He waved a black handgun at them.

"Hands in the air," Ornan said. "Now."

CHAPTER 14

Jay swung his legs into the old grave.

It's happening.

His dreams grew flesh and sinew before his eyes. With one exception. In his dreams Jay led the way. He did not bring up the rear. A lot can change in an hour.

When I am king...

The Harper's words buzzed in Jay's ear.

Another of the Harper's delusions? Or was the Teacher...? Had the Teacher...?

Impossible.

Scheme all you like, Harper. Even without John at his side, Jay would swat the tinpot king like a fly.

Jay hefted the duffel bag onto his shoulder and descended step by step.

Keep 'em where you can see 'em.

The girl's hair burned copper under his flashlight. If Jay slipped, he'd take the others down like dominos. The thought made him smile.

Far beneath the girl, the roving flashlights winked out.

"Oy!" he told the girl. "Keep it going."

The girl didn't reply. He didn't expect her to. Jay had taped her mouth and wrists himself. Good thing he had bought an insurance policy. By the end of the night he might have to cash her in.

Personally, he preferred the blond, a real hard case with her kicking and clawing, but she'd come round once his pockets filled with gold.

The stairs ended. A round tunnel bored through the rock. A few meters in, the walls fell away.

"Stone the crows," he gasped.

His flashlight beamed into the void but found no end to the darkness. Three stone steps led down to a dirt floor. The light rays of the other three men sliced through the black like lasers and pooled on the cave floor.

Jay sniffed the air. A familiar, heady scent. The smell of danger.

A fire ignited and blinded Jay for a second. Sol held a short, steel pole above his cowboy hat. The bundled rag at the end blazed with blue flame. A tin of methylated spirits sat open at his feet, where the Harper kneeled and dipped a second rag into the liquid. Sol waddled to the wall of the cave and slipped the torch into a blackened sconce chiseled into the rock.

Jay dropped his bag beside its twin and assembled another flaming torch. Within minutes, a dozen small fires lined the walls and the shadows receded. The cavern was the size and shape of an ice rink. Stalactites reached down high overhead.

Structures of varying shapes and sizes littered the floor: waist-high buildings with flat roofs, buttressed walls and towers, bridges over winding ditches. A hill rose at the back of the cave. Upon it, a square edifice, larger than the other features, commanded the miniature city, with a tall column on either side of its black rectangular mouth.

The Teacher darted between the city's features; a light-footed giant, muttering and laughing.

He turned to the Sons of Light.

"My sons." The ecstasy echoed in his voice and off the walls of the cave. He spread his arms. "Welcome to Jerusalem Below."

He pointed at the bridge over a winding trench.

"Behold the Valley of Akhor. Seventeen talents of silver under the steps. One hundred gold bars in the tomb."

He skipped toward a squat, round tower and rested his hand on the flat roof.

"Kohlit. Fourteen talents of silver in the pillar. Fifty-five in the canal."

He made an arc with his outstretched arm. "Behold Milkham. Sekhakha. Bet Shem. And of course"—he pointed at the large square building at the back of the cave—"the great Temple Below."

Jay had never heard the Teacher laugh, but now he laughed long and hard. The show of unbridled joy whispered doubts in Jay's ear.

Just how well do you know your Supreme Leader?

"Where do we start?" he asked.

The Teacher sobered. He clapped his hands together. "With the gold, shall we?"

"Gold!" Sol leaned forward on his feet like a rabid dog pulling on his leash.

The Teacher pulled a sheet of paper from his shoulder bag, unfolded it, and studied the contents.

"David." He tapped the edge of a domed building with his shoe. "Start digging here."

The Harper, who had hovered beside the girl, grabbed a shovel and scampered toward the building.

"Jay." The Teacher scraped at the dirt beside a bridge. "Ex marks the spot."

Then he trotted to another low structure and measured three paces from the wall. "Sol, this one is yours."

"And the girl?" Jay said. "Might as well lend a hand." He gave the Harper a meaningful look.

That'll show the ning-nong.

The Teacher ran a hand over his goatee. His other hand slid into his shoulder bag.

"The girl, yes."

The Harper opened his mouth to object.

"She will assist me," the Teacher said. "Hurry along, and

bring one of those black bags, won't you?" The Teacher and the girl set out across the miniature landscape.

Jay lifted his shovel and broke the ground. Not his intended result but he had given the Harper a taste of the Kiwi clobbering machine.

The sound of shifting earth echoed through the cave.

If the Harper gave any trouble, Jay would bury him here. A tomb fit for a king.

A short sprint away, Sol took off his cowboy hat and pulled his shirt over his head. The wife-beater underneath was already stained with sweat. He put his hat on and got back to work.

Jay shoveled dirt over his shoulder.

You'll do great things, his mother's voice said.

The events of his life had seemed haphazard. Random. But now he saw the hand of Providence. His mother's prophecy. Her loving hands in his hair. Coming home one day after school, finding her on the couch, surrounded by empty bottles, drowned in her own vomit. The Nazareth-House Orphanage. The man on the cross above his bed. Meeting John. Climbing together. Stealing together. Dropping out. Odd jobs. Burglaries. Stairdancing. A brush with the law. Going legit.

The big bickies came from pushing Queenstown tourists off bridges. Until that kid from Utah had stretched out his arms like the man on the cross and stepped off the ledge. Jay had checked the rope. Twice. The kid could have died. But he never woke up either. It wouldn't have been such a big deal if Jay and John had done the paperwork and gotten a permit.

Then came the signs. The voices. Wherever he turned, he saw Jerusalem. Newspaper articles. Television. Snatches of conversation on the street. Jay found a worn NIV Holy Bible in a box of his mother's things. He read in bed and mulled over the words late into the night.

Jerusalem called. Only there would he claim his destiny. Only there would he learn to wake the living dead.

One afternoon, as he chewed an egg sandwich over the

Gospel of Luke, the earth shook. He ran into the street. The buildings of Christchurch collapsed around him, and he danced. The time had come.

Jay looked up from his trench and wiped sweat from his brow. The Teacher stood at the entrance to the Temple Below at the back of the cave. He had tied the girl's hands to a stone loop above the doorway. She hung by her arms like a skinned sheep, her shirt hitching above the waistline, her shoes barely scraping the ground. Then the Teacher disappeared into the dark mouth of the Temple.

Jay's heart skipped a beat.

Where is he going?

He shook the suspicion from his head. The Teacher had led him this far. He put his shoulder into the task at hand. The pile of earth grew.

Everything happens for a reason.

The setbacks. The suffering. Even the mistakes. They were God's way of reminding Jay who he was. And, slowly, he had remembered. He and John crammed their worldly possessions into two hiking packs. They jumped bail and boarded an Air New Zealand flight.

The rest was history. *His* story. A new gospel. In school and church, children would memorize his words. The story, like any, had peaks and gullies. With each clod of earth, the climax drew nearer.

His shovel hit stone. He looked around. No one else had heard the scrape. He dropped to his knees and cleared the dirt. A flat, white circle. Too flat for bedrock. He found the edges. A stone box with a sunken lid.

"Hey," Sol called out. "I got somethin'."

Jay stepped out of his trench and ran over to the big man. The Harper joined them. A round clay surface stuck out of the ground. They worked together with their shovels. An urn emerged, double the size of the scroll jars. Sol scooped up the jar like a baby. His flabby arms deceived; the man could flip an ox like an omelet.

"It's heavy." Sol gave it a shake. Jay heard nothing. "Must

be jammed full."

"Open it," Jay said.

"The Teacher—"

"The Teacher's busy. Open the damn thing."

Sol placed the urn on its base and tried the rounded lid.

"It's stuck."

Jay ran to the duffel bag for the hammer and chisel.

The lid cracked on the first blow. Jay pulled out the fragments. The urn was packed with dirt. He chiseled out clods and spread them on the ground. No flicker of gold or silver. Just brown dirt, dry as bone.

"To hell with it," Jay said. He kicked the urn over and cracked the side open. More dirt. He gutted the jar with the shovel like a trout and spread the insides.

"Nothin'," Sol said. "Nothin' but dirt."

"Over there," Jay said. "I hit something hard. Harper, bring the crowbar."

He marched to his trench. Sol followed. The Harper sulked but did as he was told. Jay shoved the crowbar into the gap between the box and lid. A few hammer blows and the edge went in. Sol leaned on the rod and the lid gave way.

They stared into a box of brown sand.

Jay dug with his hands. He shoveled without mercy. He threw the shovel aside.

"What the...?"

Someone had gotten there before them.

But who?

He turned on the Harper. "You! What's the big idea?"

The twat reeled.

"What do you mean?"

"Did you know there's nothing here? Does the Teacher know?"

"What? No! Of course not. What are you, crazy? We came here to *get* the treasure."

"Don't call me crazy," Jay said. "You think you're the bloody Messiah."

The Harper gave him a cold, hard look. "*You* think you're

the Messiah."

"Yeah, well, I hear things. I see things. You don't know your arse from your elbow."

The Harper opened his mouth to reply but froze.

Jay heard the tinkle too. Behind them, pebbles tumbled.

Jay held a finger to his lips and pointed to the black mouth of the tunnel.

The thieves return to the scene of the crime, he thought.

With a sudden, clear intuition, he knew both who the intruders were and what he must do. He mimed instructions to the others, grabbed his shovel, and took position.

Welcome, Sons of Darkness. You're right on time.

⁓

In the Teacher's office, Dave raised his hands above his head. Shani, Ruchama, and John did the same.

Ornan aimed the gun at Dave's chest.

"They're unarmed." Ornan spoke loudly and without shifting his gaze.

Who is he talking to? Wait a minute. Is that an English accent?

Dave thought the situation had maxed out its bizarre factor, when a fourth man entered the room. He wore shorts, a T-shirt, and a City of David cap.

Dave's jaw dropped. "Ben! What...? How...?"

Ben raised his cell phone. "I got your messages. All eleven of them. A bit late, I know, but earlier I was... ah... a bit tied up."

Ben indicated John with a nod of his head.

"He the one behind this?"

"No," Dave said. "That's John. He used to work for them but now he set us free. They call themselves the Sons of Light. They left about an hour ago. They took Mandy."

Ben touched Ornan on the shoulder and Ornan lowered his weapon. The other two gunmen, the usher from the City of David restaurant and another brawny dark man, did the same. They wore the splotchy camouflage uniforms of a military unit but with no identifying symbols.

Ben read Dave's thoughts.

"Ornan's with us," he said. "Or rather, we're with him. I'll explain later." Ben smiled at the girls. "Shani and Ruchama, I presume. I've heard so much about you."

"And you must be Ben," Shani said.

Ben eyed the desk. "May I?"

He lifted the larger shards of pottery.

Dave explained. "I think I know why they wanted the scroll jars. Each jar contained another part of the Copper Scroll."

It felt strange to be a step ahead of Ben for once.

Ben grunted. He did not seem all that impressed.

"They took the fragment but we managed to read the imprint it left on the clay. We think it leads to—"

"The cemetery at Qumran?" Ben said.

Dave's jaw dropped a second time. "Yes. How did you...?"

"The stone," Ben said. "Is it here?"

Ben had told Ornan about his booty. *Is he on drugs? What the hell is going on here?* Dave studied his friend's face for clues.

"It was in the cooler with the scroll jar." He pointed.

Ben spotted the orange box beside the desk and lifted the lid. He turned to Ornan. "They must have taken it. We have to move fast."

"We're coming too," Shani said.

"It's dangerous," Ben said.

"They've got Mandy. And we can help."

Ben and Ornan exchanged a glance.

Ornan shrugged.

"Ready?" Ben said.

"How did you find us?" Dave sat with Ben, John, and the girls in the back of Ornan's A-Team van. Ornan and his men sat up front.

After a quick search of the compound, they had tied John's hands with rope and taken him along. *Just a precaution,* Ornan had said.

The van rose and fell over the bumps of the Jordan Valley road as it shuttled through the night.

"Ornan has some nifty equipment," Ben said. "As soon as you turned on your phone, he triangulated the coordinates. This is the only building for miles. Tell me about the Sons of Light."

Dave explained in broad strokes. Shani and Ruchama added the details they had learned from Mandy.

Ben spoke with a calm and modesty bordering on meekness. This was not the Ben he'd parted with outside the COD. But then, Dave supposed, he had changed too.

"The Sons of Light appear in the Dead Sea Scrolls," Ben said. "So does the Teacher of Righteousness."

"But the scrolls are two thousand years old," Dave said. "Have the Sons of Light been running around since then?"

"Unlikely. Translations of the scrolls are readily available. Perfect fodder for Jerusalem Syndromes. But these days, I suppose"—Ben glanced at the driver's compartment—"anything is possible. But why speculate. John, who is this Teacher of Righteousness?"

"Dunno. Jay found him on the Internet. An ad on Janglo was looking for the Pure of Heart to claim their Hidden Treasure. Had us chasing after the jars." John's silhouette shifted on the seat. "Sorry about your head. I tried to stop him, honest."

"Dave, did you get a look at the Teacher?"

Dave knew what Ben was thinking: was Erez moonlighting as the cult leader?

"No," he said.

Shani said, "What's the deal with the stone?"

Ben peered at the men in the front seat and said nothing.

"The magical Foundation Stone?" Shani continued, knee deep in sarcasm. "Dave already told us that much. Is it for real?"

"I told her not to open the box," Dave said.

Ben sighed from deep within his chest. "The Drinking Stone. The source of the watery depths beneath the Temple. Also known as the Weaving Stone. The point where God first wove Heaven and Earth. The doorway between the two. Wise use can effect change in the Spirit World. Overexposure drives men insane. In the wrong hands, the stone could unravel the fabric of time and space."

"*Ima'leh*," said Ruchama fearfully. The word literally meant mommy. "We sat next to it all day."

"I wouldn't worry too much. You probably won't turn into frogs. I'm sure it's just an old volcanic rock with unusual magnetic properties. Either way, Ornan wants it back and the Sons of Light might not be happy about that. They'll be disappointed as it is."

"Disappointed?" Dave said. "Because the treasure is a hoax?"

"Because the gold and silver are long gone. Dug up and spent years ago."

"Dug up? By who?"

Dave was sure a billion-dollar treasure would have made the evening news.

"Long story. But if the Sons of Light are banking on the treasure for their End of Days, they'll be desperate."

Dave swallowed hard. He had experienced their rough handling when they weren't desperate. Good thing Ornan's gang packed serious firepower. They would need it.

The van turned off the road, climbed a small hill, and passed through open gates.

Qumran.

In the front seat, Ornan's men loaded their machine guns.

Dave had not thought he would return to Qumran so soon. The dark, deserted tourist trap glowed in the moonlight and shed its daytime aura of safety and security.

Dave's car sat where he had left it. Two white vehicles parked nearby: the Hyundai van and an old Subaru. Both were empty.

"John," Ben said. "You'll have to wait here. Shani, Ruchama, you too."

"No way," Shani said. "Not until we see Mandy safe and sound."

Ben didn't argue.

Ornan led the way. He flanked the buildings, stepped over a low wall, and marched through the stony wilderness. Over the fall of the hill, the cemetery stretched out, its rows of neat cairns quiet and peaceful.

The quiet before the storm.

Ornan stopped at the edge of the third row.

The marker stones of the outer grave lay scattered beside a mound of dirt. Someone had dug deep into the earth. Ornan crouched and listened at the edge of the hole.

"They must still be inside," he whispered. He turned on a small but powerful flashlight. It illuminated a square frame of white stone three feet down and then stairs descended out of view. "Stay close. And no talking from here on."

One-by-one, Ornan and his men slipped feet-first into the hole.

"No." Ruchama shook her head. "I can't."

"Here." Ben handed her a flashlight. "Give us some light. Make sure nobody shuts the door."

Ruchama took the flashlight gratefully.

Ben disappeared into the hole.

"Don't worry," Dave told Ruchama. "We'll be right back."

His voice sounded calm and collected. Maybe it would reassure him too.

He sat on the ground and dangled his legs into the hole. His shoes found the edge of the frame. Digging his palms into the dirt, he lowered his body until he felt the first foothold.

The steps were narrow and slippery. Ruchama's yellow

beam flashed over the sides of the hole. On a shelf six feet under, a skull grinned at Dave through broken yellow teeth. He shuddered but made no sound.

You just climbed into an open grave in the middle of the night on the heels of a violent and delusional cult.

The things he did for love.

Love. That's what this was. Or stupidity. Dave saw no other explanation. He might not find Mandy. She might not want him back. For his trouble, his only reward might be a bullet in the head. But he kept going. He had tasted single-minded purpose. There was no other way to live.

Shani blocked the flashlight above and the flickers of light below faded. Dave steadied himself against the cold stone walls and felt his way, one step at a time.

The ground flattened into a tunnel. A circle of soft, wavering light surrounded the shapes of Ornan and his men. They crouched, guns at the ready, and peered into the opening. He looked over Ben's shoulder. Buildings, walls, and bridges filled the scene, and he felt as though he was sitting at the window seat of a landing airplane.

Over the breathing sounds of the men in the tunnel, Dave heard the billowing of flames. The pungent smell of alcohol invaded his nostrils.

What is this place?

And where are the Sons of Light?

A muffled whimper drew his attention. At the back of the cave, between the two pillars of a square building, a girl dangled uncomfortably by her arms like a dragon's offering.

Dave squeezed Ben's shoulder and pointed. He fought the urge to charge into the light and shout her name.

Mandy's shoulders burned. She struggled to keep her toes on the threshold. The Teacher had looped the thin rope through the tape that bound her wrists, pulling upward and pressing the tape into her flesh.

Then he'd scurried through the doorway behind her and she no longer heard his footfalls. At the other end of the cave, the three men dug furiously.

Mandy could handle the physical discomfort. What hurt more was the lack of hope.

Nobody's coming to save you, Mands.

Dave had a new girlfriend. Shani and Roo had tried to rescue her and failed, and all three sat, helpless, behind locked doors.

Mandy knew that hollow feeling well.

"Don't worry," her father had said from his hospital bed. A thin tube ran beneath his nostrils. Liquid dripped in a plastic IV bag. "I'll beat this. I promise. I'll be home by Chanukah."

Mandy had believed him. Her father had conquered Kilimanjaro. He had swum with tiger sharks in Mozambique. Next summer, they would finally fly to Israel together and follow in the steps of Father Abraham and King David.

He had probably believed it too.

Chanukah came and went and the doctors no longer smiled. The bad cells had spread. By the time the first flowers bloomed, she and her mom stood beside a hole in the ground and listened to the sad chant of the rabbi. Mandy was fourteen years old.

Movement in the cave interrupted her reverie. Jay and Damian ran over to Sol and the three men huddled together, talking excitedly.

She didn't care about their treasure. She wanted to go home. But where was home? Her tiny room on Mendele Street? Her studio on the Upper West Side? Her mom had sold their house after the funeral but Mandy could still picture her bedroom. Pink frills. Posters of winged fairies and unicorns. A part of her had never left that room. A part of her was still fourteen years old.

So that's why I'm still single.

Mandy had searched for her father in the eyes and smiles of young Jewish men and none of them had measured up. None could. But she had caught a glimpse of her father in Dave.

Heroes are dead.

She shifted her weight onto her other foot. Flakes of stone rained on her head. She looked up. The Teacher had looped the rope through a circular outcrop of stone. Strands of fiber stuck out of the rope like the feelers of an insect. Mandy leaned to one side. The rope chafed against the rough stone surface, and more strands popped.

Her heart quickened in her chest.

Heroes are dead, Mands. You'll just have to save yourself.

She seesawed her arms, pulling down on the rope, tiptoeing on one foot then the other. Her eyes stayed on her captors. The men argued inaudibly but never looked her way.

A low wall snaked away below her.

Cut the rope. Dive behind the wall. Crawl to the tunnel.

Not much of a plan but it would have to do.

Mandy looked up. The frayed ends formed bushes around the gash.

Just a bit more.

Mandy stepped up the pace of her straightjacket aerobics. She panted through her nostrils. Sweat trickled down her temples.

The three men stopped arguing and moved quickly. Mandy froze. The Sons of Light grabbed their shovels and ran for the exit.

Were they leaving without her?

But the men stopped short of the tunnel. They stood on either side of the black mouth, their backs to the wall, shovels raised like baseball bats.

A beam of light flickered in the tunnel then shut out.

Someone was coming!

But who? The tunnel was too dark to make anything out.

Her chest almost burst with anticipation. In her mind, the vision of one man rode to her rescue.

Could it be?

But if it was him, he was about to walk into a trap. And Mandy was the bait.

She squirmed against the ropes. The strip of tape still sealed her mouth shut. She had to warn him.

At the edge of the tunnel, Jay turned his head. He looked straight at her. Then he smiled that terrible smile and placed a finger over his lips.

The Teacher thumbed on his flashlight. The flat, chiseled corridor stretched into inky blackness like a mine shaft. The air was still and stale. Water dripped somewhere deep within. He advanced with care, examining the smooth, rock walls for crevices and clues.

The Copper Scroll did not specify the location of this particular treasure, but the mini Temple was the obvious choice.

Again his free hand wandered into his shoulder bag and caressed the cool surface. He found the stone strangely reassuring.

You are on the right path, it seemed to whisper.

With each step he journeyed deeper within the rock wall of the cave, toward the heart of the miniature Temple; the Holy of Holies, the sanctuary that had housed the object of his desire for millennia.

The passageway widened sharply. The Teacher followed

the wall. The beam of his flashlight fell over relief images and animated them: winged creatures with the heads of lions, eagles, bulls, and men.

Cherubs.

Goosebumps broke out over his arms and legs. He had felt the same tingle of discovery a year before in the bowels of the Hebrew University.

"You've got an hour," the clerk said and ushered him into the archive room. The small room contained a worktable and wheeled stools. A single object sat on the steel tabletop: a weathered clay jar.

"There must be some mistake," he said. "I was told I could view the scroll fragments of Cave Three."

"This is all that was authorized," the clerk said and closed the door behind him.

He approached the table. He lifted the lid of the jar. Months of tiresome bureaucracy and all they had granted him was a single, empty jar. Their arrogance knew no limits.

The mute jar mocked him. He lifted the clay vessel and ran a finger over the three letters etched in the pockmarked surface.

Then he let go. Shards of two-thousand-year-old pottery scattered over the tiled floor.

Next time they'll think twice before—

He paused, mid-thought. A sliver of metal glinted amid the ruins.

He lifted the cracked base of the round jar and crumbled the patina of clay with his fingers. A square of copper, the surface covered with tiny, deliberate markings. He drank the letters thirstily. Then he tucked the lost scroll into his shirt and, without a word, he left the campus.

The voices of the Sons of Light echoed from the cave.

Let them squabble over gold and silver.

The Teacher's treasure far out-valued anything so base.

A shaft of stone bridged the chamber ahead. Wisps of gossamer fabric hinted at embroidered curtains that had once divided the Temple into chambers.

He scanned the darkness with his flashlight. A glimmer of white stone. A raised square twenty feet ahead. And a familiar shape.

The Teacher strode toward it. His foot slipped downward. He faltered, but regained his balance. He aimed the light at the floor.

A fissure cut across the chamber and snaked up the walls on either side. Where his shoe had scraped the edge, bits of earth rolled and fell. He leaned over the rim. The gaping hole swallowed the beam of his flashlight.

Fault lines crisscrossed the Jordan Rift Valley. Their tremors and earthquakes had left scars but they had failed to destroy Jerusalem Below.

Too wide to jump; no way around.

But the Teacher had an idea.

He doubled back. At the end of the tunnel, the girl remained where he had left her. He had taken a liking to their hostage and felt a pang of regret to see her suspended by her arms. The bundle of rope lay at her feet.

The girl startled at his sudden reappearance.

"Apologies, my dear," he said. "I just need..."

Across the mini city, the Sons of Light flanked the black opening of the entrance tunnel, Jay and Sol on the left, Damian to the right, their shovels raised over their heads, ready to strike.

"What the Devil...?"

His breath caught in his throat.

Three men in army fatigues rushed out of the tunnel. The first wielded a handgun, the other two held machine guns.

Jay and Sol clunked their shovels hard on the heads of the machine gunners. Damian swung at the third. The handgun flew through the air. The gunman fell backward and clutched his arm. The other two intruders lay motionless on the ground.

Damian raised the shovel over the wounded man. "Who are you?" he shouted.

"Are they cops?" Sol asked.

Jay disentangled a machine gun. "Sons of Light. Meet the Sons of Darkness." He pulled back the bolt of the weapon and metal parts clanked. "Let the End of Days begin."

It happened fast and while Dave was distracted.

Ornan raised his hand, a signal for Ben, Dave, and Shani to wait. Then Ornan and his men filed out the tunnel.

Mandy dangled in the distance, a silver strip of tape over her mouth. A man had materialized beside her. He wore a gray hunting cap and goatee.

Erez?

Hard to tell from far away and in poor light.

Dave cringed.

Thump! Thump! Clang!

Three men with spades stood where Ornan and company had walked moments ago. Their backs faced the tunnel. The big one wore a cowboy hat and a sweaty undershirt. The second had red hair. The third man stood naked from the waist up. Dave recognized the long, greasy hair and wiry build.

Ornan had walked into a trap.

"Who are you?" the redhead said. King David, Dave guessed. Panic made his voice shrill.

"Now," Shani hissed at his neck. "Before they get the guns. Go!"

"Go where?" he hissed back.

What exactly did Shani expect him to do against a mob of lunatics?

"Are they cops?" the cowboy said.

"Sons of Light," said the man with the cruel voice, the kidnapper and self-proclaimed Jesus Christ, "meet the Sons of Darkness."

A metal mechanism clanked noisily, the sound of a machine gun preparing to fire. "Let the End of Days begin."

So much for "before they get the guns."

Dave stared at the yellow portal, frozen. Across the room, Gray Man lowered Mandy's arms and pulled her into the building like a spider retreating into a hole.

The Teacher of Righteousness.

Shani gave Dave a shove. "We can surprise them."

"She's right," Ben whispered. "It's our only chance. But we have to do it together."

Dave's eyes refused to leave the empty doorway where Mandy had stood. He tried to move but his limbs had turned to jelly.

The moment surged. The universe listened. A window had opened. Any instant, it would close. Dave knew the sensation well. All his life, he had looked on as critical moments like this passed from the world, never to return.

"Dave?" Ben's voice was faint and far away.

Jesus waved the machine gun in the air and laughed.

A shot of indignation coursed through Dave's veins. At Jay for dragging Mandy into this. At his own history of inaction. It was risky. It might fail.

It's our only chance.

"Dave!"

"I'm in." The sound of his own voice woke him from his trance. He took charge. "Ben, you take the big one. Shani, get King David." Dave balled his hands into fists. "Leave Jesus to me."

For a microsecond Dave's brain considered the words— bizarre on so many levels.

Ben touched his shoulder. "Time to get your girl."

"Ready? Set. Go!"

Ben leapt forward. Dave followed. Out the hole. Down

three steps. A shovel lay on the ground behind Jesus. Dave made for it, turning sharply and hurdling one of Ornan's men.

Ben charged at King Solomon and roared. The Sons of Light turned toward the sound of Ben's battle cry.

Dave grasped the shovel.

Ben collided with the fat man, ramming his shoulder into the cowboy's belly in a fierce rugby tackle.

Dave brought the shovel down as hard as he could on the greasy head of Jesus.

Then the room exploded.

Dave ducked. Bullets ricocheted, pelting the dirt floor and chipping clumps of rock off the walls.

The gunfire cut out. Dave's ears rang. The acrid stench of gunpowder filled his nostrils. Clouds of dust rose around him. Dave patted down his body. As far as he could tell he was unhurt. He breathed in short, quick gasps. His hands trembled.

The dust settled. Jesus lay on his back, eyes closed. Dave saw no sign of bullet wounds. The clank of shovel on skull echoed in his memory and sent a shiver down his spine.

God, I think I killed him. I killed a man with a spade. A bad man. A very bad man. But still.

Dave picked up the machine gun. It was heavier than it looked. He had never held a gun before. He brushed off the dust.

"Ow!" The barrel burned his fingertips.

King David waved his shovel at Shani like a lion tamer. His eyes moved from the pile of Jesus to the machine gun in Dave's hands. The king dropped his shovel and put his hands in the air.

"Don't shoot," he said. "I'm cool. Just don't hurt me. OK?"

Dave straightened. It felt good to be on the right side of a machine gun for once.

A groan. Ornan lay on his side and supported his right arm with his left.

"Tie them up." He winced. "I think the fool broke my arm."

"There's rope in the bag," King David said helpfully. "And tape."

"I'll get it." Shani darted to a large black duffel bag.

Dave lowered the machine gun nozzle to his captive's feet.

"On the ground," Shani told the redhead king. "Hands behind your back."

Ornan's men lay motionless on the ground.

Are they alive? How do you check for a pulse?

And Mandy! The Teacher still has Mandy.

"Ben?" Dave called. He glanced around. "Ben!"

A hand stuck out of the ground. "I'm all right." A head followed the hand and Ben climbed out of the pit. He dusted off his clothes. "Big guy broke my fall. He's taking a nap. Whoa, Dave. Easy with that thing."

Dave exhaled. He wanted to hug his burly friend.

Ben scooped up the cowboy hat, shook it off, and put it on his head. "What do you think?"

"Perfect. Now, Indy"—he winked—"let's get my girl."

"The stone," Ornan said. "Get the stone. The Teacher must have it."

Ben turned to King David. "Is this Teacher of yours armed?"

King David lifted his chin off the ground to speak. "No."

"They went in there." Dave pointed at the building at the back of the room.

Ben drew a deep breath and nodded. "Let's go."

"Not so fast," a cruel voice said.

Dave spun around.

Shani stood awkwardly on her feet. An arm locked her neck and a grimy hand pulled back on her forehead. Over her shoulder, Jesus snarled.

"Drop it," he said. "Now."

The Teacher marched Mandy down a long, dark passage. A string of loud noises erupted behind them, the nerve-grinding rattle of a jackhammer. Or a machine gun.

The Sons of Light had floored the intruders and seized their weapons. By the sound of it, they were not afraid to use them either.

Mandy had never really feared the Sons of Light. They were a quirky bunch. Misguided. At times comical. As soon as they got what they wanted, they would let her go. Unharmed. That's what she had thought. Until now.

Delusions were one thing; murder was a different ball game altogether. Their skeleton closet grew darker and deeper by the minute.

The Teacher scanned the stone floor with his flashlight and pushed ahead. He seemed as eager as Mandy to get away from his disciples.

Maybe you're not so crazy after all.

He had cut the rope that held her arms above the doorway and pulled her inside, but tape still bound her wrists and sealed her mouth.

Mandy sighed at her own naivety. She had half expected Dave to jump out the tunnel to her rescue.

Thank God he had not.

The uniformed intruders, whoever they were, could not help her now either.

The Teacher halted. A loud plastic click echoed off unseen walls. The light blinked out, and a fluorescent bar flickered to life in his hand.

They stood in the middle of a tall, wide chamber. Winged creatures watched them from the walls in the pale electric light. The jagged edge of a deep crevasse blocked their path.

The Teacher placed the light on the floor and fumbled with a black grapple hook and a bundle of thick cord.

Muffled voices drifted from the outer cave. One of them sounded like Dave.

Dream on, Mands.

She had last seen Dave in a holding cell along with Shani and Ruchama. He had tried to explain and make things right. She should have given him the chance. Dave wasn't perfect— understatement of the decade—but thanks to him, Mandy had felt love. A hot, burning, blind love. She had found her faith. She had believed in someone again even if he had turned out to be a two-timing jerk. Or was he?

Dave *had* stuck his neck out for her. What had he tried to tell her?

I've got to call for help. If I get out of this alive.

"Yes!" the Teacher muttered excitedly. The metal hook wobbled at the end of the rope.

The Teacher swung the rope like a lasso and let go. He had aimed for a finger of rock that protruded from the wall overhead, just beyond the crevasse. The grapple hook undershot the fixture and clattered uselessly on the other side of the gaping hole. The Teacher reeled in the rope and tried again. This time the hook launched over the stone beam, and the cord wrapped around the outcrop twice. The Teacher pulled back with all his weight. The hook held.

He offered Mandy the end of the rope.

You have got to be kidding.

"Go on," he said.

She peered over the edge of the crevasse. It dropped away into bottomless black. She shook her head.

The Teacher reached out and peeled the strip of silver from her mouth.

A gesture of goodwill?

Then he pulled a gun from his bag, a long-barreled silver revolver that made her think of Dirty Harry.

"Please?" he said.

We'll do it your way, then, she thought.

305

Mandy took the rope. Years ago, in a different lifetime, she had rappelled around Enchanted Rock State Park with her father. It wasn't difficult. She stepped back, stretching the cord, and placed her hands high on the rope. Then she bent her knees. Cool air brushed her face as she glided over the abyss. She looked down only when her feet touched solid ground on the other side.

Mandy flung the rope back to the Teacher.

No point being smart. He had a gun, a deep chasm lay between her and the only exit, and an army of lunatics with machine guns roamed outside. Right now, the Teacher was Mandy's only ticket out of there. Besides, give the old man a chance to fall in.

The Teacher tossed her the flashlight. He shoved the gun into his shoulder bag and gripped the rope. He froze.

"Lift your legs," Mandy said. "Gravity will do the rest."

The Teacher swung forward. Mandy stepped aside to avoid a collision. He found his feet.

"Thank you." His eyes lingered on her. His mouth curled in a bemused smile.

"You're welcome."

Knew you'd warm to me in the end.

The Teacher took the flashlight and led the way.

"This is the inner sanctum of the Temple Below," he said. "The Holy of Holies, where the real treasure lies."

Mandy had learned about the Holy of Holies in her class on the weekly Torah readings.

"The Ark of the Covenant?"

The Teacher chuckled. "No. Far more valuable."

He pointed the light at the darkness ahead. "See for yourself."

Mandy squinted. A stone altar, waist high. Fat horns marked the corners. A shudder rippled through her. A cliché of B-movies. The crazed cult member ties the young woman to his sacrificial altar and raises a large dagger over his head. Was Mandy that girl?

The moment of fear passed. An object took shape at the

center of the altar. Mandy had never seen one before but by the size, lid, and rounded shape, she made an educated guess.

"A scroll jar?"

All this for another piece of old pottery?

"*The* scroll jar. And within, the Mother of All Scrolls."

Another code word. Delusional people loved codes and riddles. The Sons of Light. The End of Days. The Mother of All Scrolls. Did a fancy name make an old pot more interesting?

"Wow." She purged her voice of cynicism.

The Teacher approached the altar. Mandy followed. A perfectly fitted, sunken circle held the base of the jar. The Teacher ran his fingers over three angled characters etched in the surface. He lifted the domed lid of the jar and peeked inside.

"Yes!" He shook with excitement. Mandy looked over his shoulder. A thick wad of rolled parchment.

"What is it?"

"The answer. The answer to all questions."

Here we go again.

He replaced the lid. "If you'd be so kind." He handed her the flashlight.

The Teacher applied both hands to the jar and pushed.

She had a bad feeling about this. In the movies, this was the point when the tomb raider pulled the lever or stepped on the trip wire. Then the walls would close in or a large stone ball would roll down the tunnel to crush them.

The jar gave way with a soft crack and separated from the altar for the first time in what she guessed was many, many years.

The Teacher hugged the jar and stepped around the altar.

"Aren't you going to read it?"

"All in good time, my dear. Come along."

Behind the altar, on the far wall, the fluorescent light revealed a low, dark crawl space.

"After you," he said.

∽

Jay closed his arm around the girl's neck. His skull throbbed. The hair at the back of his head felt damp and sticky.

Slowly, David Schwarz lowered the machine gun to the floor of the cave.

"Next time," Jay said, "hit the side of the head, not the back."

There would be no next time, of course.

The Teacher had warned him. The Sons of Darkness were always one step behind.

Ben Green wore Sol's cowboy hat. Green and his henchmen must have discovered the *Yachad* and freed Schwarz and the blond.

"Where's John?" Jay said. "What have you done with him?"

John would not have gone down without a fight.

Schwarz and Green exchanged glances.

"If you've harmed him..."

"He's safe," Green said. "Let her go and we'll take you to him."

Did they think they could turn the tables so easily? Jay had prepared for this. "Just this one? What about your lady love?"

Jay searched his peripheral vision. His insurance policy no longer stood between the pillars of the Temple Below. The Teacher must have taken her inside. All the better.

Schwarz stepped forward.

Jay tightened his grip and the girl squirmed and gasped.

"Stay where you are, Son of Darkness!"

Adrenaline pulsed through his veins. One twist and he'd break her neck.

"Please," Schwarz said. "We know the police are already looking for you. Let her go and you can leave. We won't stop you."

How does he know?

They must have tortured John, the poor bastard.

You can't trust them.

"Sure," he said. "And I'll just shake hands with the darkies waiting outside?"

The Harper wallowed on his belly, his hands tied behind his back.

"Hey," he said. "Untie me."

"Shut it, you sniveling crawler."

"Hey, I'm with you."

"Stiff kumara, mate. I've had a gutful of ya whinging. You chose Darkness. You can rot with the lot of them."

A machine gun strap stuck out under one of the downed intruders. Jay edged closer. A few more feet and he could—

Jay's eyeballs burst into flame. The world capsized. The floor rose up and slammed into his shoulder. Air seared his lungs. He convulsed on the ground and coughed in long painful spasms.

What Devil's work is this?

He pressed his fingers to the smoldering orbs in his skull but the fires raged on. Tears welled in the sockets, wetting his fingertips and pouring down his cheeks.

Hands gripped his legs and wrapped them with rope. They rolled him over, pried his arms from his face, and tied his wrists behind his back.

Jay shifted on his stomach. His eyelids twitched like egg whites in a frying pan but he willed them to open.

"...in Mandy's bag," the blond was saying. She held a red lipstick in her hand for the others to see.

Pepper spray!

How had he missed that?

Green crouched over a fallen darkie, his back to Jay. "He's coming to."

The gunman with the mustache lay on his side and clutched his arm. "Hurry. I'll take care of my men."

"And I'll handle these bad boys." The blond trained the

red canister on Jay. "Go get Mandy."

Green looked to the Temple Below. "I think I know what the Teacher is after," he told Schwarz.

What was the Teacher after?

Green and Schwarz ran toward the Temple.

Jay watched them go, straining his neck to keep his head above the dirt.

The Stone.

The plain rock Schwarz had brought to Qumran along with the scroll jar. The Sons of Darkness needed it.

Jay could use that.

The Teacher had said nothing of the stone. What other details had he left out? And what was he after in the Temple Below?

The blond picked up a machine gun and turned it over.

"Ever use one of those?" he said. "I could show you."

She slipped the strap over her shoulder, aimed it high, and pulled back on the cocking handle. She glared at him, then sauntered off to the others.

The Harper wallowed on the ground and spat dirt. "Can I have a glass of water?"

No one was listening.

"Hello-o!"

Jay craned his neck toward the back of the cave. Schwarz and Green stepped into the mouth of the Temple.

He let his eyes close, his chin drop to the ground.

A few minutes passed. The remaining Sons of Darkness licked their wounds and forgot him. The fire in his eyes burned low. He blinked them open.

He had not resisted capture. Pain had robbed his strength and gouged his eyes. But he had remembered to hold his wrists side-to-side when the unseen hands had knotted the rope. Now he rotated his wrists and the rope slackened.

On a patch of loose earth nearby lay a handgun.

Jay could use that too.

Dave walked between the twin pillars and into the dark unknown. Again.

This time he didn't need dragging. He would rescue his damsel in distress if he had to crawl through a hundred dank tunnels filled with countless invisible terrors.

Forget roses. Forget chocolates. Forget fluffy bears holding heart-shaped cushions. This was the real deal. Dave had sneaked into an ancient tomb. He had braved machine gun–toting villains. If that didn't prove him worthy of Mandy's love and forgiveness, nothing would.

Ben stopped a few steps into the dim passageway and waited.

Dave's eyes adjusted. He could make out no movement in the blackness, only the slow sway of their shadows and a faint drip-drip of water.

"Hear anything?" Ben said.

"No. Is there another way out?"

"Possibly. Probably. Damn. They're long gone by now. C'mon."

Ben's flashlight cut through the gloom like a laser. The passage widened. On the walls, grotesque faces lit up then faded to black: growling lions, eagles with sharp beaks, all winged and fierce with human bodies.

"What is this place?"

Ben inched further into the dark. "The temple of Jerusalem Below. Before the Babylonians destroyed the First Temple, the Guardians of Jerusalem built a model of the Holy City in the hope of restoring its former glory when the storm passed. They moved the Temple Treasury here for safekeeping. The landmarks in the Copper Scroll refer to Jerusalem Below, not the actual Jerusalem Above. That's why treasure hunters never found anything. They searched the Jerusalem Above using the scroll as a map, when the Copper Scroll was actually a map of a map."

Their shoes squeaked on the stone floor.

"So there's more treasure in here."

"One item in the list has no location but it's most likely in the Temple. Which makes sense because it's—"

A man's voice completed Ben's sentence.

"...the most valuable of all."

Dave had heard that British accent before.

Ben aimed the beam ahead at the source of the words. The light sketched a hunting cap, a goatee, and a girl.

"Mandy!" Dave blurted.

His feet carried him forward.

"Dave! No!" Mandy said.

"She's right," the man said. "I'd watch my step if I were you." A fluorescent light flickered to life and Dave shielded his eyes with his hand. A crevasse sliced the room in two, the jagged edge passing inches from Dave's shoes.

Mandy stared at Dave across the chasm, her eyes wide and bright in the white light.

This is your last chance, Dave. Tell her you love her. Tell her you're sorry. You'll make it up to her for the rest of your life. Tell her! Beg her!

"Mandy," he cried, overjoyed just to see her again. The words rushed out of him. "I'm an idiot!"

Mandy smiled. "I know!" She seemed to understand. Her chest heaved.

Indications of Interest! She's happy to see me! Thank you, God!

He had to get to her. The man held her close. Beside him, a rope extended from a stone beam. They must have swung across but the rope was out of his reach.

The Teacher gave a wry smile. "It seems that my escape tunnel has collapsed, and yet again, Ben, you stand in my way."

Ben inhaled sharply. "Professor Barkley? You're the Teacher?"

The Teacher pulled at his face and the goatee peeled away.

He discarded the disguise.

"You know this guy?" Mandy asked.

"Sort of," Dave said. "He taught Ben at Hebrew U."

"And a fine student you were, Ben," the professor said. "I had thought to win you over that evening when you came by and talked of scroll jars. But then your friend here tagged along and, well, loose lips sink ships."

"Did you find it?" Ben asked.

"Right here." Professor Barkley indicated the rounded jar under his arm.

"A scroll jar?" Dave said.

The professor scowled at Dave. "*The* scroll jar."

"What?"

"He always talks in riddles." Mandy spun her finger next to her ear, the universal crazy sign.

Dave laughed. "Yeah. Ben does that too."

"Yes, yes," the professor said. "You're both very happy to see each other. Now be quiet. This is the most important discovery in archaeological history. Do you understand?"

Dave shook his head.

"Tell him, Ben."

"The first Torah," Ben said. "The original scroll of Moses."

"Or a copy of a copy," the professor said. "But the earliest full manuscript. The source of all others."

Dave's confusion must have been written on his face.

Ben explained. "According to the Bible, Moses stored his scroll alongside the Ark of the Covenant."

Ben's words came slow and deliberate and Dave almost heard the cogs turning in his friend's mind. Ben was playing for time. He eyed Dave meaningfully.

Keep him talking.

Ben continued. "The Copper Scroll mentions a Copy of the Text. That could mean a copy of the Copper Scroll itself. Or it might be a reference to the Original Text."

"Very good," the professor said.

"And why is that so valuable?" Dave asked.

"Why?" The professor almost frothed at the mouth. "The original scroll of Moses? Or is it *scrolls*? Before generations of redactors merged and edited the separate and contradictory legends. The ultimate proof of the Documentary Hypothesis. Think of it. Religious laws and beliefs, pillars of faith, based on a copying error. Entire stories and characters exposed as late additions and amalgams of pagan myths. The Dead Sea Scrolls merely chipped the surface; this scroll will topple the entire edifice. The end of Western religion."

"And," Ben added, "revenge against your Christian detractors."

The professor bit his lip. "I dared to question their doctrine in my writings and they destroyed me. My tenure lost. My name ruined. This seems like a fitting comeuppance. And the world will thank me. No more religious wars. An age of pluralism and tolerance."

A shiver scuttled down Dave's spine. The Teacher had spent too much time with his nutcase followers.

"So this is your End of Days?" Mandy said.

The professor chuckled.

"The Sons of Light aren't going to like that," she said.

"I did what I had to. To acquire the other scroll jars I needed men with certain skills. The idea of reviving the Judean Desert Cult came naturally. We got carried away, I'll admit that. Kidnapping was never part of the plan."

"Then let her go, Professor," Dave said.

"And leave me to your SWAT team?" The professor leaned away from Mandy. In his hand, a silver gun glinted in the white light. "I don't think so. Here's what's going to happen. You two turn around. Tell your friends that you found nothing. The Sons of Light worked alone. Those lunatics ran amok; let them pick up the bill. They have served their purpose. When the coast clears, this dear girl will return to you while Ben and I announce our find to the world."

Fair enough, Dave thought. *Let him get away with it. I don't mind. So long as Mandy goes free. And Ben would love the limelight.*

"There's one more thing," Ben said. "The Stone."

Dave turned a violent glare at Ben.

"What, this?" Professor Barkley placed the jar on the ground. He slid his hand into his shoulder bag and displayed the Foundation Stone for all to see.

"Lovely, isn't it? Shiny. Smooth. Desirable. Seems to listen, to suck in everything around it. Could it be your Foundation Stone? Who knows? Either way, you'll never prove its provenance. The stone is worthless, Ben. A mere artifact. A rock like any other. What really matters is this." He pointed at the scroll jar. "The written word. The spirit of men long-dead heard across the millennia."

"All the same," a voice behind Dave said. "I'll have them both."

Not again.

Jay padded down the passageway and into the circle of light. He had a gun and he pointed it at the professor. At Mandy.

"Lunatics, you say? Served our purpose?"

Oh, crap.

Dave edged out of the line of fire. The gunman did not seem to see him.

"You." Jay's voice quavered. "Teacher. You said you believed in me. My time had come. I was The One. Did you tell all of us that? Keep us out in the wop-wops, play us against each other while we kept our vows of silence?"

Dave looked around for a gun, a spade, anything. He met Mandy's frightened gaze. She stepped away from the former Teacher.

"It's not what you think," the professor said. "Put that down." He had lowered his voice to a commanding tone but the sway he had held over this particular Son of Light had evaporated.

"Thought you'd pull a swiftie, did ya? And by-the-by, the cave's a skinner. Not a skerrick of your gold or silver. Don't act surprised. You knew it all along. That's why you came in here for the real treasure."

"This is all part of our plan. I'll explain later."

"Not this time, Teach. My eyes are open. For the first time, I see things the way they really are. Not the lies you fed us."

Dave studied Jay.

Their main opponent had shrugged off his delusions. Jesus had been unstoppable; Jay would respond to reason. A peaceful end glimmered on the horizon.

The Teacher feigned insult. "I never lied to you, my son. We must defeat the Sons of Darkness with deception. Surely you understand?"

Jay shook his head. "I trusted you but in the end *you* were from Darkness."

Hope fled Dave like air from a balloon. So much for a peaceful solution.

"I thank you for one thing," Jay continued. "Whatever your intentions. You showed me The Way. But now *you've* served *your* purpose. Put the stone down next to the jar."

Professor Barkley glanced at the stone, shocked. "What? This old rock?" His tone became nonchalant. Reckless. He tossed the Foundation Stone lightly in his hand. Dave remembered the careful respect with which Ornan had handled the stone, like a technician defusing a bomb. The hairs on the back of Dave's neck stiffened.

He flashed a look at Mandy and tipped his head to the side.

Get as far away as you can.

Mandy nodded, then shifted her glance to the rope beside her. She had a point. The rope was the only way over the abyss.

"This stone means nothing, Jay. Don't let them fool you."

"All the same." Jay waved the barrel of the gun. "Drop it."

The professor smiled. His eyes glittered. "As you wish."

The Foundation Stone slipped from his fingers, bounced once on the stone floor, and rolled over the edge.

"No!" Ben said.

Dave's stomach convulsed with each clink of the stone

316

against rocky outcrops, each softer than the one before, until the sound faded away.

"That's a long way down," Professor Barkley said.

"What is it?" Jay asked. Fingers of muddy sweat trickled down his face. "What does it do?"

"What *did* it do?" the Teacher said. "The same as all religious artifacts and relics. Nothing."

The Teacher stepped sideways. He wrapped an arm around Mandy's waist and aimed his gun past his human shield.

"Now my turn. Put the gun down, Jay. I'll only ask once."

Mandy stared at Dave. Her chest rose and fell quickly. Her eyes shouted Help! Or was it Goodbye?

Dave's throat dried up. He had no weapon; he had lost the element of surprise. He stood no chance against Jay.

His feet moved as if they had a will of their own. He took one step forward, then another, along the edge of the crevasse until he cast a weak shadow over Jay.

Dave stared down the barrel of the gun. It jiggled irritably.

"Out of my way, Schwarz."

Dave swallowed hard but shook his head. "Not Mandy. Please."

The gun stayed on target. At this range Jay had no way of missing. One squeeze of the finger and it was game over.

Dave had his back to Mandy now. At least she wouldn't see the fear on his face. He braced himself for the blast and pain in his chest. The earth seemed to shudder beneath his feet.

"Did you feel that?" Ben asked.

The ground trembled again.

Jay lowered his gun. "It's happening." He was actually smiling; his face glowed under the sheen of grimy sweat. "The End of Days is upon us. Teacher, prepare to meet your Judgment Day."

A low hiss and a swish. A stormy sea crashing over rocks. The sound grew louder. The room danced like an airplane shifting through air pockets.

Dave turned around as a huge column of white erupted from the crevasse. The force knocked him off his feet. He landed hard on his back. Darkness. Cold spray covered his face and drenched his shirt and jeans. The roar of rushing water blotted out all sound.

He shot to his feet.

Mandy. Have to get to Mandy.

He stepped forward, his eyes closed against the spray.

The chilly water seeped into his shoes, splashed at his ankles, then climbed his calves. He waded on, against the torrent, toward the deafening jet; a mouse trapped in a water pipe. The fountain floored him again. When he rose, the waters sucked at his waist. A loud crack. A tall wave broadsided him. Dave tried to find his feet. Blackness all around. He was floating. The mighty swells swept him back, back, back.

"No!"

He paddled fiercely but the current swept him away. His body spun. Then a watery hand dashed his head against a wall. Pain flared in his skull. He sank beneath the surface and knew no more.

The ground teetered beneath Mandy. She closed her hand over the hanging rope. For a split-second, a white jet of water shot from the crevasse like lightning. Then the fluorescent light shattered and plunged the Holy of Holies into darkness.

The blast wave shoved her backward, into the Teacher, whose arm slipped from her waist.

She clung to the rope for all she was worth. Jets stung her arms. The white noise of ferocious waters surrounded her. She swung sideways, then forward in the dark, buffeted by the powerful flow of an upside-down Niagara Falls. Then her forward movement slowed. Her legs dipped in water and found the floor of a knee-deep river.

She sensed that she had rounded the fountain and crossed back over the gaping crack.

"Dave!" she cried.

She could barely hear her own voice.

A clap of thunder and then a large swell lifted her off her feet and urged her forward.

Mandy heard her father's voice. They were swimming in the sea at Galveston.

"If a wave sweeps you out," he said, "don't fight it. The ocean is stronger than you. You'll tire fast and sink."

"What should I do, Daddy?"

"Just float. Keep your head above water. Breathe. The current will bring you back in the end."

Mandy lay back. She drifted feet first. Her sopping clothes stuck to her body and made floating difficult. She spread her arms, feeling for obstacles. A window of yellow light rushed at her. Then she dropped off a cliff and splashed into a pool of water.

She got to her feet and swept the damp strands of hair from her face. She stood in a large pond of shallow, muddy water. Flaming torches burned along the walls.

The cave!

Water gushed from the Temple behind her and from other holes along the walls, like faucets over an immense bath.

"Mandy!" Shani waded toward her and stumbled over a sunken house. "Thank God, you're OK. We have to get out of here. Now." She pointed at the entrance tunnel behind her.

The waters lapped at the steps. In a filthy sleeveless undershirt, his hands tied behind his back, Sol ducked his head and staggered into the dark mouth. A small, mustachioed man in army fatigues assisted him. Mandy squinted at him in the flickering flame light. He looked like the manager of the restaurant in the City of David.

Mario?

Mandy let the question go. "Dave," she said. "Have you seen Dave?"

"No. He went after you. Then all hell broke loose."

"I have to find him."

Shani studied Mandy's face, then kissed her on the cheek. "See you outside."

Mandy turned back. The faux Temple was a flowing waterfall. The rapids discolored as a human shape dropped into the deepening pool.

Mandy ran.

A man got to his feet and gulped air.

"Ben." She gripped his shoulders. "Where's Dave?"

The soaked man glanced around. His bald head glistened. "Couldn't see a thing."

She watched the fountain at the Temple mouth and panted. The wetness crept up her legs.

She sloshed around the choppy pool and scanned the waterlogged scenery. "Dave!" she called over the roar of the rapids.

"Dave!" Ben joined the search and they split up.

The heads of miniature buildings poked above water level and blocked Mandy's view. Dave might have washed up before her. If he was hurt, every second counted.

"Mandy!" Shani stood in the mouth of the tunnel. The flood level washed over her feet. Shani beckoned her to follow.

"Dave!" Mandy shouted.

She'd find him. She had to. Dave had bared his heart. He had risked his life for her. She could forgive him anything. She had held out for a hero and Dave was her hero.

A human form beached on a hilltop. An arm stuck out of the water. Limp.

Mandy waded toward it, then dove in and swam. She

turned the body over and cradled the head in her arms.

His eyes were closed, his face blue and cold.

"Dave!"

Mandy dug her heels into the ground and pulled his body onto her and out of the water.

Strands of her wet hair caressed his face. His neck warmed to her touch.

Ben splashed toward her. "Is he breathing?"

Mandy barely heard him.

Don't die on me, Dave.

She lowered her face to his. Their lips touched for the first time. She opened his mouth with hers and gave him her life's breath.

Don't die, Dave. I won't let you.

His chest rose. Mandy came up for air and repeated the procedure.

After the third lungful, Dave convulsed. She tilted his body to help the liquid drain from his lungs.

How long had he been under? A few minutes without oxygen spelled brain damage. The blue eyes opened. Mandy searched them for a sign.

Dave, are you still there?

He stared at her, his eyes glazed over.

Then he blinked.

"You saved me," he said.

A short sound burst from Mandy's chest.

Thank the Lord!

Tears streamed down her face. Or was it floodwater? It didn't matter. Dave was alive.

"Easy," he said. "I'm not used to girls drooling over me."

"Jesus, Dave," Ben said. "We thought you had drowned. Can you walk?"

Dave never took his eyes off her. His lips curled in the most beautiful smile she had ever seen.

"I'm perfectly comfortable right here."

"Mandy!"

Shani's voice was a high-pitched shriek. The waters had

reached her friend's ample chest. Soon, the only exit would be completely submerged.

"Get up," Ben said. "Now."

Dave got to his feet with difficulty. Mandy and Ben supported him on either side and walked, then dragged him toward the closing tunnel mouth. The water helped. A flaming torch sizzled and died in the rising water. The flickering light dimmed.

Mandy, Dave and Ben slipped into the tunnel. They pressed their heads together and gulped air at the ceiling like hungry catfish in a pond. Shani's flashlight danced ahead. The stairs were damp and slippery. Mandy and Dave climbed together, step by step, toward the square of pale blue.

Shani and Ruchama grasped Mandy's hands and pulled, then Ruchama locked Mandy in a bone-crushing bear hug. Dave collapsed on the dry loose earth beside the open grave. He smiled at her.

Dawn broke over Qumran. The Jordanian Valley glowed in the warm rays of a new day. And behind them, from the car park, came the blue-and-red flicker of strobe lights.

The Teacher of Righteousness opened his eyes. Pale blue skies. Dry desert breeze on his face. A gentle, flowing sensation around his body.

Is this Heaven?

A heaviness in his chest. He coughed. Water spilled from his mouth and over his cheeks. He tried to lift his head but it was no use. The ground at his back felt hard but agreeable.

He heard the crunch of gravel underfoot, then silence.

A face filled the blue. A woman of middle age, her blond hair cropped short and sharp. The eyes peered at him with concern.

The angels of Heaven, it would seem, used hair salons and makeup. And spoke with a British accent.

"Are you all right?" she asked.

The Teacher wondered whether he was. He felt fine apart from the fact that he could not move. It took time to adjust to incorporeal existence.

"Over here," she said, louder.

More crunching of gravel.

"Is it him?" a man's voice said.

"No."

A man joined the woman. Were all angels British and middle-aged? Worry filled their eyes. Or was it disappointment?

"What's your name?" the woman-angel asked.

The Teacher searched his mind, which was blissfully white and clean.

"Teacher." His throat was rough and parched. "Teacher of Righteousness."

The woman-angel smiled. "You just rest here. Everything will be all right."

She kneeled beside him and dripped cool, clear water into his mouth from a plastic bottle.

Images flashed in his mind.

The scroll. He had found the Scroll of Scrolls. The End of Days. A World of Peace.

He felt about for the earthen jar but his hands returned empty. Water trickled around the edges of his recumbent body.

No matter.

He had merged with the scroll. They were one now. Nothing would separate them again. The One Scroll would speak through him.

"What's this?"

The woman-angel reached out of view. She stood and brushed lumps of wet sand from a circular black stone.

The man-angel fished reading glasses from his shirt pocket and studied the smooth stone.

"Nothing," the Teacher answered. "Absolutely nothing." The thought made him laugh, although he could not recall why.

A mobile phone rang.

"Yes?" the woman said. "Oh, thank God. Steven, they've found him. We're on our way. Oh, and we found another one." She considered the Teacher. "Yes. And a little confused. All right."

The angelic couple held the stone between them and paused to exchange a soft glance. Then they walked off together. As they disappeared from view, they held hands.

How sweet.

The Teacher returned to his sky of endless blue.

Two men in navy uniforms arrived. They lifted the Teacher onto a stretcher and into the air like an emperor.

Inside the van, a woman in a blue dress shirt sat beside him. She connected a tube to his arm and smiled gently.

Then he was floating again, this time on a wheeled bed, toward a large, square building in white Jerusalem stone.

"Yes!" the Teacher exclaimed. A tear blurred his vision but he managed to read the legend above the wide doorway. *Shaare Zedek*. The Gates of Zedek. The Gates of Righteousness.

Home.

At last!

CHAPTER 15

It was the happiest day of Dave's life.

As he stepped forward, the chorus line of friends and relatives in suits and smiles stepped back. A trumpeter kept pace and blared his song.

Od yishama / Again shall be heard.

Be'arey Yehuda / In the cities of Judah.

Uvechutzot Yerushalayim / And in the yards of Jerusalem.

Kol sason vekol simcha / The sound of joy and happiness.

Kol chatan vekol kalah / The voice of bride and groom.

Dave wore a long white *kittel* over a blue suit and white tie. His mother, in a salmon evening dress and wide-brimmed hat, locked his left arm in hers, and his father gripped his right.

His parents beamed at him and at each other. Their recent behavior mystified him. He had caught them winking at each other and whispering sweet nothings. In public! Dave wasn't entirely convinced that his nuptials alone had rekindled their love.

The wedding parade rounded a corner of the Dan Hotel lobby. An expansive balcony came into view and there it was. White silken sheets formed the canopy and colorful bouquets adorned the corner posts. Behind the *chuppah*, in the soft hues of the setting sun, lights sparkled over the rise and fall of the

Jerusalem skyline.

The dancers dispersed. Dave and his parents walked the long, white carpet, passing between the rows of chairs. Under the *chuppah*, Mishi greeted them with his furry *shtreimel* and toothy grin.

Ben stood by, packed into a tuxedo like a celebrity bodyguard. He patted his breast pocket and pretended to have misplaced the wedding band.

Dave had seen little of Ben over the last three months, but today Ben had picked him up first thing in the morning. His duties as best man included occupying the groom on the day of the wedding, assisting with errands, and generally making sure that the scatterbrain made it to the *chuppah* on time. Or at all. As Ben pointed out, the job was known as *shomer*, or "guard," and probably served to prevent a skittish groom from fleeing the country.

The day kicked off with morning prayers at the Western Wall. Skipping breakfast—many couples fasted on their wedding day—Ben drove them in his Yaris past the Jerusalem Biblical Zoo and onto a bumpy dirt road. He followed the winding contours of the untamed hillside and parked in a clearing among the tall grasses and wild shrubs. The two friends grabbed their towels and hiked the short trail to *Ein Ya'el*.

A thin, bearded man walked the other way on the dirt path. He wore clothes of white flannel and a large, knitted *kippa*. He wrung water from his blond earlocks and smiled as he passed them by.

The waters of the natural spring trickled into a deep, square pool outlined by large slabs of plastered rock and hedged on one side by a wall of rough stone.

Dave had never gone skinny-dipping before. This was to be a day of many firsts.

Ben dive-bombed with a glorious splash. Dave slipped into the chilly water, held his breath, and went under. He assumed a loose fetal position, then broke the surface, reentering the world and gasping, fresh and pure as his first day. He counted three immersions, and then joined Ben, who rested against the side of the pool, his arms spread along the edge. He was thankful for the thick green water of the back-to-nature *mikva* and their privacy. Tuesday was a slow business day for the spring.

Bushes rustled in the breeze and the leaves of trees played with the sunlight. Birds sang and dove overhead. Images sloshed in Dave's mind like the waters around him. Between viewing wedding halls, tasting entrees, and buying suits and rings, his thoughts had often returned to Qumran. The Internet had helped him put some of the pieces together.

Professor Edward Barkley had taken up residence in the Kfar Shaul Mental Health Center. A fellow archaeologist had taken over his restoration project of a British Mandate–era outpost in the Jordanian Valley. Two of his fellow patients, both Texans, had responded to treatment and returned to their anxious families abroad.

The police, however, deported John White to New Zealand where he awaited trial.

Jason "Jay" Smith had disappeared and was presumed drowned. The details of the orphaned criminal's life had moved Dave. Delusions aside, he and Jay were not all that different. Most people Dave knew in Katamon were running from something: their families, their past, their future. Unlike Jay, Dave had found something real to run toward.

He read about the Documentary Hypothesis. What if Barkley was right? What if the Bible was a mix of earlier myths and legends? What if the Torah was not dictated word for word to Moses as Dave had learned in kindergarten? Would his life change? Not much. Thousands of years of shared experience, longing, and sensibility did not stand or fall on one text or another. His understanding of the Bible would have to evolve, for sure, but, as he had learned, nothing in life or love slipped easily into the tidy little box of his expectations.

Dave also discovered that the Greek word Katamon meant "beneath the monastery," a fact that dovetailed well with his recent escapade in Jerusalem Below but, he had to admit, ultimately meant nothing.

Other questions remained unanswered and as he relaxed they bubbled to the surface.

"Ben. You never explained about Ornan."

The waters lapped lazily against the edge of the pool.

"Ben?"

"OK," Ben said. "I'll tell you. But if you ever breathe a word of this to anyone—"

"I know, I know. You'll kill me."

Ben leaned back and read the answer off the clear blue sky.

"Three thousand years ago, King David, having united the tribes of Israel, needed a new capital. The ideal city would be central, fortified, and with a ready supply of water."

Dave gazed at the grassy hillocks. In his mind's eye, a young King David and his warriors scaled the low erosion walls of ancient stone and surveyed the landscape, swords and spears at the ready.

Ben continued. "Jerusalem had all that and more. From time immemorial, the city had served as a cultic center, and tradition long tied the site to the forefathers. Abraham's Mount Moriah. Jacob's House of God. But Jebusites held the city."

Dave knew the story well. "The blind and the lame."

"Most commentators," Ben said, "saw that as a taunt. *Our walls are so strong, even cripples can defend them.* But they got it wrong. The blind and lame were a warning. Beware. Enter at your own risk. For the Jebusites believed they guarded a great spiritual force, a power too dangerous for man to wield."

Dave hazarded a guess. "Our Foundation Stone?"

Ben's eyebrows jumped twice. "The Jebusites opened the city gates to David but the young king took no heed of their warnings. He made his home there, and soon the City of David filled with allies of all races from across the kingdom. One fateful night David came across a sealed room at the top of the citadel. He forced his way in and discovered a plain-looking stone. As he examined it, he glimpsed, through the window, a young woman bathing on a rooftop."

A tingle traced up Dave's spine and it had nothing to do with the cold water of the spring.

"You mean... Are you trying to say that Bathsheba...?"

"So the story goes. And that would explain a few things. Anyway, King David learned his lesson. He reinstated the Jebusites as Guardians of Jerusalem's Secret Treasures. Days became years, years centuries. The sacred trust passed from father to son. Then the Babylonians marched against Jerusalem. If the city fell, Jerusalem's treasures and the all-powerful Stone would fall into enemy hands.

"The Guardians took precautions. They built Jerusalem Below and secretly transferred the Temple's wealth. They altered holy texts to cover their tracks. The site of the Foundation Stone became the threshing floor of Aravna the Jebusite, they transformed the Welcoming of David into the Daring Conquest of the Jebusite city, and King David was recast as a common adulterer.

"In case their followers dispersed and forgot their traditions, they recorded their treasures in the Copper Scroll. They baked key sections of the scroll into jars, each marked with the letters Tsadi-Dalet-Qof, the sign of the founder of their order."

"Zadok the High Priest?"

Ben grinned but shook his head. "*Malki-Zedek*, King of Shalem. In the book of Genesis, he greets Abraham after the battle of the Four Kings. *Shalem* became known as *Uru-salim* and even later as..." He paused for dramatic effect.

"Jerusalem," Dave said. He connected more dots. "So Ornan is..."

Ben nodded. "The faithful heir of the Jebusite Guardians of Jerusalem. They kept David's trust ever since, even during Second Temple times, awaiting the full restoration of Jerusalem. Empires came and went. The Temple's gold and silver helped fund their order and convince those who wandered too near to look the other way. Three thousand years of bribes adds up and the treasure ran dry. They had to resort to threats of violence, or they released minor artifacts, like the scroll jars, to divert attention away from the City of David. On occasion, they welcomed enlightened outsiders into their fold. Archaeologists, mostly."

A lightbulb flared in Dave's memory.

"Kathleen Kenyon dug the City of David but never published her findings."

"Right. The same with Father de Vaux and Qumran, and *he* dug the *entire* cemetery, blocking that path to future archaeologists."

"And now the illustrious Ben Green."

Ben looked away but Dave saw the smug grin.

Dave's fingertips were turning into prunes. It was time to get out and towel down, but he had to settle one more nagging question.

"So the stone was real after all?"

Ben made a doubtful groan. "I wouldn't go *that* far."

"But what about that flashflood? The *Drinking Stone*? The source of the watery depths?"

"Cold-water geysers are a well-documented phenomenon, especially along fault lines."

"Come on, Ben. You don't really believe that."

"Water rich in carbon dioxide, trapped beneath strata of—Hey! Stop splashing!"

Under the *chuppah*, Ben found the gold wedding band in its box and winked at Dave.

Your secrets are safe with me, Ben.

Friends and relatives peered expectantly from the rows of chairs and filled the wings. At the end of the white carpet stood the bride. She held a round bouquet to her bosom. A man and woman stood on either side. A gauzy veil hid the bride's face.

She floated toward him.

A stab of sudden panic pierced his chest.

Oh, God. Is this right?

The trumpet played a slow, calming tune. *Tov Lehodot / It is good to give thanks.*

As his bride approached, the veil melted away and Mandy held his gaze. She radiated happiness. The crowd, the music, the rabbi, the hotel, everything faded. All Dave saw, all that mattered, was the girl he had chosen. She rose before him. Her perfect auburn curls flowed over her shoulders. Her bright eyes drank him in. Her sweet perfume filled his head. She circled him. She stood beside him.

The ceremony flew by: the wine, the ring, the wedding contract, the Seven Blessings, more wine, Mishi's short, cryptic speech in pseudo-English. They sang the sad *Im eshkachekh Yerushalayim / If I forget thee, Jerusalem.*

Then Dave crushed a glass cup wrapped in foil beneath the heel of his black dress shoe, and the band erupted in joyous sounds.

Dave hugged his wife. He hugged his family and friends. They walked the carpet, bride and groom hand-in-hand, and the sea of well-wishers parted for them. A wall of dancing men formed two steps ahead.

Dave waved at Ruchama, who stood beside a man with earlocks and a straggly beard, the mythical neighbor Mandy had invited for her flatmate. Dave nodded at Ornan and his entourage. They wore dark suits and glasses and inclined their heads. At the bar, Mike the eternal bachelor chatted with Shani, who curled a finger through her Marilyn Monroe hair.

The parade reached the bridal chamber, where the newlyweds would enjoy a moment of quiet and hors d'oeuvres before rejoining their guests in the banquet hall.

As the door closed behind them, one journey ended and another began. Dave didn't know where this adventure would lead or how it would end. No matter. He and Mandy would figure it out. Together.

ALSO BY DAN SOFER

An Unexpected Afterlife
The Dry Bones Society, Book I
Coming March 2017

ABOUT THE AUTHOR

DAN SOFER writes tales of romantic misadventure and magical realism, many of which take place in Jerusalem. His multi-layered stories mix emotion and action, humor and pathos, myth and legend—entertainment for the heart and soul. Dan lives in Israel with his family.

Visit **dansofer.com/list-alab** for free bonus material and updates on new releases.